CAUGHT IN PASSION'S SPELL

Rye's black eyes lit with a fire Aerial didn't recognize, yet could only imagine must match the light in her own. Inadvertently, she drew closer to him.

She knew, somewhere deep in her conscience, that she was supposed to push herself away from him, maybe even slap him for standing so close to her, for touching her. At the very least, she shouldn't be caressing his cheek or reveling in the feel of his strong arms around her. But for the life of her, she could not think of a single reason to move away . . .

D1041175

LOVE'S WINDSWEPT EMBRACE

MICHALANN PERRY

ZEBRA BOOKS
KENSINGTON PUBLISHING CORP.

ZEBRA BOOKS

are published by

Kensington Publishing Corp.
475 Park Avenue South
New York, NY 10016

First printing: July, 1990

Printed in the United States of America

DEDICATION

To Dolly Teeter Perry and Donna Perry Willy, two great Iowa ladies who are gone from this world but who continue to be a loving influence and source of strength in my life.

And to the rest of the Perrys and Teeters, as well as to the citizens of Fairfield, the Best Little City in Iowa!

Prologue

The black-haired eleven-year-old, Rye Berenger, studied his catch of fish and sighed. Damn, he'd already caught six medium-sized fish from the pond, the exact number his mother had sent him to bring home for supper.

Disappointed, Rye sagged against the tree trunk, wishing he could stay just a little longer. When he was here, lulled by the whisper of the breeze rustling the leaves overhead and the hypnotizing dance of sunlight on the water, he could think and dream about the future without anything more distracting than the buzz of insects or the occasional leap of a fish from the water to interrupt his daydreams—not like at home, where there was always someone talking to him and giving him chores to do.

Sitting up straight, he cast a furtive glance around the woods behind him. Reaching the hoped-for conclusion that he was alone, he grinned mischievously. What would it hurt if he stayed just a bit longer? There would still be plenty of time to chop the wood for supper before dark. Working quickly, he unhooked three of the fish he had caught and pitched them back into the water.

"I saw that!" a high-pitched child's voice accused from behind a bush. "And I'm gonna tell!"

"You little sneak!" Rye growled, springing to his feet and taking off at a run.

"I'm going to tell Mama!" the girl squealed, turn-

7

ing to take flight.

In only a few strides the boy's long legs brought him within reach of his eight-year-old sister. "If you do . . ." He grabbed one of her flying black braids and jerked her to a halt. Flipping her to the ground, he straddled her and circled her skinny waist with his hands to tickle her, a ferocious scowl on his face. "You're gonna be real sorry."

"Stop!" the little girl giggled, squirming to escape.

"Not until you give me your word you aren't gonna tell!"

"All right! I won't—"

The sound of gunfire cracked through the air, bringing the children's horseplay to an immediate end. They froze, their identical black eyes round with fear.

"What was that?" the little girl asked in a breathless whisper.

"It came from the field Pa is planting this afternoon. He's probably just shooting crows," Rye answered, the dark facial features he had inherited from his Lakota Indian mother intense as he listened for a second shot. When none came, he released his sister and stood up. "That's all it is, but I'll go check. Now go on home and tell Ma I'll be along soon."

Her dark eyes glistening with tears, the little girl laced her fingers into her brother's protective grip. "Come with me."

"Aw, hell, Ginny. Don't start that. I told you it was Pa shooting at a crow. Now go on before we both get a lickin'." He grimaced, now regretful of his frivolous actions. "And I've got three more fish to catch before supper."

"But I'm scared. Just go with me to the edge of the yard. Pleeeezz."

Rolling his black eyes in disgust, Rye tightened his hold on her delicate hand. He prayed no one ever found out what a softie he was when it came to his little sister. But every time he vowed never to give in to her again she would look at him with big, pleading eyes, and he'd find himself doing exactly what she wanted—again.

"All right," he grumbled, "but one of these days you're gonna have to quit being such a baby. Hell, Ginny, I won't always be here to take care of you."

Ginny directed a teary smile up   her lanky brother. She knew differently. And what's more, she knew that he knew she knew. "You better not let Ma hear you swearing."

Hand in hand, the two dark-skinned children walked through the woods in silence, each warm and secure in the other's company.

Just as they reached the edge of the woods, another shot cracked through the air. Before Rye could react or determine where it had come from, Ginny pitched forward onto the ground. Instinctively he dropped to the ground beside her—only an instant before the sting of a bullet sliced its way across his scalp. Then he tumbled into the oblivion of unconsciousness.

When Rye awoke, he had no idea how long he'd been out or what had happened. All he knew was that his head hurt worse than anything he'd ever felt. Curious, he reached up to touch his hair. At the familiar, sticky feel of blood, a rush of memories and terror crowded into his brain, snapping his eyes open.

Horror and reality hit him squarely in the chest, and he shook with trepidation. *No!* his mind keened as the truth stared at him from his sister's lifeless eyes.

"Ginny?" he whimpered, his lips barely moving. "You can't be dead. Say something." Weeping silently, he gathered the limp body into his arms and rocked her. "Oh, please don't be dead."

As if to confirm what Rye already knew to be true, a loud burst of laughter reverberated through the air. Forcing his blurred gaze away from his sister's face to the cabin three hundred feet from where he lay, Rye started in surprise. Coming from the entrance to his family's cabin was the shabbily dressed man Rye recognized as the town drunk, a man who was said to have lost his entire family five years earlier, when the Eastern Sioux had gone on a rampage in Minnesota, killing almost five hundred settlers.

"An eye for an eye!" the man bellowed, turning back to face the open door with another demented laugh as he raised a fist high in the air and shook it. "And a scalp for a scalp! Now I'm goin' to pay those two half-breed nits for what you bastard savages did to my family."

Rye's horrified gaze flew to what the man clutched in his fist, and every nerve and muscle in his body cramped and quivered with nausea.

No! he protested, unable to free the air trapped in his lungs.

It had to be a trick, a dream. That couldn't be his mother's long black hair he could see hanging from the man's fist. The colored streamers entwined with the braids were not the same ribbons he'd seen his mother braid into her hair that morning, they couldn't be . . .

He squeezed his eyes closed, determined to blot out the nightmare that held him in its grip. It would be that simple. He would just keep his eyes closed until the ugly vision went away—or until his pa came to wake him up as he did every morning with his loud and cheerful, "Rise and shine, boy!"

The thought of his father flicked Rye's eyes open and forced his reluctant gaze back to the man's hand. It was then he saw a familiar flash of orange-red intermingled with his mother's hair and ribbons, and at last the total, awful truth speared viciously

10

into his brain. He wasn't dreaming. He was wide awake, and that was his father's scalp clutched in the man's fist with his mother's.

The first shot he'd heard from the field hadn't been Pa shooting at a crow at all, he now realized. It had been the sound of his father being killed by this man. The same man who would have killed him too if he hadn't stooped to check on his sister at just that instant.

A terrible guilt washed over him. It was all his fault. If he hadn't been dallying at the pond he would have at least been there to protect his mother, maybe even his father as well. If not for him, his mother and sister might still be alive. But as it was. . . .

Rye's natural instinct for revenge yelled at him to rise and charge the vicious animal approaching the spot where he lay, but a second instinct told him that if he did the man would kill him before he could take three steps. And if he died there would be no one alive to seek revenge for what this villain had done.

Praying the spirits of his parents and sister weren't watching him, certain they would surely think he was a coward for running away, the boy stealthily dragged himself back into the safe shadows of the woods. And then he ran and ran and ran — until he could run no more.

ST. LOUIS, MISSOURI; 1875

Fifteen-year-old Aerial Windsor watched bitterly as the enormous red and gold gas-filled balloon ascended from the cliff overlooking the Mississippi River. It rose to the fanfare of an exuberant brass band and the cheers of hundreds of spectators who had come to witness the aircraft's departure.

Her lips compressed in a thin, stubborn line, Aerial crossed her arms tightly over her chest. *It's not fair. I've worked just as hard as they have for this, They have no right to go without me.*

She glared up at the man and woman smiling and waving from the basket of the rising balloon. *I didn't see them so concerned about my safety when I risked my life daily on a trapeze bar at every carnival and fair in the country for the last eight years to raise money for this.*

A flash of recollection brought to mind the almost invisible safety lines that had been attached to a harness under her costume every time she had climbed out of the tethered balloon to perform two hundred feet above the crowd, but she promptly ignored it.

Right then, she was in no mood to give her parents the slightest bit of credit, so it was easy to relegate that memory to the back of her brain and tell herself, *If they really cared, they wouldn't have left me behind. They would have found a way for me to go, too! All they were worried about was protecting their star performer, and how large the day's receipts would be. But now, when they're about to do something really magnificent and become famous, suddenly it's "too dangerous" for me to go with them.*

Watching the ascent in spite of her vow not to, Aerial couldn't help the ripple of pride she felt. As much as she hated to admit it to herself, her parents really were an imposing sight. With the afternoon sun causing her blond hair to glisten pure gold, her mother looked like a heavenly apparition in her flowing white chiffon, and her father, tall and handsome in a conservative black suit and hat, looked like a rich gentleman out for a Sunday stroll.

Certainly, no one would take either of the two people in the balloon for a pair of daredevil aeronauts who intended to spend the next twenty-four hours several thousand feet in the air, in an attempt to break the distance record of 809 miles in nineteen

12

hours and fifty minutes, set in 1859 by John Wise on a journey begun in this very city.

"Wise made a mistake when he took extra passengers and too much baggage," she remembered her father saying. "And his lavishness forced him to spend most of his ballast during the night so they could ride the high-altitude current. But we're going to travel with the minimum of weight so we can save our ballast for the other end of the trip if we start to descend before we've outdistanced Wise's flight. *And* we're going to land with our balloon intact, rather than crash to the earth in tattered silk like he did."

Aerial's expression grew more dismal and her bottom lip began to quiver. She could already imagine the reception her parents would receive when they stepped out of the balloon basket on the East Coast tomorrow afternoon, the holders of a new world record. There would be more brass bands and even bigger crowds of people. Everyone who was anyone would be there to greet them—everyone, that is, but Aerial Windsor!

A sudden gasp from the crowd brought Aerial out of her reverie, and she focused on the balloon which had drifted out over the Mississippi River. As she watched in stunned immobility, the balloon dropped a hundred feet closer to the water, as if a huge hand had reached up and snatched it from the sky.

"Mama! Papa!" Aerial ran to the edge of the cliff as she watched her parents frantically tossing their precious sandbag ballast over the side in a desperate attempt to reverse the effects of the downdraft that had obviously taken them by surprise. But their efforts were hopeless, and the balloon dipped closer and closer to the brown water below—as though a second hand held it down from above.

"Jump!" Aerial screamed. But even if her frenzied cries could have been heard, they were too late. The balloon plunged so close to the water that the wicker passenger car toppled onto its side and immediately filled with water, as if it were a huge ladle skimming the river's surface.

The crowd watched in disbelieving silence as the balloon, still inflated with its full load of gas but anchored to the earth by the weight of the flooded basket, began to drift across the river, dragging its unwieldy cargo with it.

After a seemingly indeterminable length of time, when the balloon's passengers had failed to bob to the surface of the water and wave that they were safe, the spectators suddenly broke into action. Newspaper men raced to be the first to get the story of the unfortunate disaster to their papers. Others rushed to their carriages to get down to the bank to be there when the rescue boats brought in the bodies. Policemen shouted for order. Women cried. Men placed bets on how long it would take to find the victims. Others, who had bet against the success of the Windsors' journey, rushed to find their bookmakers and collect their winnings.

No one seemed to notice the slender blond girl who stood alone on the cliff's edge, staring down into the muddy water below.

How could I have let them leave without even telling them how much I loved them?

Chapter One

Her tights-clad legs artfully crossed at the ankles and one hand held above her head, Aerial Windsor posed, waiting for the applause from her last stunt of the afternoon to taper off. Smiling down on the cheering crowd from her perch on the steel trapeze bar dangling from the huge red and gold balloon hovering over the town square, she was reminded of a gay field of flowers blossoming and swaying in celebration of life, and a surge of excitement filled her chest.

This was actually it. The moment she had worked for since the day of her parents' deaths five years ago was finally at hand. And with it, fourteen grueling years of performing for carnivals, county fairs, and celebrations throughout the Midwest was coming to an end.

Inspired as she hadn't been in years, she made a decision. Not only would this be her last performance from the *Wind Rose,* but it would be her most spectacular as well. She would give this audience a stunt they would remember and talk about long after she was gone.

Aerial's face grew serious; a hush immediately came over the crowd as they concentrated their attention on the woman in the air. Gaily hatted women ceased their gossiping with friends; farmers and businessmen grew quiet; children stopped running and giggling; babies cut short their crying; and even

15

the barking dogs grew silent. It was as if every living thing on the ground sensed they were about to witness something more special and daring than anything they'd ever seen.

Satisfied that she had the undivided attention of her audience, Aerial positioned her hands on the trapeze ropes. Her expression now intent, she rocked her hips side to side, making certain her balance and placement on the bar were perfect.

Taking a deep breath, she bent one knee back, released her grip on the ropes and propelled her body over backward. Instead of catching herself by hooking her bent knee over the trapeze bar, as she had done to end her act in the past, she straightened her leg and deliberately slid off the bar into an unsupported fall.

A united gasp rose from the crowd. Frozen, the spectators watched breathlessly as she plunged toward the ground.

Knowing she had teased her audience enough, Aerial reached across the carefully calculated space to catch the drag rope that paralleled her free-falling descent.

Sighing with relief, the stunned gathering gaped in awe as she grabbed the rope with both hands and quickly twisted one leg into it, stopping her fall as suddenly as it had begun.

Silence continued to grip the crowd as they waited to see if she would lose what appeared to be a tenuous hold and continue her drop to her death.

Then, to their amazement, Aerial slipped her foot into a stirrup they hadn't noticed on the rope before that moment. She then held up her free hand in the pose that signaled the end of each stunt.

Though the people were slow to understand that the fall had been deliberate and that the lovely aeronaut was truly safe, Aerial held her pose with a teasing grin until they did.

16

Starting with the barest smattering of hesitant applause, the clapping and cheering from below crescendoed to a wild roar of approval as realization worked its way through the crowd.

Tossing back her blond head, Aerial gave a triumphant laugh and called up to her assistant, who peered over the basket rim, a disapproving scowl on his weathered face. "Let the rope out, Arnold. But take it slow. I'm going to milk this bow for all it's worth." She gave a jubilant giggle. "Because as of right now, I am officially retired from the county fair circuit!"

His emotions a strange mix of disappointment and relief, Rye Berenger stared down at the filthy body at his feet. How could this have happened? Was Fate so cruel that it had allowed him to spend all these years searching for the murderer of his family, only to deny him his reward by killing off his enemy in this Iowa alleyway only hours, maybe just minutes, before he arrived to confront him?

A surge of optimism suddenly lifted Rye's feelings of defeat. Maybe the old derelict wasn't dead after all. Maybe he had simply drunk himself into such a stupor that he only appeared to be dead.

Knowing in his heart he was deluding himself, but unable to stop, Rye hunkered his lanky six-foot frame down beside the vagrant and roughly flipped him over onto his back.

Startled by the pale, dead eyes that stared up at him from the gaunt, skeletal mask, Rye was hit by a wave of disgust and confusion. How could this shrunken, foul-smelling collection of bones and skin even be a human being, much less the murderer he had dedicated the past thirteen years to finding and killing? The man he remembered had been tall. True, he'd been lean, but at least there had been muscle

17

between the skin and bone. He'd been nothing like this pitiful dreg of humanity, whose body had obviously outlived his soul by many years.

Suddenly it was easy for Rye to see that maybe Fate had not played a cruel trick on him after all. Instead, it had given his family's murderer a slower, more agonizing death than Rye could have imagined even in his darkest, most hatred-consumed hours of preparation for his revenge.

"Heketchetu," he heard the voice of his mother whisper in the language of her people, who continued to refer to themselves as Lakota, despite the white man's insistence they be called the Sioux.

"It is finished," he repeated in English, as a sense of release melted over his strong body. It was finished. For the first time since that terrible day, he could finally allow himself to think of a life beyond this moment.

He heaved a sigh. Maybe he would go west, possibly to Kansas or Colorado, and homestead. Or, he might work as a cowboy to raise enough money to buy a small ranch in Texas or New Mexico and start a herd of cattle or horses. Or he could go back to South Dakota, to settle near his mother's relatives. But wherever he went, the past was finally behind him.

"Yes, *Ina,* at last it is finished," he said aloud.

Energized by his newfound freedom, Rye started to rise. But something caught his gaze, stopping him. Without thinking, he ripped back the dead man's tattered coat.

Renewed misery assaulted Rye's brain. Tears filled his black eyes. After all these years, the bastard who'd murdered his family still wore the knife his father had fashioned with his own hands.

Desperate to remove the stench of human filth from the only thing that remained of his family, Rye wrenched the knife free of the grimy leather sheath

18

strapped to the emaciated waist. Crazed by the horrible visions brought on by the sight of the knife, his actions were automatic.

No longer in control or even able to think clearly, he grabbed a shock of thin, gray hair and slapped the knife to the man's forehead at the hairline. "A scalp for a scalp, you bastard!" he growled ferociously, throwing the dead man's own words from long ago back at him.

"No, son," he heard his mother's spirit plead. *"Heketchetu."*

His face twisted with rage, he shook his head. "No, *Ina,* it is not finished yet."

Aerial viewed the scene below as her assistant slowly lowered her toward the cheering crowd. Without understanding why, her gaze suddenly veered away from the spectators to the streets and stores that surrounded the town square where she had performed from the *Wind Rose* daily for the past week.

Then she saw what had arrested her attention—a lone man dressed all in black, kneeling in the alley beside the dry-goods store—and her curiosity overcame all her other thoughts. She straightened her spine and stretched her neck to better see.

What was he doing back there, when everyone else in town was in the square watching her? And what was he hunched over and studying so intently? It looked like a pile of rags or garbage.

Her inquisitiveness piqued, she signaled her assistant to stop her descent. She squinted her eyes for a better view.

Suddenly, as if he'd been shot from the ground, the man leaped up and bolted from the back end of the alleyway at a dead run.

"Oh, my God!" Aerial gasped, as she saw what the man had been bending over. Not garbage. Not rags.

19

But a human body. Her panicked gaze fixed helplessly on the fleeing man, just as the sun sent a reflection flashing up at her from something metal in his hand. And what he'd been doing in the alley became completely clear to her.

"Stop that man!" she screamed, pointing and waving wildly. "He stabbed someone in that alley!" she yelled to the crowd. "Hurry! Get me down from here!" she ordered her assistant.

As one, the spectators turned their heads in the direction Aerial was indicating, their expressions puzzled, though no one below seemed inclined to move. "Do something!" she begged. "He's getting away!"

Taking care to keep the escaping man in her sights, she deliberately made herself more aware of his clothing and build as she was lowered to the ground. Just before he would have disappeared from view by ducking behind the hotel, he stopped and turned his face in her direction. His expression hard, he fixed a threatening frown on her. Then he was gone.

A chill of dread shimmied up Aerial's spine. He had looked directly into her eyes, as if telegraphing a threat to her through some invisible line. A threat that she would be next to feel his wrath . . .

Try as she might to convince herself there had been no deliberate threat in the man's stare, and that he hadn't been sending her any message at all, she couldn't shake off the ominous feeling. It had been filled with so much hatred and anger.

"Well, I'm not going to wait for you to come after me," she mumbled with more bravado than she felt as she realized the spectators were still staring incredulously at the general store, trying to grasp what had her so agitated.

"Why isn't somebody doing something?" she asked impatiently as she was lowered to within five feet of the ground. Not able to wait any longer, she disentangled her foot and leg and jumped the rest of the way down. "Where's the sheriff?"

"Right here, Miss Windsor. What's the trouble?"

"I saw a man run out of that alley carrying a knife!" she gasped. "Hurry. You've got to go after him!"

The sheriff scratched his chin and shook his head, an amused grin on his round face. "Well, now, miss, running with a knife ain't exactly a crime, now is it?"

Exasperated by the man's attitude, Aerial shoved her face up to the lawman's and spoke through her teeth. "But using it on another human being is! And he . . ."

"What?"

Yes, what Aerial? Looked at you? Threatened you with a magical telepathic message? Her expression was momentarily confused. "He . . . left someone lying in the alley. Maybe even dead. Now, will you please do your job and go arrest him?"

The sheriff's expression grew serious. "Are you saying that you saw someone stabbed from up there?"

Aerial drew in a deep breath and balled her fists in an attempt to check the anger the man was causing to boil in her. "Yes, that's exactly what I'm saying." She paused and thought for an instant. "Well, that's not exactly what I saw. But I did see a man dressed all in black stooping over a wounded or dead man. Back there." She pointed to the alley next to the general store. "Then I saw the same man run out of the alley with a knife in his hand. He disappeared behind the hotel. You've got to go after him. You can't let him get away."

"Go check the alley, Rolf," the sheriff ordered a young deputy, who took off at a run. "Don't worry, Miss Windsor. I'm sure it's nothin'. The afternoon sun causes the shadows to play tricks on us all, but we'll check it out anyway."

"Don't be ridiculous! This was no case of shadows playing tricks. I had a perfect view, and I'm telling you I saw a man, a flesh and blood man, running away from that alley. And he was carrying a knife!"

"You'd better come see this, Sheriff!" the deputy shouted from the alley, then ran toward the back of the general store. "Looks like she was right!"

As one, the spectators made a rush for the alley.

The sheriff whipped out his sidearm and fired it into the air. "You folks go on about your business!" he bellowed, bringing the surging crowd to a standstill. He grabbed Aerial's arm with his free hand. "You come with me."

Running to keep up in spite of her unwillingness to go, Aerial tried to protest. "What do you need me for?"

"If there's been a murder, I'll need you to make a statement."

"I can't go with you," she panted, wrenching her arm free. If there was anything she didn't want to do right then it was view a dead body at close range. "I need to secure my balloon. My assistant can't do it alone. Besides, I've already told you everything I saw, but if you want to talk to me again, I'll be glad to help."

The sheriff thought for a minute, then nodded his agreement. "I guess that'll be okay, but don't go anywhere before I talk to you again and get a full description of what you saw."

Relieved, Aerial held up her hands in a sign of surrender and shook her head as she took a step backward. "Oh, I won't, Sheriff. I'll be right here with the *Wind Rose!* You have my word on it!"

"Hold it right there, mister. You're not goin' nowhere!"

His saddlebags draped over his shoulder, Rye hesitated in mid-step on the end of the hotel porch, though his first impulse was to make a run for freedom. "Are you talking to me?" he asked, slowly turning to face two young deputies who advanced across the deserted porch toward him, their revolvers drawn.

"We ain't talkin' to the wind," the smaller of the two answered, looking uncertainly to his partner. "Whadda ya think, Zeb? Is he the lowdown skunk what killed and scalped that poor drunk in the alley?"

Zeb nodded his head, his pimpled face splitting in a triumphant grin as he examined Rye from head to foot. "If he ain't, I'll lead the parade tomorrow wearin' Miss Hattie's red petticoats." He motioned to Rye with the revolver. "Drop them saddlebags, Injun, and lemme me see you reach for some sky."

Frustrated and angry, Rye sliced a glance toward the town square. When he spotted the same gasfilled balloon he'd seen hovering over the town all the day, *Wind Rose* written in huge black letters on its bloated girth, he was hit with a sinking feeling of defeat.

Dammit! Of all the dumb luck! The woman who had spotted him from the sky had seen him well enough to give the sheriff a description.

Halfway surprised not to see the gloating aeronaut still pointing her accusing finger at him from the wicker car of the great balloon, Rye quickly razed his dark eyes over the mob of people watching the drama on the hotel porch from the center of the square, but she was nowhere in sight. Still, he knew she was there, watching him, waiting to tighten the noose around his throat, the noose she had put there with her interference.

He shook his head in resignation. Who was he trying to fool? There was no one to blame but himself. When he had realized he'd been seen, he should have just kept on going. What had he been thinking when he had wasted valuable time stopping at the hotel to collect his belongings? There certainly wasn't anything in his saddlebags worth hanging for, and from the glint in the deputies' eyes, that was exactly what he was going to do. Unless he did some fast thinking.

Doing his best to remain calm until the right moment came and he could make a break for freedom, Rye lowered the saddlebags to the porch. "I don't know who you think I am, but you're making a big mistake. Now, why don't you put those guns away and let's forget this ever happened. I've got a train to catch and don't want to miss it."

There was something in the hard gleam in Rye's dark eyes that made the two inexperienced deputies glance at each other hesitantly. "He sure don't talk like a Injun, Zeb."

Snorting with disgust, Zeb shook his head. "How many Injuns you heard talk, Jase? This ain't exactly been Injun country the last thirty years!"

Jase's skin color deepened to an embarrassed red. "None, but . . ."

"Well, it don't matter anyhow. He matches the description that Windsor gal gave the sheriff, and we're takin' him in. Get his gun."

Obviously uncomfortable with the idea of putting himself within touching distance of the prisoner, Jase snatched Rye's gun from its holster and jumped back.

Having decided his best defense was no resistance—for the time being—Rye did nothing. After all, maybe he could take on the two seemingly inept deputies, but what kind of chance of escaping would he have with the entire population of the county looking on? No, he was better off waiting and picking his own moment to make his move for freedom.

* * *

24

"I still don't see why I must go to the jail and identify him face to face, Sheriff," Aerial said, testing the weight of one of the sandbags arranged around the outside of the balloon's passenger car. She still hadn't completely shaken off the memory of the hard look the knife-toting man had directed at her from a distance, and even though he was safely behind bars, she didn't particularly want to feel the effect of that threatening glower at close range.

"I already told you he was the man I saw running out of the alley, when your deputies arrested him outside the hotel yesterday afternoon. Besides, since I didn't see his features all that distinctly," she lied, continuing to circle the square wicker basket to check the equipment and supplies tied to its sides, "my facing him would serve no purpose whatsoever."

"No purpose except maybe saving your life."

Aerial stopped her nervous fidgeting with her balloon netting and jerked her head around to look at the lawman, her blue eyes wide with apprehension. "What do you mean?"

The sheriff shrugged and held out his hands in a motion of helplessness. "Just that you're my only witness—and he knows it. And a man lowdown enough to kill and scalp a defenseless drunk in an alley wouldn't think twice about killin' the one person who could send him to the gallows—first chance he got."

Aerial gulped and instinctively clasped her throat with her hands.

"But, much as I hate to do it," the sheriff went on, turning slowly away from her and starting to walk away, "if you refuse to come to the office and identify him officially, I don't have a choice but to turn him loose."

Dropping her hold on the netting that spread over the entire balloon to distribute the weight of the gondola evenly, Aerial called out, "Sheriff, wait." She hurried after him. "I'll do it! Just don't let him out of jail!"

"All I want you to do is look at him and tell me if you're sure he's the man you saw running out of the alley. Then, after you sign the deposition, you're free to leave town right on schedule."

Aerial nodded her head, her eyes riveted to the door through which a deputy had disappeared when the sheriff had sent him to "fetch" the prisoner moments before. "What if I'm not sure?"

"I think you know the answer to that question, Miss Windsor."

A sick feeling of dread washed over her. "You'll release him," she said with resignation, "whether he's guilty or not."

"Without a witness, I can't do nothin' else."

Suddenly, the door leading from the cells burst open, and a handcuffed prisoner stumbled into the office, evidently pushed from behind by the deputy who followed him into the room. "Here he is, Sheriff."

In an involuntary reaction to the captive's abrupt presence, Aerial shrank back in her chair. The sheriff's office suddenly seemed much smaller than it had before the prisoner had come in. A shudder of fear ripped through her, and she crossed her arms over her chest, hugging herself protectively. He was even more dangerous looking here in the sheriff's office than he'd appeared to be when she'd seen him from the *Wind Rose*—and so much bigger.

Over six feet tall, she was certain, the man was decidedly the tallest person in the room; and it was impossible not to sense the controlled strength in his muscular frame. Though he was the perfect picture of submission with his hands secured behind his back and his head bent forward so that his dark hair hid his face from her view, he still presented a picture of deadly power just waiting for the right moment to be loosed on its enemies—like a snake poised to strike. A chill of apprehension broke out on Aerial's arms.

"Well, Miss Windsor, is this the man you saw running out of the alley after killing that old drunk yesterday?" the sheriff asked gruffly, his voice sending a new wave of fear flooding through her. The clothes were the same, but she just couldn't be certain.

"I'm not—"

"Show her your face, half-breed!" the deputy snarled, grabbing a handful of raven black hair and jerking the prisoner's head back.

"But I didn't see . . ." she started, her words dying off as her gaze was captured and held by eyes the color and hardness of coal. Paralyzed by the unspoken threat in the man's expression, she knew again the full heat of the damning stare that had literally burned its way onto her memory the day before.

"Well, is it him or not?" the sheriff asked again, his tone becoming impatient.

Aerial nodded her head so subtly that no one saw her motion, no one, that is, except the prisoner, who narrowed his eyes menacingly, silently daring her to say the words out loud.

With all the force she could muster, she wrenched her gaze free of the intimidating glare that held her powerless, and she nodded her head again. "Yes," she rasped, her voice the barest whisper. "He's the same man I saw running away from the alley."

The lawman's face broke into a satisfied grin and he motioned toward the exit with his head. "That's all we need. Take him back to his cell, Rolf, and I'll have Miss Windsor sign the deposition so she can be on her way." He tossed an offhand glance at the clock in the corner. "It's gettin' pretty close to four o'clock, and I hear the band already startin' to warm up for her big send-off."

"Sure thing, Sheriff." The deputy gave Aerial a polite nod and grin. "Nice meetin' you, Miss Windsor. Let's go, Injun!" he said, prodding Rye from the room.

Once the door slammed behind the two men, Aerial let out a loud relieved sigh. "What will happen to him?" she asked, taking the pen the sheriff offered her and surveying the papers he had shoved across the desk toward her.

"You don't need to worry about him. That's one murderin', thievin' Injun that won't be botherin' decent, law-abidin' folks again. Just as soon as we can get him tried and convicted, he'll get hung like he deserves."

A frisson of guilt charged through Aerial. On her word alone a human being was going to die. Her hand paused on the legal document and she stared at the pen. What if she was wrong? What if it was just a coincidence that the prisoner and murderer looked alike? Was she so positive he was the same man she had seen running out of the alley that she was willing to be the one responsible for his death? She had to be sure.

Closing her eyes, she deliberately brought forth the picture of the murderer's hard glare and again compared it to that of the prisoner. There could be no doubt. Not where a man's life was at stake.

"Is there a problem, Miss Windsor?" the sheriff asked, his voice an abrupt intrusion on her concentration. "You're not havin' second thoughts, are you? He is the same man you saw, isn't he?"

She thought for a full minute longer before answering. "Yes," she finally managed. "There is absolutely no doubt in my mind your prisoner is the same man I saw leaving the alley."

An hour later, dressed in flowing pink silk chiffon and a large matching hat, Aerial climbed a portable staircase and stepped into the cramped wicker car she had spent the early morning hours outfitting for this big moment.

Already exhausted, she managed to hold the smile that had been frozen on her face for the past hour and a half. She had smiled as the high school band played through its repertoire of marches and waltzes, some of them twice. She had smiled as young children had brought her bouquets of flowers. She had smiled through endless speeches by the mayor and every other city and county bigwig who could fit on the speaker's platform. And she had smiled through the long-winded and flowery presentation of a bottle of champagne and a sack of mail for her landing on the East Coast by the representative of the Chamber of Commerce, Chester Hagen, who'd been instrumental in getting her flight to originate in Fairfield at the conclusion of the Fourth of July celebration.

But now it was finally over, and she could leave.

She held up her hands to silence the music and the applause. "Good citizens of Fairfield, Iowa, I thank you for this wonderful day." She nodded to the young men who had all been given their instructions earlier that day. As one, they scurried to their stations around the balloon car, where a circle of sandbags had been arranged on the ground to anchor the *Wind Rose* until it was time to lift off.

"As I embark on this record-seeking flight, I want you to know that wherever the wind carries me, and no matter how many achievements may be attained with this flight, I will carry the memory of Fairfield in my heart for all time. Gentlemen, untie the ropes, please."

The ground crew quickly untied one of each pair

of sandbags, but retained the freed end of the ropes. When every alternate bag had been untied she gave a last wave to the audience and cried, "Good-bye, my friends."

In unison, the crew relaxed their holds on the freed ropes and sat down on the sandbags that were still tied to the other ends. The ropes silently slid through the special rings around the basket, then fell to the ground to be caught and rolled up by the workers below as the majestic red and gold balloon lifted its wicker car off the surface of the earth for its last and greatest flight.

"Daddy, this is for you and Mama," Aerial whispered, her eyes filling with tears as she lifted them heavenward. "Never again will you be the butt of other people's rude jokes."

Chapter Two

Aerial snapped out of her reverie with the realization that the *Wind Rose* was already slowing its ascent—much too soon. Spinning around to the spot where she had secured her instruments, she checked first the altimeter, then the clock.

Immediately alarmed by the ratio of achieved altitude to the number of minutes registering on the face of the clock since takeoff, she hurried to open one of the canvas sacks of sand hanging on the outside of the basket. "I don't understand. How could I be carrying too much weight? I planned so carefully."

Unwilling to risk precious seconds with the scoop she ordinarily used to remove small amounts of ballast, she burrowed both hands into the pouch. With frantic purpose she pitched as much sand overboard as she could manage, then dug in the bag for more. After the release of the second handful of sand, she gave the altimeter a hopeful glance.

"Damn!" Though the dial was creeping upward, it wasn't nearly where it should be. It was imperative that she reach the higher altitudes, where the unpredictable winds that had sent her parents plummeting to their deaths were practically nonexistent.

Anxious, she looked around the supply-crammed basket. There had to be something big she could throw overboard that would make an immediate difference, without wasting a grain of her valuable sand ballast. It was imperative that the ballast be saved for the landing.

For the first time she noticed a crumpled tarp in

the corner. That was odd. The tarp had been folded when she had arranged and checked her supplies that morning. In fact, now that she thought about it, when she had packed the car there had been more space to move about than there was now.

A sense of irritation washed over her. Obviously someone had been in the basket while she was at the send-off ceremonies and had either rummaged through her things or put something else on board— like a stowaway!

"Arnold!" she said to the tarp, certain now that she knew who was under it. "I told you I had to do this alone."

With no time to contemplate why her determined assistant had come against her orders, Aerial ripped back the heavy canvas, knowing exactly what, or to be exact, *who* would be the first to go over the side.

"Miss Windsor, I believe," a deep voice bit out caustically.

Staring into eyes so black the irises and pupils seemed to be one, Aerial took a step back, unable to muster more than a strangled, choking sound.

"You look as if you've seen a ghost," Rye said with a bitter chuckle as he shoved the tarp aside and rearranged his large frame into a more comfortable position on the floor of the basket. "Sorry to disappoint you, but I'm still alive. No thanks to you."

Her heart pounding at a painful rate from the shock of finding herself trapped hundreds of feet above the earth with the murderer she had thought to be safely secured behind bars, Aerial managed to speak. "A-a-are you going t-t-to kill m-m-me?"

Rye deliberately lowered his eyes to the revolver he had aimed at her middle, then raised them to her frightened face. A lazy grin stretched across his mouth, a grin that contained no mirth. "Well, now, I guess that's up to you."

"W-what do you m-m-mean?" If only she could

break free of the intense gaze that held her paralyzed with fear, maybe she could think of what she should do.

Rye gave her a taunting smile, showing white teeth in a way that seemed positively deadly. "I won't kill you if you do what I tell you and get me to safety in this gas bag of yours." He shrugged. "On the other hand, if you give me trouble . . . But we don't need to talk about that, do we? Because you're not going to give me any trouble, are you, Miss Windsor?"

Aerial shook her head, almost as hypnotized by the calm, velvety voice as she was by her captor's black eyes.

"Good. Now that we have that understood, is that dial supposed to be going down . . ." He indicated the instrument panel to his left with his head. ". . . instead of up?"

Aerial's panicked gaze flew to the altimeter. "No! We're going back down because we're carrying too much weight!" she shouted, her fear of the weapon not nearly so incapacitating as the fear of meeting her parents' fate. She rushed to the open sand pouch and threw an entire sandbag over the side, knowing that just a little bit of sand could make the difference.

Rye's complexion blanched perceptibly, and he levered himself to a kneeling position. "What can I do to help?"

She gave him an intolerant glance. "You can get out of my balloon! That's what you can do. It's your weight that's causing the problem." She pointed to a bundle resting on a wicker picnic basket. "You can use the parachute." She cast a quick look at the altimeter, relieved to notice the balloon was slowly rising again, though not fast enough to allow her to relax.

"But since I doubt you're willing to be so accommodating, you can at least help me get rid of this."

33

Stooping down, she strained to lug a corner of the weatherproofed canvas onto the rim of the basket.

Ignoring the sarcasm in her tone, Rye holstered his revolver and pushed her aside to gather the entire square of heavy canvas in his arms. With ease, he heaved it over the side, then automatically glanced at the altimeter to see if there had been any change. "The dial's going up," he announced, his voice triumphant.

Aerial bit back the damning retort that came to her mind. "For now," she mumbled, tossing another handful of sand over the side for good measure. "But as we go higher, the gas loses it's lifting power and—" She spun around to face him, her expression challenging. "If you'll use that parachute, I swear I won't tell a living soul you were ever here, or where you are."

Rye stood up and peered over the side. His stomach did a sudden somersault, and the bones and muscles in his legs felt as if they had turned to a quivering mass of jelly. He grabbed the basket rim with both hands to steady himself. He'd no idea how far above the earth they were. In the balloon car, there was no awareness of any movement whatsoever. Not up or down or sideways.

With blurred vision, he stared helplessly at the vast acres of green Iowa farmland passing slowly beneath them, the rippling fields of corn and wheat moving in a haunting dance that only added to his weakness. Swallowing back the wave of nausea that rose to his throat, he tore his gaze away from the mesmerizing scene below. "Lady, you must be crazy if you think I'd ju—"

She pointed eastward and spoke as if she hadn't heard the refusal. "The Mississippi River is ahead. That means we're almost to Illinois, and once you're over the state line, it will be safe to jump."

"I told you, I'm not jumping!" he shouted. "Now

shut up about it."

She studied his determined face for a moment. Then understanding hit her. The bronzed complexion she remembered from when she saw him at the Fairfield jail was now a grayish green. "You're afraid, aren't you?" she accused with a triumphant sneer.

Rye narrowed his eyes and cocked the hammer on the revolver. "You don't learn too fast."

The sneer slid from her face. Now she'd done it. Why did she have to make that taunt about his being afraid? She had better think fast if she was going to undo any of the harm caused by her careless remark.

She sucked in a deep, fortifying breath, determined to hide the fear pulsing through her brain. "If you kill me," she started, struggling to make her voice sound calm and natural, "you'll kill yourself as well. If that's your intention, why did you bother escaping from jail?"

"What are you talking about?"

"For one thing, if you ever want to feel solid ground beneath your feet again, you can't kill me, I'm the only one who knows how to safely land the *Wind Rose*."

The expression on his face became even more uncertain.

"And for another," she went on, enjoying her "captor's" misery. "Before you pull that trigger, I think you should know that the balloon over your head is filled with enough coal gas to burn this entire craft to a crisp in a matter of seconds. All it would take to turn us both into cinders would be one spark from your revolver."

Rye couldn't resist shifting his worried gaze up to the underside of the balloon. After all, nothing could be as bad as looking down. Besides, he knew she was bluffing. "I don't believe you."

Aerial shrugged, his growing uneasiness restoring the tiniest bit of her confidence. "You probably think the gas is all trapped in the balloon and can't possibly be a danger to us down here. But that's because you don't know anything about ballooning — or coal gas." She pointed upward.

"See that tube up there? That's the inflation appendix. Not only is it used to fill the balloon with gas from the public gas mains, but since it must stay open to let the gas back *out* when it expands, the *highly explosive* combination of hydrogen and methane is escaping all the time we're rising."

She stooped to pick up the parachute and held it out to him, hoping that her technical description would be sufficiently frightening to her unwanted passenger. "Sure you don't want to use this?"

Ignoring her snide suggestion, Rye reholstered his gun. After all, there were other ways to kill a person — if it came to that. "Just shut up and start thinking about a place to bring this thing down once we get past the river."

"No! I can't."

"What do you mean, you can't?"

"Because . . ." She cut her words short. *Think, Aerial! It won't matter a bit to him that ending your flight so soon will only give your father's critics something else to laugh about. In fact, that would probably make him doubly determined to do it, just to get back at you for getting him arrested.*

It occurred to her that if she was forced to land at gunpoint people would certainly understand, but as quickly as the thought occurred to her, she dismissed it. Did she really expect the murderer to hang around after they landed to corroborate her story? To the public it would seem that she, like her parents, had simply failed.

She shook her head. No! She refused to disgrace the Windsor name a second time. One way or another she would make this flight. Even if it meant spending hours with a gun-toting murderer, she would not land before she had reestablished her father's good reputation!

However, she knew she had better convince her abductor that staying aloft was to his advantage, not hers. He already looked as if the height were making him desperate enough to gamble on blowing himself to smithereens if that was the only way to get his feet on solid ground again.

"Well," she began, her mind racing for a reasonable excuse to keep him aloft. Suddenly, she was struck with inspiration. "Unless you want to be caught, you can't land in Illinois."

"Why not? You said it yourself, I'll be safe once I'm out of Iowa."

Aerial winced, damning herself for putting the idea of landing in Illinois into his head. Well, that couldn't be helped now. She would just have to give him a new idea! "The river isn't more than forty or fifty miles from Fairfield, and a posse could cover that distance in just a few hours."

"But they won't. They don't even know I'm with you."

"Are you so sure?" she asked with a smile she hoped looked as if she knew something he didn't know, deliberately meaning to work on the insecurity so obvious in his tone. "But even if they haven't figured out how you got out of town, it's only a matter of time until they do. And then it will be too late for you if you're on the ground."

"What are you talking about?"

"A balloon this size can't exactly drop out of the sky unnoticed. In fact, every farmer for miles around will see us coming down long before we land, and they'll all be there to meet us. Towns all along our expected path have been warned to watch for the balloon so they can report my progress back to Fairfield as well as warn the next town that I'm heading in their direction. You can be sure they'll send a wire

37

back to Fairfield telling them where I've made any unscheduled landing. *And* that I'm not alone. And you can bet the Fairfield sheriff will come running, especially after the way you made a fool out of him by escaping."

Struggling to think around the lightheadedness that threatened him, Rye tightened his grip on the rim and forced himself to peek over the side at the landscape passing lazily beneath them. "I'd still have a five- or six-hour start before they could get there," he mused, almost as if talking to himself.

"Not if they've already realized you escaped in my balloon. In that case, they've already wired everyone to be on the lookout for you if I should land prematurely. If they have, the local lawmen will be waiting to take you into custody. Besides," she added for good measure, "if you did get away, you'd be on foot. They'll have horses."

"Damn," he mumbled, knowing she was right. Gladly removing his attention from the ground, he faced her squarely, though never loosening his death grip on the side of the car. "How long before we get to Indiana?"

Victory resounded through Aerial's blood. The kidnapper had become the kidnapped, for the time being at least. Of course, she would feel better if she had the gun, but for now this was definitely better than the alternative. She'd think about the gun later.

"Indiana?" She opened the lid on a wooden box bolted to the rim of the basket, exposing a map board. "I'll have to check the map and calculate it."

After several minutes of careful studying and figuring with pencil and navigating instruments, she looked up at Rye. "Of course this is only an educated guess, but if we gain some altitude, increase our rate of speed, and stay on this same course, we should cross out of Illinois in about six or seven hours."

Rye took out his pocket watch and flipped it open. "Six or seven hours would put us there about ten or eleven thirty, right?"

Aerial nodded, letting him have a moment to come to his own conclusion. "Give or take an hour or two."

"Can you land this thing in the dark?"

Just like stealing candy from a baby, she congratulated herself. "I see no problem if the conditions are right and I can see where I'm going." She would wait until later to tell him that there was no balloonist in the world who would land in the dark on strange terrain—unless forced down. For now, she just wanted him to opt for staying aloft a little bit longer.

"And in the dark, no one would be able to see us coming down, would they?"

"I don't see how."

"Then we'll wait until we pass over Illinois."

Struggling to hold back the smile of relief that threatened to erupt on her face, Aerial snapped her map board shut and spun away from her passenger. "Whatever you say, Mr. . . . Uh, do you have a name?"

She quickly dumped the remaining sand in the first bag overboard, pouch and all. Now that she was free to work, she intended to make up for time lost dealing with her uninvited passenger. She only wished he could be the extra weight she was dropping over the side, rather than the precious ballast she had planned to save to keep the balloon aloft longer, once it started its inevitable descent at the end of the flight.

"Berenger. Rye Berenger," he answered, sliding down to the floor of the basket and leaning back against the wicker wall, as if his decision had cost him the last of his energy.

"Rye Berenger?" She studied him curiously over her shoulder. "They said you were an Indian. That

39

doesn't sound like an Indian name."

"On my mother's side. My father was white."

"I see," she responded, abruptly returning to her work. What was wrong with her? What had possessed her to even ask his name, much less make an attempt at conversation? What difference did it make to her? She already knew as much about him as she needed to know. He was a murderer and she was stuck with him for the next twenty-four hours. Pure and simple.

Promising herself she would only speak to the man if it was absolutely necessary, she emptied a second and third bag of sand into the air, then checked her altimeter. "That's more like it," she said to herself as the dial finally began to rise at a more aggressive rate.

Taking a deep breath, she looked back toward Fairfield, realizing that the town was now completely out of sight. Suddenly she felt good. Despite the unforseen complications, she was still in the air and gaining altitude. Nothing—and no one—was going to stop her now.

Her spirits were so lifted she couldn't stop the happy grin that spread across her face. Forgetting her vow, she wheeled around to face Rye. "We're going to ma—"

His head slumped forward so that his chin rested on his chest, his fingers laced across his lean middle, Rye Berenger was sound asleep.

Unexpected disappointment flashed in her head. After all the trouble he had caused with the departure, he could have at least stayed awake long enough to share her good news.

Shocked by the preposterous thought, Aerial slapped her hands to her chest and pivoted around so her back was to him. What was she thinking? This man was a murderer. He had been going to kill her. He could still be planning to do it once he had no more use for her. And she was wanting to share her good news with him?

Lord, all the thin air I've been breathing at high altitudes has finally caught up with me. How could I even be thinking of talking to that murderer, much less "sharing" anything with him?

She hastily scanned her instruments, then turned back to her map board. Well, that inclination may have occurred in a very weak moment of exhilaration, but it wouldn't happen again. Her intent had been to make this flight alone, so she would simply go on as planned. Well, almost as planned. If she totally ignored Rye Berenger's presence, it would be close enough.

During the next hour Aerial managed to become so involved with her charts and instruments that she actually forgot her unwanted passenger for a while.

Drifting at an ideal thirty miles per hour in the absolute silence forty-five hundred feet above the gently rolling hills of northwest Illinois, she was suddenly overwhelmed with a sense of loneliness greater than any she had ever felt.

She had no one. Her family was dead. She had never stayed anywhere long enough to have established any real friends. In fact, she could just keep flying higher and higher and never go back down, and it would make no difference to anyone on earth.

The truth sent a violent chill shuddering through her.

"Stop feeling sorry for yourself," she scolded aloud, wrapping her arms around herself. *It's that way because I want it that way. When you care about people, losing them is too painful.*

Rubbing her hands up and down on her arms to get warm, she realized for the first time that she was still wearing the pink chiffon she had worn for the send-off. "No wonder I'm cold," she exclaimed with a quick look at the red-tinged setting sun.

Opening a small trunk, she whisked out a long-sleeved white cotton blouse, a plain brown skirt, and a jacket. Once she got into more practical clothing she would feel much better, and this ridiculous wave of self-pity would disappear. She hurriedly unfastened the buttons at the nape of her neck, then crossed her arms in front of herself to grab hold of the sides of her bodice at the waist.

A vision of her unwanted passenger zipped across her mind, catching her just as she would have whisked the dress off over her head.

A flicker of hope that the entire incident had been a bad dream ignited in her head, and she whirled around to check. But of course, it was no dream.

Frustrated, she stared at the sleeping man in disgusted silence. What was she supposed to do now? How could she change clothes with him only three feet away and apt to awaken at any moment? For that matter . . . She took a desperate glance at the small wicker commode in the corner that disguised her chamber pot.

Her chill temporarily forgotten, she faced the immediate problem. Searching for an answer to her predicament, she studied Rye Berenger, really seeing him for the first time.

An odd feeling of confusion washed over her. Asleep, he didn't look nearly so vicious or threatening. In fact, he seemed vulnerable and defenseless, like a lost little boy who needed someone to take care of him, despite the broad shoulders that seemed to span more than half the four-foot wall of the basket.

His thick and slightly wavy hair was long. It hung over the tops of his ears on the sides, past his shirt collar in back, and over his forehead in front. And black! She had never seen hair so black. A description she had read in a romance novel long ago flared in her mind, and she now knew exactly what it meant. He had hair "blacker than a raven's wing."

Why, he's actually handsome, she realized with surprise, noting straight black eyebrows, well-shaped full lips, high, pronounced cheekbones, and a firm jawline darkened only slightly by a shadow of beard.

In fact, now that she had time to study him so closely, she decided Rye Berenger's nose was the only thing that kept his features from being too good-looking to be masculine. Not overly large or obviously hooked, his subtly aquiline nose bore obvious testimony to his Indian heritage. It gave him the rugged look of a man who was not only capable of taking care of himself, but of anyone he loved.

Shocked at the unseemly turn her thoughts had taken, Aerial gasped and tore her gaze free from the sleeping man. Determined to force her concentration back to the problem at hand, she flipped open her trunk and snatched out her rain poncho.

Her actions frenzied, she divided the basket diagonally with a curtain made by stretching the poncho between support ropes. Listening for sounds that indicated Rye had awakened, she waited several minutes to be safe. When she determined that he was still sleeping soundly on the other side of the curtain, she hurriedly changed her clothes and made use of the commode while her privacy lasted—keeping her eyes glued to the curtain every minute.

Once her needs had been taken care of, she faced the curtain, wishing she could leave it up until the end of the flight. But of course, that wouldn't be very practical. Not only did it cut her sphere of vision in half, but half of her supplies were on the other side too, her food in particular. Suddenly she was very hungry. She'd been too busy and excited about the launch to eat a bite of food that day.

Resigned to the impracticality of leaving the divider up, Aerial untied one end and pitched the poncho into the corner.

Her concentration on Rye, she crept over to the

picnic basket beside where he slept, his shoulder touching its side. Squatting down carefully, she eased out a jug of coffee that had been wrapped in several layers of thick towels in a burlap bag. It wouldn't be boiling hot anymore, but it should still be warm. Besides, cold or hot, it would certainly help her stay awake during the long night ahead.

In the narrow space between Rye's large form and the wall of the balloon car, it was a struggle to unwrap and open the jug. But she was determined to have a cup of coffee. Unfortunately, there was even less room than she had anticipated, and she accidently brushed her hand against him.

Automatically swerving her eyes to the side to see what she had touched, her gaze fell on her passenger's holstered revolver. Excitement charged through her. If she could just get that gun . . .

Balancing the coffee jug precariously on her knees, she looked up at the man's face. Relieved to see that he still slept soundly, she carefully put the coffee back into the basket.

Her eyes zigzagging back and forth between the sleeping man's face and the revolver, she slowly moved her hand toward the weapon.

Just as she wrapped her fingers around the butt of the gun, the balloon basket lurched. Before Aerial could catch herself, the back of her hand nudged him in the ribs.

"Ahhh!" he yowled, jerking awake. His features, so handsome in sleep, were now contorted with pain. "What are you doing?"

Startled, her hands flew to her mouth and she fell back on her bottom, the gun no longer within her grasp. "I'm sorry! I didn't mean to wake you up. I just wanted some coffee and something to eat," she choked out. "I thought I could . . ." She stopped. "Wait a minute. What am I explaining to you for? You're the intruder here, not me!"

Wincing, Rye inserted his hand under his jacket to touch his side where she had bumped him. His face twisted in a hapless grimace, he raised black, hurting eyes to her face, then lowered his gaze as he removed his hand from inside the jacket.

Instinctively, Aerial looked downward too. "Oh, my goodness! You're bleeding!"

"So it would seem."

Chapter Three

"How can that be? I barely touched you!"

Rye gave her a grim smile, his struggle to hide his pain obvious. "Relax. You didn't do it. It's just a little scratch I picked up on my way out of Fairfield."

The slick red stain on his fingers gave testimony to the fact that his wound was much more serious than he was letting on. "Little scratch? Since when do scratches bleed like that? I'd better look at it."

Forgetting for the moment that Rye Berenger had threatened to kill her an hour earlier, she reached for his jacket front.

His face dark with anger, he grabbed both her wrists. "So you can finish off the job?"

He knew! He knew she had been going to steal his gun! Now what was she going to do?

Calling on all her inner resources, she returned his determined glare with her own willful gaze. "I don't know what you're talking about, Mr. Berenger. All I want to do is see if I can help you," she said evenly. "Now, are you going to let me look at it or are you going to sit there and finish yourself off by bleeding to death?"

His lip curling bitterly, Rye gave his revolver a meaningful glance, then looked up at Aerial. "Funny, I got the distinct impression that wouldn't upset you too much."

Inexplicably hurt that he thought she actually wanted him dead, Aerial fought the urge to deny it. "It wouldn't . . . as long as you do it somewhere else. I just don't want the blood stains all over my basket.

46

Besides, as inconvenient as it is to have you alive in my balloon, I don't particularly want to explain a dead body when I land. Of course, if you weren't too big for me to lift, I could just dump you over the side and my problem would be solved, but since you are, and I can't, why don't you stop being so ridiculous and let me do something about that 'scratch'?"

He studied her face for several minutes, his own features filled with distrust. Finally he dropped his grip on her wrists and held his hands out in a sign of surrender. "Go on, but it's not that serious. And don't try anything stupid."

"I . . . I've no intention of doing anything stupid," she rasped with confused relief. She could still feel the heat of his fingers raging up her arms from her wrists. Trembling with the effort to function, she shoved his jacket front aside.

"Oh!" Aerial's dismayed eyes focused on the bright red stain plastering the once-tan material of his shirt to his side.

Rye surveyed his own wound. "It looks a lot worse than it is," he said with a grunt.

"I find that difficult to believe," Aerial commented, her tone distracted as her natural instinct to perform in an emergency took over. "The first thing we must do is take off that jacket and shirt so I can determine just how seriously you're injured." She released her hold on the jacket front and reached for the buttons on his shirt.

"I can do it." His tone testy, he brushed her hands aside.

She hesitated for a moment, then stood up and turned away. If he wanted to be stubborn, it was no skin off her nose. "In that case, I'll get my medical supplies." She leaned forward and retrieved bandages and a bottle of carbolic wash from a canvas bag strapped to the side.

When she turned to face him again, she sucked in

a loud gasp of air before she could stop herself. Though she had told him to remove his clothing, nothing had prepared her for the impressively muscled expanse of male chest that assaulted her eyes. Suddenly it was very warm in the balloon car.

"If you're going to stand there gawking while I freeze to death, I'm putting my coat back on."

Realizing that her lower jaw had dropped an unattractive two inches, Aerial snapped her teeth together. "I wasn't gawking," she protested with an indignant sniff, her face hot with embarrassment.

Rye nodded, his knowing eyes telling her he knew exactly how he had affected her. "Whatever you say."

Aerial took a deep breath and knelt down beside him again. "First I need to clean this up," she explained, tipping the water jug onto a white folded cloth.

"Lift your arm," she ordered stiffly, sure his nearness was hiking her temperature by several degrees. What would it do to her when she actually touched his flesh? She wished now she had taken his word for it when he had insisted the wound was not serious.

Complying with her instructions, Rye raised his arm, and Aerial immediately forgot her own uneasiness.

The wound he had labeled "a little scratch" was an eight-inch diagonal slash that stretched from a point a few inches below his underarm to within a hand span of his belt. "How'd this happen?" she asked, pressing the wet cloth to the cut.

"Damn! What're you trying to do?" he bellowed, his reflexes making him jerk back from the cold and grab her hand.

"What did you expect?" she asked with a humorless chuckle, keeping the cloth to his side despite his hold on her wrist. "We're not exactly equipped with facilities for heating water up here, Mr. Berenger. Besides, the cold will help stop the bleeding. So quit being such a baby and let me clean this up and get a bandage on it."

Gritting his teeth, Rye relaxed his muscles ever so slightly, but he retained a loose hold on her wrist. "Okay, but make it fast."

When Aerial had finished cleansing and wrapping Rye's injury, she released a long sigh. "That should take care of you until you can get to a doctor."

"Thanks," he said, reaching for his shirt.

"What are you doing?"

"I'm getting dressed. Before I catch pneumonia."

"You can't put that back on," she said, snatching the bloody shirt away from him.

"Hey! Give me my shirt." Making a grab for his shirt, Rye lunged forward.

Unprepared for the force and speed of his charge, Aerial toppled over onto her back. Her breath taken away, she didn't move.

Stunned, Rye scrambled to Aerial and hovered over her. "Are you all right? I didn't mean . . ."

Though she had successfully avoided looking directly at his face while she'd worked on his wound, now she was unable to resist raising her blue eyes to his. "I . . . I think so," she answered breathlessly. "How about you? I hope you didn't open your cut again."

His black eyes never leaving her face, he patted the fresh bandage and shook his head. "Looks like you did too good a job taping me up," he said with a sheepish smile, his voice hoarse. "Here, let me help you up." He grasped her upper arms and hauled her to a sitting position before she could protest. "Are you sure you're not hurt?"

An incredible feeling of lightness washed through her. His face was so close to hers she could barely breathe, much less speak. All she could do was nod.

The warmth of his breath soughed gently over her face, and she was sure she had to be unconscious

49

and dreaming. Never in her life had she felt so help-less, so protected. It was as though her will and bones and muscles had all turned to air. In fact, she had the distinct feeling that if she weren't anchored in the balloon car by the iron grip that held her, she could easily float away and dissolve into the clouds.

"You don't look so good," Rye said, his voice sounding far away. "Did you hit your head? Maybe you should lie back down."

Unable to pull her gaze away from his concerned face, not even wanting to, she managed a weak smile. The mere thought of how long it had been since anyone had looked at her that way suddenly made her want to cry. He seemed so much younger and gentler than she had judged him to be. How could this be the face of a murderer?

No sooner had the question formed in her mind than reason rose to combat it. *Of course he's a murderer!* a scolding inner voice insisted. *You saw his victim with your own eyes!*

Her head cleared slightly by the ugly reminder, she wrenched her beguiled gaze away from the dark face that watched her with such intense concern.

"Please take your hands off me," she said through clenched teeth, bracing herself for the familiar soli-tude she knew would again envelope her the instant the physical contact ended. "I don't need your help."

Surprise registered on Rye's face as though she had kicked him in the stomach, surprise that was quickly veiled behind a hard mask of indifference. "What-ever you say, lady. But give me back my shirt."

Remembering the struggle that had caused her fall, she looked down at her hand. She was surprised to see that she still clung to the bloody shirt. "You really will freeze if you put it back on. It's not even dry." Without waiting for his response, she tossed the shirt aside and scooted shakily to her small trunk. "I have a blanket you can use to keep warm.

At least until your shirt dries out."

The idea of wearing a wet shirt was only slightly more distasteful than huddling in a blanket like an old Indian chief whose day had come and gone, yet Rye realized he had little choice. He was already cold, and the sun was only beginning to descend. He could just imagine how cold it would be once it was dark. Anyway, he wasn't going anywhere for a few more hours. He might as well be comfortable, as comfortable as he could be trapped in a basket and floating hundreds of feet above the earth. His empty stomach did a somersault at the reminder of where he was.

"Thanks," he grunted, snatching the offered blanket from her and draping it around his shoulders. "Did I hear you say something about coffee and something to eat?"

Her expression registered annoyance. Hadn't she done enough for this overbearing oaf? Now he expected her to feed him as well. She was tempted to tell him he had imagined her mention of food. But of course she couldn't do that, not unless she wanted to go hungry herself.

Besides, if he had a full belly maybe he would fall back to sleep and she could delay the battle they were sure to have when she refused to land the balloon later that night.

"Help yourself," she offered coolly, indicating the picnic basket in the corner. "The good ladies of Fairfield were quite generous. They must have known I was going to have an extra mouth to feed."

"What do you mean, we can't land before daylight?!? You said the dark wouldn't be a problem!"

Annoyed that Rye Berenger hadn't done her the favor of sleeping through the night, Aerial shook her head and removed her attention from the dials of the instruments she'd been reading by the light of the full moon.

"I said *if* I could see, and *if* we stayed on the same course," she stated calmly, doing her best to hide the uneasiness she felt inside. She knew she mustn't make him so angry he would force her to land despite her arguments against it. She had to make him see the advantages to staying aloft. "Unfortunately, neither of those conditions exists, so we can't possibly land."

Rye inspected the small car, surprised to notice how well-lit it was. In fact, he was amazed to see he could make out every detail around him. "What are you up to? It's bright as day up here."

She shrugged and gave him a helpless grin over her shoulder. "Up here, perhaps, but if you'll look over the side, you'll see that's because we're above the clouds. I have no way of seeing what it's like on the ground. Besides, as close as I can determine, we're over the southern end of Lake Michigan right now."

"Oh?" he asked, his dark brows arched suspiciously. "And exactly how did you reach that conclusion if you can't see the ground?"

Aerial went back to her instruments, relieved to bring the conversation to an area where she felt secure. "For one thing, instead of moving due east, as we did before we left Iowa, we've been traveling at a northeasterly angle most of the time since we crossed the Mississippi. Like this." She placed a straightedge on her map at the same angle they had drifted from the river.

Knowing he couldn't see what she was doing, she examined him where he continued to sit beside the picnic basket. An idea hit her. "If you want to understand this, you're going to have to stand up and look at the map."

Rye took an uneasy look side to side, then raised his eyes to her expectant face. He couldn't miss the challenge in her expression. He had ignored her first reference to him standing up, but she obviously didn't intend to quit until he started squirming so she could make another snide comment about his being afraid.

Damned if he was going to give her the satisfaction of knowing how right she had been. "Sure," he agreed, grabbing hold of the basket rim. Making every effort to convince himself that his earlier vertigo had been the result of twenty-four hours without sleep or food, as well as a loss of blood, he hauled himself to his feet.

The surprise on Aerial Windsor's face was enough to confirm that he had read her intent correctly. He couldn't resist giving her a triumphant grin and arch of his brows, and he was sure he heard a peeved snort as she presented the back of her head to him again.

Viewing her from behind, he was free to appreciate the way the bright moonlight turned her hair to a shimmering halo of gold. Her rigid posture as she pored over her maps made him think about all that had happened to her and how bravely she had taken it.

Most women would have screamed, pleaded, or wept — or all three — if they'd found themselves the prisoner of a man they believed to be a murderer, but not this one. Even when she had obviously been frightened, she had looked him straight in the eye and stood her ground.

He was hit with the odd thought that he wished they had met under different circumstances, but he quickly tossed it aside.

"Are you going to stand there clinging to the rim for dear life, or are you going to come over here and let me explain how I know where we are?" Aerial asked without looking at him. "You don't need to be afraid. It's really quite safe."

Damn! He hadn't fooled her at all. Even without seeing him, she knew he was still uneasy as hell in this basket. It was obvious she intended to take advantage of that knowledge every chance she got.

He glanced down at his hand. At the thought of losing the security of his grip on the rim he was tempted to sit back down. What difference did it make to him what she thought about him? He didn't care if she knew he was afraid. Besides, what *normal* person wouldn't be nervous up here?

But for all his rationalizing, he still couldn't bring himself to admit his fear by backing down.

All he had to do was keep his eyes straight ahead and not look over the side or think about how far the fall to the ground was, and he could do it. He *would* do it!

Silently, he willed the muscles of his fingers to relax one at a time until he could drop his hand to his side.

He hesitated, testing his balance. Hit with the realization that his footing was quite steady and that he wasn't going to tumble out of the basket, his face split in a victorious grin.

"Well?" a chiding voice asked, dampening the flicker of elation he was feeling. "Do you want me to explain this or not?"

"Yes," he answered, dropping the blanket from around his shoulders. Two could play this game, and he knew just how to unhinge this particular enemy. He'd seen it in her expression earlier. Miss Aerial Windsor might not be afraid of heights, or even his gun, but there was definitely one thing that frightened her. He stepped across the basket in one determined stride. "Explain it to me."

At the unexpected feel of him so close behind her, Aerial jumped and twisted her head around before she could stop herself. "Oh!" She was surprised to find her nose only inches from the coppery male chest that had unnerved her so severely before.

"Did I frighten you?" he asked, enjoying her obvious discomfort.

Her gaze vaulted up to his face, forcing her to tip her head back. He was much taller than she had realized. "N . . . no," she answered, her voice a raspy whisper. She ran her tongue nervously over her lips to wet her mouth. "Of course not."

His mouth stretched in a lazy smile that said he knew she was lying, but he let it drop. "In that case, suppose you 'show' me why we can't land in Indiana as we planned."

Determined to regain control of the strange emotions assaulting her, Aerial wrenched her eyes away from the dark face that loomed over her. She wouldn't allow herself to think about the heat of his body, so close to her that she suddenly felt as if she were standing in front of a stove. And she would ignore the tangy, salty smell of his flesh that seemed intent on blinding her senses to anything but him.

She pointed a shaky finger to a spot on the map. "According to my calculations, we should be about here."

"And where is that?" he breathed, bringing his mouth near her ear and his muscled chest flush against her back as he leaned forward to grip the basket rim on either side of her map board.

Trapped in the circle of his arms, Aerial was overwhelmed with an incredible desire to relax back into the security of his embrace. It might be nice to be able to lean on someone else for just a while.

Tensing at the ludicrous thought of relying on a murderer like Rye Berenger for anything, she stiffened and spoke. "Must you stand so close?"

"If I don't, I can't see the map."

Scrutinizing the supplies stacked on either side of where she was standing, she realized he was telling the truth. Unfortunately, that didn't help. She would just have to pretend he wasn't there.

She wagged her pencil up and down over an area of the map. "This is Lake Michigan," she said, hating herself for the tremble in her voice.

She adjusted her straightedge on the map. "And this is the approximate route we've taken from the Mississippi." With her pencil, she indicated a point at the southern end of the lake where her straightedge crossed it. "We should be about right here. So you can see it would be very wet, and deadly, to land now."

"How do you know?" he asked, his voice rough. All of a sudden he was very warm. What had started out as a plan to make her uneasy was definitely having its effect on him as well. But he wasn't so uncomfortable that he could bear the thought of taking a step backward. Besides, he really wanted to understand this balloon flying. The more he knew about it, the less he would be at her mercy until they landed.

"I know because it's my job to know," she said haughtily, obviously insulted that he would question her ability.

"Suppose you explain it to me in a bit more detail," he said caustically.

"I keep track with my compass and other instruments. Also, not long before you woke up, there was a break in the clouds and I saw the lights of Chicago below. And since it's on Lake Michigan, I'm reasonably certain my calculations are accurate."

"What makes you so sure it was Chicago and not some other city?"

She heaved a sigh obviously meant to relay impatience with his stupidity. "Because Chicago is the only place big enough to be seen at night from this altitude. Other towns, if you see them at all, are just occasional dots of light."

His body tensed and his grip on the basket rim

tightened. "What does that mean? Just how high up are we?"

"Are you sure you want to know?" she asked, sensing that she had just regained some leverage in this silent war for control.

"Of course I want to know. How high up are we? A thousand feet?"

"More like ten," she said with a gloating smirk.

Rye gulped. "Ten *thousand?* You mean we're almost two miles off the ground?"

Aerial nodded. "Give or take a few hundred feet." She was really enjoying the panic she heard in his voice. It served him right for what he was doing to her. "You're not afraid, are you? You don't need to be, you know. As long as we're up this high, we're perfectly safe. It's only when we get closer to the earth that there's any real danger."

Just don't look down, he told himself again, forcing his eyes back to the map.

Suddenly, something caught his attention, and he pushed his fear to the back of his mind. Squinting to be sure of what he was seeing, he brought one hand to the map board and pointed to the northeast route she had indicated they were traveling. "This looks like we're heading into Canada."

A charge of electricity sizzled up her arm from where his inner arm grazed her sleeve. Holding her breath to keep back the moan that threatened to escape from her lips, she studied the map much longer than necessary to answer. Finally, she managed to speak.

"If we stay on this same course, we are. On the other hand, we may turn more eastward again and remain on the United States side. With a balloon, you never know."

"Can't you steer this thing at all?"

"No better than we can steer the wind. Up here, we're part of the wind and go wherever it takes us.

57

That's why you don't feel any sense of moving."

Still peering over her shoulder, his ear close to her cheek, his hand a scant inch from hers on the straightedge, he ran his finger up the ruler to the map of Canada. "If we do go into Canada, we could land on the east shore of Lake Huron, couldn't we?"

Her skin tingled from her scalp to her toes, as if she were connected to him through thousands of electric wires. She was completely engulfed in his presence. It was horrible. It was wonderful. And she had the sudden wish that the moment would never end.

"We can't land there," she managed to say, wishing her voice didn't sound so breathless. Thank heavens they were discussing something she could talk about in her sleep. If she had to think to speak, she was sure she would become a stammering idiot.

"If we tried to land on the peninsula between Huron and Erie, we could be swept right into Lake Ontario if anything went wrong." With a shaking finger, she backed up her statement by pointing it out on the map. "To be safe, we'll have to stay aloft until we're farther into Canada."

Rye didn't say anything for several seconds, though Aerial could have sworn it was minutes—minutes of glorious, unbearable torture, with his warm breath on her cheek, her sleeve only a fraction of an inch from the inside of his bare arm.

"Even though I'll be farther east than I intended to be, it might work out for the best if you can get me to Canada before we land. No one is going to cross into Canada to track me down. I'm not that important."

"What if we don't go into Canada?"

"You just keep watching those charts and instruments and hope we do, because I don't intend to rot in some Iowa jail or get hung for something I didn't do."

Shocked by his words, Aerial snapped her head around to stare at him. "Didn't? But I saw y—"

Rye's black eyes narrowed angrily. "I know exactly what you saw, Miss Windsor. Don't forget, I saw you, too. You didn't see me killing that old drunk, and you and I both know it."

"If you didn't kill him, why were you running away?" she asked, her own eyes searching his face for answers. Something inside her wanted desperately to believe him. "You had a knife."

"And don't forget the most obvious proof I killed him. I'm an Indian, therefore I must be guilty. So you left me there to hang without giving a thought to the possibility that I might be innocent."

Shocked at the hurt and bitterness in his tone, Aerial defended herself. "I didn't know you were an Indian until the sheriff told me you were," she said, remembering the soul-searching she had done before she had signed the deposition against him. Had she been wrong?

His lip curled distastefully. "But since everyone knows the Indian is always guilty, once you found out, it didn't matter if you actually saw me kill that sorry excuse for a man or not, did it? One way or another, you were doing your patriotic duty. Whether or not I was guilty, it was a chance to rid the world of one more filthy red man, so you signed that deposition against me saying you saw me murder him, even though you saw nothing of the sort."

"That's not true. I told the sheriff I didn't see the actual murder, just you leaving the scene with a knife. But he told me he knew you were guilty and that if I didn't sign, he would have to let you go since I was the only witness." She sucked in a deep breath and bit her lip, feeling more worried by the minute that she had made the wrong decision in the sheriff's office.

"He said you would come after me and kill me

too, since I was the only one who could put you at the scene of the murder. I couldn't take that chance. Anyway," she added, turning her face away from his, "I was . . . am . . . sure it was you I saw bending over that body before you ran away."

He cupped her chin in his strong grasp and forced her head back around so she had to look at him. "And of course it didn't occur to you that I might have just discovered the dead man and be checking to see if he was alive, did it?"

Her eyes wide with apprehension, she formed a silent *no* with her lips.

"Of course it didn't. You just wanted to wash your hands of the situation, so you signed that deposition. It didn't matter to you if an innocent man got hung, did it? After all, it was just another Indian."

"Stop saying that!" Aerial twisted her head to free her face from his grip, but it did no good. "That thought never crossed my mind. I was convinced you were guilty. I still am. I saw what I saw, and nothing you say can change that. You killed that man and then you—" She swallowed back the nausea that rose in her throat. "Then you sc . . . scalped him."

As though she had kicked him in the belly, Rye Berenger seemed to wilt. The hard, hate-filled expression on his face turned sad and vulnerable. He dropped his hold on her jaw and his grip on the rim of the basket. "Yeah, I scalped him."

Unable to believe her ears, Aerial stared in amazement. "Why would you do such a horrible thing?" burst from her mouth before she could stop herself.

Rye's black eyes bored into hers, as though he was about to tell her something. Then he shook his head and said, "You wouldn't understand."

He seemed so sad, and for a brief moment Aerial had an overwhelming desire to wrap her arms around him to comfort him. "I might."

"It's a very long story." Rye pivoted away from her

and stepped to the other side of the basket. With a tired groan, he slid down to the floor.

At the loss of his nearness, a chill passed through Aerial. Not questioning her need to recreate the first sense of closeness she had felt with another human being in years, she crossed over and sat down beside him.

"We've got all night," she said, leaning back against the picnic basket. Wrapping her arms around her bent knees, she rested her chin on them and stared straight head. "And I'm a good listener."

When he didn't respond, she rolled her face to the side and smiled sympathetically, her cheek pressed to her knees. "Why don't you tell me your side of what happened in Fairfield."

He cast a skeptical glance in her direction. "Why bother? You saw what you saw."

"I know that's what I said, but don't you think you owe it to yourself to convince me I made a mistake? Besides, what have you got to lose? You're stuck here tonight, so you might as well use the time to your advantage."

"You won't believe me."

"I might surprise you. Anyway, if I'm willing to give you the benefit of the doubt and listen to what you have to say, can't you bring yourself to give me that same consideration? Who knows? We both might learn something. You might realize I'm not the heartless bigot you've decided I am, and I could discover you're not the murderer I accused you of being. But there's only one way it's going to happen."

His expression a mix of hurt, anger and distrust, Rye studied her face for a full minute before he spoke. "I guess you're right. What have I got to lose?"

Chapter Four

Rye inhaled deeply. "I don't know where to begin."

"You could start at the beginning. What were you doing in that alley?"

Rye stared at her long and hard, his aching black eyes boring into her and touching something so deep inside her that she trembled with the impact.

"What happened in that alley wasn't the beginning," he said flatly. Rolling his head back against the basket wall, he gazed at the underside of the balloon overhead. "It was supposed to be an ending to something that began thirteen years ago. But it looks like Cletus Hackmore—that was his name—isn't through ruining my life, even though he finally got what he deserved."

Aerial's eyes widened in stunned disbelief. Disappointment squeezed at her insides. She had really wanted him to convince her he was innocent. "So you did kill him."

The muscles in Rye's jaws bunched, but he didn't look at her. "No, I didn't kill him. I wanted to, and that's what I was in Fairfield to do, but someone else got there first."

Confused, Aerial frowned. "But why would anyone want to kill a harmless old man like that?"

Rye's upper lip twitched up and down, as if the words on his tongue were making him sick to his stomach. He rolled his dark eyes down to study her out of the corner of his eye, then directed them upward again. "Thirteen years ago that 'harmless old man' came to my family's farm in southeastern Nebraska and murdered and scalped my parents and eight-year-old sister; then he shot me."

"Oh, my God!" Aerial choked back the bile that rose in her throat, wishing she didn't have to hear the rest of the story, but knowing she must. "What happened? How?"

Rye bit his lower lip, which, by the light of the moon, she could see was trembling slightly. It was all she could do to keep herself from reaching out and touching his arm to comfort him, but she knew instinctively he would resent any show of sympathy on her part. Besides, he could be lying. So she said nothing.

He lifted his shoulders with pretended indifference, then relaxed them. "He was said to have lost his family in '62, when the Eastern Sioux rebelled in Minnesota and killed hundreds of whites. I guess he resented the fact that my family had what he had lost, so he decided to kill us. But whatever his reason was, he took my family away from me. Since then, I've known there was only one reason I survived. I knew if I waited long enough and searched far enough, the day would come when I would make him pay."

Tears filled Aerial's eyes, spilling over her lower lids to trail down her cheeks. The agony and pain on Rye Berenger's face made doubting his incredible story impossible. "You poor thing! You must have just been a little boy thirteen years ago. How did you escape?"

Rye studied her, momentarily surprised and puzzled by the tone of caring he heard in her voice. Deciding it had to be his imagination, he returned his attention to the balloon.

"I was eleven. Because my sister and I were mixed blood—our mother was Lakota, that's Sioux to the whites—we never had much to do with the townspeople, and they left us pretty much alone. Ginny and I were so secluded on the farm we never really thought much about being different or hated because of our Indian blood. Not until that day when Cletus Hackmore decided to pay us a call. That was the day I realized hate existed, and I swore I'd avenge the deaths of my family if it took my entire life to do it."

"If that man did what you say, what was he doing in Fairfield? Why wasn't he hung thirteen years ago? Anyone committing such a horrible crime should have been arrested and hung right then."

Rye shrugged and released a snort of derisive laughter. "Don't forget the white man's first rule about who's always guilty, Miss Windsor." He pressed his hand against his bandaged side and shifted his body restlessly.

"Evidently, when Hackmore realized his shot had only wounded me, and that I had gotten away to tell the story, he headed back to town and told the law that he had seen me kill and scalp my family and then set fire to the house. Tell me, who do you think they would have believed if I had gone to them with the truth? Assuming, of course, I could have gotten as far as the sheriff's office before some vigilante group lynched me."

"You were only eleven. Couldn't they see that a child wouldn't have been capable of doing such a thing."

"Believe me, it would have made no difference. I was Indian, Hackmore was white. Age and size play no part in the logic whites use to decide what is true where an Indian is involved."

"Then what did you do? You were too young to strike out on your own!"

"I don't remember how I got there, but somehow I managed to get to a neighboring farm, where a family of Quakers lived. They had always treated us fairly, and I knew I'd be safe there. I had done odd jobs for Friend Padluck; when the townspeople told my parents that it would be 'better for all concerned' if Ginny and I didn't attend the school in town, Mrs. Padluck even invited us to the classes she conducted in a room off her kitchen for Quaker children in the area. They were good people, and I was sure they would be able to tell me what to do."

"And did they?"

He nodded. "If it weren't for them, I'd be dead. They said when I arrived at their farm, bleeding and near collapse, I gave them a vague idea of what had happened, then passed out cold on their back porch. When I woke up three days later I was upstairs in a big bed and found out that between my ramblings and the riders who showed up at their farm looking for me the next day, they had pieced the rest of the story together."

"Did they tell the posse they had you?"

"No, they could recognize a lynch party when they saw one. They'd seen too many during the years before the war, when they were active in the Underground Railroad, not to see this one for what it was. They just thanked the riders for warning them and promised to be on guard in case I showed up."

"What happened then? How long did you stay there?" Aerial asked, her heart breaking for the child who had been so cruelly wronged. No wonder he found it impossible to trust whites.

"The Padlucks kept me hidden until my wound healed, but we all knew I couldn't stay there indefinitely without being discovered. It wasn't as if I could just blend into their blond family and help work their farm—which was all I knew how to do. So, once I was strong enough to travel, they smuggled me into Dakota territory to live with my mother's people on the reservation."

"And you've been there all this time?"

"No. By the time I was eighteen I had almost reached my full height and weight and had learned

65

how to take care of myself, so I knew the time had come to find Hackmore. It took me six years to track him down, but I finally did."

"In Fairfield," she said softly, already knowing the end of the story.

"In Fairfield," he repeated, his voice hoarse and rough with regret. "But I was too late. Someone had beaten me to him and robbed me of my revenge."

"Then you really were just checking to see if he was alive when I saw you bending over him? But what about the knife?"

"It belonged to my father. He made it himself, and when I saw it in that bastard's belt . . ." Rye squeezed his eyes closed and rocked his head from side to side against the basket wall, his pain obvious. ". . . I could only think of making him pay the way my family paid. I couldn't kill him, but I could . . ."

". . . take his scalp," Aerial finished for him, her stomach churning with revulsion, even though she was surprised to realize she understood completely why he had done what he'd done. In fact, she wasn't sure she wouldn't have done the same thing.

"I took his scalp," he confirmed. Raising his black eyes, glistening with unshed tears, he fixed an accusing glare on her. "So, now that you know 'my side' of the story, do I still have your 'benefit of the doubt?' "

Aerial sniffed and wiped the backs of her index fingers beneath her eyes. He had to be telling the truth. Surely no one but a professional actor could lie so convincingly. Still, she couldn't bring herself to admit she was inclined to believe him. "Yes, Mr. Berenger, you still have the benefit of my doubt."

Without thinking, she gave him a trembling smile and placed her hand on his arm. At the unexpected physical contact, the subject of their discussion was temporarily forgotten.

Neither of them able to move, they stared help-

66

lessly at the spot where her pale fingers touched the contrasting dark flesh of his corded forearm.

They looked up at the same time, her flustered blue eyes locking with his bewildered black ones.

In a panicked attempt to escape his intense stare, Aerial inadvertently dropped her eyes to his naked chest, dark and muscular above the bright white bandage that circled his ribs. The heat in her face doubled.

All the time he'd been talking, her full attention had been on his words, and she had forgotten that he had dropped the blanket when he'd come to look at her map. But now . . .

"You probably should put the blanket back around your shoulders," she said, her voice a hoarse whisper that sounded unfamiliar to her own ears. "You must be cold."

"Are you?" he asked, straightening his back so that he was no longer relaxing against the basket side.

Her gaze dropped to his mouth. She licked her own lips nervously, then looked back at his eyes. "A . . . am I what?"

"Cold." His upper body leaned toward her.

Cold? As a matter of fact, if she didn't know better, she'd swear she was on fire. She shook her head slightly, her eyes riveted to his face. Her gaze flicked over his mouth again, and like the proverbial moth to the flame, her torso leaned of its own will toward him.

Realizing just in time what she was doing, she stiffened her spine and tore her hand away from his arm. "Maybe your shirt's dry!" she blurted out, grasping at anything to take her mind off the inappropriate trail it seemed determined to take. "While you were asleep, I rinsed it out. It must be dry by now."

Desperate to get as far from Rye and her unfamiliar feelings, Aerial bolted up from the floor and literally leaped across the car.

"Of course," she went on nervously, making a fist around a clump of the shirt she had hung from the balloon rope to dry, "it won't be completely clean because I didn't have any water to waste. Water is too heavy to carry much extra on a trip like this, but I think I got most of the blood out. If it goes untended, blood stains so badly you might never get it all out, but if it's washed out right away with cold water, it usually doesn't ruin—"

"Miss Windsor," a deep voice crooned from behind her, as two familiar tanned hands grasped her upper arms.

The breath caught in her lungs. Both fists clenched into the damp material of the shirt. "W . . . what?"

As if she had no more control of her actions than a puppet on a string, she felt her feet move as he pried the shirt from her hands and turned her around to face him.

"Thanks," he said huskily.

"It was nothing," she answered, her attention on the well-shaped lips that hovered only inches above her own mouth. "It would be a shame to let a perfectly good shirt—"

"Not for the shirt."

"Not for the shirt?"

He shook his head, and a hint of a smile formed on his lips. "Not for the shirt."

"Then for what?" Her question was spoken so softly that almost no sound came out. If it hadn't been that high in the sky the slightest sound carried clearly for great distances, he might not have heard her at all.

"For believing me."

"I didn't say I believed you," she whispered, valiantly fighting the urge to move closer into the security of his embrace. "I only said . . ."

He smiled knowingly. ". . . that you were giving me the benefit of the doubt. I know. But that's a lot more than any other white person has ever given me—except for the Padlucks—and I thank you for it."

The thought of the lonely half-Indian boy who had lived all those years with hatred and the memory of his murdered family tugged anew at Aerial's heart. For the first time since her parents' deaths, her own loneliness seemed less severe. She was no longer alone.

Without thinking about what she was doing, she lifted her hands from her sides and caught his face between her palms. "There's no need to thank me."

His black eyes clouded with bewilderment, then suddenly lit with a fire Aerial didn't recognize, yet could only imagine must match the light in her own eyes. Inadvertently, she raised herself on her toes and drew herself closer to him.

She knew, somewhere deep in her conscience, that she was supposed to push herself away from him, maybe even slap him for standing so close to her, for touching her. At the very least, she certainly shouldn't be holding his face or reveling in the feel of his strong grip on her upper arms. But for the life of her, she could not think of a single reason to remove her hands from his cheeks or break out of his hold on her.

His eyes never leaving her face, Rye wrapped his arms around her and splayed his large hands over the narrowness of her back.

Aerial was conscious that what she was doing was totally out of character for her, but she couldn't stop herself. It was as though she were controlled by a power other than her own. Burrowing her fingers through the thick hair at his temples, she laced them together at the nape of his neck.

He lowered his mouth to her upturned face, gently drawing her against the hardness of his body as he did. He hesitated a scant fraction of a second, then brushed his lips lightly across hers.

The brief touch of his mouth on hers sent waves of electricity charging through her. Every nerve, every hair, every inch of her skin surged to life.

All thoughts of right and wrong, should and shouldn't, were driven from her mind. The only thing she knew was that right here, at this very moment, she was truly alive for the first time since the day her parents had died, and she wished with all her heart the feeling could last forever.

But of course nothing lasts forever, a nagging inner voice reminded her. *You know the only way to protect yourself is to not let anyone get close.*

Frantic to disprove what life had taught her so convincingly, she tightened her hold around Rye's neck and eagerly sought his mouth with hers. Even if it didn't last past this moment, she had been on the outside looking in at life too long to give up this chance to experience it.

Rye's hands on her back ceased their circular caresses, and he drew back his head to study her suspiciously. He could tell by her innocent kiss that she hadn't had much experience with men, if any at all. On the other hand, the way she was clutching at his hair, pressing her slim body against his, her mouth pleading to be properly kissed, told him an entirely different story.

Tentacles of disappointment spiraled through him. Miss Aerial Windsor was evidently no different than the dozens of white women he'd met in his travels, women who wanted to experience the thrill of being taken by a "real live Indian."

Who knew why they wanted their secret liaisons with him? Curiosity? Forbidden fruit? A sense of danger? Whatever it was, it had insured an abun-

70

dance of bed partners over the years, though he had to admit, never one as young or inexperienced as this one seemed to be.

But far be it from him to let a "lady" down, especially one as beautiful and ripe for the picking as Aerial Windsor.

Driven by desire and an anger he couldn't explain, Rye lowered his hands to grip the firm mounds of her bottom. Hauling her against him, he brought his mouth down on hers, hard and punishing. If she wanted to know what it was like to be with a "savage," he was more than willing to oblige.

Nothing in Aerial's twenty-years of life could have prepared her for the bolt of lightning that shot through her as Rye's mouth captured hers. No longer gentle, as his first kiss had been, this kiss was rough and demanding, frightening her at the same time it thrilled her.

Dropping her hands from around his neck, she flattened her palms against his chest, trying to push him away. "Stop," she moaned, wrenching her mouth free.

"What's the matter, Miss Windsor?" He gripped her chin in hard fingers and forced her head back around so she had to look at him. "Have you changed your mind? Or is this just part of the game?"

Her eyes widened in surprise, not only at his words, but at the hatred in his expression. "Game? I don't understand."

"You can drop the pretense now. You and I both know this is what you want." He tightened his grip on her bottom and thrust his hips forward, grinding against her. At the same time, he slid a hand down her chest to clutch and squeeze her breast as he captured her open mouth with his, plunging his tongue deep within.

Horrified he could think she could have wanted to

be treated like this, she squirmed to free herself. "Mmm," she moaned, twisting her head from side to side to end the kiss, and shoving at the hard, satin-skinned chest beneath her palms.

Suddenly he released her mouth and reared his head back, sliding an arrogant glance down his nose at her. "Too rough for you, Miss Windsor?"

Her eyes bright with tears and rage, she lifted a hand from his chest and pressed the back of it to her violated mouth.

"Isn't that what you wanted? You didn't really expect a 'savage' to be a gentle lover, did you?"

"Surely you don't think I wanted this to happen. I only wanted . . ."

She couldn't finish. Was she lying to herself? Was he justified in assuming she had wanted more than just to be held and kissed? Was that why the strange feelings she'd been experiencing had urged her to toss all caution to the wind and throw herself at him? Was that why he had behaved and spoken so cruelly?

A seed of self-doubt and conscience began to sprout in Rye's mind. Had he misread the situation? Suddenly he was not so sure. Apprehension ruling him, he dropped his hand from her breast to her waist. Bringing his other hand around from her bottom, he made her look at him by taking her chin again, though more gently than before.

His black eyes narrowed into gleaming points of granite, and he scrutinized her harshly, searching her tear-filled, frightened eyes for the truth. "You really didn't want this?" he asked suspiciously.

She shook her head vehemently "No! How could you think such a thing?"

"Believe me, it wasn't too damned difficult. Not with you climbing all over me like you were. What was I supposed to think?"

Aerial sucked in a horrified gasp. "I wasn't climbing all over you!" she said indignantly. "I was just . . ."

"Just what?"

Her face grew hot. How could she tell him what had happened when she wasn't even sure herself? How could she explain that she had expected a second kiss to be similar to the first; sweet and romantic, not cruel and punishing. "I just wanted to . . . to make you feel better."

"Make *me* feel better?"

She nodded feebly. It wasn't a total lie. She had been very touched by his story. "What happened to you is so sad," she went on, her voice growing stronger. "You seemed so alone, and I . . ."

"Pitied me!" he finished for her, his tone accusing and filled with loathing, as though she'd committed the worst crime. He tightened his hold on her chin and lowered his face to within an inch of hers. "Well, lady, you can keep your pity and lily-white charity. I don't need it."

Aerial stiffened, his unexpected reaction restoring some of the pluck she had temporarily misplaced in the aftermath of his kiss.

"Actually, the thought of pitying you never entered my mind," she said with an indignant sniff. "But now that you've brought it up, you're right. I do pity you. But not for the reasons you think. It's true you've had a hard time, but who hasn't? No, I pity you, Mr. Berenger, because you're so wrapped up in bitterness and self-pity that you can't accept a simple offer of compassion and kindness for what it is."

The tightness in her chest suffocating her, she made a half turn away from him and snatched the almost dry shirt from the balloon rope. "Here," she said, jabbing the wadded material at his middle. "Now, if you'll excuse me, I've learned my lesson. Until we land, I'll keep my sympathy and assistance to myself. And if you ever touch me again, I'll freeze

73

in hell before I'll withdraw that deposition I signed in Fairfield! Is that clear, Mr. Berenger?"

Momentarily silenced by her angry retort, Rye made room for her to squeeze past him so she could return to the balloon's instrument panel. Only vaguely aware of what he was doing, he slipped the shirt on, his expression a mix of confusion and disbelief. He didn't know what to do.

For the first time in thirteen years — since the last time he had seen the Padlucks — he had met a white person who had been willing to accept him as he was without wanting something in return, and what had he done? He had destroyed any seed of trust and belief she might have, had proved to her that he was no better than the lowlife animal the rest of the world said he was.

Chapter Five

Wincing with distaste, Aerial lowered the metal mug from her lips. If there was anything worse than the last inch of coffee in the pot, it had to be the last inch of coffee in *yesterday's* pot. In fact, the jug of coffee she had brought from Fairfield was so cold and thick with dregs she would have preferred drinking one of the foul-tasting medicinals her mother had spooned down her throat at the first sign of sickness throughout her childhood.

She cast a resentful glance at Rye, irritated to see he was silently watching her, as he'd done off and on all night long. *When he wasn't sleeping, eating or helping himself to another cup of my coffee!*

It was bad enough that shortly after midnight his extra weight had made it necessary for her to discard a hundred and seventy-five pounds of precious sand ballast so she could reach the faster, more predictable westerly currents of the higher altitudes. But this . . .

She glared at the black sludge in the bottom of her cup. This was really the final straw. He, who could have slept throughout the entire flight without being missed, had drunk all the coffee, leaving her nothing but the oozy dregs, when she needed the energizing effect of the coffee more than ever to stay awake.

A low, involuntary growl issued from her throat, and she hurled the cup, dregs and all, out of the balloon. Too bad she couldn't get rid of Rye Berenger that easily.

Heaving a frustrated sigh, she checked the clock on the instrument panel. A shot of adrenaline surged through her veins. Eagerly looking toward the eastern horizon, she confirmed what she suspected. It was almost dawn! That meant if she kept the balloon afloat for only six more hours, she would best Wise's record for hours in the air by ten minutes, hopefully equaling his distance record as well.

In fact, now that the end, and daylight, were in sight, she had no doubts about staying awake—coffee or no coffee.

Reinspired, she stepped back to the map board and opened it to study the course the balloon had taken during the night. According to her computations, instead of passing over into Canada as they had seemed destined to do, they had pretty much followed the United States/Canadian border up the center of Lake Erie for its entire length.

The last time there had been anything other than water below had been a little past midnight, when the *Wind Rose* had drifted over the city of Toledo. But if her figures were correct, within the hour, they should site land at the northeastern tip of the lake in New York, the state where John Wise had ended his record-setting flight twenty-one years before. Suecess was definitely within her grasp now.

As if sent to remind her there were still too many things that could go wrong for her to be counting her chickens, a blast of cold air hit her.

She cast a worried glance at the barometer on the instrument panel, instinctively dreading what she would find. "No! It can't be!" She peered frantically over the side of the car, searching for an explanation of what she'd discovered.

With disbelieving eyes, she stared down onto a boiling mass of ominous black clouds overtaking them from the west. The cold moist air over the

76

lake, accompanied by the balloon's natural descent after so many hours, was causing them to lose altitude prematurely. "Why now?"

"What is it?" Rye asked, sitting up straighter, the alarm in her voice causing him to break his night-long silence. "Is something wrong?"

Shooting Rye an angry frown that implied, *This is all your fault,* she quickly went to work releasing sandbags from the outer wall of the basket in a desperate rush to lighten the balloon's load.

"No, nothing's wrong," she spit out harshly. "Not unless you want to count the fact that we've dropped five hundred feet in the last five minutes and that there's a huge storm moving in below that's going to dash us to pieces if we continue to descend."

Doing his best to forget his fear, Rye gripped the rim and heaved himself to his knees. "What can I do to help?"

Annoyed that he couldn't figure it out for himself after all the hours he'd spent watching her jettison ballast, she eyed him bitterly over her shoulder. "On your knees? I guess you could try praying." She returned her attention to untying a third sandbag.

Drawing on a reserve of courage he only hoped was there, Rye hauled himself to his feet and moved with determination to where she leaned over the side to reach the bottom row of sandbags.

"Here," he said, peering over the edge with resolve. Swallowing back the nausea he felt at the sight of the churning black clouds below, he covered her hands on the sandbag with his own. "I'll do this. You probably need to be doing something else, like checking those dials you're always watching."

Surprised, Aerial stared at the dark hands on hers, then looked up, her eyes bright with confusion. "Are you sure?"

He shrugged and gave her a hapless grin. "How

many bags do you want dropped?"

Knowing she had no time to spare, Aerial withdrew her hands from his and straightened her posture. "Just one for now. I'll check to see if it and the other two I released did any good at all. We can't use any more than absolutely necessary. We don't have any to spare."

"That's good," she said finally after they had worked together for close to an hour, with Aerial watching the instruments and shouting repeatedly for him to release another bag of sand as the needles on the dials dipped lower and lower. Rye silently followed her orders. "It looks like we're stable. For the moment anyway. Are you all right?"

Breathing more easily, Rye rolled his shoulders back and forth to work out the tightness. "Couldn't be better," he lied, his heart pounding with the realization that he hadn't fallen out of the basket or disgraced himself by fainting or getting sick to his stomach. There had been several moments when he hadn't been sure he could keep up his facade of bravery. Pleased with himself, the thought crossed his mind that he might get the hang of balloon flying yet. He might even grow to like it!

He contemplated the idea for a minute, then shook his head. *Naagh. If I ever set feet on solid ground again, I'm never going higher than the second story of a building—and then only if it's a matter of life and death!*

"Any idea where we are?" he asked, peering over her shoulder and doing his best to keep up the casual pretense.

"My guess would be that we're somewhere between Lake Erie and Lake Ontario around Buffalo or Niagara Falls." She indicated their estimated location on her map. But I can't be sure because I can't see through the storm to spot any familiar landmarks. I can't even use the moon and stars to plot our course since they're gone. All I can be sure of is that we're still heading northeast and will probably spend the next few hours over Lake Ontario."

In response to her statement, Rye looked toward the sun, still low on the eastern horizon, but fully risen. "So that means we won't be landing for a while yet," he said with resignation.

Aerial studied the map a moment longer, then shrugged and shook her head. "Not unless the storm disappears and the wind decides to change course and send us due east over land instead of the lake, which doesn't seem too likely at this point."

Realizing the casualness her conversation had assumed, Aerial deliberately changed her tone. "Instead of worrying about when we land," she said with a sneer, "you'd better just hope we manage to stay aloft until that storm has run its course. Because once we get over the lake, if we get pulled down into it . . ." Tilting her head to the side and hunching her shoulders in surrender, she wrinkled her face meaningfully, allowing her eyes to finish her statement for her.

Rye stared at her, stunned. "Surely it won't come to that. Didn't you just say we were stable?"

"For now, but once we're over Lake Ontario, the cool air will undoubtedly cause us to drop unless we can lighten the load a lot more, and we don't have that many sandbags left."

"You knew this could happen, didn't you?" he accused. "That's why you parted with every bag of sand like it was a personal friend."

She couldn't help bristling at the accurate analogy. "I hardly think I'm that bad. But you're right. I knew this could happen, or something like it. No long-distance trip is without its dangers. A storm with heavy ground winds just happens to be one of the more serious dangers for even the most experienced balloonist."

"Yet you set out on this trip without any help, in spite of what you knew?" he asked, his face twisted with anger. "What were you thinking? How could your family let you take such a dangerous chance? What if I hadn't been here to help you?"

Tears sprang to Aerial's eyes at the mention of her family and the reminder of how much she still missed them. She turned her face so Rye couldn't see how his words had hurt her. "I'd like to point out, Mr. Berenger, that if I'd made this trip alone, as you may recall was my original intent, I wouldn't be in any danger now. If I hadn't been *forced* to use most of my ballast during the first half of the trip to make up for your unwanted presence so we could reach ten thousand feet, I would have had more than enough ballast to keep me well above the storm until it blew itself out. But because of you . . ."

A wave of shame washed over Rye. She was right. Because of him they were probably both going to be killed.

Then he remembered what—and who—had gotten him into this mess in the first place, and the instant of guilt he had felt was immediately displaced by renewed anger. Whose fault was it that he was helplessly trapped between heaven and earth in a flimsy wicker basket, on the verge of dying a very unpleasant death at any moment? Certainly not his!

"Hold on there, lady! Don't put the blame on me. You got yourself into this fix all by yourself with your lying and meddling. If you'd just kept your mouth shut and hadn't lied on that deposition, I sure as hell wouldn't be here keeping you company. I'd be on my horse heading west, instead of—"

"Keeping me company!? Is that what you call ruining my one and only chance at making this flight and breaking a record that has stood for twenty-one years? A record, I might add, that I've worked and saved and planned on conquering since my parents were killed five years ago trying the same thing. Well, I hope you'll excuse me if I don't thank you!" She took a deep breath, then added, "And I wasn't lying. I told the sheriff exactly what I saw!"

She returned her attention to her instruments. "Keeping me company, indeed!" she mumbled with a sniff. "I'd rather have a bushel of rattlesnakes for company. At least they'd make my death quick, instead of dragging it out for thirteen hours. In fact, now that I think about it, I should have let you blow us up in the first place. That way, I wouldn't have wasted my last hours on earth trying to save a flight that was doomed from the moment you set foot on board!"

Suddenly, as if it had been punched, the balloon gave an unexpected downward lurch.

Both Rye and Aerial grabbed for support to keep from falling, their eyes simultaneously leaping to the needles on the altimeter.

"I guess I'd better let another sandbag go," Rye said, moving to lean over the side again, though the thought of looking down into the storm was every bit as unsettling as it was before.

Aerial nodded her agreement. "Better make it two," she said, experiencing her own kind of apprehension. "I have a feeling the worst hasn't even begun, but the longer we can ward off the storm's downward pull, the more chance we may have of outlasting it. Though I don't hold out much hope."

The next two hours bore out Aerial's prediction. Not only did they exhaust their supply of sandbags in the battle to remain beyond the storm's ominous reach, but it grew more impossible by the minute for the helpless balloon to resist the wind's demanding call from below.

Aerial squatted down to open her trunk. "Let me get the life preserver, and then we can get rid of this," she said. "It's pretty heavy."

As she dug in the trunk's contents, her hand paused on the filmy pink fabric of the dress she had worn to start her journey. A wave of sadness rocked her as the unadulterated truth slammed her in the chest.

All her plans and dreams were lost. They had blown away in the storm: the showy landing she had envisioned making dressed in flowing chiffon and spotlighted in sunlight, the moment when she would have publicly reclaimed her father's good name at last. There would be no cheering crowd to welcome her, no newspapermen to write an accounting of her adventure, and John Wise's record would continue to stand.

The car shuddered violently and tilted as the wind picked up speed, sending its passengers and remaining contents slamming to one side.

"Damn!" Rye cursed, grabbing frantically at the rim to right himself. "Looks like we're descending even more."

Breathless, Aerial worked her way out from under the supplies that held her pinned to the basket wall. "If we can get rid of more weight, we might still be lucky enough for the wind to carry us past the lake so we can at least go down on solid ground."

"From this high up, land doesn't sound a lot better than water," Rye grunted, dragging the trunk away from the lower side of the basket to lift it.

"It's not," she answered, straining to help him with the trunk. "Either way, we'll probably be killed." Groaning with the effort, she lifted her end of the trunk up to the ledge and gave it a decisive shove overboard.

Out of habit, she checked the altimeter to see if

the weight loss had made any difference. Seeing that the effect had been minimal, she canvassed the car for something else to go.

"Dead is dead." He picked up the picnic basket and raised his eyebrows in a silent question. "So what difference does it make how we get there?"

Nodding her agreement that the food was no longer necessary, she hefted the sack of mail the Fairfielders had sent to their friends in the east and pitched it out of the basket. "I know dead is dead, but as far as I'm concerned, being dead on land is by far more desirable than being dead at the bottom of Lake Ontario, our bodies never to be found again, or even worse, washing up on shore three days from now all bloated and . . ."

Her inadvertent description of her parents' fate hit her with cruel force. Her bottom lip began to tremble. Was this how it was going to end? Was she going to die, too, with no one to even witness the fact that she'd gotten this close to John Wise's record? Would she just disappear into the lake and never be heard from again? What's more, who would care? Even the people in Fairfield who had expected her flight to put their town on the map would only mourn the loss of their own gain, not her as a person.

Stop it! she ordered herself. *Don't you dare start crying and feeling sorry for yourself.*

Determined not to give up without a fight, she hefted her mackintosh to jettison over the side next, deliberately forcing the conversation back to a more optimistic vein.

"Besides, if we crash on land and by some miracle survive, we can walk to safety. Or if we can't walk, we can just wait to be found. My father's friend, John LaMountain, crashed in the Canadian wilderness and was rescued after four days. How long do you think we'd last in the lake?"

Rye tipped his head to the side, indicating the commode leaning at a precarious angle in the corner. "What about that?"

Despite the fact that they should be long past embarrassment at this point, she blushed profusely. Unable to look him in the eyes or to watch as he disposed of the unmentionable article, she mumbled, "Yes," running her nervous gaze over the stripped car in search of something else to toss out. Finally, her gaze focused on her instrument panel and map board.

Quickly getting rid of the chamber pot and cabinet, Rye paused for a moment to study her from behind. She really was something. Any other woman would be hysterical right now. She certainly wouldn't be standing there considering throwing out her charts and instruments.

Without being told, he sensed they meant more to her than anything else she owned, and suddenly he knew he couldn't let her give them up. If they were going to die anyway, why shouldn't she keep something she treasured with her to the end?

"Don't," he said, covering her hands as she reached to untie the instrument panel first. "They don't weigh enough to make any difference. What about that coiled rope on the side? It must weigh two or three hundred pounds. And if we come down on land, you might need some of those things to figure out where we are—in case we have to walk."

He could have sworn he felt her sag with relief, but before he could be sure, she withdrew her hands from the instruments and out from under his.

Now soaked to the skin by the torrential rain the balloon had descended into, she narrowed her eyes angrily. "I told you not to touch me ever again or I'd . . ."

"Kill me," he finished for her, a half smile turning up the corner of his mouth. "But I thought it was just a figure of speech. I didn't think you were really planning to do it."

Unable to resist the grim humor of his wry remark, she couldn't stop herself from smiling too. "Well, now you know I'm a woman of my word, don't you?"

For a long moment, they stared at one another, their eyes locked in understanding. As one, they reached across the narrow space that separated them.

Unable to deny herself the sanctity and comfort of another human being's embrace any longer, Aerial moved into Rye's arms.

Oblivious to the chilling rain pelting her skin and plastering her hair to her face, she clutched the soaked shirt at his back, clinging to him with desperate hunger. Determined to block out everything else, she buried her face in the hollow of his throat.

"There, there," he soothed, splaying one hand over her narrow back to haul her more securely into the protection of his body. Cupping the back of her head with the other hand, he pressed his mouth to her sleek, wet hair and breathed in deeply. Lord, she smelled good, like damp flowers after a gentle spring rain.

"You're not giving up, are you?" he asked, his voice husky and gentle. "That doesn't sound like you. I figured you would still be fighting with your last breath. And who knows? We could already be over land. With as much speed as we've picked up, I wouldn't be surprised to find out we've left Lake Ontario completely behind us. We could be well into Canada."

"Or for that matter, halfway across New York," Aerial said against his neck, taking heart at the possibility. It was so much easier to think optimistically in the warmth of his arms, the comforting sound of his heart pounding in her ear. "John Wise, he's the man who holds the record for distance and hours in a balloon, only made it to Henderson, New York, on the eastern shore of the lake. If we've gone beyond that point . . ."

"Or even New York," Rye conceded, though as long as he was making wishful calculations regarding their situation, he would continue to hope for Canada. "Now, what about that rope? Shouldn't we get rid of it?"

"It's called a drag line," she said, delaying the moment when she would have to leave the sanctuary of his arms, though she knew there was no time to waste. "It's used to control landings. When we're closer to the ground, if we want to stay up longer, we can let it out, and the balloon is relieved of the weight of the part of the rope that rests on the ground. Then, when we want to go lower, all we have to do is pull the line off the ground to make the basket heavier."

"So our problem seems to be deciding when the rope can do us the most good—now or later."

As much as she hated giving up the security in the shelter of his arms, she released her hold on his shirt and stepped back. "Getting rid of the rope now *could* buy us a little more time. And since it's not very likely there will be a controlled landing of any kind, it probably won't give us much help later."

Reacting to the sudden loss of her warm body pressed to his, Rye tensed. Unable to move, he stared helplessly at Aerial.

Limp strands of drenched blond hair hung in her face and down her back; her nose and cheeks were chafed a raw, uncomfortable-looking pink; and the wet, loose-fitting jacket she wore gave her the look of a bedraggled urchin. Still, she was the most appealing woman he'd ever seen. And God help him,

86

he wanted her. Here. Now. Storm and imminent death be damned!

Rye staggered back a step, his senses assaulted by a vision of himself embedded deep inside her, his hips cradled securely between her silky thighs as the balloon plunged to the ground.

The collision of his backside with the wicker rim of the basket brought his erotic imaginings to a halt long enough to give him the strength to turn away from her.

Leaning over the side to untie the drag line, he paused, his hands on the rope. This was the first time since he'd been in the balloon car that he hadn't experienced nausea and lightheadiness when he'd looked down toward the ground.

His upper lip curled bitterly at the irony. Quite frankly, right then he would have welcomed a bout of dizziness. It would definitely be easier to cope with than the particular agony he was feeling. But then so would falling out of the balloon!

God! Had he ever wanted any woman the way he wanted this one? Surely, he hadn't. *At least not without doing something about it!* he commented silently.

Concentrating on the rope, he hurried to work it free, but no amount of effort was capable of easing the growing desire consuming his senses.

What's wrong with me? I'm probably going to die in a few minutes, and all I can think about is making love to a woman who has made it clear she wants nothing to do with me!

He moved faster to work the line loose, fighting the vision of himself locked inside her body, his fevered motions matching the storm's wild abandon as they plummeted back to earth in a final, climactic explosion.

Maybe it's what she wants too, a desperate inner voice whispered inside his head.

At the thought, Rye relived the feel of her nails clawing at his back just minutes before. Or had it been hours? His torture and longing had grown so intense that he couldn't be sure. He'd lost all track of time.

He closed his eyes and sucked in a deep breath. His conscience at war with his desire, he worked furiously to free the last tie on the drag line. *That wasn't passion,* he told himself. *That was fear. She's afraid. She just wanted to be held. That's all.*

So, why not give her what she wants? And at the same time you ease her fears, she can help you forget yours.

I can't.

Then you'll both die without having the one thing that could make dying a little less difficult. When it is right here for the taking!

"Dammit!" he growled as the drag line dropped into the churning abyss of rain and storm clouds, disappearing almost before it had cleared the bottom of the basket.

"What is it?" Aerial shouted over the wind from her station at the instrument panel. "Do you see something?" Hand-over-hand, she dragged her way down the precariously tilted floor of the balloon car to where Rye stood staring over the side. "Is it land?"

Clinging to a suspension rope to retain his balance, Rye turned his head and stared at her as though he was surprised to find her standing beside him.

The anguished expression on his face tugged painfully at her heart, and guilt gnawed at her insides. He was right. Largely, this was her fault. If only she hadn't let that sheriff talk her into signing that damned deposition! But she had, and because she had, this man, who had already known more suffering than any human should endure, was going to die, as surely as if he'd stayed in Fairfield and been hanged.

Without thinking about whether or not it was right, she reached up to fingercomb several dripping strands of black hair off Rye's rain-drenched face, her open palm lingering to caress his cheek. She shook her head sadly. "I'm so sorry."

Her cool touch on his fevered skin drove him over the edge of rational thinking. All he could hear was the beating of his own heart, the demand of his own desire. He could no longer help himself.

Desperate need controlling his actions, he sandwiched her face between large palms and lowered his mouth to hers. With a crushing kiss, he threaded the fingers of one hand into her hair, clutching a handful of the heavy wet silk at the back of her head. With desperate, clumsy motions, he slid his other hand down her neck and into her jacket, shoving the heavy, clinging wool off her shoulder.

"I have to," he whispered, covering her face with intense kisses, her eyelids, her forehead, her cheeks, her ears, her neck. "God forgive me, I have to do this."

Chapter Six

A need of overwhelming intensity pulsed in Aerial's veins, transforming her limbs to liquid, her thoughts to erotic visions, and silencing any protests her conscience might have.

As unprepared for Rye's passionate assault as she was, she was even less prepared for her own reaction.

In that instant she knew with all her being that this was what she wanted . . . needed . . . had to have! Even at the risk of paying with her immortal soul, she couldn't, wouldn't, ignore her final chance in this lifetime to know the joy of being loved, no matter how fleeting that joy might be. No matter if it wasn't forever. *Dead* was forever. But right now she was alive, and now was all she would ever have if the storm had its way.

Lips parted and pleading thirstily for his kiss, she moved into the hard curve of his body.

Releasing his hold on her hair, Rye peeled the jacket from her shoulders. His actions frantic, he covered her neck and shoulders with ravenous kisses, then dropped to his knees before her.

Oblivious to the wind whipping wildly around them, he buried his face against her breasts, kissing them through the wet, clinging blouse, thrilling as her nipples, already erect from the cold, hardened and pressed forward against his mouth.

She had thought nothing, absolutely nothing,

could make her feel more loved and protected than just being held in Rye Berenger's arms, her face pressed to his chest, blotting out the doom that surrounded them. But now she knew she had been wrong.

This was what it was to be loved, needed, alive! *This* was the feeling of completeness she had longed for her whole life through, and this was her one chance to know it.

With the battering, swirling rain adding ever-increasing desperation to her need, Aerial dug her fingers into Rye's thick, wet hair, clutching his head to her breast, as the balloon twisted and spiraled closer to its destruction.

A shudder tripped through her as he caught her ankles beneath her wet skirt. Her heart jumped painfully in her chest, and every muscle and nerve in her body tensed. Her breathing became shallow, her mouth dry. Gasping for air, she tightened her hold on him to steady herself, her fingers curling greedily into his hair. She couldn't get close enough to him.

Kneading her limbs with desperate roughness, Rye moved his hands up the backs of her legs until he cupped the round firmness of her bottom in his hands. Beyond thinking, he hauled her hips forward, pressing the juncture of her thighs to his chest as he arched her upper body back with the urgent pressure of his mouth at her breast.

Death hovered all around them, threatening to put an end to their torture with each raging gust of wind, with each violent jerk and plunge of the helpless balloon car. Frantic to win the race with the sadistic storm, he ripped her wet skirts upward with one rough, passion-ruled motion. His actions clumsy and desperate, he grappled with the tapes at the waist of her drawers, tearing them down her slim hips and thighs and tossing them aside.

Dragging her to the floor of the gondola, he silenced her startled protests by plunging his tongue deep into her mouth as his hand fumbled to undo his trousers.

Driven by a hunger that ravaged his senses with a velocity matching the destructive force of the storm all around him, he separated her thighs with his hand and lunged onto her, pinning her beneath him.

With minimal guidance from his hand, he located the dewy entrance to his salvation and pressed into her, ultimate grace within his reach at last.

The deafening roar of the building storm, both inside and out, grew to thought-destroying proportions, pulsing, throbbing, demanding, devastating. The instant of rationality he'd experienced dissolved as swiftly as it had occurred.

No more able to silence the inner storm that had him in its control than he was able to stop the wind and rain from hurling him to his death, he lifted his hips slightly.

With one strong thrust, he broke the virginal barricade.

"Aagh!" she gasped, wrenching her mouth from his as the unexpected pain shot through her. "It hu—"

"Shh, shh," he whispered, recapturing her mouth with a series of light, consoling kisses as guilt and blame crashed through his blinding desire. "It'll go away," he promised. "Just give it a minute."

His passion on the verge of exploding, he steeled himself to wait, giving her a chance to adjust to him. There was no rush. He had won. He had beaten the storm. He was safely locked inside her. It no longer mattered when the wind hurled him to his death. He was already in heaven.

As the shock of the surprising pain subsided,

Aerial felt her own desire reflame, bringing with it a new kind of agony, a marvelous kind of agony that made her body want to match his gentle, rocking movements inside her.

Instinctively bending her knees, she flattened her booted feet on the gondola floor and worked her hands under his shirt to caress the wet, muscled flesh of his back.

When he felt her stir beneath him, her arms twine around his waist, Rye began to move ever so slowly in and out of the blissful fire of her body. He'd heard that a woman's first experience was rarely a good one, but since this was not only her first time, but quite probably her last as well, he knew he owed it to her to hold off his own release as long as possible so she could experience the same fulfillment he sought.

However, for all his noble intentions, with each slow stroke he took, the sensuous, untutored motions of the woman beneath him made his vow to take his time more impossible to keep.

Now! his passion screamed above the wails of the storm.

Not yet! his conscience countered.

The battle raged on inside him as over and over, Aerial lifted her hips upward, each time inviting him deeper into her heat, each time making it more impossible to ignore his own body's demands to force his full length into her before she was ready.

Then it was happening and he couldn't stop himself. The agony of his desire had risen to such heights there was nothing he could do but follow it. "Yes! Dammit, yes!!!" he roared, silencing his conscience once and for all as he buried himself inside her.

Covering her mouth with deep kisses, he ran his open hands under her, lifting her hips to meet his urgent thrusts.

Never in all her imaginings had Aerial anticipated the absolute rapture that exploded inside her at the moment when Rye spilled his seed into the convulsing, clenching heart of her sex. It was so overwhelming, so all-consuming, she forgot where she was, forgot that only hours before she had hated this man, had sworn to kill him if he so much as touched her. She even forgot that she would no doubt be hurled to her death in the next instant.

"Ohhh!" she shuddered as the climaxing muscles of her passion gave a final convulsive jerk, wringing the last of his strength from him.

"Oh, God!" Rye moaned, collapsing his full weight on her. Suddenly he was thankful for the cooling rain that pelted him with ever increasing vengeance.

Their hearts beating in syncopated rhythm, their rapid breathing slowing in united bliss, Rye and Aerial clung to each other as the balloon continued its tumultuous descent.

The realization that they were still alive crept over them as they slowly became aware of their surroundings again. The creaking and moaning of the wicker basket and suspension ropes, unnoticed during their lovemaking, sounded as if the entire craft would break apart at any moment without waiting for the final crash to earth, but the rain seemed to be lighter, the wind not quite so fierce.

The first to notice, Rye lifted his head to test the surroundings. "Damn, I think it's letting up." His expression splitting into a grin, he eased off her to a sitting position. "You don't suppose . . . ?" Rising up on his knees, he dragged his pants up over his bared hips as he peered cautiously over the rim.

Still more than a little stunned by what had

happened, Aerial was slower to react to the change in the weather. Once she realized that the basket was no longer riding at the perilous, tilted angle behind the balloon, but had assumed a more normal vertical position beneath the balloon, hope seared through her. Was it possible? Had they actually survived the storm?

In her hurry to know if they'd been saved, she experienced only a slight twinge of embarrassment as she hurriedly covered her bared legs with her skirt. Scrambling on all fours over to the instruments, she discovered the entire panel miraculously intact.

A quick inspection of the map board told her she hadn't been so fortunate in that area. Though the box where she kept her oilcloth-wrapped maps and charts was still attached to the gondola, it clung to the rim by one unstable, tattered thong, its lid open and flapping against the side. Of course, all the fragile contents were long gone.

"Land!" Rye shouted, leaping to his feet, buttoning his pants as he rose. "We're over land!"

"Thank God," Aerial cried, her face splitting in a radiant smile as she pulled herself to her feet. "How close are . . . Oh, my God!" she shouted, her elation turning to horror as an entire forest loomed up from the ground in front of the rapidly dropping craft. "Get down and hang on," she screamed at Rye, crouching down in the basket, her grip on the rim frantic, her eyes squeezed shut.

Every muscle in her body braced for the impact, she clung to the rim with all her concentration. To the explosive crack of breaking tree branches, the basket tipped momentarily on its side, sending her feet sliding out from under her, showering her with pine needles, cones, and twigs. Still she hung on with knuckle-whitening, finger-cramping tenacity, knowing if she let go, she would surely be hurled to her death.

Then, just as suddenly as they had slammed into the trees, the balloon received an unexpected spurt of new life and rose into the air.

It took an instant for Aerial to realize that they had been given a reprieve. They weren't going to crash into the trees after all—at least not yet. "We're airborne again!" she announced gleefully, crawling clumsily out from under the debris that had fallen on her during their momentary brush with the treetops. "I may be able to claim the record after all!"

Brushing the thick tangle of blond hair out of her eyes, she turned to Rye, her face radiant with relief.

Cold, clammy fingers of terror coiled and knotted inside Aerial. "Mr. Berenger?" she asked, her head swiveling from left to right as her brain struggled to absorb what her eyes were telling her.

"Rye!" The truth pounded violently in her head as she realized what had given the balloon its second wind.

Rye Berenger had been thrown out of the basket when they had hit the trees!

She rushed to the spot where he'd been standing just before the impact and peered down on the receding trees. There was no sign that Rye Berenger had ever been there. In fact, the only thing she saw that might indicate the entire incident wasn't a figment of her imagination was the hole the basket must have made when it had hit the otherwise unbroken span of green—a hole big enough to swallow a falling man, without leaving a trace that he had ever existed.

Paralyzed, Aerial stared in numb silence for half a minute, unable to believe what had happened.

"No!" She refused to accept the thoughts colliding in her head. "You can't be dead! You can't!"

She had to do something, and fast. Every instant she delayed, the balloon was carrying her farther away from Rye.

Slicing a frenzied examination over the surrounding terrain, she quickly realized there was nothing but trees as far as the eye could see. There was no place to set the balloon down without at very least injuring herself so seriously that she wouldn't be able to save either of them. There had to be another way.

Think, Aerial. Dammit, think! There's got to be something!

Remembering her parachute, an instant of relief washed over her, but it was immediately quelled as she recalled that the parachute had been jettisoned with her trunk. Dejectedly, she looked at the now useless life preserver she had kept.

With no safe place to land for miles around, and no parachute on board, there was only one other choice. Unable to bear the thought of leaving Rye, no matter how many times in the past twenty-four hours she had wished he would disappear from her life, she made her decision.

Whatever the consequences might be, she had to take the gamble and land in the trees—now. If she waited any longer she might as well not land at all. As it was, she might never be able to find him in the acres of uninhabited forest.

Panic raging relentlessly through her, Aerial used both hands to yank one of the two ropes hanging down from the inflation appendix of the balloon.

Almost immediately, she heard the thankful whoosh of gas rushing to escape through the long, narrow, triangle-shaped slit she had torn open in the top of the balloon.

Called the rip panel, the flap was used to collapse a balloon rapidly once the balloonist was committed to a landing site. With the sudden escape of its remaining gas, the balloon could parachute sharply to the ground with a minimum amount of drifting away from its target. Also, if it got caught in a gust of ground-level wind, it wouldn't lift off again to go "hedgehopping" across the land. Of course, she was quite sure that dropping onto a dense tangle of forest in the middle of nowhere hadn't been in John Wise's plans when he invented the handy device.

The pardon it had stolen with the loss of Rye's weight rescinded, the hardy balloon gave up its gallant battle to survive. To the hiss of escaping gas, it arrowed downward, plummeting back toward the forest it had escaped only moments before. This time there would be no last-minute reprieve.

Her arms locked around one of the ropes that secured the gondola to the failing balloon, Aerial watched the approaching treetops as long as she could, desperate to find a sign that she hadn't drifted so far from where she had lost Rye that she wouldn't be able to find him.

At the thought, her insides curled protectively into themselves. Was this her punishment for what had happened in the balloon? Could God be so cruel that He would give her a second chance at life by allowing her to survive the wicked storm, then snatch it back by destroying the one person who'd shown her what it was to be alive?

Bracing herself as best she could for the impact, she prayed. She had to find Rye Berenger. She couldn't lose him now. She just couldn't . . .

His senses assaulted by the sweetly familiar smell of rain-washed vegetation and rich damp earth, Rye opened his eyes sleepily. *Where the hell am I?* he wondered, slowly becoming aware of the pine and spruce duff his cheek was pressed into.

Then it all came back to him with overwhelming clarity: the feeling of exhilaration he'd known when he had spotted land beneath the descending balloon, the sudden rush of greenery that exploded unexpectedly up from the earth before he realized what was happening, the feeling of lightness as he'd been hurled into the air, the cracking sound of breaking tree limbs, the bellow of his own voice as he fell, the high-pitched scream of a woman calling his name . . .

"Oh, my God!" he shouted, bolting up from the ground, his frantic gaze roving dizzily over the immediate area as he brushed at the forest debris clinging to his face and mouth. Aerial! Where was Aerial?

Certain she and the remains of the balloon and basket had to be close by, he scoured the surroundings, desperate to find a sign — any sign — that he wasn't alone. "Aerial!"

The only answer to his frantic call was the rustle of the wind in the trees overhead and the soft slurping sound of his own footsteps sinking into and slogging out of the spongy, rain-soaked ground.

A new fear gripped his gut. Had she been killed in the crash that had ironically left him only scratched and bruised? Was that why she didn't answer him?

No! his mind protested vehemently, never wondering why the possibility of Aerial Windsor's death brought him such pain, while the fact that he was alive and virtually uninjured brought him no joy or relief whatsoever.

"She can't be dead!" he insisted aloud, taking an indecisive step first in one direction, then in another. "She's got to be here. The ground didn't just open up and swallow her."

That's it! he told himself excitedly, as the memory of his last moments in the gondola flashed in his mind.

He laughed nervously, raising his gaze up to the thick covering overhead to confirm what reason told him was true.

Relieved to find it was as he had suspected, he heaved a sigh of relief. No wonder he couldn't find the balloon and passenger basket on the ground. It was easy to see that the huge, clumsy *Wind Rose* couldn't have made it through foliage so thick that only occasional small patches of sky were even visible from where he stood.

She was holding on when we crashed! he remembered jubilantly. *So it stands to reason if she didn't fall out when I did she's probably still up there in the basket—trying to figure out how to get down.*

"Aerial!" he shouted. "Aerial Windsor!"

However, after calling her and searching the treetops overhead for several minutes with no sign of the red and gold silk balloon, it became more and more difficult to ignore the niggling inner voice that kept telling him that somehow her balloon-flying expertise had allowed her to keep the balloon in the air and that she had gone on alone, just like she wanted all along. *Without even checking to see if I was dead or not.*

Disgusted with himself for the sudden feelings of betrayal and abandonment that gnawed at him, he tried to convince himself he was relieved to be rid of her. After all, wasn't this what he wanted, too?

He should just be thankful to be safely back on earth and, except for a few minor cuts and abrasions, all in one piece. Besides, she had saved him the trouble of dealing with her and what had happened in the balloon. The only thing he had to worry about now was figuring out where in the hell he was and where he was going from here.

Rye surveyed the spruce, pine, and hemlock trees that surrounded him. God, he hoped he was in Canada. He didn't need a confrontation with a United States lawman right now. Though the way his luck had been running ever since he rode into Fairfield two days before, he was probably within a few yards of an entire regiment of them.

How could she just dump me and take off without giving a second thought to whether I was alive or dead? his injured ego asked, bulldozing its way back into his thoughts despite his efforts to ignore it.

"What difference does it make who dumped who?" he asked himself irritably. "I was going to leave her the minute I set foot on solid ground anyway. At least this way I don't have to worry about feeling some crazy sense of obligation to her."

Yes, this way was definitely for the best. A nice, clean break, with no emotional millstone to hold him back.

Still, she could have at least made sure I was alive before she left.

Aerial sat up straight, checking her arms and aching body for injuries. A combination of amazement and relief washed over her as she accepted the fact that except for a bruise or two, she had landed completely unharmed.

At the thought, she raised her eyes to see if her unexpected good fortune had extended itself to her balloon.

Though she had known landing in the forest couldn't possibly leave her balloon unscathed, she was unprepared for the total destruction that greeted her eyes.

The instant of optimism she'd felt at her own safety dissolved into depression at the sight.

Impaled on the jagged tops and branches of the conical pine and spruce trees around her, the once magnificent *Wind Rose* was now reduced to shredded strips of red and gold pongee silk, its ragged remains draped over the needled branches of the trees in a goading reminder of past glory.

A wave of grief swelled in her chest as painful memories assaulted her. The gallant balloon she had spent months patching and reconstructing after her parents' deaths had truly flown its last flight.

She remembered how after the crash she had fought to stop her father's backers from selling the wrecked balloon to salvage at least a part of their losses. Fortunately for her, they had been so anxious to regain their full investment she'd been able to convince them to sell her the balloon for an amount equal to six times what the rag buyers would have paid for the silk, and at an exorbitant interest rate.

Of course, they hadn't thought she would be able to repay them, but on the off chance they could fully recoup their losses, they had agreed to the loan, with the understanding that if she missed a single payment they would immediately repossess the balloon and get what they could out of it.

She couldn't help the sad grin that crept across her face as she thought of the surprised look on banker Watson's jowly face every time she'd made another payment. He and his partners had been so sure she couldn't do it. But she'd fooled them all.

Oh, it had been close sometimes, especially in the beginning, when bookings for her balloon act had been hard to come by because promoters hesitated to deal with a "mere girl." More than once in the past five years she'd slept in the gondola to save the cost of a hotel room for the night, or skipped a meal rather than eat in a restaurant if a local family in the town where she was appearing didn't invite her to dinner.

But now it had all paid off. At last, the balloon was truly hers, free and clear. Wincing, she rolled her eyes back up to the tattered silk streamers that waved from the treetops. At least what there was left of it was hers. Unfortunately, even the rag buyers wouldn't want it now.

Hauling herself to her feet, she shook her head with regret. Losing the balloon wouldn't be nearly so catastrophic if there were witnesses to testify when and where she had landed. However, by landing this way, not only had she just destroyed her option of selling the balloon to finance a new start in life if she didn't succeed, but she had made sure that even if she *had* created a new distance record, there would be no ten thousand dollar reward promised her by the citizens of Fairfield, for there were no witnesses to her landing. Wise's record would stand, the Windsor name would go unredeemed, and once more, Aerial Windsor was penniless and alone, with no way to buy that little house and settle down the way she had always dreamed.

"There you go, crying over spilled milk again," she admonished herself as she peered over the rim of the gondola.

Right away her thoughts turned to a more immediate problem. The basket was wedged in the branches of a giant, long-needled pine tree, a good thirty feet off the ground.

She tugged the ripcord that hung from the higher branches, drawing both its ends into the basket. Quickly tying one end of the rope to the trunk of the pine tree, she hurriedly tested her knot for strength, then tossed the other end to the ground.

She took a deep breath and climbed out of the basket and started down the tree. Using the rough branches for foot holds and the rope to steady herself, she dropped from limb to limb, doing her best to protect her face from being scratched as she descended.

"Well, hello," a deep male voice greeted her as she jumped the last few feet to the ground.

Relief exploded inside Aerial, and an elated smile spread on her face. "Rye!" Dropping her grip on the rope, she spun around. "Thank God! I was afra—"

Her words dried up in her mouth and her smile dissolved into shock at the sight of three rifle-toting men who looked to be in their mid-twenties. "Where did you come from?"

"Seems like we oughta be askin' *you* that question, pretty lady," the redbearded man said with a chuckle and a sly grin at his comrades.

Aerial glanced up the tree she had just descended, then back to the three men. "Why I . . ." Suddenly it occurred to her what she had here, and a surge of excitement exploded inside her. Not only could these men help her find Rye, but they were witnesses to her success. "Where exactly is this?"

"She must a angel," the only clean-shaven man in the group said, ignoring her question. "A fallen angel," he added with a snide chuckle.

Aerial gave an embarrassed laugh and shook her head. "Don't be silly. I'm not an angel. I'm just an ordinary. . . . I mean I'm not from . . ."

Frustrated and suddenly frightened by the strange way the three were watching her, as though they didn't understand a word she was saying, she started over.

"I came here from Iowa, not Heaven!" She laughed nervously and pointed up to the basket. "See? I was in that balloon. It crashed."

"A answer ta our prayers," the mustached man said, nodding his head enthusiastically, his pale eyes gleaming hungrily. "After a week in these woods trackin' that killer black bear, you're shore a sight for sore eyes."

"Will you stop that and listen to me?" Aerial said. "Once and for all, I'm not an angel or the answer to anyone's prayers. I'm just a woman in a very unfortunate predicament and in dire need of your help. I've just set a world's record and need you to verify that fact to the authorities."

The bearded man moved toward her, his grin a definite leer. "Honey, you come ta the right place. There ain't a feller in the Adirondacks who wouldn't give a month's profit for a go at helpin' a fine lookin' gal like you."

Frightened by the strange light in the redhead's eyes, Aerial moved back. "What are you doing?"

"Jest what the Good Lord intended Adam to do to keep Eve happy when he put her in the Garden of Eden with him."

"No!" she gasped, fully understanding now. What a fool she'd been. She'd actually thought these barbarians would help her.

Turning, she tried to make a run for safety.

"Where ya goin', gal?" the mustached man chuckled. Reaching out, he curled a burly arm around her waist and drew her against his chest, his free hand cupping her buttocks. "I thought ya wanted our help with yer pree-dic-a-ment."

"Let me go, you pig!" Aerial screamed, kicking and punching her captor with all her strength.

"Not 'til we hep ourselves to them heavenly charms o' yers."

"Help!" she shrilled. "Somebody help me!"

"Sugar, that's jest what we intend to do! Jest as soon as you help us out o' our pree-dic-a-ment."

Chapter Seven

Tensing, Rye stopped in his tracks. Was that a man's voice he had heard? Cocking his head, he squinted his eyes in concentration and listened intently, a frisson of apprehension kicking his heartbeat into a higher gear.

All he needed right now was a confrontation with some landowner who might start shooting the minute he recognized his trespasser as an Indian. Unless he wanted to add to the growing list of places he was already wanted for murder, he couldn't let himself be forced into a position where he had to defend himself, so it would definitely be better to avoid all human contact until he figured out where he was.

When he heard the voice again, this time accompanied by raucous laughter, he relaxed slightly. *Just some hunters having a good time,* he assured himself, doing his best to ignore the uneasiness he continued to feel. However, since it was obvious there were at least two people, that was all the more reason to avoid them.

Because the voices were coming from his right, he knew as long as he kept going in the direction he had determined to be north there was nothing to worry about. They wouldn't even have to know he'd been here.

"Help!" a high-pitched voice cut into Rye's thoughts, creating in him a feeling of dread the likes of which he'd never known.

His keen senses leaped to attention, and he spun around, his entire body quivering with foreboding. *It can't be her!* he told himself emphatically. *She's miles from here by now.*

Whipping his revolver from its holster, he quickly checked the load, shaking his head at his own stupidity for even considering getting involved in what was probably nothing more than a squabble between a man and his wife. But no matter how impractical or dangerous involvement could prove to be, he knew he couldn't walk away.

"Somebody help me!"

Even if it wasn't Aerial Windsor, he couldn't bring himself to leave a woman in trouble without trying to help her — or at least checking to see if his help was needed. If only he'd been there to respond to his mother's screams, maybe he could have . . .

Shaking his head in a futile attempt to shrug off the guilt that still plagued him after all these years, he took off at a run.

"Get your hands off me, you filthy animal!" the woman screamed.

The terrible suspicion that the mysterious woman was Aerial immediately amplified, charging his run with even more speed.

"Come on, sugar. Don't be like that. You know you like it!" the man's voice coaxed.

Despite Rye's continued efforts to brush the possibility aside, with each long-legged stride he grew more afraid his initial hunch had been right.

"Eeeeow," the unseen man screamed in obvious pain. "You little bitch! I'll teach you . . ."

The recognizable sound of flesh slapping flesh sliced through the air. Rye's control, already stretched to the point of snapping, tensed even more, especially when he heard the woman's startled cry that followed the slap. *I'll kill him!* he swore, already forgetting his vow to avoid all trouble.

Rye's immediate urge to crash ahead without thinking was checked by another voice. "Hey, Clem, watch it! Don't mess up her face."

A modicum of coolheadedness restored by this sobering reminder that there were at least two men to contend with, Rye dropped to a crouch and moved quickly into the shadows of the surrounding brush. He had to know what and who he was up against before he did anything.

"The goddamned bitch clawed me! Look! I'm bleeding!"

"And I'll do it again if you touch me," threatened the woman. Rye no longer had any doubt it was Aerial.

His senses heightened to razor-edged sharpness by the confrontation, Rye inched forward, his black eyes taking in every detail of his surroundings. He had no doubt he could have easily handled one man. But two? This was going to take some planning. He couldn't just go in there shooting.

Cautiously, he moved a branch aside to better determine the situation.

"I'll hold her for you," the second voice offered. "Jest don't mess up her—"

The man's words were cut off by a surprised grunt just as Rye spotted the preoccupied group of men immediately ahead.

Damn! It was worse than he had expected. There were three of them, including one who was doubled over and holding his belly as though he'd just been hit.

"Next time, I'll aim lower!" the woman threatened in a low, guttural growl.

A flash of blond hair appeared, then disappeared behind the larger man who had his back to Rye. Rye's heart plunged into the pit of his belly, taking with it his last granule of hope that it wasn't Aerial.

Every fiber of his anger wrenched at his self-restraint, but his basic intelligence prevailed. As long as they had Aerial in their midst, he knew he had to wait and pick his moment carefully.

His jaw knotted with tension. His knuckles whitened as he gripped the revolver with one hand and a sapling trunk with the other, yet he willed himself to stay put until the time was right, as his mother's father, Night Arrow, had taught him to do.

Not certain how long he could live by his grandfather's rules of patience, he scoured the area for an answer to his dilemma. There had to be something. Inadvertently, he glanced upward.

Spotting the tattered remains of the *Wind Rose,* he winced at the final proof that the men before him did indeed have Aerial Windsor at their mercy.

"Now you done it, girlie," rasped the bearded man Aerial had elbowed in the belly. He ripped open the fly of his own pants. "We was tryin' to be nice, but if you want it rough, that's what you're gonna get."

Rye's anger roared to volcanic proportions and his grip on his revolver, slippery with sweat, tightened with deadly purpose. His bead on the bearded man's head, he exerted pressure on the trigger.

Not yet, his inner voice repeated. *They're so close together, the bullet could pass through and hit Aerial. You've got to wait until you can get a clear shot.*

The bearded man grabbed Aerial's arms from

behind and jerked her back against him. Rubbing himself against her backside, he laughed and tightened his hold on her upper arms, forcing her breasts to thrust outward. "Lift her skirt, Sid," he ordered the younger, beardless man. "We'll show her."

Determined to die before she would give in to these animals, Aerial let a bloodcurdling scream. Twisting furiously against the iron grip that held her upper arms, she kicked at the fumbling hands on her skirt and the man groping at her chest. If it took her last breath, her last ounce of strength, she would fight them.

With surprising force, she clipped the man at her feet under his chin with the toe of her boot. Caught off guard, Sid sprawled back on the ground.

Before the other two could react, she leaned forward, clamping her teeth closed on the exposed neck of the man in front of her with the ferocity of a dog protecting a bone. At the same time, she brought her hands together behind her to use them as a crushing vice on Deke's most vulnerable parts.

A duet of shocked, masculine yowls and curses reverberated through the air. Forgetting their fallen comrade, each of the two men automatically dropped his grip on Aerial to wrestle free of the agonizing pain they were enduring.

"Get down, Aerial!" Rye shouted, crashing into the tiny clearing, his revolver ready.

Reacting instinctively, Aerial freed her "prisoners" and made a break for safety.

Before either of the would-be rapists could retrieve a weapon, Rye fired twice, his aim rapid and purposeful.

The look of shock on the bearded man's face was one of sheer disbelief as he stared at the spreading red stain at the juncture of his thighs. "Oh, my God," he moaned as reality set it. "Oh, my God!" Gripping himself, he fell to his knees weeping. "OHHHHHHHH, MY GOOO-OOOOOOOD!"

"My fingers!" the other wounded man wailed, staring incredulously at his bleeding hand. "You shot off my goddamned fingers."

"You've got more," Rye said, his tone cold and deadly. He indicated the bearded man with a tilt of his head. "Too bad your friend wasn't so lucky."

"Rye! Watch out! He's got a gun!" Aerial pointed at Sid, who, unnoticed during the brief skirmish, had recovered from the blow to his chin.

With rattlesnake speed, Rye spun to the side, his revolver discharging as he did.

Letting a piercing shriek, Sid dropped his gun and slapped his hand against the side of his head. Where his ear had been only a moment before, he found only bloody pulp in its place. "My ear!"

"If you don't want the next one between the eyes, I suggest you get over there with your pals."

Rye glanced at Aerial, the hard expression in his black eyes immediately softening. "Are you all right? If they hurt you, I'll kill . . . In fact. . . ." He lifted his revolver and aimed it at the frightened, wounded group who huddled together a few feet away.

"No!" Aerial cried, frightened by the vengeance reflected on Rye's features. It was almost as if he had been personally wounded by what the men had tried to do to her. She ran to him and clutched his arm. "I'm not hurt."

Rye looked down at the pale hand on his sleeve, his expression tender again. "Are you sure?" he asked, his voice softer, his eyes traveling over her to confirm for himself that she was safe.

"I'm sure," she said, his gentle tone temporarily erasing from her mind the violence she had just witnessed.

Suddenly, her own expression grew anxious, her eyes widening with dismay. "But what about *you?!*" She had been so relieved to see Rye that only now did she notice the torn and bloodied state of his clothing and the scrapes and cuts on his face and neck and hands. "You're hurt! And your side is bleeding again! It needs to be taken care of right away."

Rye glanced down at his blood-soaked shirt, his expression showing more pain than he intended. "There's no time for that now. We've got to get out of here before anyone else comes."

Her attention shot back to where the three who had tried to rape her sat moaning and crying. A chill shuddered up her spine at the thought of what would have happened if Rye hadn't come to her rescue when he did. She was struck by the fact that she felt no guilt or sympathy for the pain they were suffering. Inadvertently, she shielded herself slightly behind Rye.

"Do you have any idea where we are?" he asked her.

"They said something about the Adirondacks," she answered in a hoarse whisper, continuing to watch the three attackers suspiciously. "If they were telling the truth, we're in northern New York."

"New York? Are you sure?" He glared at his captives. "Is she right? Are we in New York?"

Still gripping his torn ear, Sid nodded.

Rye clicked his tongue impatiently. "How far is it to Canada?" he asked Aerial out of the corner of his mouth.

Aerial shrugged, hurt by his gruff tone. "I have no idea."

"What about you?" he asked the three men. "Any of you know how far it is to the Canadian border?"

"Maybe fifty or sixty miles," Clem answered, pointing northward with his uninjured hand, his sweating face contorted with pain. "That way."

Rye heaved an exasperated sigh and glanced briefly at Aerial, then back at his prisoners. One hand keeping the revolver aimed at the men, he retrieved his knife from a boot and handed it to Aerial.

"Cut down that rope . . ." With a tilt of his head, he indicated the rope she had used to descend from the balloon. ". . . and tie them up. We've got to get going before anyone else comes along."

The three men immediately began to howl in protest. "You can't just leave us here like this. These woods're crawling with panthers and wolves and black bears. We been trackin' one killer bear for a week now and know he's close by."

Rye's lip curled with hatred, his menacing glare directed at the three men. "Getting eaten by a bear or a pack of wolves would be better than what your kind deserves. With my luck, these woods are filled with bastards like you, who'll be along any minute to help you out. And I don't intend to be here when they do."

He observed Aerial, the tenderness he had shown earlier gone. "Now, are you going to tie them up like I told you, or should I just finish the job with this." He tightened his grip on the revolver.

Aerial stared aghast at him. It was difficult to imagine this unfeeling man was the same man who just ten hours before had so heartrendingly relayed to her the tragic story of his parents' deaths. Last night she had been ready to believe he had never killed anyone, including that man in Iowa. Now she wasn't so certain.

Maybe he was a cold-blooded murderer after all. The look in his hard black eyes certainly made it easier to believe that than to believe he was innocent of all wrong doing. But whether or not he was telling the truth about what happened in Fairfield, she had no doubt he would kill the three wounded men if she refused to do as he said.

Unable to stand by and watch human beings deliberately killed, no matter how terrible they were, Aerial scurried to retrieve the rope. "All right! I'll do it! But I can't help but wonder why a man who claims he was wrongly accused of murdering that man in Iowa is so anxious to commit the same crime in New York."

Rye's scowl darkened. "And I can't help but wonder why a woman who was nearly raped is so quick to rush to the defense of her attackers."

Aerial opened her mouth to argue, then stopped herself. What good would it do? For now, the best thing would be to keep her mouth shut and do what he wanted. If she made him even more angry than he was, there was no telling what he would do.

When she had tied the last knot, Rye squatted down to test the security of her efforts. "That ought to keep them out of trouble, at least long enough for us to get out of here." He holstered his own gun and quickly rounded up his prisoners' weapons: three rifles, three hunting knives, and one revolver. "Let's go."

"Wouldn't it make more sense to wait here until someone does come," she suggested hastily, not only balking at the idea of leaving her attackers

115

at the mercy of the forest but suddenly hesitant to go anywhere with this seemingly ruthless man. "That way they can help us get these three to jail for what they did," she suggested in what she hoped was a sensible tone.

Rye looked up at her from where he had hunkered down to fashion a harness out of the leftover rope, his expression disbelieving. "You haven't understood anything I've said, have you?" He shook his head hopelessly. "By the time those three tell their story, it'll be *me* who attacked you, and they'll be the ones who came to your rescue."

Aerial shook her head incredulously. "Why would anyone believe their lies when I'll be here to tell them what really happened."

Adjusting the rope harness on his back, Rye released a bitter chuckle and stood up. "Well, I don't intend to hang around here just to prove to you how things are in the real world." He started out of the clearing. "You do what you want."

Aerial stared after him, stunned. He was actually going to leave her here to deal with this alone. *Well, let him go. I don't need him. He's brought me nothing but trouble since the first moment I laid eyes on him. I'll just wait until someone comes looking for me. Surely these three aren't the only ones who saw my balloon go down. By tonight I'll be safely in the nearest town being toasted as the new world record holder for distance traveled in a balloon. And Rye Berenger will still be tramping around in the woods cold and hungry and lost!*

An unwanted vision of the passionate moments she had spent in Rye's arms, his lips on hers, flashed in her mind. Even on the verge of death, she had felt more alive with him than she ever had in her life; right then, she knew she would never again know that feeling if she let him walk

116

out of her life.

She started after him, then stopped herself. What was she thinking? She would be a fool to run after him now. If he really wanted her with him, he wouldn't have left her.

Even if she dared to believe their lovemaking had meant anything to him other than an outlet for his lust, any fool would know she would be better off if she never had anything to do with him again.

Why, he was nothing more than a common criminal. He was a wanted man, roaming from one place to another, always a scant step ahead of the law, certainly not the industrious store-keeper or reserved banker or hardworking farmer she had always dreamed of marrying and building a life with. A woman who cared for a man like Rye Berenger would never know the satisfaction of living in one place in a house filled with happy, loved children.

No, Rye Berenger was definitely not the kind of man she wanted to spend her life with. Caring about him would only mean a lifetime of heart-break and misery, and the sooner she forgot him, the better it would be.

Aerial gave the three bound men an uneasy glance, then quickly looked away. She couldn't look at them without remembering what they had threatened to do to her—and without remembering how glad she had been to see Rye's tall, lean form materialize in time to save her.

All I have to do is wait, she reassured herself, bravely fighting the sense of loss she was experiencing, a sense of loss that had nothing to do with her destroyed balloon or the distance challenge she had met for naught. *I'll be just fine. Someone will come soon.* She paced back and forth for a second, then stopped, her face contorted with indecision.

What if no one comes? a little voice asked inside her head. *Or what if I have to stay here all night with them?* She took another nervous look at the threesome, less confident by the instant that the ropes binding them were secure. *What if they figure out a way to untie themselves? Or what if that bear gets here before anyone finds me? Maybe even a pack of wolves?*

She looked around apprehensively, suddenly feeling danger lurking behind every tree and bush.

Then the ultimate fear exploded in her mind. What if the people who came looking for her were no better than the three who had found her first? Without Rye Berenger to step in, she would be utterly helpless. He hadn't even left her a gun to protect herself!

"Lady," Sid asked, "can you loosen the ropes a little bit? They're awful tight."

Damn you, Rye Berenger! she swore silently, refusing to acknowledge that Sid had spoken. *You cost me everything. And then you just walked out and left me as if I never existed. How could you do that? It's not bad enough that because of you the record I set probably won't get official recognition; I don't even have my balloon anymore. You took it all, my record, my balloon, my virginity—and my self-respect. And then you left. Damn you! You owe me for all you've stolen from me, and I swear if I ever lay eyes on you again, you're going to pay.*

"All right! That's it!" Rye announced, shattering her vengeful thoughts into a storm of shock as he crashed back into the clearing.

Relief erupted in Aerial's chest, all thoughts of revenge leaving her. All she could think of was that he hadn't left her after all. "You're back!"

His dark face scowling, Rye grabbed her arm.

"Whether you like it or not, you're coming with me."

"Let go of me!" she shouted, instinctively fighting him in spite of how glad she was that he was back.

"You had your chance to come willingly. Now you don't have a choice. You've already cost me too much time."

Torn between indignation for the way he was treating her and elation that he hadn't walked out of her life after all, Aerial dug in her heels and struggled halfheartedly against his hold. "I told you, I can't leave. I have to stay with my balloon so that when the rescuers arrive, I'll have witnesses to the fact that I've broken the distance record. I won't let you steal that from me, too."

A moment of guilt rushed through Rye's head. He knew how important this record was to her, and he hated to deprive her of the chance to have it, but dammit, this was a case of survival. He sure as hell couldn't stay here, and he couldn't leave her behind.

He cast an angry glance at the three men he had wounded. If only he had just killed them in the first place, when his rage at finding Aerial in their clutches was at its peak. It would have been easy then. But now that time had cooled his anger slightly, he realized that the sense of honor instilled in him by his peace-loving father wouldn't permit him to shoot helpless, bound men in cold blood—even if they deserved to be dead.

Unexpectedly, gunfire cracked through the air, causing the heads of all five people in the woods to jerk around.

Excitedly thinking, *We're saved!* Aerial's immediate inclination was to call out to whoever had fired the shot, but Rye's reflexes were too quick for her.

Clamping one hand over her mouth, he whipped his revolver from his holster and aimed it at the bound prisoners. "First one that makes a sound is a dead man!" he warned through his teeth.

A second series of shots exploded through the woods, followed by the sounds of rough laughter and comments. "Oooeee, I got him." "I reckon this is about the biggest one we ever bagged." "Thought sure when we heard them shots earlier that Deke 'n' the boys'd be collectin' the bounty on this one."

Clem, who continued to hold his bleeding hand against his chest, managed a cocky sneer. "Now who's the dead man? That's our partners, and they're gonna be all over you like flies on manure in about two minutes."

Hit with the realization that the new arrivals were friends of the three who had attacked her, Aerial clutched at Rye's arm and stared up at him.

Looking down into the frightened blue eyes that pleaded with him for protection, Rye was filled with indecision. On an emotional level, the thought of running away from danger brought back such painful memories that he was tempted to stay. Yet his sense of survival reminded him that even if he weren't weak from his fall and the loss of blood, it would be impossible to hold off several attackers for very long if they came at him from more than one direction. All it would take would be one lucky shot and Aerial would be totally at their mercy.

The vision of the bear hunters even touching her, much less raping her, sent a surge of revulsion slamming into his gut, and he knew he had no choice. Guilt and memories be damned, he

120

had to stay alive until he got her to safety.

Releasing an angry growl, he wheeled about, scooped Aerial into his arms, and took off at a run.

Chapter Eight

Rye strained to increase his gait, knowing he had to put as much distance as possible between himself and Aerial's attackers before their shouts for help brought their friends to free them.

It had already been several minutes since he'd left the bound men, but between the higher altitude and his already weakened state, the strength had drained from his limbs. Already, his lungs felt as if they would burst, and his side cramped painfully. Each stumbling step he completed threatened to be his last, but still he continued, determined to stay on his feet.

Her ear pressed to Rye's heaving chest, Aerial quickly became aware of what was happening. From the sound of his rapidly pumping heart and his labored breathing, it was obvious he was in no condition even to be standing, much less running or carrying her added weight.

Struck with a horrible picture of what it would mean if Rye was forced to protect himself from Deke and Clem and Sid's cohorts, Aerial was shaken from the temporary sense of safety she had felt when Rye had whisked her up in his arms.

She couldn't let them hurt Rye, not after he had risked his own life to save her. She had to do whatever it took to protect him from them.

She squirmed in his arms. "Stop! I don't need

to be carried."

"Can't stop," he panted, stumbling, but managing to stay upright and continue his slow, staggering run. "Can't let them have you."

"Rye!" she said, demanding his attention by catching his cheeks between her palms and forcing him to look at her. "No one's going to hurt either of us if you'll just listen to me." She hesitated a second to determine if her words were even getting through to him. "Are you listening?"

He nodded feebly, his run slowing to a walk.

"Look at yourself. You're on the verge of collapsing. You've got to put me down before you drop me."

He continued on as though he hadn't heard her, his desperate walk through the abundant fern and ground pine that covered the forest floor fueled by sheer willpower.

"Rye!" she hissed, slapping his face to shake him out of the stupor he'd worked himself into. "They're going to kill both of us if you don't put me down right this minute. Is that what you want?"

Whether it was the slap or her words that got through to him, she didn't know or care. She was just thankful when he stopped and let her slide from his arms.

"You're right," he admitted breathlessly. "I can't make it. You go on without me. I'll hold them off as long as I can."

Before her eyes, Rye grew shorter as his knees began to buckle.

"Oh, no you don't!" She slipped her arm around his waist to stop his fall. Flinching as her hand slid over the sticky area of his shirt where his reopened wound continued to ooze blood, she wedged her shoulder under his arm and bolstered him up.

"After all you've cost me," she grunted, starting him forward, "if you think I'm going to let you take the easy way out, you'd better think again. Whether you like it or not, we're in this together. Now, walk!"

Hating himself for not having the strength to protest, Rye did as she commanded, concentrating on not leaning on her too heavily, though somewhere in the back of his mind he was surprised by the physical strength she possessed.

"No good," he mumbled after wading only a few steps through the thick foliage. "You've got to go on without me. I can't go any farther."

As much as she hated to admit it, Aerial had to agree with Rye. It was a miracle that he hadn't already passed out. She paused, listening for sounds that indicated the bear hunters had found their wounded partners and were on Rye and Aerial's trail.

Determining that the bound men were still yelling for help, she heaved a sigh of relief for the slight reprieve and scanned the area for a place to hide until Rye could regain his strength.

She eyed one of the many raspberry brambles that contributed to the tangle of vegetation surrounding them. With a wince of distaste, she immediately relegated that idea to last place on the list of possibilities. Only as the most desperate resort would she consider crawling into one of the larger brambles. If the thorns weren't enough, the thought of the insects and rodents who must call the brambles home convinced her she had to come up with something else—and fast. If only there were a cave.

Just then, shouts from behind them told her the bound men had been located by the others. Her time was up. She had to do something now. "Looks like the raspberry brambles are our only choice."

Resigned to her fate, she hurriedly scoured the area to decide on the best bramble for their hideout. Zeroing in on a likely candidate, she noticed a particularly dense covering of ferns between the bramble and a stand of spruce trees that appeared to be fifty or sixty feet high.

"Perfect!" She checked Rye, who was obviously struggling to stay conscious. "Just stay awake for a few more minutes," she coaxed, prodding him toward the ferns. "And then you can sleep all you want."

By sheer will, Rye managed to stay upright, only dropping to the ground when Aerial told him it was all right to do so.

"That's right," she told him, though she knew he no longer heard her. "You just sleep." She quickly removed his bundle of weapons, then stood up to be certain the wild, knee-high ferns hid the guns and Rye's prone body. Satisfied, she turned her head in the direction from which they had come. All she could do now was wait for the danger to come. An angry shout from the hunters told her that moment wasn't far away.

Reacting automatically, she fell to the ground and burrowed her way under the ferns, doing her best to disturb the protective camouflage as little as possible. Praying Rye would stay quiet and that nothing that would give away their location was showing through the sprays of long leaves above them, she held her breath.

Almost immediately she heard men's angry voices and the sounds of heavy boots tramping through the dense brush.

Evidently, the disturbance penetrated Rye's sleep. "Aerial?" he muttered, lifting his head off the ground to look around with frantic, unseeing eyes.

Panicked, Aerial pulled him into her arms and held his face to her bosom. "Go back to sleep," she whispered against his ear, afraid he would start thrashing around if he realized how close the danger was. "It's all right. I'm here."

Seemingly appeased by her voice, Rye nuzzled his face between her breasts, gave a low, contented moan, then went back to sleep.

Too afraid for her life to examine the sense of fulfillment holding him made her feel, Aerial stroked Rye's coarse black hair. "Shh, shh."

"How much longer we gonna look for 'em?" a man's voice asked, startling Aerial by its very nearness.

Not daring to move, she tightened her hold on Rye and peeked through the holes of light in the ferns. She swallowed back a gasp as she caught sight of a trouser leg not more than six feet from where she lay. It didn't matter that she and Rye must be hidden completely from view. All the trackers had to do to find them would be to take a few steps in this direction and they would trip over them!

"Jest as long as is necessary," a second voice responded.

"But Clem said the Injun was askin' 'bout gittin' to Canada. You ain't gonna foller 'em that far, are ya? What about our bear?"

"To hell with the bear. Someone's gotta make that lowdown Injun pay for what he done to my brother."

"You might be willin' to walk off and leave the thirty dollars for that bear, but not me. I say we go back, collect the bounty, then go lookin' for the Injun what done in Deke. Whadda ya say?"

Barely registering the fact that one of the three men who had attacked her must have died, Aer-

126

ial watched as the trouser leg turn slowly to the right. Sure the owner must be exploring the area for a clue as to which way to go, her imagination immediately ignited with a vision of an obvious path of trampled ferns leading the enemy directly to their hiding place.

Knowing discovery was just a moment away, she held Rye closer, not daring to even breathe. If only she had taken the time to check the trail behind her.

"I guess you're right," Deke's brother conceded. "It's pretty near impossible to track a feller through all this brush. No sooner do ya lift your foot off the ground, and these damn ferns close in over your track."

Aerial opened one eye suspiciously, refusing to believe her luck. Was it really possible they couldn't see the trail she was sure she and Rye must have left?

" 'Specially if the feller yer trackin' happens to be a Injun."

Aerial opened her other eye, but she still held her breath and listened.

"Come on. Let's go skin that bear and git our bounty. But I don't mind tellin' you, I ain't lookin' forward to tellin' Ma the Injun bastard who killed her baby boy and shot up cousins got plum away. She's gonna be fit to be tied with grief."

Continuing her soothing stroking on Rye's hair and back to insure that he would stay quiet, Aerial stared with disbelieving eyes as the trouser leg disappeared from her view. She stayed there long after the conversation and movements of the two men could no longer be heard.

At first she was simply too afraid to move, but then as the truth that the danger was gone sank in, she realized she couldn't yet bear to give

127

up the sweet feeling of holding Rye in her arms. So she decided to stay put just a few minutes longer—to be on the safe side.

Aerial didn't know at what point she fell asleep or how long she slept, but when she awoke it was with a lazy, contented grin, as if she had just had the best night's sleep of her life and didn't have a problem in the world. But it was only a moment before the seriousness of her predicament came crashing back into her consciousness.

Glancing down at Rye, she determined that he was still sleeping, though more fitfully than before. Suddenly aware of how intensely she was perspiring with his body pressed against hers, she put her hand on his forehead in an effort to ease her arm out from under his head. It was then she noticed his skin was hot, as she was sure hers must be. But unlike hers, his was dry except where he was touching hers. And he was shivering.

She sat upright, fear enveloping her. "You're burning with fever!" she said aloud, her panic increasing.

What if Rye was seriously ill? Should she try to go for help? She thought about that for a moment, then shook her head. Leaving him was out of the question for the simple reason that she would never find her way back to this spot, assuming of course that she made it to safety in the first place. There had to be something else she could do.

A quick look at the afternoon sun reminded her that whatever she decided to do it needed to be soon or they would be stuck here for the night. Cautiously, she stood up and glanced around, afraid the hunters might be back.

When she heard nothing but the buzz of insects and the gentle rustle of the ferns, she grew more confident. "Stay right there," she said to the unconscious man. "I'm going to look around."

Picking out the tallest spruce tree in the nearby stand, she grabbed hold of one of its drooping branches and ducked under it.

Moments later, Aerial peeked through the branches near the top of the tree to survey her surroundings. Far to the east she saw a giant strip of water, gleaming gold in the rays of the sun. "That must be Lake Champlain," she said to herself, mentally reviewing her maps. She knew the area to be dotted with thousands of small lakes, but only one was as big as the one she saw.

All around her there were other roundtopped mountains, each of them crowded so close to the others that it seemed as though they were holding each other up. Glancing farther up the mountain on which she and Rye were stranded, she saw that the evergreens, so tall and abundant where she was, became a tangle of stunted pines and spruces that gradually decreased in height until the surface of the mountain was entirely bare, with the exception of what looked like mosses and small plants.

Quickly retracing in her mind what she had learned about the Adirondacks in preparation for her trip, she came to the conclusion that they were on Mount Marcy. At an altitude of over five thousand feet, it was the highest peak in the Adirondacks, and the only one to have a definite timber line.

She scrunched her face in disgust, displeased with her discovery. What was she supposed to do now? Mount Marcy was virtually uninhabited. That meant that if she was right about where they were, the only available help would be in one of the tiny towns at the base of the mountain.

Resigning herself to leaving Rye to go for help, she started back down the tree. Before she had climbed more than a few feet, the sun reflected off something to the north. Hit with the sense that whatever she'd seen wasn't part of the mountain's natural decor, she squinted to see better.

Strain as she might, she saw nothing but trees. On the verge of crediting wishful thinking with whatever she had seen, she moved her head up and down one last time, hoping to achieve just the right angle to see the mysterious thing again. Even if it were a dead tree, she would feel better making sure. Then she saw it again and her heart leaped in her chest.

"That's no dead tree!" she muttered, finally able to make out a few definite details. "That's some kind of building!" Knowing a structure in the woods meant people, she was assaulted with a combination of relief and apprehension. The presence of people indicated one of two things: either help for Rye was just over the next rise or danger was lurking only a few feet from where he slept, too sick and weak to protect himself!

Slipping and leaping from branch to branch, Aerial climbed back down the spruce tree and ran to where she had left Rye. Finding him still asleep, she decided not to wake him. If she hurried, she could check out the cabin she had spotted and be back before he knew she was gone.

Crouching low, she quickly worked her way through the ferns and brambles toward the section of the woods where she had determined the cabin to be. Again and again she glanced over her shoulder, not only to make certain no one

130

was following her, but to keep a grasp on her bearings. The ground was so thickly covered that it would be easy to become lost only a few feet from her destination. Hopefully, as long as she kept the spruce tree she had climbed in sight, she should be able to find her way back to Rye.

In a matter of moments the building she had seen suddenly materialized before her eyes, as though rising from the greenery surrounding it.

Dropping to a squat, she stared at the cabin. Its aged walls were tilted and splintering with neglect, and it looked as if it were being held up by the trailing vines and brambles that wound over its surface, making it almost invisible even at this close range. In fact, if she'd been walking any faster, she could have easily passed right by without seeing it.

Creeping in for a closer look at what appeared to be a deserted shack, she spotted a chimney peeking out of the bark roof and a small stream careening down the mountain to join the Hudson River, that is, if this was truly the southern side of Mount Marcy.

"All the comforts of home," she mumbled, taking a quick glance up at the sky to determine how much time was left before dark. Confirming that she still had a few hours, she stood up, ran over to the cabin, and knocked on the door, which hung precariously on one leather hinge. "Is anybody home?" she called out nervously.

Certain she'd have run like a frightened rabbit if anyone had answered her, she heaved a sigh of relief when no one did. Calmer now, she swung open the rickety door and peeked inside.

The agitated chatter and squeaks of small animals filled the air as the sudden sunlight inside the cabin's one room sent a raccoon, several mice, and one or two other furry critters Aerial couldn't identify scurrying past and over her feet.

Screaming in spite of herself, Aerial jumped back as the cabin's tiny inhabitants disappeared into the woods. Inclined to do the same thing, she started back the way she had come.

Before she had gone more than a few steps, common sense stopped her retreat. She turned around and faced the cabin again.

Maybe she should reconsider. After all, hidden the way it was, the shack would certainly be safer for Rye than where he was now. Besides providing a roof in case of rain, it had the added bonuses of fresh water and a fireplace for cooking. If she had anything to cook or even knew how to cook it!

Keeping her concentration on the ground in case any late-departing "guests" should come out, she picked up a long stick and approached the structure again. Using the stick, she removed two tattered pieces of what appeared to be waxed burlap from the windows on each side of the door and flung them aside. Peering inside, she found that exposing the room to the sunlight was no help whatsoever. If anything, it was worse than she had expected it to be.

A dirt floor, torn blankets and mattress, a crumbling fireplace, one rusty iron pot, a tin cup filled with dirt, and more rubbish than she'd ever seen: this was the sight that met her gaze. Aerial knew she would stay out in a thousand rainstorms before she would sleep in this filthy place.

She contemplated the cheerful stream, then studied the cabin again, reminding herself that she wasn't the one who had the fever and needed shelter for the night, no matter how foul it might be.

Resigned to what she had to do, Aerial took a

deep breath and went inside the hut to retrieve the tin cup. Holding it out in front of her with two fingers, she made a face and ran to the stream to wash the cup out as best she could before filling it with water.

Carefully holding the cup in both hands, Aerial hurried back to where she had left Rye. Relieved to find him still there, she knelt beside him and lifted his head into her lap.

"Rye, you have to wake up now. It will be dark soon and I need to get you somewhere dry."

Smacking his parched lips, Rye looked at her with a cloudy, disoriented stare. "Water," he croaked.

Aerial produced the tin cup proudly and held it to his lips, pleased with herself that she had done the right thing—for she had never in her life taken care of a sick person.

"When you're finished, I'll take you where you can have all the fresh water you want," she promised, urging him to hurry and spilling half the water down his chin.

"Not so fast," he protested, raising a weak hand to indicate he had to rest.

She was relieved to see that his bleary eyes were slightly clearer, as if he might know where he was. But he was still shivering. "Rye, I've got to get you off this damp ground. Do you think you can walk?"

"Walk?" he asked, as though the word had no meaning to him. "Water," he said, lifting his head again and reaching for the cup in her hand.

"Yes, water," she repeated, holding the cup just out of his reach. "When we get you under some shelter, you can have all the water you want. Now, come on."

133

Working her way to a standing position, she held out one hand to him while holding the water in the other. "Sit up and take my hand, Rye, and I'll give you more water."

Straining, he managed to do as she ordered. As a reward, she gave him a couple of sips of water, then placed the cup out of his reach, again. She rewarded him with another sip when he stood up, then with still another when he took his first steps.

Supporting him with her arm, she walked him laboriously back to the cabin, reclaiming the scraps of her skirt fabric she had left to mark her trail.

At the woodland hovel once more, she regarded the building, disappointed to find it looked no more livable than it had before. She sat Rye down and let him lean back against a tree while she ran to the creek for more water.

Back at his side, she dropped to her knees beside him, her brow furrowed with worry. "Drink this," she said, holding the cup to his lips. "It'll make you feel better."

Covering her hands on the cup with his own, Rye gulped greedily at the cold mountain water. "Where are we?" he asked when he had emptied the cup.

"I think we're on Mount Marcy in the Adirondacks."

"I mean, where exactly are we?" he asked, lifting a limp hand and waving it toward the shack. "Who does that belong to?"

Aerial gave the dilapidated cabin an embarrassed glance and shrugged. "Us, I guess, at least for tonight, since it looks like no one else has plans to use it. Wasn't I lucky to find it?" she asked, her tone and smile artificially cheerful.

His breathing shallow and rapid, Rye gave her

a weak nod, his eyes opening and closing slowly. "Yeah, real lucky."

"I know it doesn't look like much now," she said defensively, hurt in spite of the fact that she knew it was his fever talking, "but once I clean it up you're going to thank me, especially if there's another storm."

"I bet," he mumbled, the trip to the cabin finally taking its toll on his strength. With a shudder, he lay down on the ground. "Especially when the roof collapses on me," he added, curling himself into a ball for warmth, his eyes already closed. "I'll just stay here."

"It would serve you right if I did just leave you there," Aerial threatened. She knelt beside him and began unbuttoning his shirt so she could wash the cuts on his face and arms and rebandage the knife wound in his side.

Once she had taken care of Rye's injuries and had washed and hung his shirt to dry, Aerial used the remaining daylight to shake out the tattered blankets left in the shack, remove trash and debris from inside, and beat the forgotten mattress ticking until the little stuffing it had in it was no more.

In the midst of all the filth, she found several treasures: a tin plate, an animal trap, a china cup, only slightly cracked. Best of all, there was a broken shovel and an old broom, which she immediately put to use removing animal droppings, nests, cobwebs, and more than one questionable item she decided she was better off not identifying.

Once the dirt floor was swept clean and the ticking and blankets laid out neatly in the center of the room, she managed to get a fire started in the fireplace, using dry kindling and tinder she'd found in the rubbish she had removed from the cabin and the two sulphur matches she'd found in a glass jar in the corner.

As the last seconds of twilight faded into darkness, Aerial surveyed the interior of the cabin, more than pleased with the results of her first homemaking efforts. Clean and lit by the crackling fire, it looked quite cozy, she decided.

A smile on her face, she hurried to where Rye still slept; and again using water as the proverbial "carrot," she coaxed him into the cabin and down onto the mattress ticking.

"Here, drink this tea I made," she said, lifting his head and holding the china cup to his lips. "It will help you get your strength back."

Rye took a sip, then shuddered with distaste and tried to push her hand away. "What is that? Are you trying to cure me or kill me?"

Her own supply of energy exhausted, Aerial had no more patience to give her cantankerous companion. Who did he think he was? Dropping his head back onto the ticking with a thud, she stood up.

"That's it! I've had enough of your rudeness. For your information, you're not the only one who's unhappy about being here. Because of you I've lost everything, but I still worked my fingers to the bone to protect you and make you comfortable. Fever or not, you could at least be civil and show a little appreciation. From now on," she said angrily, flinging open the one-hinged door, "I'm going to worry about my own needs, and you can starve or bleed to death for all I care. You're on your own!" She stepped outside, slamming the door behind her.

Staring after her, his fevered brow wrinkled with confusion, Rye tried to understand what had just happened. "What'd I say?"

"And another thing!" Aerial shouted from outside the door. "I made that tea with raspberries because that was the only thing I found that I knew wouldn't poison you. Next time I won't be so cautious!"

Chapter Nine

Her anger tempered by a reviving bath in the stream and the several handfuls of raspberries she had eaten, Aerial stood over Rye, who slept on his side, his face to the fire. Studying his sleeping features, she was again amazed at how much younger he looked when he was asleep. It was as if he were two different people. Like this, it was easy to imagine he was the most innocent of men, but remembering how he'd been with her attackers, she knew she didn't dare trust what her heart was wanting her to believe.

Noticing the empty china cup in front of him, she glanced at the pot of raspberry tea she had left beside the fire and realized that most of the tea was gone.

She smiled, forgetting the frightening side of Rye and concentrating on the vulnerable man before her. Evidently, something she'd said had gotten through to him after all. Whatever the reason, he had consumed the tea and was sleeping more normally than before, his shivering all but stopped.

Pleased with her instinctive nursing skills, she stooped to cover his bared chest and shoulder with one of the tattered blankets she had aired out, for his washed shirt had been too wet to put back on. Pausing to feel his forehead, she was happy to discover that, though not entirely gone, his fever seemed to have lowered somewhat, a fact for which she gave her tea full credit.

A chill suddenly shook her and she tightened the second blanket around her own shoulders and stood up. It was going to be a long, cold night wearing nothing but her chemise and a ragged scrap of blanket. But she didn't really have any choice. Her clothes had been stiff with dirt and blood, and if she had waited until morning to wash them she would have been forced to forfeit all sense of modesty in the light of day—not to mention spending the night in the filthy clothing!

Moving closer to the fire, she reaffirmed her decision. A night of being cold was definitely preferable to spending the day so scantily dressed. Besides, if Rye was better in the morning, they would want to be on their way—wherever they were going.

Just then, Rye bolted upright on the pallet. "Noooooo," he wailed in the most tortured moan Aerial had ever heard. "Gotta get help. Gotta get help."

"Rye!" she cried, rushing to his side and kneeling beside him to grab his shoulders. "What is it? What's wrong."

His gaze glassy, Rye stared, obviously not recognizing her. "Gotta help . . ." He frowned, as if trying to remember something. "Gotta . . ."

Realizing he was talking in his sleep, she tried to get him to lie back down. "There, there. Go back to sleep. It's just a dream."

Fighting her, he remained sitting. "Help . . . Gotta get help . . ." His confused frown deepened, and he licked his parched lips. Then his entire face seemed to crumble into a look of horrified anguish. "Noooooo!" he bellowed. "Dear God, noooooo! Oh, please, no!"

In his struggle to stand up, he flailed at Aerial with his arms. "Gotta do something . . . Gotta . . ."

Frightened that he would hurt himself if she didn't stop him, Aerial drew back one hand and slapped him across the face, yelling, "Rye! Wake up! It's all right now. It's just a bad dream."

Suddenly Rye stopped thrashing and stared at her. "Aerial?" he asked, directing his tear-filled gaze to her frightened face. "Oh, my God," he sobbed, gathering her into his arms, "I thought you were . . ." He gripped handfuls of her blond hair and buried his face in it.

"I'm fine," she answered, stroking his head. "No one hurt me. It was just a dream, Rye. Just a bad dream."

"So real," he muttered into her ear. "He had you and I couldn't get to you. I ran and ran, but the more I ran toward you, the farther away you were."

"Don't think about it. I'm here now, and no one's going to hurt me." Gently she guided him down to the mat on the floor. "Just go back to sleep."

He nodded his head. "So real," he murmured, lying the rest of the way down and closing his eyes, but keeping hold of her wrist.

"It's all right," she soothed, prying his fingers open.

Just as she was free, his head popped up from the mat, the look in his black eyes frantic as he scanned the small room. "Where are you going?" he asked, the fear in his voice touching something very deep inside her.

"I'm not going anywhere," she answered,

brushing his hair off his forehead and coaxing his head back down to the mat.

"Don't leave me," he pleaded sleepily, her hand on his forehead immediately appeasing him.

"I won't. Now, you go to sleep. I'll be right here when you wake up."

"Mmm," he moaned, dozing off. "Right here."

A warmth she didn't understand enveloped her heart as she watched him sleep peacefully. Finally, after a few soul-searching minutes, she turned back to the fire. What did it mean that he'd been dreaming about her? Was it just a feverish nightmare? Or could it mean something else?

If she was nothing to him, would he have risked his life and come back to save her from her attackers when it would have been easier to just walk away from her?

Stooping to add more wood to the fire, she couldn't resist smiling. Would he have been so frightened when he dreamed she was in danger? Or so glad to find her safe? Was it possible that what had happened in the balloon had been more than just lust on his part? Maybe . . .

She bolted up from the floor. *Stop it! It was the fever talking! He doesn't care about you. You're nothing to him—except maybe a way to clear his name, here and in Iowa. Once you testify that he shot those men in your defense and that you didn't actually see him kill that drunk in Fairfield, he'll walk out of your life without a backward glance! He's just afraid he'll lose you before you can get him out of trouble, and the sooner you get that through your head, the better off you'll be!*

She wheeled around and glared angrily at Rye. Look at him! How dare he lie there, totally oblivious to how much he had cost her and to the

141

havoc he had reaped on her well-planned life. *I should have left him when he fell out of the basket. He wasn't hurt that badly, and I'd still have my balloon! Now that I think about it, if I had a lick of sense, I'd walk out that door this minute, before he has a chance to steal my heart along with everything else he's taken from me* . . .

"Aerial?" Rye whimpered, his voice slicing into her thoughts. "Where are you?" He rolled his head restlessly from side to side, his actions increasingly agitated. "Can't see you . . . Aerial? Aerial! I need you!"

Despite the fact that she knew that every minute she spent responding to his needs she was opening herself to more heartache, Aerial rushed to Rye and dropped down beside him. "I'm still here. I'm not going anywhere," she told him with resignation.

At the sound of her voice, he immediately reached for her.

Knowing there was only one way he was going to sleep restfully, she lay down beside him and drew him into her embrace.

After all, he *had* saved her from the three hunters, so she at least owed him the same kindness she would give to anyone who was sick and in need of help. Anyway, if she planned to walk down the mountain in the morning, she could use a little sleep herself.

Aerial opened her eyes lazily, then closed them again. *Just a few more minutes,* she thought, fighting her return to reality. She would lie here and rest her eyes a little longer. Then she would get dressed and go make her last-minute preparations before leaving.

She smiled contentedly in her sleep. After tomorrow, her father's good name would be restored and she would be famous in her own right for having achieved the new world record for cross-country miles traveled in a balloon. But best of all, after tomorrow she would finally be free to settle down in one place. Never again would she have to wake up in a strange bed in a strange town and experience that moment of panic at not knowing where she was.

At the thought, she blinked sleepily.

Suddenly, every horrible event of the past forty-eight hours crashed into her memory with volcanic force. She bolted upright, fully awake to the harsh reality of her whereabouts.

Disheartened at not finding herself in the Iowa hotel room she'd been dreaming about, she lashed her alarmed scrutiny over the dimly-lit interior of the deserted Adirondack shack. The cabin she'd deemed "quite cozy" last night by firelight, showed itself for what it was: a dank, dimly-lit pile of rotting logs on the verge of collapse.

Giving the ceiling an uneasy glance, she wondered at their luck that the roof hadn't caved in on them during the night. Well, hopefully, Rye was better this morning and they could start down the mountain right away, because this place was probably going to crumble any minute. Shaking her head at their luck, she turned to check on Rye.

It took an instant for her mind to register the meaning of the rumpled ticking where she had expected to find Rye sleeping.

"Rye?" Desperately fighting the panic that immediately began to pound in her chest and temples, she whipped another inspection around the cabin. He had to be here. He wouldn't have just

143

left her here alone. "Rye!"

When she received no immediate answer, she bolted up from the mat on the floor, the obvious conclusion ringing in her ears. With a night to recover and to rethink his situation, Rye Berenger had decided his chances for survival were better if he went on without her. He had left her defenseless and alone, and this time for good!

She stared at the empty cabin long and hard, struggling to ignore the tentacles of fear coiling in her belly. After all, this wasn't exactly the first time in her life she'd been forced into circumstances where there was only herself to depend on for survival. When her parents left her alone without warning, she'd taken care of herself, hadn't she? Of course! And she could do it again. She proved that yesterday!

Suddenly she was struck with the memory of the attack by the hunters and the fact that their friends were looking for her. And a whole new list of dangers reeled off in her head. What if the hunters came back? What if she encountered a wild animal? What would she eat? Or what if she wandered around in these woods for days without ever finding her way to a town!

Faced with the very real possibility that surviving on her own in the wilds of the Adirondacks would be impossible, she lunged at the cabin door and flung it open. If she hurried, maybe she could catch Rye. Even if he refused to take her to the nearest town, she certainly would be safer with him than she would be alone!

"Rye!" she screamed, darting out of the cabin.

A revolver drawn, his face pinched with worry, Rye rounded the corner of the cabin at a run. "Aerial? What's wrong?" he asked, his alert eyes skimming over the yard.

"Thank heavens!" she cried. Running to him, she slammed against his muscular chest and threw her arms around his neck. "I thought you had left me!" she babbled, covering his chest and shoulders with tearful kisses.

Puzzled by the zealous greeting, Rye grabbed her upper arms and held her away from him. "Did you really think I'd leave you alone up here?"

Confused by the hurt she saw in Rye's black eyes, Aerial tried to explain. "When I woke up and you weren't there, I . . ."

"Automatically thought I'd run out on you," he finished with a sneer. "You really *don't* trust me, do you?" Before she could answer, he hauled her hard against the wall of his chest and pushed his face down to within inches of hers. "For the record, Miss Windsor, I thought you might be hungry this morning for something besides raspberries. So, while I was washing up, I decided to snare a rabbit for your breakfast."

"I didn't know," she whispered contritely.

"Well, now you do," he growled, dropping his hold on her and taking a step back.

Only then did Aerial realize Rye was wearing nothing but an Indian breechcloth and the white bandage she had tied around his middle the night before. His inky black hair, shiny with water from his bath, was fingercombed back from his angry face, emphasizing the hurt in his dark eyes as he glared accusingly at her.

"Yes, now I know," she murmured. Her face growing hot, she gaped helplessly at the naked expanse of bronzed skin in front of her.

Unable to stop herself, she took the few steps that separated her from Rye. All sense of what was proper or improper evaporated from her mind. She only knew she must ease the pain in

145

Rye's eyes, the pain she had put there, the pain she was certain he managed to disguise from the rest of the world but couldn't hide from her.

Reaching up, she clasped his cheeks between her palms. "I'm sorry. I was wrong. Can you forgive me?"

The heat of her hands raced through Rye's body from his face to his toes. Suddenly the fever of the night before seemed mild in comparison to what he was feeling now.

Hauling her to him, he slanted his mouth over hers in a kiss that was at once desperate and punishing.

The unexpected intensity of his embrace startled Aerial, causing her instinctively to drop her hands from his face to his shoulders and to resist. But no sooner did the impulse to escape occur than it dissolved into a longing she couldn't deny.

Opening her mouth wider to receive his full kiss, she raised up on her toes and wound her arms around his neck. Burrowing her fingers into the damp hair at the back of his head, she moaned, helplessly moving her thinly clad body against his.

Logic and reason screamed at him to stop. They had already lost too much valuable time. The hunters who had come to the rescue of Aerial's attackers could find them at any minute.

But the feel of her warm, slim body pressed against him, not to mention the demanding need swelling in him, negated any arguments his conscience might create.

Claiming her mouth with his tongue just as his desire cried out to claim her body, he molded his hands to her buttocks, lifting her hard against his passion. Then, unable to bear the waiting any longer, Rye scooped Aerial into his arms and

146

strode purposefully into the cabin, his mouth still sealed to hers.

He gently lowered her to the makeshift bed and lay down beside her, shaping his lean body to hers. Spanning her midriff with one large hand, he trailed a fiery line of kisses down her neck and over her shoulders.

As his hand massaged and caressed its way upward, his mouth tickled and nipped its way down her chest. Catching her breast from the underside, he squeezed softly as his lips came down on its erect peak, hungrily sucking it despite the thin white chemise she wore.

Jolts of electricity streamed through Aerial, filling her entire soul with magnificent light. Every thought she'd ever possessed disappeared. Every fear, every worry, every sad memory, every moment of loneliness. All of them miraculously gone.

Instinct telling her what she needed, she searched for his breechcloth string with clumsy hands.

He lifted his head from her breast. "Easy, easy," he murmured, removing her hands from between them and securing them in one strong fist above her head. "I don't want to rush this time."

In the back of his mind, the remaining fragment of good sense he possessed reminded him that time was of the utmost urgency and that he was crazy not to take her right then. But even if it meant his death, this time he knew he could not hurry. He had to see all of her, touch all of her, savor every delectable moment with her.

Using his free hand, he whisked her chemise upward, dragging it along the length of her arms, stopping at her wrists.

"You're so beautiful," he moaned, his eyes

gleaming with lust as he surveyed her breasts and brought his hand back down to knead and manipulate a nipple.

The sudden exposure sent a wave of embarrassment rippling through Aerial, and she tried to lower her arms to cover herself.

"No, Wind Flower, don't hide yourself from me." He tightened his grip on her wrists. When she stopped struggling, he moved his free hand down the slender length of her body.

Instinctively, Aerial rolled her hips to the side in an attempt to protect the most personal part of her body from his view.

Allowing her to stay twisted to the side, he dipped his head to kiss her exposed underarm, imitating the circling motion of his tongue with his fingertips on her breast. Continuing his deliberately tormenting caresses at one breast, he trailed his tongue to the peak of the other and sucked it into his mouth.

Aerial couldn't fight the delicious languor swelling inside her as he bathed her breasts with his kisses, and she slowly relaxed her defensive pose and relaxed onto her back. "Oh, Rye," she sighed, arching her body toward his mouth.

The slow movement of his hand on her flesh was so soothing, so subtle, that when he inserted his fingers into the downy, dark blond patch at the juncture of her thighs she automatically lifted her hips, offering herself up to his caress, begging for it.

Dewy with desire, Aerial opened her thighs, and he slid his fingers into the hot creases of her sex. Anxiously bucking upward at his intimate pleasuring, she rocked her head back and forth between her raised arms, moaning unintelligible little sounds.

Suddenly, her entire body felt as if it were going to explode into a million fragments. Every nerve and muscle in her concentrated on that one small center of her existence, on one purpose.

Her body jumped spasmodically against Rye's hand as he continued his gentle stroking. Breathlessly, she wrenched her hands out of his fist and the tangled chemise and wrapped her arms around his neck and shoulders.

Unable to put off his own release any longer, Rye ripped off his breechcloth and rolled onto her. Cradling himself between her thighs, he poised the tip of his passion at the brink of the undulating entrance to her body for only the briefest instant.

With a moan of thanksgiving, he sank deep into the grasping tightness as she lifted her hips up to meet his thrust. "Oh, my God," he groaned at her eager reception, ramming uncontrollably into her.

Greedy to possess all of him, Aerial wrapped her calves over his perspiring thighs and dug her nails into the straining muscles of his back.

Panting for air, she cried out her glorious anguish as she spiraled into ecstasy for the second time.

With his mouth stretched in a pained grimace, Rye released an agonizing groan. Tossing back his head to swallow huge gulps of air, he slammed into her one last time, his own shuddering body filling her with his virility.

His energy depleted, he rolled away from her and flopped a forearm back over his eyes. "I'm sorry," he said, his voice rough, his breathing labored. "I didn't want that to happen again." His eyes covered, he placed his other hand on her stomach. "Are you all right?"

Her euphoric mood crashed to reality with a

brutal thud at his hurtful words. He was sorry! He hadn't wanted it to happen again!

The truth cut devastatingly into her. She had given him her innocence, sacrificed her balloon to save him, protected him from the hunters, nursed him back to health, and it had meant nothing to him. She was no more to him now than she had been the first minute they'd met.

Overwhelmed with shame and embarrassment, she curled away from him, reaching for a blanket to cover herself as she did. "I'm just fine," she answered, her voice cracking with self-recrimination.

Had she really thought her own wanton behavior would have brought about different consequences? Had her pride and self-worth sunk so low that she'd lost all sense of good judgment? Had she become so starved for love that she had given herself to a man who cared nothing about her? A man she would never see again? A man who was probably a murderer? A man who had taken what rightfully belonged to the man she would marry?

She felt dirty, used, and foolish—and more lonely than she'd ever felt in her life. After this, she couldn't even dream of settling down with a husband and raising a family, because no decent man would want her.

Snatching up her discarded chemise and clutching the blanket around her naked body, Aerial dashed from the cabin.

"Hey! What's the matter? Where are you going?" Rye called after her, raising his head and shoulders off the mat and staring at the open door.

"To bathe!" she hurled back at him. "Suddenly, I feel very unclean."

"Oh," Rye said, lying back down with a groan,

otally exhausted. Such strenuous activity on the heels of his illness had probably been too much for his fever-weakened body. Maybe if he just slept a few minutes he'd be able to get back the vigor he'd felt when he had first awakened.

He closed his eyes. Oh, yes, that was what he needed. Just a little bit more sleep.

He lay there for several minutes, not thinking, not feeling, yet not quite asleep. Then, slowly, very slowly, he became aware of Aerial's parting word chanting repeatedly in his head. *Unclean . . Unclean . . . Unclean . . .*

"Unclean?" he asked aloud, opening his eyes wide as the thought finally worked its way to the front of his consciousness.

He sat up again and stared at the door, his confusion clarifying into hurtful understanding. Aerial Windsor hadn't been referring to her physical condition at all! She felt unclean because she'd been with him. That was why she had rushed out, so desperate for a bath. She felt "unclean" because she had been with an Indian!

Recovering from his momentary lapse, Rye bolted up from the mat. Far be it from him to stay with a woman he made feel "unclean." There were too many in the world who would beg him to make love to them. And once he got to Canada, he intended to spend the next two months obliging them!

Quickly reclaiming his breechcloth, he took his knife and stormed outside to dress the rabbit he'd killed for breakfast. Spotting his shirt where she'd hung it after washing it the night before, he paused to see if it was dry.

She must have scrubbed this until her hands were raw to get all that blood and filth out, he thought, surprised to see how clean the shirt was. He fingered the material absently, his hurt

151

and anger unexpectedly reverting to confusion.

Why had she done it? Why had she protected him from the bear hunters then acted as though he carried a disease? What had made Aerial Windsor, a white woman, take care of a man she undoubtedly considered a filthy savage in such a manner that she'd not only found him shelter and cared for his wounds but she had actually washed his clothes?

Puzzled, he stared off in the direction of the creek, where he could hear the splashing sounds of Aerial's bathing. A glimmer of hope rekindled inside him. Could it be that she actually cared about him?

No! he growled to himself, swerving away from the shirt. *Whether I live or die doesn't mean anything to her. She just wanted to keep me healthy because she knows I'm her only hope of getting out of these woods. The only reason she dirtied her hands was to save her own skin! But I guess sleeping with the Indian to keep him in line turned out to be too big a sacrifice for her delicate tastes.*

He strode angrily to where he'd hung the rabbit he'd snared. He raised his knife and deftly decapitated the dead animal. Grumbling at what a fool he'd been to have let himself think for even a moment that Aerial Windsor would judge him for what he was as a person, he made four efficient cuts in the rabbit's front and hind legs. Then, in one quick, vengeful motion, he turned the hide inside out, stripping it off the body and forelegs like a glove.

To hell with Aerial Windsor, he decided, slitting the skinned carcus down the center to remove the entrails. If his own belly weren't so empty he wouldn't even waste time on breakfast before he figured out where the nearest town was so he could get rid of her once and for all and be on his way to Canada.

Behind him, the snap of a breaking twig interrupted his thoughts. Certain it was Aerial returning from her bath, he tensed.

"All right, Injun. Drop the knife and turn around nice and slow!"

Chapter Ten

Aerial's fingers froze on the tip of the blond braid she was securing with a strip of petticoat. She cocked her head and listened, unable to contain the optimistic thought that popped into her head: if the voices she heard were a search party from a nearby town who had come to save her, her record could still be salvaged.

Flinging the braid back over her shoulder, she checked to be certain her almost-dry dress was fully buttoned, then started for the cabin.

"Where's the girl, Injun?" she heard a deep, frightening voice ask from the front of the cabin. She slowed her step, doubt replacing her initial hopes.

"Hell, Sheriff, don't waste time talkin' to the likes o' him. He probably already killed her like he did Deke!"

Aerial's heart leaped into her throat and she stopped in her tracks. Though she wasn't certain, she could swear that voice belonged to the bear hunter she and Rye had fled from the day before. If so . . .

"I say we hang him right here," another rough voice suggested, completing the panicked thought her mind had begun to conjure up.

The man's words squeezed the life from her hopes, constricting her lungs and trapping the air in them. Frantic, she scanned the area, searching for a way to help Rye.

"Hold on there, boys. You don't have no proof

he's the Injun who shot Deke."

Aerial released a sigh of relief. Thank God. A voice of reason! She started forward again. Once she explained what had really happened—

"He's the one, all right, Sheriff," confirmed a new participant in the drama she could hear unfolding.

Aerial felt the color drain from her face. There was no doubt in her mind she recognized *that* voice. In fact, she'd never forget it. It belonged to one of the men who had attacked her! The one the others had called Clem! The one who had put his filthy hands on her breasts!

Her insides curled defensively as every horrible moment with the men in the woods flashed through her mind. Overwhelmed by the vile memories, she forgot everything else. Self-preservation became her only thought. Her eyes wild, she searched for a place to hide until they were gone.

"Are you sure, Clem? All these savages look pretty much the same," the sheriff said.

The lawman's words eased Aerial's panic—at least enough to stop her instinctive run for cover.

"Hell, yes, I'm sure. He was havin' a go at that poor little white gal who crashed in the balloon. She was fightin' him like a wildcat. 'Course, she wasn't no match for him. Then when we tried to git him off her, he killed Deke an' shot me 'n' Sid."

"You lying bastard," Aerial heard Rye growl. His voice sounded strained, as if he were fighting restraints of some kind. "That's not what happened and you know it!"

"Who you gonna believe, Sheriff? Me or a filthy Injun?"

"You know the answer to that, Clem. But we still gotta take him in. The law says he's got a right to a trial."

"Law, hell!" snarled the man she was pretty sure was the bear hunter. "Since when've Injuns got rights? He killed my baby brother and he's gonna pay! Git the rope!"

"No" Aerial screamed, fear for Rye overriding her fear for herself. Her mobility restored, she wheeled around and broke into a frantic run for the shack. "You can't hang him!"

The eight men in the yard, including Rye, stared in disbelief as Aerial rounded the corner of the cabin.

"He's innocent, Sheriff!" she announced. "He was defending me from those three animals when they were going to . . ." She couldn't finish her sentence.

The sheriff rushed forward to greet Aerial. "Miss Windsor! You're alive!"

"Of course, I'm alive. Thanks to—" She stopped, her brow creasing with confusion. "You know who I am?"

" 'Course we do. The telegraph wires 'a been jumpin' with your name ever since your balloon was spotted comin' off Lake Ontario yesterday mornin'. You're famous. Folks 'a been trackin' your trip 'cross the country since you left Ioway two days ago. Fact is, just about the whole town o' Keene Valley was out watchin' for you when some hunters on Big Slide Mountain seen your balloon go down and brought us the word."

"They were?" she asked, momentarily unable to concentrate on anything but this newest development. "Then that means the time and place of my landing is official—"

"To tell the truth, Miss Windsor, when our search party ran into Clem 'n the boys and they told us how this filthy Injun took you prisoner, we was sick. We didn't hold out much hope o' findin' you alive."

The sheriff's words sent shame rocking through Aerial. She'd been so excited by her unexpected good fortune that she had temporarily forgotten what should have been her first priority.

She shot a contrite glance at Rye, who continued to stand beside the cabin, his hard expression giving no clue to what he was thinking. Squaring her shoulders, she turned her attention back to the sheriff.

"I'm afraid you don't have the facts right, Sheriff. This man didn't—"

"We gonna stand around jawin' all day, Sheriff?" Clem interrupted loudly.

"I say we hang him right here," Ned growled. Bringing forth a prepared noose for the others to see, he advanced purposefully on Rye.

"Yeah!" the men cheered loudly, starting to close in on the prisoner, their eyes bright with excitement.

"No!" Aerial stepped between Rye and the rope-toting vigilantes that surrounded him. Her expression wrathful, she pointed at Clem. "If anyone should be hung, it's that animal and his vile friends. They were going to . . ." Her face colored with embarrassment. There were certain words a lady just didn't say no matter what the circumstances. She lowered her eyes and stared down at her interlaced fingers. "This man was defending me from them."

"Ain't you got it backwards, gal?" Clem asked with a meaningful leer. "Now, jest move aside and let us do what we come here to do." With a powerful, sweeping gesture, he hit her on the arm with the back of his hand, knocking her to the ground.

A wild animal sound issuing from his throat, Rye lunged at Clem and grabbed him by the neck and squeezed.

Clawing frantically at Rye's iron grip, Clem's eyes bulged with the pressure of Rye's fingers on his windpipe.

Acting quickly, the sheriff brought the butt of his gun down on the side of Rye's head.

For the briefest instant, Rye's black eyes widened with surprise. Then they closed as every muscle in his body relaxed. With a grunt, he dropped unconscious to the ground.

"Now you see why we gotta hang him, Sheriff?" Clem wheezed, his hand on his own throat. "The bastard's a vicious killer!"

Deke's brother hunkered down and lifted Rye's head by his hair. "Clem's right." He started to put the noose over Rye's head. "Let's git it over and done with here."

"No!" Recovering from her fall, Aerial flew at the bear hunter's back and brought her hands around to claw at his eyes. "You're not going to hang him!"

"Aieee!" He shot up off the ground, unable to shake Aerial off his back. "Git this crazy woman off me," he yowled, blindly trying to escape her the fingernails digging into his eye sockets.

The explosion of a revolver fired into the air brought everything to a halt. "You can let him go, Miss Windsor. There ain't gonna be no hangin' today, or any other day, if what you say is true."

Aerial hesitated an instant, then relaxed her hold on her "prisoner" and stepped away.

At the same time, Clem wheeled to face the sheriff, his hand hovering close to the butt of the revolver riding on his own hip. "You gonna b'lieve that crazy wildcat over me, who you know'd all my life? Why, I went to school with your boys!"

The sheriff's eyes narrowed with purpose as he

clicked back the hammer on the gun he had aimed at Clem. "You ain't gonna give me much choice, son, if you do somethin' dumb like go for that piece."

When Aerial was spotted among the posse that rode into town in mid-afternoon, the news spread up and down Main Street in a matter of moments that the daring balloonist had been found and was alive.

Men, women, children, and barking dogs rushed forward to greet her. "Miss Windsor, is it true you come all the way from Iowa in under twenty hours?"

"What was it like?"

"Bet you was scared."

"It's a miracle you wasn't killed!"

"Did you ever think you'd get this far?"

"You poor dear, are you all right?"

No sooner would Aerial turn to locate whoever had asked the question than another was fired at her from somewhere else in the crowd, two and three at a time. All she could do was nod and shake her head and smile.

"We thought you was dead for sure."

"There's a nice clean room waitin' for you at the hotel."

"We had 'em do it up—just in case."

"You'll feel much better once you have a hot bath and we get you some clean clothes."

"Mrs. Thomas, the storekeeper's wife, is gonna round up something for you to wear."

"Can I have your autograph, Miss Windsor?"

"Have you eaten?"

"We're settin' up at the Presbyterian church to have a social in your honor."

"How long you been flyin' in a balloon?"

She had known there would be a big fuss over her accomplishment, for America was fascinated with aeronauts and considered them all celebrities no matter what they'd done; but the acclaim, even the feat itself, had lost its importance for her. In fact, she was suddenly possessed with a desire to take Rye and escape back into the woods. "Sheriff?" she asked, her blue eyes raised to his in a helpless plea.

The sheriff gave her a sympathetic smile, then raised his hand to silence the crowd. "Come on, folks. Miss Windsor's had a rough coupla days. Let's give her a chance to catch her breath before you hit her with all your questions."

"I got a question for *you,* Sheriff!" an angry woman cried from the sidewalk. "Why ain't that Injun what killed my boy dead?"

His presence having gone unnoticed by the crowd in the excitement of having a celebrity in their midst, Rye became the sudden focus of the surrounding mob.

"Yeah, Sheriff! What about that Injun?" someone shouted.

"Why'd you bring him here? Why didn't you hang him and leave him where you found him after what he done to Deke and the boys?" another yelled.

His brow furrowing angrily, Sheriff Hawes tightened his hold on Aerial's shoulders as she tensed and opened her mouth to protest. "I'm sorry 'bout your boy, Mizz Wilkes," he told the haggard, gray-haired woman in black who stood on the boardwalk beside Deke's brother, Ned. "But like I told your boy there, the law says a man's innocent 'til he's proved guilty."

"A white man, not a Injun!" someone hollered.

"What more proof do you need, Sheriff?" someone else yelled from the back of the crowd.

160

"Deke Wilkes is laid out at the funeral home, and Clem and Sid saw that Injun kill him. I say we hang—"

The sheriff whipped his revolver from its holster with an exasperated shrug. The instant the lawman's gun appeared in his hand, his three deputies made a protective circle around Rye, their backs to their charge, their rifles aimed at the crowd.

"We already been through this, but I'll say it again. There ain't gonna be no hangin' today. This Injun's my prisoner, and it's my sworn duty to keep him alive and see that he gits a fair trial, even if I gotta shoot someone to do it. Now, why don't you folks go on 'bout your business and let me get back to mine—which is upholdin' the law."

Hawes stood his ground for a full minute as the crowd paused to consider his words. Finally they decided he meant what he had said. As one, they began to back away, grudgingly clearing a path for Aerial, the sheriff, the deputies and Rye to make their way toward a log building labeled "JAIL" in black letters above the door.

Once they were inside the office, Rye spared Aerial a single now-do-you-see-how-it-is? look and peacefully allowed himself to be escorted by the deputies into a cell, as the sheriff directed Aerial into a wooden chair beside his cluttered desk with a rather ungentlemanly prod.

"Why are they putting him in a cell?" she asked, her momentary relief at getting away from the crowd turning to apprehension and worry. "I'm telling you he was only defending me from those men. He was my assistant on my flight. We got separated for a few minutes when we crashed. That's when those three men found me and assumed I was alone and defenseless."

The sheriff's face grew tight with distaste, what he was thinking clearly evident. "You mean you was travelin' alone with that Injun?"

Embarrassment roiled through Aerial's blood. The sheriff's insinuating tone made her feel as if she were wearing a scarlet letter on her chest and that everyone knew about her wanton behavior with Rye. Part of her wanted to run and hide, but she knew she couldn't.

"The point is," she went on, jutting her chin to keep from ducking her head, "he works for me and was defending me. My traveling arrangements aren't the issue here. I demand that you release him immediately and arrest the men who attacked me."

"Go round up Clem and Sid and get 'em over here, pronto," the sheriff barked at one of the deputies, ignoring Aerial as he slapped his hat onto a hook on the wall. "And while you're at it, send a wire to the folks in Iowa and let 'em know Miss Windsor's safe."

Sucking in a deep, weary breath, he lowered his large body down into his chair. Obviously, learning that Aerial had been with Rye of her own accord wasn't what he'd wanted to hear. Threading his fingers through his hair, he finally spoke.

"Look, lady, there's only two reasons I didn't let them folks outside have that Injun. One, 'cause it's my job to watch out for him whether I like it or not; and two, 'cause for the life o' me, I can't figger out why you'd be protectin' him if you wasn't tellin' the truth."

"Exactly! Why would I lie to defend a man who attacked me? It doesn't make sense."

"Course it don't make sense," the sheriff agreed, his voice sounding as if he were talking to himself rather than to her. "Not to a sane person, anyhow."

He squinted his eyes and thoughtfully studied Aerial for several seconds before going on. "But to a gal crazy enough to go flyin' 'cross the country in a balloon, lying 'bout what happened might make all the sense in the world. Wait a minute!" he interrupted himself, leaning forward in his chair, his expression suspicious. "Are you one o' them bleedin' hearts who's always tryin' to help the Injuns and nig—"

"Will you stop it! I'm not crazy. I'm not a 'bleeding heart.' I'm simply telling the truth. That man is not guilty of anything but defending me, and you've got to release him!"

"Sorry, Miss Windsor, but by the same token I ain't hangin' that Injun 'til someone shows me some proof he's guilty, I ain't lettin' him outta that cell 'less I got proof he ain't."

He stood up and took her arm, trying to draw her from her chair, obviously satisfied with the decision he'd made, which was not to make a decision at all. "Now, why don't you let one o' my boys take you over to the hotel so you can clean up and git some rest before the celebration they're plannin' for you tonight."

Aerial wrenched her arm free and leaned back in the chair. "I'm not going anywhere until you release him, and that's all there is to it!"

With a loud crash, the door to the street burst open. "Here they are, Sheriff," the deputy announced, allowing Clem and Sid to precede him into the office. "Oh yeah, I sent that wire to Io-way."

"That's good," the sheriff said, waving the two wary men inside. "Come on in, boys. Let's talk this out and see if we can't figger out what really happened up there in the woods."

"I already told you what happened!" Clem and Aerial said at the same time.

163

"I know you did, but since your stories don't agree, suppose you tell me again."

"Like I said," Clem started first. "We was out huntin' that bear for the bounty when we come up on that Injun in there havin' a go at this gal. She was fightin' him, so we pulled him off her. He shot all three of us, then took off with her. And that's the God's truth, ain't it, Sid?"

"Well, Sid?" the sheriff asked. "Did it happen like Clem says?"

Sid, his head wrapped in a white bandage, glanced hesitantly at Aerial, then back at his partner.

"Go on, Sid," Clem coaxed through his teeth, giving his partner a nudge in the ribs. "Tell the sheriff it happened jest like I said it did."

Sid studied his lap, then the ceiling. Finally he nodded. "Yeah, that's what happened all right."

"You liars!" Aerial gasped, leaping out of her chair and flying at the two men. "You were the ones I was fighting against. He shot you to save me from *you!* If I'd had a gun, I would have put a bullet in each of you myself."

Grabbing her from behind, the sheriff lifted the struggling, kicking Aerial back into her chair. "Now, stay put," he ordered, then redirected his attention to Clem and Sid.

"Well, boys, whadda you say to that? Seems mighty strange, don't it? Why would this little lady stick up for the feller you say tried to take her by force and want to shoot you, who you say saved her?"

The color drained from both men's faces, but Clem quickly tried to hide his uneasiness behind a wicked laugh. "Hell, Sheriff, how do we know what's goin' on in her head? Maybe he gave her some Injun potion and it got her confused."

The sheriff arched his eyebrows. "You don't re-

164

ally expect no one to believe that, do you, Clem?"

"Well, uh . . ." Clem shot Sid a nervous glance, then turned back to the sheriff. "Don't forget she spent the night with that Injun, Sheriff. I hear once a white woman's been with a Injun, she'll do anythin' he tells her to—even lie for him."

Aerial sucked in a loud, indignant gulp and pushed herself up out of the chair. "Why, you filthy, lying—"

"Sit *down,* Miss Windsor," the sheriff ordered testily. "You'll git your chance. But I wanna set a coupla things straight first."

Knowing Rye's situation would not be aided by making the sheriff angry with her, Aerial bit her bottom lip to keep from saying more. Curving her fingers over the arms of the chair in tight, self-restraining fists, she forced herself to sit back down.

"Good," the sheriff acknowledged, then returned his attention to Clem and Sid. "I'm still not sure how this all came about. You say you were just walkin' through the woods when you come across the Injun attackin' her."

"Right," Clem said. "An' she was fightin' him off, kickin' an' scratchin' an' bitin' an—"

"Screamin'?" the sheriff asked. "I bet she was really screamin'."

"Like a banshee," Clem confirmed with a relieved grin. "I hate to think what that bastard woulda done to her if we hadn't come along when we did."

"That brings me to the part I'm not too clear on. If she was screamin' for help, seems to me like you boys would o' spread out and snuck up on the Injun so you could git the drop on him, 'stead o' him gittin' the drop on you. But you didn't. Why not?"

Sid and Clem looked at each other nervously, each obviously expecting the other to have a good answer to the sheriff's question.

"Uh," Clem began, "I guess maybe we was talkin' an' didn't hear her 'til it was too late."

Sid nodded his agreement. "Yeah, we was talkin'."

The sheriff wiped his large hand thoughtfully over his day-old beard. "I see. 'Course that brings up another question. If you was makin' so much noise you couldn't hear a woman screamin', how'd you 'spect to sneak up on that bear you was huntin?" Without waiting for an answer, he went on. "Or for that matter, how'd you git close enough to that Injun to see what he was doin' before he heard you? Seems to me like even a deaf man would 'a heard you comin' and would be waitin' for you. An' considerin' a Injun's keen sense o' hearin', why do ya suppose he didn't do that?"

Another nervous shifting of eyes between the two men. Sweat beaded profusely on their brows and upper lips. "How the hell do we know?" Clem answered, moving restlessly in his chair and lifting the flannel collar of his shirt away from his neck. "Maybe he was gruntin' and breathin' so loud he jest didn't hear us. He was goin' at her pretty hard."

"I guess that could explain it. 'Specially with her screamin' an' fightin' him like you say she was," the sheriff commented.

"Sure it could!" Clem said, standing up, his relief obvious. "Now, can we go? We need to make a call on Deke's poor mama."

"Sure you can. Just give me a couple more minutes."

The relief on their faces slid to misery. "Sure, Sheriff," Clem said, "but can you hurry it up?

166

It's awful hot in here." He fidgeted with his collar again.

The sheriff studied the profusely sweating man, his own expression disappointed and filled with disgust. "I'm just wonderin' how a man who was so caught up in what he was doin' he didn't hear three noisy hunters come up on him managed to draw a gun and shoot all three o' you without one o' you gittin' away?"

"He's fast!" Sid said, touching the bandage where his ear had been. "I never seen a man that fast."

"No doubt. Still, I never heard of a feller so fast three men could come up behind him and he could still outdraw all three of 'em and get away—carrying a prisoner—without at least one o' those crack riflemen puttin' a single bullet in him."

"Us either," Clem offered, "but that's what he did."

"Sounds almost like he caught *you* by surprise 'stead o' the other way 'round." The sheriff went on as though Clem hadn't spoken. "Don't it?"

"You sayin' we're lyin', Sheriff?" Clem asked indignantly. He stood up to go, pulling on Sid's arm. "Come on, Sid. We don't have to stay here an' listen to this garbage."

The sheriff nodded his head, indicating the office door. A rifle-toting deputy immediately barred Clem's retreat.

"Not so fast, boys. I ain't sayin' you're lyin'. I'm just tryin' to get to the bottom of a puzzlin' situation."

"All right," Clem snarled. "But I'm warnin' you, I've had enough o' your questions. If you're accusin' us o' somethin', then say it."

The sheriff shrugged. "Fair enough. No more questions. Jest a coupla observations."

"What's that?" Clem asked, his tone suspicious.

"Jest that I couldn't help wonderin' how you got them scratches on your cheek there. Looks like you met up with a wildcat or a mad wo—"

"You're barkin' up the wrong tree, Sheriff," Clem interrupted. "A man's bound to pick up a scratch or two when he's been out bear huntin' for over a week."

"I s'pose you're right about that. And is that the reason for the bandage I seen on your neck when you was tuggin' on your collar?"

Clem's hand flew to his neck to touch the bandage. "Hell, this is nothin'! Just a little cut. Not worth mentionin'."

"Cut, huh? Mind if I take a look?" The sheriff lumbered out of his chair, a deliberately disarming grin on his face.

"Yeah, I do mind!" Clem spat, holding his neck and backing toward the door—and bumping square into the deputy blocking his exit.

"Why's that, Clem?" the sheriff asked, reaching out to lift the bandage away from Clem's neck. "You ain't hidin' somethin', are you?" He angled his head to the side to better see, then shook his head. "Mmm, mmm, mmm. That's a real nasty lookin' bite you got there, Clem. Not to mention them scratches on your face."

"So what? It still don't prove nothin'."

"Maybe not. But by your own admission, Miss Windsor was bitin' and scratchin' her attacker." The sheriff indicated the door to the cells with his thumb. "An' that Injun in there ain't got a bite mark on him. You, on the other hand, got as nice a set o' teethmarks as I ever seen on your neck. Whadda you think the chances are o' them marks on your neck matchin' Miss Windsor's bite?"

Clem opened his mouth to argue, then seemed

168

to think better of it. "Hell, we was just havin' some fun with her. There wasn't no cause for that Injun to shoot off my fingers and Sid's ear and Deke's . . . You ain't thinkin' o' lettin that Injun go free, are ya, Sheriff? He killed Deke, and I wanna know what you're gonna do about it!"

"I got no legal cause to hold a man, even a Injun, for killin' a man in defense of a lady's honor."

Aerial sagged back in her chair with relief. "Thank heavens!"

Clem narrowed his eyes at the sheriff. "Come election next month, you're gonna find yourself out of a job if you side with Deke's killer aginst your own kind."

The sheriff shrugged his shoulders wearily. "You're probably right, son, but the law's the law, and as long as I'm wearin' this badge, I'm gonna uphold it best I can. Now, why don't you run along and see to your auntie."

"We will, but we'll be back. You can be sure o' that! Come on, Sid." The deputy stood aside and silently allowed the two men to pass, then followed them outside.

Aerial stared aghast. "Why didn't you put them in jail? They were going to . . ." She still couldn't bring herself to say the word *rape* out loud. ". . . hurt me."

"But they didn't actually, uh . . . hurt you, did they? Besides, it's your word against theirs, and to tell you the truth, no jury in this town's gonna convict two o' their own on the word of a woman who'd go gallivantin' across the country with a Injun 'assistant'."

The sheriff's tone of voice and facial expression left no room for Aerial to wonder which side he would be on if she insisted on making official charges against Clem and Sid.

"My advice to you," the sheriff went on, "is just to take your Injun and git outta town before those two boys get any more folks riled up 'bout the fact I ain't gonna hold Deke's killer, because to tell you the truth, I ain't all that sure I'd be willin' to fire on my friends and neighbors to protect no Injun."

A frightening picture of a wild mob attacking the jail and overwhelming the sheriff flared in her mind, convincing her that any thought of standing her ground and arguing with the sheriff about his sworn duty was not only impractical but stupid. "I appreciate your honesty," she conceded bitterly.

She walked over to the door of the cell where Rye sat silently watching and listening to all that was transpiring in the small office. Holding out a bundle she'd brought from the shack in the woods, she spoke coolly. "If you'll let me give my assistant . . ." she couldn't disguise the sarcasm in her tone, ". . . the rest of his clothing, we'll leave immediately. I certainly wouldn't want to test your vow to uphold the law any further than it has already been tested."

The sheriff eyed Rye's clothing in her arms, a regretful smile on his face. He snatched a key ring off a nail on the wall over his desk. "You got a lot o' spunk, Miss Windsor. It's a shame you decided to throw yourself away on a Injun," he said, joining her at the cell door.

"Just release him!" Aerial demanded.

"Sheriff!" shouted a deputy rushing into the office from the street and waving a paper in the air.

"What is it, Hagerty?" the sheriff asked impatiently, inserting the key in the lock.

"We just got a wire from the folks in Ioway, an' you ain't *never* gonna guess what it says!"

"Jest spit it out, boy. It's been a long day, an' I

ain't in no mood for guessin' games."

A sly, victorious grin slid over Hagarty's face. "Seems they're lookin for a *Injun* who kilt and scalped a man in Fairfield, then escaped without a trace at the *exact same time* that balloon gal left town! *And* there's a five hundred dollar reward for him. Dead or alive!"

Both men turned their triumphant expressions on Aerial, who stood with her mouth open, her eyes frantically inspecting the small office for an escape.

"Well, Miss Windsor," the sheriff said with a satisfied smirk. "That sheds a different light on things, don't it now?" With an exaggerated flourish, he scraped the key from the lock and jabbed it into his pocket.

Chapter Eleven

Dropping the bundle of Rye's belongings to the floor, Aerial slapped her fingertips to her mouth.

Say something! she commanded herself, her eyes wide with shock and panic. *You can't just stand here with your mouth hanging open!*

But what could she say? If she tried to convince them that Rye wasn't guilty of killing the man in Fairfield, it would be the same as admitting she had known all along that he was wanted for murder. And given the sheriff's already low opinion of her, not to mention the whole town's bias against Indians, they would automatically pronounce her guilty of helping a criminal escape. And that would mean jail for her, as well as for Rye.

A shudder went up her spine at the thought of being confined in a jail cell. Her breathing accelerated painfully in a desperate attempt to overcome the sudden feeling that she couldn't breathe.

She had to think of another way to help Rye, because one thing was certain. She couldn't give the sheriff any reason to put her in jail.

Praying she could communicate with her eyes the fact that she wasn't forsaking him, she looked at Rye. He watched her through the bars from the cell's single cot, his expression cold and detached.

Hurt that he wouldn't even spare her some sign of understanding for the situation she was in, or even a glimmer of thanks for trying to help him,

172

she turned away from his hard black glare.

"How could I have been so blind?" she wailed, hoping the look of surprise on her face was convincing. "When I think what he might have done if you hadn't found me . . ." Throwing herself at the sheriff, she wrapped her arms around his neck and clung to him, the tremble in her voice genuine. "Oh, Sheriff, how can I ever repay you for saving me?"

Momentarily nonplussed, Sheriff Hawes shot his deputy a questioning eye, then hesitantly closed his arms around Aerial's trembling back and clumsily patted her. "There, there, little lady. You don't owe me nothin'. I was jest doin' my job."

"To think, I actually defended him . . ." She paused, closing and opening her eyes as if she were fighting sleep. "How could I have been such a fool? And I judged you so harshly. Can you ever forgive . . ."

With a helpless moan, she fluttered her eyes shut, then went limp.

"Oh, shit! She fainted," the sheriff muttered, sweeping Aerial up into his burly arms and starting for the door. "You keep a eye on that Injun while I git Doc Simmons to have a look at her."

Dammit, Rye cursed silently, his hooded gaze on the deputy who stood in the doorway facing the street. *Why'd she have to tell them I came with her from Iowa? That sheriff would have figured out the truth about Deke without that damaging bit of information. If she'd just kept her mouth shut, I would have been out of here and on to Canada by now.*

Uttering a disgusted hiss, he stood up and walked over to the cell door. As long as he was

173

stuck here, he might as well take advantage of the deputy's inattention and check the building for escape possibilities.

He gently shook the cell door on the off chance that it wasn't locked. Of course, it didn't budge. He shrugged indifferently. He hadn't really expected it to.

Next, he leveled his attention on the nail over the sheriff's cluttered desk where the cell key had been kept until Hawes had stuck it in his pocket and left the building with it. Without that key, there was no other way out of the cell, unless he could suddenly shrink and squeeze through the tiny barred window high on the back wall of the cell.

Surely there wasn't just a single key. There had to be at least one more. He studied the deputy standing in the doorway, his attention leveled on the man's belt. There, as he had hoped, was the second key. Maybe the gods had decided to give him a chance after all.

Rye narrowed his eyes thoughtfully. If he could get the deputy to come over to the bars, he just might be able to grab him and get that key.

Rye's attention flipped to the bundle of clothing Aerial had accidentally dropped in front of the cell when she'd heard the information contained in the wire from Fairfield.

His mouth quirked in a humorless grin. It sure hadn't taken long for her to switch sides and start playing up to that sheriff when she thought she was going to be exposed as her "assistant's" accomplice.

Of course, what had he expected from her? Obviously, anything she'd ever done for him had been only because she was looking out for herself. Why should she change now? She'd hidden him from

Deke's friends because she didn't want to be raped. She had taken care of him when he was sick because she knew she couldn't survive in the woods by herself. And she'd only defended him against the charge of killing Deke because she had wanted revenge against Sid and Clem for what they had tried to do to her.

But the minute it became obvious she could end up in jail herself if she told the truth about what had happened in Iowa, she had been all over that sheriff like honey on a biscuit.

"To hell with her," he mumbled under his breath, again scrutinizing the office for a possible way to escape.

"Howdy, Miss Melanie." The deputy's voice cut into Rye's concentration, causing him to jump in spite of himself. "Nice evenin', ain't it?"

Rye stood motionless, waiting for the sound of a woman's footsteps to pass on by. It would be tricky enough getting that key from the deputy. He didn't need any screaming female to alert the entire town.

"Sure is, Tom," a coy female voice answered. "I thought you might like some company for a bit. I brought hot coffee and fresh-baked cookies right out of the oven."

No! Rye ordered silently. *Tell her no!*

"Gosh, Miss Melanie, that sounds mighty temptin'. You know I always like settin' with you and uh . . ." Tom looked back over his shoulder at Rye's cell. "But I'm the only one on duty, so I'd better not. Leastwise, not 'til the sheriff gits back."

Good for you, Tom. I always admired a man who stands by his duty. Now, tell her to go home!

"Being on duty never stopped you from sittin' out here on the porch with me before, Tom Ha-

175

garty! Have you got another girl?"

"No, 'course not, Melanie! You're the only gal for me. It's jest that we got a real dangerous prisoner here, and I can't take no chances on him escapin', so you better not stay. If it ain't too late when Beck relieves me, maybe I could come by your house."

That's right. Set a date for later, Rye encouraged the deputy.

"Well, if you *really* don't want me to stay, then I suppose I'll go on home. But don't come by later. I'm sure by then I will have found someone who's not too busy for me."

Knowing Tom's valiant defenses had been destroyed even before the deputy took a hasty step out onto the porch, Rye groaned in disgust and swept his scrutiny over the office, hoping against hope that if there were two keys to the cell, there might be yet a third.

"Wait a minute, Melanie," the deputy whined. "I don't guess it'd hurt none to sit here on the porch for a couple o' minutes. That Injun ain't goin' nowhere, not as long as I got the only other key to his cell 'sides the sheriff's. Anyhow, the sheriff probably won't be back before mornin'. He had that look in his eye when he left here like he gets when he wants a drink real bad. Fact is, I wouldn't be a bit surprised to find out he dropped that Windsor gal over to Doc's and jest kept on walkin over to the Ace High for a night o' serious drinkin'."

"Congratulations, Deputy." Rye chuckled bitterly. "You just put the clincher on my day!" Disheartened, he hunkered down and stretched his arm through the bars to retrieve his things. At least if he wasn't going anywhere right away, he could put on his boots, shirt and trousers so when—and if—

he finally got his chance to get a jump on the deputy he would be ready to leave.

Aerial peeked out of the shadows of the alley alongside the jail building and watched as Deputy Hagarty and a pretty young woman sat beside each other on the wooden bench in front of the sheriff's office.

It's about time my luck changed! she told herself, elated that at least one problem she'd anticipated had taken care of itself. Now, if only the sheriff would live up to the deputy's prediction and stay out drinking all night it would be perfect. But of course, she couldn't count on that.

The most she could hope for was the few minutes she'd bought herself by sending the sheriff over to the Presbyterian church with her apologies for not being up to the big celebration the town had planned for her that night. Fortunately, the doctor had backed her up by blaming her fainting on exhaustion and then prescribing a good night's rest.

Running stealthily, she made her way down the alley to the back of the jail. She immediately located the small, barred window she had noticed earlier that was shared by the jail's two cells. All she had to do now was get Rye's attention. Scanning the ground, she found several pebbles and picked them up.

One by one, she pitched them at the window, hoping they would get Rye's attention when they landed on his cot, but one by one she missed the opening. Her first handful of pebbles exhausted, she gave up on that idea and studied the alley for another way to get Rye's attention.

Spying a wooden crate across the alley, she

177

quickly dragged it to a position under the window and scrambled up onto it.

"Psst, Rye," she whispered, peeking into the window. Since her view of the cell was severely limited, it appeared to be empty. She assumed he must still be on the cot beneath the window. "Rye, answer me."

Maybe he's asleep, she told herself, growing more uneasy by the instant. What if she was too late? What if the sheriff had figured out what she was planning to do and had moved Rye before she got here?

Stop it! Why would the deputy tell his girlfriend he was guarding a dangerous prisoner if they had taken Rye somewhere else?

"Rye!" she called as loudly as she dared, nervously checking the open front door on the chance the deputy or sheriff would suddenly appear to investigate. The reassuring hum of Hagarty's conversation with Melanie eased her tension just a bit.

Dammit, what had she done to deserve becoming involved in such a mess? All she'd wanted to do was restore her father's good name and then spend the rest of her life living quietly in one place, and here she was on the verge of committing a crime by breaking a man out of jail.

When Rye still didn't answer, she decided to try one last thing. Digging in her pocket, she brought out a handful of coins, then poked her arm between the bars of the window. *If this doesn't wake you up, you're on your own, mister,* she threatened silently, releasing all the coins she held at the same time. "Rye, it's me. Wake up!"

"What are you doing here?" a rough voice snarled from inside the cell as an angry face popped into view, scant inches from her own frightened face.

Releasing a startled squeal, she took an instinctive step back. An iron grip clamped around her wrist inside the cell, checking her inevitable fall from the crate.

Recognizing the face in the window now, she relaxed. "Rye! You scared me to death! Why didn't you answer when I called?"

"I repeat, what're you doing here? Come to gloat? Or just to make sure I don't tell the sheriff you knew all along that I was wanted in Iowa?"

Hurt he could think such a thing after all she'd done for him, Aerial pushed her face close to the bars and spoke resentfully through her teeth. "I came to help you escape. But if you'd rather stay here and wait for the lynch mob I overheard the doctor and the sheriff worrying about, then let me go and I'll go back to the hotel and get a decent night's sleep."

Rye released a harsh laugh. "So you're here to help me escape, are you? Just how do you plan to do that? And more importantly, why?"

"Why?" Aerial repeated. Hadn't she asked herself the same question a dozen times on the way over here? This man was responsible for ruining everything she'd ever wanted, and here she was risking her own arrest to save him from a hangman's noose.

"Yeah, why? I got the idea that you'd jump at the chance to be rid of me permanently."

A terrible emptiness swelled in her chest at the thought of never seeing Rye Berenger again. But no matter how painful the idea was, she refused to give him the satisfaction of knowing how she felt. "Believe me, I'd like nothing better than to see the last of you, but not so much that I'm willing to stand by and let you be hung without a trial."

Struggling to control the tears that threatened to

spill from her eyes, she wrenched her hand free and withdrew it from between the bars. "Now," she said, digging into her pocket again, "do you want this or not?" She poked her hand back into the cell, a key on a metal ring in her fingers.

The tiniest bit of satisfaction washed through Aerial at the confused surprise in Rye's black eyes.

"Where'd you get that?"

"The answer to that oughta be plain as the nose on your face, Injun," Sheriff Hawes said, stepping out of the shadows, his revolver drawn. "I'll take my key back now, Miss Windsor."

Unable to move, Aerial stared at the gun barrel aimed at her. "You knew?" she asked, her shocked words breathless as she slowly withdrew her hand from the cell.

The sheriff stepped closer and reached for Aerial's arm to help her off the box. "Let's just say when I found my key missin', it waddn't too hard to figger out who took it—and where I'd find it."

"What are you going to do with me?" She stepped off the box, doing her best to disguise the fear rampaging through her. Her heart feeling as if it would explode through the wall of her chest in the next minute, she held out the key ring to the sheriff.

"Hell, lady, you don't give me a choice." He prodded her toward a rear door to the jail building. "In case you don't know it, helpin' a prisoner break out o' jail is a criminal offense."

"You mean you intend to lock me in a cell?"

The sheriff nodded, his expression disgusted. "That's what we do with folks who break the law."

"But I can't go to jail! You can't do this to me! What about the publicity? What will people think?"

"You should 'a thought o' that before you stole

180

that key. You got no one to blame but yourself, little lady. I gave you every chance to be taken at your word, but you jest couldn't stay away from this heathen, could you?" He pounded hard on the door.

Slightly relieved that he was at least taking her in through the back way so no one would see her, Aerial did her best to think of a way out of the latest trouble Rye Berenger had gotten her into.

"Since this man has committed no crime in your state, I wasn't aiding a criminal, so you really have no right to hold either of us!" she pointed out in a last ditch effort to stay out of jail.

"The folks in Ioway asked us to keep the Injun under lock an' key 'til they can send someone to collect him, and to escort you back to Fairfield for a big hoo-ha they got planned to celebrate you settin' a new world record in that balloon o' yours."

A sick feeling squeezed at Aerial's stomach. Look what she had done. Instead of redeeming her father's reputation with her flight, she had managed to make things worse. No matter what she had to do, she couldn't let the people from Fairfield find her in a jail cell.

"Zat you, Sheriff?" Hagarty's voice called from the other side of the door.

"Who the hell do you think it is? Open up!"

The scrape of a metal bar sliding across the other side of the wooden door sent new fear churning through Aerial. If she passed out again, this time it would be no act.

"It's about time," the sheriff bellowed, shoving her past Hagarty, whose mouth hung open in surprise at seeing Aerial.

"What's she doin' he—?"

"Don't stand there gawking," the sheriff ordered.

"Bar that door. Then git back out front and keep a eye on things."

"We expectin' trouble, Sheriff?" Hagarty asked, removing his revolver from his holster and checking its load. "Zat why she's here?"

Sheriff Hawes shifted his eyes from Hagarty to Aerial, his frustration and indecision obvious. "It's probably nothin'," he finally said, "but Clem and his pals're down at the saloon talkin' 'bout payin' us a visit. They're probably jest lettin' off steam, but I sent Beck down to check it out. I figger it don't hurt to be ready in case they decide to—."

"Decide to what?!" Aerial asked nervously. "You're talking about a lynch mob, aren't you?"

"There, there, Miss Windsor," Hagarty soothed, obviously unaware that Aerial's "visit" was for any purpose other than her protection. "Don't you worry your pretty head 'bout it. Me and the sheriff ain't gonna let it come to that" His chest puffing with male bravado, he opened the front door and stepped out onto the porch.

Aerial stared at the front door for a moment then turned to face the sheriff, her expression suddenly triumphant. "Why didn't you tell the deputy I was under arrest?"

Surprise froze the sheriff's tired, leathery face. Finally he spoke. "It didn't come up!" he grumbled, looking down at the toes of his worn boots.

"That's not why, and you and I both know it. Isn't the real reason you didn't tell Deputy Hagarty about me is because it could mean your job if it got out that your carelessness allowed me to steal your key?"

When the sheriff didn't answer, Aerial was convinced she had backed him into a corner. "Well, don't worry, Sheriff," she said, unable to keep the slight gloating tone out of her voice. "Your se-

182

cret's safe with me. Just let us slip out the back door and no one ever has to know about your temporary lapse. I swear I'll carry your secret to my grave."

"Dammit, gal!" The sheriff grabbed her upper arm and spun her toward a cell. "I guess you ain't gonna be satisfied 'til I lock you up, are ya?" He yanked open the second cell and gave her a rough push inside, then slammed the door behind her and locked it.

Caught off guard by the sheriff's sudden tirade, Aerial lost her balance and sprawled out flat on the jail floor.

"You bastard!" Rye yelled at Hawes, flying at the bars of his own cell beside Aerial's, his face contorted with rage.

"I'm warnin' you, Injun. You and that Injun-lovin girlfriend o' yours have pushed me 'bout as far as I'm gonna be pushed. One more word outta either one o' you and I'm gonna forget my thirty years o' honest sheriffin' an' give you both to that mob down at the saloon."

"Both of us?" Aerial said, unable to stop herself from speaking, despite what her common sense and the sheriff's grim expression counseled her to do. She scrambled to her feet and rushed forward. "What are you talking about? What would they want with me?" She twisted toward Rye, who stood only inches from her on the other side of the bars. "Do you know what he means?"

The sheriff shook his head in obvious disbelief. "You still don't get it, do you? Your Injun ain't the only one in trouble here. That bunch at the saloon is sayin' it's jest as much your fault Deke's dead as it is the Injun's, 'cause you're the one what brought him here."

Aerial's eyes widened in dismay. Without thinking, she clasped her hands to her throat. "But that's impossible. They wouldn't hang a woman!"

The sheriff shrugged. "Don't guess they think a gal who travels alone with a Injun deserves the same consideration as a decent woman would."

But . . ."

"I kinda hoped I could keep from addin' more fuel to the fire by not tellin' Hagarty why I brought you here," the sheriff went on. "I was hopin' I could jest keep a eye on you 'til the folks git here from Ioway and can take the two o' you off my hands. I figgered I'd let them worry 'bout you since it was *their* prisoner you was breakin' out, and not mine."

Aerial directed her frightened eyes to Rye, then back to the sheriff. "Would they really hang us?"

"Depends on how much they've had to drink. So far, they're jest talkin', but if word gits out you tried to break that Injun outta here, I got a mighty strong feelin' they're gonna be in the mood to do a lot more than jest talkin' before the night's over."

"What are you going to do? You've got to—" A sudden memory of the sheriff's earlier words hit Aerial and stopped in mid-sentence. "You don't intend to do anything to stop them if they come for us, do you?" she asked, her accusing voice trembling. "You're going to let them hang us, aren't you!?"

"Nobody's hung nobody yet!"

That might have appeased Aerial if the sheriff had been able to look her in the eyes. "But if they should decide that's what they want to do, you don't intend to fight them, do you?"

The sheriff didn't answer.

"I didn't think so. Tell me, Sheriff, were all those things you said about upholding the law and

184

honesty and duty a lie? Or are you just so weak that you can destroy the thirty-year record of 'honest sheriffing' you bragged about by forfeiting the lives of two innocent strangers rather than stand up to the actual lawbreakers simply because they're people you know?"

Sheriff Hawes studied Aerial with a long, resentful expression, then gave her a dismissive wave of his large hand and nodded at Rye. "I'm startin' to feel some respect for you, Injun. Any man who could come all the way from Ioway with a gal who talks as much as this one does has a lot more patience than me. I don't know how you stood it. I would a jumped outta that balloon before we'd been gone a hour." He presented his back to them and opened the front door. "I'm going to step outside and give my ears a rest."

"Why you weak, patronizing old—"

Rye reached through the bars and caught Aerial's hand with his to silence her. "Enough! Can't you see you're making things worse on yourself?"

"Oh, am I?" she sputtered. She wrenched her hand out of his and pushed her face up to the bars separating them. "At least I'm trying to do something! Which is more than I can say for you! I don't see you making much headway at getting us out of here with your silent, wait-until-the-rope's-around-my-neck attitude!"

"No one's going to put a rope around your neck, but if they did, it would be your own fault."

"*My* fault? My fault indeed! This is the thanks I get for saving your rotten life more times than I care to remember? I'm stuck in this filthy cell waiting for a mob of drunks to hang me because I tried to save your ungrateful neck one more time, and it's *my* fault?!"

"No one asked you to save my ungrateful neck.

185

In another few minutes, I'd have gotten out of here and been on my way to Canada. But now, courtesy of your bungling attempt to break me out, I not only have to get past *two* armed men instead of one, but I've got to take you with me when I go!"

"Why, you arrogant, self-righteous boor! I wouldn't go with you if it were the last way on earth I could save myself! In fact, I'd rather take my chances with that mob than to spend another day in your presence!"

Undaunted by her spiteful words, Rye held up his hand to silence her and focused his attention on the door to the street. "Listen," he ordered.

"What is it?" Aerial whispered, anxiety overwhelming her ire. "Oh, my God! They're coming, aren't they?"

Rye turned to face her, a cold, sardonic smile on his face. "Sounds like you're going to get your wish, Miss Windsor. You get to face your mob, and you won't be forced to spend any more time with me."

Before she could respond, Tom Hagarty burst into the office. He slammed the door, shutting out very little of the commotion coming from the street. His young face a mask of worry, he stomped across the sheriff's office and stood in front of the cells, the key in his hand.

"What are you doing?" Holding the bars with a knuckle-whitening grip, Aerial had to shout to make herself heard over the loud yells filtering into the office from outside. "Are you going to give us to those lunatics?"

"No, ma'am," Hagarty said, inserting the key in the door to her cell. "Sheriff says for me to take you out the back way. He says he and Beck'll try to hold 'em off 'til I git you back to the hotel."

Stunned, Aerial flashed her eyes to Rye. As desperate as she was to get away from the lynch mob, and as infuriated as she was with Rye Berenger for all he had cost her, she knew she couldn't leave him. "What about him? You can't let them hang him!"

Shaking his head, Tom swung open the door to her cell and stepped aside for her to exit, instinctively backing to within inches of Rye's cell. "Sheriff says we gotta—"

With the speed of a rattlesnake, Rye's arm shot through the bars and whipped around Hagarty's neck, dragging him back against the bars with a choking hold that cut off the rest of his sentence.

Reacting spontaneously, Aerial grabbed the key from the startled deputy and hurried to unlock the second cell.

"Make a sound and I'll break your neck," Rye told the young deputy as he took his gun from him. Holding Hagarty's own revolver on him, Rye released some of the pressure on his neck. "From the sound of that crowd out there, I don't have anything to lose if I kill you, do I?"

Tom shook his head, his eyes filling with tears. "I won't give you any trouble."

Rye let go of him. "Smart man. Now get in this cell and keep quiet if you don't want that little girlfriend of yours to visit you in a casket the next time she comes calling."

Tom hurried to obey.

"Bring me that rope," Rye said to Aerial as he took off the deputy's neck bandana and gagged him with it. "And bar that front door."

Knowing her own situation was growing more disastrous by the instant, Aerial paused. If she helped Rye escape she would be as much a criminal as he was.

187

She looked back at Rye and the truth hit her with staggering force. Right or wrong, she had to help him. Even if it meant she would go to jail — or worse — she could not let them hang Rye Berenger.

Chapter Twelve

A few minutes later, Rye led two saddled horses out into the alley where Aerial waited. "We're in luck," he whispered tersely. The stable owner must be out front watching the show at the sheriff's office." He caught her around the waist and started to lift her onto the roan mare. "Let's go."

Knowing what she had to do, Aerial pried his hands from her waist and took a step back. "I'm not coming with you."

He stopped, his bronzed face a mixture of disappointment and anger. "What do you mean, you're not coming with me?"

"I'm going to stay here and wait for the people from Fairfield to come for me in a few days."

Rye heaved a frustrated sigh. In his brain, he knew he should be relieved by her decision and should just get on the horse and ride out of town. But in his heart . . .

"Once that mob out there in the street finds out you helped me escape, do you think they'll wait until your friends get here from Iowa to do something about it? Or maybe you want to be hung. Is that it?"

"Don't be ridiculous. They're not going to hang me and you know it. Especially when I tell them the reason I helped you escape was because I was afraid you were going to kill the deputy."

"And what will you tell them your reason was for stealing the cell key and bringing it to me in

189

the first place?" he asked, his mouth curled in a bitter snarl. "Whose life were you trying to save then?"

Aerial was hit with a crazy, unexpected desire to cry out, *Mine! I was saving my own life because I can't bear the thought of living without you!*

She shuddered slightly in an unconscious attempt to ward off the ridiculous thought. What was she thinking? She could live perfectly well if she never saw Rye Berenger again. In fact, that was what she had every intention of doing once she got him safely out town and out of her life.

"My own life!" she spat out, using every modicum of will she could muster not to throw her arms around him and tell him she wanted to go with him. "I only tried to help you because I felt I owed you something for saving me from those men, and because I knew if you got out of jail I would be rid of you once and for all!"

Rye stared at her long and hard, his features twisted with irritation and an emotion Aerial couldn't quite read. Before she could contemplate the meaning of the strange look, he grabbed her around the waist and whisked her up onto the saddled black gelding.

"What are you doing?"

"Lady, in case you've forgotten, there's still the matter of that deposition you signed against me in Iowa." He climbed into the saddle behind her, trapping her between his arms as he reached around her to hold the reins. "So you might as well sit back and relax, because you're not rid of me yet, not until the entire debt is paid!"

Unable to fight the overwhelming relief that washed over her, Aerial sagged back into the curve of Rye's body. No matter what his reason was for taking her with him, she had been given a reprieve from the desolation she had already begun to feel at the thought of letting him ride out of her life forever.

His face flushed with fury, Chester Hagen glowered down at the Fairfield sheriff. "Damn those fools! Their incompetence has ruined everything! How could this have happened?"

The sheriff shrugged and indicated the wire on his desk with a nonchalant sweep of his callused hand. "You know as much as I do, Mr. Hagen."

Hagen ran his fingers through his thick white hair and paced over to the window to gaze out onto the deserted town square. "Well, I'll tell you one thing, Sheriff. I'm not going to stand still while that Indian bastard destroys everything I've worked for."

The sheriff frowned. "You sound like it's somethin' personal between you'n that Indian."

Chester jerked his head around and stared at the lawman, the color on his face darkening to an even deeper shade of red than before.

"It *is* personal, Sheriff Riley," he finally admitted. "Not only will this publicity reflect badly on our city's good name, which, I shouldn't need to remind you, I've worked diligently for years to promote as the president of the Chamber of Commerce. But when I think of that sweet, innocent girl in the evil clutches of that filthy savage it makes my blood boil." His large body shuddered dramatically.

"That fine young woman gave us the opportunity to put our city on the map with her flight, and we had a duty to protect her from vicious animals like the one who abducted and no doubt raped her." He swallowed distastefully at the thought.

"Now, instead of attracting new residents and

businesses to Fairfield because it is the city the famous Aerial Windsor chose to originate her balloon flight in, we'll be known as the city where Indians are allowed to kill innocent citizens and abduct women off the streets." He paused and took a deep breath. "Yes, Sheriff, I take it *very* personally that Rye Berenger is at this moment a free man instead of hanging from the end of a rope, as should every decent, concerned citizen of Fairfield, seeing as how it is our jail he broke out of in the first place!"

The sun rose with dramatic effect, magically highlighting a slash of glistening water that cut across the width of the horizon to dissect the seemingly endless forest ahead with golden splendor.

"Now what?" Aerial asked, ignoring the beauty in the distance and concentrating on the place where Rye had reined the horses to a halt after their all-night ride.

His concentration intense, Rye shook his head with disgust as he watched the churning river rush past them and plunge at least a hundred feet over steep falls before continuing its northeastward journey. The friendly river that had led them out of Keene Valley toward Canada was no longer a friend. It had just become the opposition.

"I've heard of a great falls on the Canadian border they call Niagara Falls," Rye mused, his brow furrowed as he considered their few options. "You don't think . . ."

Aerial shook her head decisively. "It's not."

"Are you sure?"

Though there was no doubt in her mind, she squared her shoulders and mentally compared the terrain with the maps of New York and Canada she had diligently studied in preparation for her flight. "For one thing, we're farther north and east than Niagara; and for another, I saw Niagara when I was a little girl when my father ballooned over them at a big celebration. Believe me, this is nothing compared to Niagara Falls. They're so huge, there are actually two falls, one on the Canadian side and one on the American side. Combined, they're nearly half a mile wide!"

"And I guess it's too much to hope this is another set of falls on the Canadian border, isn't it?"

Aerial shook her head, unable to resist giving him a sympathetic smile. "I'm afraid so. I'm willing to bet we're still in New York. In fact, if I'm not mistaken, that lake down there is Champlain, the boundary between New York and Vermont." She paused, then added in an optimistic tone, "But if you follow it north, it will take you to Canada."

She pointed toward verdant mountain peaks in the distance, rising from and fading into the morning mist east of the lake. "And those must be the Green Mountains of Vermont."

"Vermont," he grunted. "That's just great."

Knowing how disappointed he must be to realize they were still miles from the Canadian border, she turned in the saddle to face him. For the first time, she became aware of the dark circles beneath Rye's eyes. She had slept most of the night, safe in the circle of his arms, while he had stayed awake.

"Maybe we should stop and rest. It won't seem so far after a few hours of sleep."

Rye checked over his shoulder, searching for signs they were being followed. "We can't stop. They could be right behind us."

Fear ran through Aerial at the thought. Not for herself, but for him. She knew if Clem and his

193

mob caught up with them, there would be no stopping the lynching a third time.

"Certainly, they wouldn't try to follow us in the dark. Don't you think they would have at least waited for daylight when they could see any trail we left behind?"

"You're probably right, but I don't intend to take any chances. A man wouldn't need too many brains to figure out we don't know the area and would be forced to follow the river north out of town if we wanted to get to Canada."

He nudged the gelding in the sides and veered him away from the falls. "Now that the sun's up, though, we don't need the river. We can head straight north, instead of wasting time following all it's twists and curves."

Aerial turned back around to face the front, knowing his mind was made up but unable to keep her comments to herself. "I suppose you know best, but if they're able to figure out that you're trying to get to Canada by following the river, won't it be obvious to them which way we went when we reached the falls?"

Rye halted the horses. "Have you got a better idea?"

Excited that he respected her enough to at least listen to her suggestions, Aerial turned to face him again, her expression conniving. "What if we worked our way down to the bottom of the falls and followed the river the rest of the way to the lake? We could cross over into Vermont before we continued north to Canada. They'd never expect that, would they?"

Rye thought for a moment, his black eyes scanning the thickly forested surroundings. "It might work," he conceded. "But it's too risky. It's too steep here to use the horses, and I don't want to end up on foot this far from Canada. No, I think we're better off if we stick to the most direct route, even if it is the most obvious. If they decided not to start after us until first light, they're only now getting underway, and we could be over the border by the time they get to this point."

"In that case, can we at least stop for a few minutes?" Aerial asked, seeing his practical point, but a little hurt that he hadn't been interested in her tricky scheme. "I really need to . . ." Blushing profusely at what she'd been about to say, she cut herself off by nervously clearing her throat. ". . . freshen up."

Rye grinned in spite of their dire circumstances. "Yeah, me too. And I could use a bite to eat. How about you?"

"Oh!" Aerial slapped her hand to her abdomen and rolled her eyes toward heaven. "Right now, I'd kill for a piece of stale bread."

Rye threw back his head and laughed at her dramatics. "Well, you're in luck," he said, swinging down off the horse and reaching up for her. "That's all I found at the stable where I 'borrowed' these horses. And you don't even have to kill for it!"

Supporting herself by placing her hands on Rye's shoulders, Aerial allowed herself to be lifted off the horse. When it was just the two of them like this it was awfully easy to forget that he was a wanted man and that by bringing her with him he was destroying her chances of ever having the life she had dreamed of. All she was aware of was how right and natural it seemed when they were together. "You mean my stomach has been growling all night and you had food the whole time?"

Rye idly investigated the area for the safest place to rest. "I guess I wasn't listening to your stomach. Did you know you talk in your sleep?" He led the horses toward a particularly thick stand

195

of trees, leaving a stunned Aerial staring after him.

"You're lying!" she accused, running to catch up with him. "I don't talk in my sleep."

"You don't?" Rye asked with a knowing arch of his brows as he secured the stolen horses to graze in a hidden grassy area. He lifted his broad shoulders in an indifferent shrug and started back toward the trail. "My mistake. It must have been the wind."

"Well, I might have mumbled a little bit," she conceded. "Who doesn't? But I bet I didn't say anything that made any sense."

Without acknowledging her comments, Rye retraced their step from the road, his alert eyes scanning the area for any telltale signs that might give away the fact that they had turned off the trail at this spot.

She followed him again. "Well, did I?"

"Did you what?" Backing toward the hidden horses, he brushed a stick over the ground to cover the occasional track they had left in the damp soil and to ruffle the trampled foliage.

"Did I make any sense?"

"When?"

"When I talked in my sleep!" she squealed.

Sparing her an evasive smile, he shoved her behind him, then whisked his branch over the spot where she had stood. "I thought you said you don't talk in your sleep."

Exasperation reaching its limit, Aerial stopped, blocking his backward progress. "Stop it! What did I say?"

"Don't worry, Miss Windsor, your secrets are safe with me!"

"Secrets?" Suddenly, her dreams of the night before flashed across her conscious mind, and her skin began to burn with embarrassment. Cuddled safely in Rye's arms throughout the night, her slumber had been filled with dreams of him. Holding her. Kissing her. Making love to her! Surely, she hadn't . . . "What secrets??"

Rye dug into the bag he'd brought from the stable and produced a loaf of bread. "Here," he said, breaking off a chunk and offering it to her. "I thought you were hungry."

Momentarily taken back by the way he'd changed the subject, Aerial stared at the bread in Rye's outstretched hand before she accepted it. "Thanks," she finally said. Tearing off a bite, she popped it into her mouth, then slowly began to chew the tough, tasteless lump, her suspicious gaze never leaving his face.

"We'll let the horses rest for an hour," he said, his manner serious now. His black eyes no longer contained even a glimmer of the teasing glint she had been sure she'd seen in them only a moment before.

"Once we get to Canada, what are we going to do?" she asked, taking another bite of bread, relieved to let the subject of talking in her sleep drop.

"That depends on you," he said, thoughtfully watching her mouth as he chewed his own meager breakfast.

"On me? How?"

"If you're going to withdraw that deposition you signed against me in Fairfield, we'll wait a spell and then head back to Iowa to clear my name."

"And if I'm still not convinced that withdrawing my statement is the right thing to do, what then?"

A flicker of something Aerial couldn't identify skittered across his face, but he quickly hid it behind his mask of indifference before Aerial could examine it more closely.

He shrugged. "Then I guess we're stuck with

each other until you're convinced." He narrowed his eyes in a menacing glare and lowered his face to within inches of hers. "Because no matter how long it takes or how unpleasant it gets for either of us, you're not going to see the last of me, or the United States side of the border, until you admit to those people in Fairfield that you lied when you said you saw me kill that old man!"

His hurtful words echoed loudly in Aerial's mind. *Stuck with each other!? Unpleasant!?* So that was how he really felt about her. And to think that during the night she had actually let herself imagine how wonderful it would be to spend every night for the rest of her life safe in the shelter of this man's arms. She had even fantasized about how they would clear his name, get married, then settle down on a farm and raise children like she'd always planned on doing.

What a joke! Men like Rye Berenger don't "settle down." Well, her little girl ideas of having a Prince Charming whisk her away on his magnificent charger to live happily ever after had made a fool of her for the last time!

Rye Berenger was no Prince Charming; he was a criminal. The stolen horses from the stable in Keene Valley weren't magnificent; they were both quite ordinary. She was no longer a little girl; she was a grown woman. And this was no fairy tale; this was real life.

Once and for all, she had to face the truth. If there was a happy ending in her future, it would never be with Rye Berenger!

"In that case," she finally said, jutting her chin in a defiant effort to keep from crying, "you just convinced me, because no one wants an end to this 'unpleasant' association of ours any more — or any sooner — than I do."

Rye stared at Aerial for a long moment, wishing

198

he could take back the words he'd said that had put that wounded look in her eyes. But he couldn't. Not if he wanted to keep his own emotions at bay. And certainly not if he intended to destroy any romantic notions Aerial Windsor's naive mind might be concocting about him.

He hated himself for hurting her. Even now he longed to take her in his arms and kiss away the hurt he had caused her, the hurt he could see she was trying so valiantly to hide from him.

Once he had recognized that look a woman gets when she thinks she has found the man for her, he had realized he had no choice. He had to make her see that he was the wrong man for her.

Aerial Windsor should be with a man who could give her a house and children and *respectability*. She deserved better than a rootless halfbreed who had no place in either the white man's world or in the Indian's, and who had nothing to offer her. Nothing, that is, except the bitter life of ostracism that would automatically accompany the disgrace of being an Indian's woman and eventually destroy any feelings she had ever had for him.

Again he chastised himself for taking advantage of her innocence. God, he hoped she wasn't pregnant. If he knew his baby was growing in her belly, he didn't think he would have the strength to leave her, and he couldn't bear the thought of knowing what it would do to her if he stayed.

Rye cleared his throat noisily and turned away from Aerial. "Good, I'm glad to hear it. Since we both want this over with as soon as possible, let's finish up here and get going."

"It's about time," a familiar voice drawled. "We been waitin' for you."

Startled, Aerial and Rye stared as Clem and Sid

199

stepped out of the brush and rocks that sided the road a hundred feet ahead, their rifles aimed directly at the two riders.

"You look surprised, Injun," a third man said, stepping into the open and joining his partners. An ugly grin slithered across the face of the man they both recognized as Deke's brother, Ned. "Didn't expect to see us agin, did ya?" He leveled his rifle and vengeful glare on Rye.

Berating himself for his own stupidity, Rye rapidly scoured the area for an escape. How could he have overlooked the fact that the locals would not only anticipate the route he and Aerial would take once they reached the falls, but that they would know a shortcut that would make it possible for them to get ahead and cut them off?

Aerial tightened her already desperate grip on the saddle horn of the mare on which she had ridden alone since their rest stop. "What are we going to do?" she rasped, her words barely audible.

Rye turned his head slightly and whispered out of the corner of his mouth, his lips barely moving. "We're going to make a run for it."

Aerial's eyes widened with terror. "I can't!" she gasped. "I'll fall."

"When I tell you, lie as low as you can over the mare's neck and just hang on! I'll do the rest."

Taking care to keep his hands out of the view of the approaching men, Rye checked his grip on his own reins and shifted the lead rope on Aerial's horse to his left hand as he slid his right hand toward the butt of his revolver.

The three men ambled forward, their smugness making them careless. "This is gonna be the easiest money we ever made," Clem bragged. "And the most fun."

"But we don't have any money," Aerial said, her

voice shaking. Stinging sweat poured into her eyes and her fingers began to cramp on the saddle horn.

"It ain't your money we want," Clem said, glancing at his partners with a snide grin. "We're gonna get that reward they're offerin' for your Injun's dead body back in Ioway. It's been upped to five thousand dollars!"

"But he's not wanted for anything in New York," Aerial protested.

"Oh, we ain't gonna *hang* him," Clem offered.

"Hangin's too quick for the likes o' him," Ned injected. "We're gonna let him die nice and slow, while we give him a taste o' what it was like for Deke to spend his last minutes on earth knowin' he was only half a man."

Clem snickered. "And while he's dyin', he's gonna watch us take his woman over and over in every way we can imagine, all the time knowin' that even if he lived he'd never have you or any other woman again."

Waves of nausea rocked through Aerial as understanding exploded in her mind.

"Now!" Whipping his revolver from the holster, Rye released a barrage of bullets on the bounty hunters as he simultaneously leaned forward, kicked the gelding in the sides and jerked on the mare's lead rope.

At the sudden forward lunge of her horse, Aerial was thrown back, then was snapped forward by her own death grip on the saddle horn. Reacting mechanically, she flattened herself over the horse's mane.

To keep from being trampled by the two horses thundering toward them and to evade the flying bullets, the three men on the ground dove to the side of the road.

Bounced and jostled like a rag doll tied to the

201

pommel, Aerial hung on for dear life. She tried with all her strength to tighten her legs around the mare's girth to keep from flopping up and down so much, but to no avail.

With all her concentration centered on staying in the saddle, it was a moment before she realized the bounty hunters had evidently recovered and were firing their rifles.

All around her, she heard the zing and whoosh of bullets whizzing past. And then she heard nothing.

His naturally protruding eyes bulging even more than usual, Hershel Zimmermann brought the newspaper closer to his face. "I'll be damned. Will you look at that!"

"What is it, Hershel?" the red-headed waitress asked, pouring fresh coffee into the half-full mug on the counter in front of the restaurant's only customer. "You look like you just discovered a gold mine."

"I may have, Pearl," Hershel answered absently, continuing to scan the print on the newspaper page excitedly. "I just may have."

Pearl put the coffeepot back on the stove, then turned back to face the wiry, black-haired man. For years, he had come into her Brooklyn coffee shop for breakfast every morning, always wearing the same frayed black gabardine suit.

There was no doubt Hershel had seen better days, and that his clothes were left over from those days. But unlike other down-in-the-heelers she met, Hershel was always clean, and he carried himself with the confidence of a man who was just around the corner from striking it rich. His black hair—dyed, she suspected—was always neatly parted in the middle and combed down with hair oil; his mustache was trimmed regularly; his worn, white shirt front was never dirty; and he always appeared to be freshly shaven. Besides, he was good company.

"Well," she finally said, resting her hands on her wide hips, "are you going to share this great news with me? Or are you going to just sit there grinning and staring at that newspaper?"

"Mmm," Hershel said, taking a moment to finish reading the article that had caught his interest before he peered up at her. When he finally did, his face broke into a huge smile. "You remember me telling you about those balloon-flying clients of mine who crashed and got killed in the Mississippi a few years back?"

Pearl smiled. How could she forget the story about the Windsors. Hadn't he mentioned them at least once every day over the five years he'd been coming into her place? "Sure, I remember. They were the ones you spent everything you had promoting, and then caused you to lose it all when they crashed and didn't make the flight."

Hershel's face clouded over. "They made me look like a fool. From that day on, I couldn't get any decent acts to sign with me. They thought I was bad luck. And the acts I did sign, I played hell getting booked anywhere."

"But all it would take would be just one good act and you could be on top again," Pearl said, her tone encouraging.

Hershel's expression lightened again. He jabbed his finger at the newspaper on the counter. "And now, after all those years of searching for that one great money-making act, I've finally found it practically in my own back yard!"

Pearl turned the paper around so she could read the headline he was indicating. "Daredevil Female Balloonist Creates New World Record for Distance," she read aloud.

She looked up at Hershel, her expression worried. "But Hershel, you told me yourself that no balloonist in the country will even talk to you. That's why you started handling singing and juggling and animal acts for variety shows and beer halls."

"This one will talk to me. She at least owes me that much. Keep reading." His eyes twinkling like those of a young boy, he patted the newspaper.

"On July 5th in the year of our Lord 1880, female aeronaut Aerial Windsor . . ." Pearl looked up at Hershel. "Windsor?"

"Their daughter," Hershel confirmed. "Go on."

Pearl returned her attention to the article. " . . . landed her balloon, the *Wind Rose,* on Mount Marcy in the Adirondacks, after traveling 926 miles from Fairfield, Iowa, in only twenty-one hours, making her the first person to ever attain such a distance in a balloon. Until Miss Windsor's amazing feat this week, the previous record of 809 miles set in 1859 by the renowned aeronaut John Wise has been challenged many times, but never met."

Pearl stopped reading and grinned up at Hershel. "Do you really think she'll see you?"

"Of course she will. Why, I bet right about now she'd jump at the chance to talk to someone who knew her parents, and to have someone take some of the problems of her new celebrity status off her shoulders. If anyone ever needed a manager, she does. The offers for her to appear places are probably already pouring into that town of Keene Valley where they took her."

"How do you know she doesn't already have someone?" Pearl asked, hating to see Hershel get his hopes up. He'd been disappointed too many times.

"The article didn't mention a manager or booking agent. It just says she was sponsored by that town in Iowa. No, I'm willing to wager everything I own that she doesn't have anyone handling her affairs for her."

Pearl opened her mouth to point out he didn't have much to wager, but Hershel stopped her by covering her plump hand with his and looking up at her with beseeching gray eyes. "I have a real good feeling about this one, Pearl."

Pearl didn't speak for a minute. She had never seen Hershel so excited. Who was she to spoil it for him? And maybe he was right. Maybe his luck was about to change. Maybe something good was finally about to happen to Hershel Zimmermann.

"Then I feel good about it too." She turned her hand over beneath his and squeezed his fingers affectionately. "But I don't mind telling you, Hershel, I'm going to miss you."

Hershel looked deep into Pearl's green eyes. "I'll miss you too, Pearl O'Hara. But I'll be back. And this is the first place I'll come."

Pearl smiled, her ruddy face blushing schoolgirl pink. "You just see that it is, Hershel Zimmermann."

Chapter Thirteen

"Oh," Aerial moaned, attempting to lift her head off the ground, but dropping it as something that felt like an electric shock shot up her spine.

Rye appeared at her side immediately. "Don't try to sit up," he told her.

"What happened?" she asked, unable to remember. Every bone and muscle in her body ached so severely she couldn't think. Her head felt as if a stick of dynamite had gone off inside her skull; the muscles of her thighs felt as if they had been stretched to the limit, then shattered to fragments; her backside felt as though it had been beaten to a bloody pulp with a railroad tie; and her entire spine and neck felt as if they would snap if she moved. Even her fingers felt cramped and useless. But worst of all was the unbearable throbbing in her right upper arm. "Did I fall?"

"No, you didn't fall," Rye said with a grim smile. He shook his head. "Though only God knows how you stayed in the saddle." He picked up one of her hands, still frozen in the grip she had used to cling to the saddle horn. "You were amazing," he whispered, bringing her bent fingers to his lips and kissing them one by one.

"Then why do I feel like I've been run over by a train?"

"Shh. We'll talk about it later. You need to rest

now."

She blinked her eyes slowly and ran her tongue over her dry lips. "I'm thirsty."

No sooner did she say the words than Rye was lifting her head and holding a cup of water to her lips so she could drink.

"Mmm," she managed to moan between greedy gulps.

"Easy now. There's no hurry."

"Thank you." Allowing him to lower her head back down to the ground, she closed her eyes. Maybe it wouldn't hurt so much to think if they were shut. "Where are we?" she asked after several minutes of silence.

"We're in a boathouse on that lake you told me about, the one between New York and Vermont. It must belong to someone with a place on one of those islands out there."

She listened for a moment, noticing for the first time the sound of water lapping against the shore and boathouse. "Lake Champlain? How did we get here?"

"I didn't know how much longer you'd be able to stay on that mare. So when we got far enough ahead of Ned and his pals that they couldn't see us, I sent the horses on in one direction, and we came down to the water."

"But how? Wasn't it too steep?"

"Not as bad as back at the falls. Anyway, I didn't have much choice. I had to get you where I could look at your arm."

"My arm?" She didn't need to ask which arm. The throbbing was more intense now than when she had first awakened. In fact, now that she thought about it, the pain in her arm actually made the aches in her head, hands, bottom, legs, neck and back seem less severe. Automatically, she raised her head to see. "Is it broken?" she asked, realizing that her arm was bandaged in what looked like the remains of her petticoat.

Rye hurried to calm her. "No, don't worry, it's not broken."

"Then what?" The small amount of effort to look had taken a toll on her strength.

Rye winced nervously. "You were shot."

"Shot!?" Her eyes snapped open wide. "I don't understand!"

Then it all came back to her: the meeting of the three bounty hunters, their vile threats, the bruising ride to escape, the fear that she would be thrown off the mare, and finally the white-hot pain that had seared through her arm before she lost consciousness. "Am I going to die?"

"No, you're not going to die, but you may wish you had in the next few hours. I got the bullet out and I don't think it hit a bone. But it's still going to hurt like hell. I don't have anything to give you to ease the pain. I used the little bit of whiskey I found in the bottom of that boat to wash out the wound."

Touched by the worry and tenderness in Rye's voice and on his face, Aerial lifted her uninjured arm and caressed his cheek. "It already feels better," she lied. "Just knowing you're taking care of me helps."

Covering her hand on his cheek with his own, Rye brought her palm to his lips and kissed it. "I should have let you stay in Keene Valley. Can you ever forgive me for forcing you to come with me?"

Surprised to see a sheen of tears glistening in Rye's black eyes, Aerial couldn't help smiling. "There's nothing to forgive. What I wouldn't have forgiven would be if you had left me behind."

His black eyes bright with longing, Rye was silent for several moments. Then, his face filled with resolve, he removed her hand from his face and placed it on her chest. He stood up and strode away from her. "I guess it's a good thing I didn't have enough whiskey for you to drink. You're talking crazy enough without it."

"Am I?" She studied him from behind, her heart swelling with joy at what she had seen in Rye's eyes. It didn't matter what he said or did. She knew the truth.

Whether he admitted it, or even knew it, Rye Berenger hadn't brought her with him just to make sure she withdrew that deposition. The simple truth was that he hadn't been *able* to leave her behind. He cared for her!

"Try to get some sleep," he said, his tone gruff and raspy as he made a point of changing the subject. "As soon as it's dark we're leaving."

"Shouldn't we leave now?" she asked, taking his cue. "Won't they find us?"

"By the time they find this boathouse, we'll be gone."

"Are you sure?"

Rye peered through a dirty window toward the wooded hill leading away from the water. "As sure as I can be under the circumstances. We got a pretty good lead on them before they stopped firing their rifles and came after us. By the time they find our horses and realize we're on foot, they won't know if the horses ran a few feet or a few miles after we ditched them. So they'll have to backtrack to look for signs, signs I tried not to leave."

He turned back to face her. "Hopefully, they'll give up or at least decide to make camp for the night and get a fresh start in the morning. Don't forget, they didn't sleep last night. They're just as tired as we are."

"Where are we going?" Aerial asked sleepily,

not really caring, just liking the way the word *we* sounded when she said it, just loving the way it made her feel to hear him say it.

"Once it's dark, we'll take the boat and cross the lake into Vermont. Then, the first town we come to, I'm getting you to a doctor and I'm going on into Canada."

Aerial bolted upright, reviving every ache in her body, but none of them were as great as the one he had just created in her heart. "Without me?"

"It's the only way. I shouldn't have brought you in the first place."

"But what about the deposition?" she asked, grasping for a reason for him to keep her with him. "I thought you said we were stuck with each other until I withdrew it."

Rye shrugged. "You can wire your people in Iowa to come for you, and you can cancel it when you get back to Fairfield."

"How do you know I won't change my mind and let my testimony stand?" she asked, her bottom lip trembling slightly.

"You won't," he said, his black eyes very tired and old looking. "No matter how you feel about me, I know you'll do the right thing, which is to admit that you didn't actually see me kill anyone."

"I wouldn't be so sure about that if I were you," she said, lying back down. "I just might surprise you."

"That's a chance I've got to take, because in the next few days I'm going to cover a lot of miles, and I don't intend to let you slow me down again."

Well, we'll just see about that, Mr. Berenger. We'll just see.

* * *

210

"Aerial, wake up. It's time to go." Rye gently shook her.

Aerial came instantly awake, her eyes frantically searching the dark boathouse for a clue of where she was. "Rye? Is that you?"

"Were you expecting someone else?" he asked, obviously pretending to be in better spirits than he was in. "Do you want me to carry you, or can you walk?"

"I can walk," she bragged stubbornly. "Just help me up."

Doing as she requested, he eased her to a standing position. The instant he removed some of his support, her knees buckled.

"So much for walking." With a disgruntled snarl, he caught her and scooped her up into his arms. "I don't suppose you have any idea how wide this lake is, do you?" he asked as he lowered her into the boat.

"Fourteen miles at its widest point," she answered without even thinking about it. "One hundred and seven miles in length," she went on. "Lake Champlain lies in a broad valley between the Adirondacks in New York and the Green Mountains in Vermont, and it empties into the St. Lawrence River in Quebec, Canada. It has a number of large and small islands, the largest and most famous being Grand Island in the upper half of the lake. It is the main route . . ."

Rye chuckled and shook his head in amazement. "And I was worried because we lost your maps. But who needs maps when I have a walking, or at least talking, geography book with me?" He climbed into the boat and picked up the oars.

She scooted back in the bow of the boat so that she could sit up. "Does that mean you've decided not to leave me in Vermont and go on without me?"

Scowling, Rye used an oar to shove out of the boathouse. "I was making a joke," he grunted, expertly using one oar to bring the boat about in the water. "I don't need a map or a geography book to get where I'm going. All I have to do is follow the lake north to its end, then head due west. Once I'm in Manitoba, I'll know exactly where I am, and it will be a simple matter of turning south and locating my mother's people in South Dakota."

"Due west will put you in the middle of Lake Huron or Lake Superior," she told him smugly. "Do you plan to swim them, row across them, or go around them?"

Rye frowned his annoyance. "I knew that, and I'll decide what to do when I get there." He pulled harder on the oars, the boat's speed picking up quickly.

Before Aerial could respond with another snide comment, she became aware of the dark choppy water surrounding them. As if she'd been kicked in the head, her fear of drowning rose inside her. Her heart pounding painfully, she gripped the sides of the rowboat. "Are you sure this boat is safe?"

Rye studied her face, then smiled. "You're not afraid, are you?" he asked, seizing the opportunity to repay her for the way she had goaded him in the balloon. "I didn't think anything scared you."

"I'm not afraid," she said defensively, but her eyes shifting nervously from side to side made a lie of her words. "I told you, I just don't like the idea of drowning. If I'm going to die, I want to do it on dry land."

"Well, you're not going to die—in the water *or* on land, so just sit back and enjoy the ride. It's going to be a long night."

Aerial forced herself to do as he said—sit back, that is. "Enjoy" was another matter all together. Doing her best to seem casual, she looked around her, then back over her shoulder toward the boathouse. A new surge of fear sizzled through her as she realized the boathouse was already out of sight. That meant—

Don't think about it! she ordered herself. She looked back at Rye and concentrated on his muscular shoulders as he strained over the oars. *He won't let me drown. He won't let me drown. He won't let me drown.*

For what felt like hours, Aerial fought to keep control over her warring emotions. It would help if there were a moon and stars out. She could at least use them to determine the time, how far they had gone, and in what direction. Maybe then she wouldn't feel so isolated or helpless, as if she were a prisoner condemned to spend forever in the black void of purgatory.

However, with nothing to take her mind off her fear except the sound of the wind and the rhythmic creak of the oars as they moved through the water, the torture was fast becoming unbearable.

She shuddered, longing to hug herself for warmth but afraid to let go of the sides. A large drop of rain hit her in the face, then another, and then another. "It's raining," she wailed, wiping her face with her uninjured shoulder while maintaining her clutch on the boat sides.

"I can see that," Rye grumbled.

"Maybe we should go back to the boathouse," she shouted over the wind that had picked up greatly in the last few minutes. Her fear of drowning was fast overwhelming her tenuous grasp on sanity. It was squeezing the breath from her lungs.

"We can't. It's too far. Besides, we already spent more time there than we should have." He lifted the oars out of the water and leaned forward over them, then sank them deep into the water and pulled. "But don't worry, the way the wind is picking up from the west, we should be able to make it across the lake in record time."

As if in response to his statement, a distant flash of lightning lit up the black sky.

"Oh!" Aerial screamed, curling into a ball on the floor of the boat and covering her head with her arms.

"Relax. That lightning was miles from here."

"Oh, Lord, please help me. I don't want to drown."

The sky lit up again, and Rye looked back over his shoulder toward the center of the lake. "All right!" he surrendered. "It looks like there's an island not far ahead. We might be able to make it there before the storm gets too bad. Can you hold on that long?"

"I'll try," Aerial whimpered. Ashamed and embarrassed by her own outburst of panic, she did her best to regain some semblance of self-control. "But please hurry."

During the next hour and a half, Aerial huddled silently in the bow of the boat as Rye rowed them farther and farther out into the lake with each turn of the oars.

Fortunately, the approaching downpour held off, and he was able to keep his bearing on the island whenever lightning lit the sky, despite the increasing winds, the dangerously rough water and the fact that the island took longer to reach than he had anticipated.

"Are you all right?" he yelled over the deafening sounds of the wind and the waves crashing higher and higher around and into the little boat.

"We're almost there, just another hundred yards or so."

He didn't hear a response, but then who could hear anything? Besides, he was having too much trouble controlling the rowboat now. The closer to the island they got, the rougher the water became. It was as if for every three feet he rowed toward the beach, they were washed two feet back out into the lake whenever he lifted the oars for the next stroke.

Then, as if the rain clouds were water-filled balloons timed to burst simultaneously, the entire sky released the rain it had held in check.

Without warning, a loud thunk accompanied a violent jolt of the small craft. Caught by surprise, Rye lost his balance and was pitched over backward. His grip on the oars was the only thing that kept him in the boat.

To the grating sound of shattering wood, he struggled to right himself as a jagged boulder tore upward through the floor of the rowboat. Almost as if it had never been there, the rock disappeared beneath the water that rushed through the huge gash in the bottom of the boat.

"Aerial!" he shouted, diving for the bow. But Aerial wasn't there. His heart pounding with uncontrolled fear as he realized what had happened, he frantically searched the murky waters around him.

"Rye! Help m—" Aerial's voice screamed from his right, before it was cut off.

"Aerial!" he shouted, jumping into the water toward the spot where he thought she had gone under.

"Rye! I can't s—"

Now, she was to his left. "Oh, God! Help me find her!" he moaned, treading water and swiveling his head from left to right.

Suddenly she was there. All over him. "Rye! Help me!" she choked, her arms in a strangling hold on his neck, her fingers clutching at his hair, her legs tangling around his legs and waist as if she were climbing him.

"Aerial! Let go of me," he coughed, struggling to free himself from her crazed hold as they both went under.

"You're going to drown us both!" he sputtered as they came up.

But she wouldn't release him, and they sank below the surface of the water a second time.

Knowing he had no choice, Rye sucked in a quick gulp of air when they resurfaced and deliberately took her under again.

Frantic to get to air, she released him and started flailing her arms in an attempt to reach the surface.

Free, Rye broke the water behind her and grabbed her by the hair. Holding her face above the water, he swam toward the remains of the rowboat impaled on the submerged rock.

Balancing himself on the boulder and the wreckage, he hauled her to him and held her head and shoulders out of the water. He pressed her cheek to his heaving chest and buried his face in her wet hair. "Are you all right?" he panted, the scare she had given him contributing even more to his shortness of breath than the struggle to save her.

She nodded feebly, her desperate gasps for air making it impossible for her to speak.

Assaulted by the vicious truth of what had just happened, he clutched her to him in a frantic hug and covered her face with kisses. "Thank God! I don't know what I'd do if . . . He tightened his embrace. "Oh, God, Aerial, I thought I'd lost you."

216

The dark freezing water crashed all around them, and the torrential rain battered them mercilessly, but neither of them expressed any fear. They stayed that way for several minutes, silently taking the time to revive their strength from each other's presence. Finally, Rye made the first move.

"We can't stay here any longer, Aerial. We need to swim the rest of the way to the island."

New fear jolted through her and she gripped him harder. "I can't swim!"

"You don't have to. I'll swim for both of us, but you've got to help."

"I can't!" She was fast becoming hysterical again. "I told you, I can't swim!"

"Aerial!" he shouted sternly. "Get control of yourself! You're only making it worse! I'm not going to let you drown. Now, are you going to trust me and do what I tell you, or are we going to sit out here until we both drown?"

All the times Rye had saved her flashed through Aerial's mind: the hours he'd spent helping her keep the *Wind Rose* aloft despite his own fears of falling; the way he'd endangered his life and freedom to save her from being raped; the moment when he had plucked her from the angry waters of Lake Champlain.

"I trust you," she answered meekly.

"Good," he sighed, prying her arms from around his waist and turning her around so that her back was to him. "Now, what I want you to do is just relax your body and lie back on me. I'll do the rest." He brought a strong arm over her chest from behind and grasped her under the arm.

Aerial tried, but nothing happened. It was one thing for her to tell herself to relax, but quite another to make her body obey. There was suddenly a nudge at her buttocks and she felt her body and legs being lifted upward.

"See?" Rye asked, removing his hand from under her. "The water will hold you up if you don't fight it."

Aerial nodded her head, trying to convince herself that she believed what he was saying. "You're not going to let go of me, are you?"

"Not for anything in the world. But I can't swim in these choppy waters if you're struggling. So it's very important that you just lie there and don't fight me or the water. Do you understand?"

"I understand," she answered, using her last remaining ounce of strength not to resist.

"In that case let's go." He shoved off from the submerged rock and started swimming for the island.

"What do we do now?" Sid asked, shading his eyes against the glare of the morning sun as he stared out over the lake.

Clem shook his head in disgust. "If they was out on the water durin' that storm last night they're dead by now — sure as we're standin' here."

"We don't know they was on the water." Ned searched the lake for a sign. "They mighta come as far as the lake, then decided to foller the shore north."

"If they did, their tracks was washed away in the rain," Sid pointed out. "How're we gonna find 'em now?"

Clem nodded his head in agreement. "On the other hand, if they found a boat, they mighta got across the lake before the storm come up."

Ned squinted to see farther, his expression contemplative. "I'm willin' to bet they wouldn't try to make a crossin' before dark, if they tried to make one at all. They woulda been sittin' ducks in the daylight. No, if they found a boat, I'd stake my reputation as the best bear tracker in these parts that they didn't use it until after sunset."

"Then there's a real good chance they was out in the middle o' the lake when the storm hit," Clem pointed out again. "And died."

"They ain't dead," Ned insisted.

Clem shrugged. "One way or another, it looks like they outsmarted us. If they're dead, we got no way to figure out where the bodies'll wash up—or if they even will. And if they *ain't* dead, we got no idea what side o' the lake they're on, an' no way o' trackin' 'em after last night's storm."

Ned shook his head resolutely. "We ain't outsmarted. Mark my words. We're gonna find 'em yet."

"But how?" Sid insisted. "We don't know where to look!"

"That's the trouble with you two. You don't think. 'Stead o' worryin' 'bout what we don't know, let's think on what we do know."

"And what's that?"

"Well, we know that Injun was tryin' to git to Canada, don't we?" Ned asked thoughtfully. "And by the blood on that mare's saddle, we got good reason to b'lieve the gal took a bullet."

"He coulda figgered to take her on up to Plattsburg to find a doctor," Clem suggested excitedly.

Sid's eyes lit up. "Or if he got a boat, he might count on findin' a doc in a town on t'other side."

Ned flashed a triumphant, yellow-toothed grin. "But whatever side they're on, we know one thing for certain."

"What's that?" Sid and Clem asked together.

"If he's alive, that Injun is gonna keep workin'

219

his way north toward Canada."

Sid and Clem stared at Ned, waiting for him to continue.

Sparing his partners an impatient look, Ned cleared his throat and spat a stream of tobacco juice onto the ground. "Don't you see? It don't matter what side o' the lake they're on right now; sooner or later they're gonna wind up at the upper end o' the lake. All we gotta do is git there first, an' be waitin' for 'em to show . . ."

Chapter Fourteen

Aerial opened her eyes to brilliant sunlight streaming through fluttering white lace curtains playing in the breeze. Relieved, she smiled at her own foolishness. It had been just another nightmare: the gunshot wound, the boat wreck, almost drowning. It didn't occur to her to wonder where she was because she was used to not knowing where she was when she first awoke. It would come to her in a minute.

It all seemed so real, she thought, squeezing her eyes closed tight to erase the horrible memories. *My body even aches as if—*

Jolted to full alertness, she came the rest of the way awake. Her eyes round with confusion, she took in the unfamiliar lace and yellow-chintz surroundings. She moved her eyes downward, finding that she was clad in an equally unrecognizable white nightgown. The lower half of her body was covered with a white sheet and yellow blanket.

"This doesn't make sense," she murmured, her eyes making a frantic search of the room for anything that might give her a clue to where she was. "This isn't where I went to bed last night. I should be . . ." She frowned, suddenly frightened.

She couldn't remember where she'd gone to bed last night. Fully awake, she still had no idea where she was supposed to be! Lord! Had it finally happened? Had she gone to sleep in one too many strange beds?

The thought that she was still dreaming whipped

through her mind, appeasing her fears momentarily. *That makes sense. After all, this is exactly the kind of room I've always dreamed of having some day.*

But the more her uneasy glance surveyed the beautiful room, the harder it was to convince herself that this wasn't real.

She rubbed her hand idly over the soft cotton of the clean nightgown. It certainly felt real. She breathed in deeply, noticing the sweet scent of fresh, rain-washed earth and honeysuckle wafting into the room from outside. It smelled real. She listened intently, suddenly aware of the cheerful chatter of birds outside her window announcing a new day. It sounded real. In fact, it sounded heavenly.

Then another possibility hit her. Had she died in the boat wreck and come to Heaven?

Her emotions a tangled mix of alarm and excitement at the thought of seeing her parents again, she bolted upright in the bed. "Mama? Papa?"

The instant she came up off the bed, the joy on her face became a look of distress as blinding pain exploded in her head and arm, bringing with it the truth.

Suddenly, warm, familiar arms wrapped themselves around her shoulders. Gently, they eased her back down onto the pillow. "I'll get you something else for the pain."

"Don't leave me," she whimpered, clutching at the naked arms.

"I'm not leaving," Rye answered, relaxing back onto the pillow next to hers. "I was just going to get you another dose of pain medicine from over there on the wash stand." He pointed across the room. "See?"

Aerial opened her eyes and located the brown medicine bottle he was indicating. "What is it?"

222

He kissed the top of her head and carefully rearranged his body along the length of hers and gathered her into his embrace. "I'm not sure. I found it in the medicine chest with a label on it that said it was for pain. It must work pretty well. You've slept all day."

"All day?" she asked, nuzzling her face contentedly into the curve of his shoulder. Already the pain was subsiding. Just lying safe in the security of his arms and filling her nostrils with the sweet scent of him acted as a panacea for all her physical miseries. "Medicine chest? I don't understand. Where are we?"

"Do you remember when our boat crashed?"

All the terror she had felt surged into her memory. Shivering, she instinctively snuggled closer to him and nodded weakly. "I was hoping it was a nightmare."

He grunted ironically. "It was that, all right. And do you remember swimming to the island?"

"I swam? That's impossible. I don't know how to swim."

He chuckled again and stroked her cheek with the backs of his fingers. "Believe me, I know that. Actually, I did the swimming for both of us."

"Is that where we are now? On the island? Whose house is this?"

Rye shrugged. "It must belong to some rich people who only use it for vacations. It looks like no one's been here for a while. All the furniture was covered with sheets and the windows are boarded up."

Aerial's gaze flew automatically over the cheerful room and to the open window.

"I opened this room and the kitchen," he answered her unspoken question. "There's a fully stocked pantry."

"And a wardrobe full of clothes?" she asked,

indicating the nightgown she wore.

"You didn't want me to leave you in the wet rags you were wearing, did you?"

"No, but what if the people who own this place come back? Aren't we breaking the law?"

"We'll worry about that when — and if — the time comes. In the meantime, let's just think about getting you well. Which reminds me, I've got a rabbit stewing in a pot of dried vegetables I found in the kitchen. Think you can eat some? It's pretty good, if I say so myself."

"You cook?"

Rye shrugged, seeming to be embarrassed. "When you've been on your own as long as I have, you learn to do a lot of things you might not have known how to do otherwise."

Aerial smiled weakly, feeling safe and pampered for the first time since her parents had died, maybe even longer than that. In fact, if she really thought about it, she had to admit that though her parents had always seen to all her needs, it had been different with them. They had always been so consumed with their work and each other that most of the time she had felt as if they only cared for her out of duty and in order to safeguard their own careers, since she was an integral part of their act.

But with Rye, it was as if he really cared about her. As if he . . .

She stopped herself. She was doing it again. Her imagination and wishful thinking were running away with her. Rye Berenger hadn't done a thing for her that any decent human being wouldn't have done for another. Sure, he'd saved her from drowning; and he'd taken care of her while she was sick. But he would have done that for anyone. *And he would have cooked for them, too!*

"Stew sounds good." She rolled away from him,

224

determined to forget her foolishly romantic thoughts. "Thank you. I'm sure I'll feel much better if I eat something. And maybe a little more of that medicine wouldn't hurt."

"What do you mean, she's not here?" Hershel Zimmermann asked the desk clerk at the Keene Valley Hotel. "Is there another hotel in this town?"

"Nope. This is the only one."

"Then where is she?"

"She left town a coupla days ago."

A tight claw of pain clenched at Hershel's midsection. His face red with frustration and disappointment, he slapped a newspaper down on the counter. "That's impossible. It says right here in the paper that she was going to stay here until someone from Iowa came to escort her back to Fairfield. They couldn't have gotten here already, could they?"

"No," the clerk said with a smug grin.

The pain in Hershel's gut intensified. "Then why isn't she still here?" he asked, his voice rising with each word.

"Can't rightly say for sure." The clerk's eyes roamed curiously over Hershel, as if he were sizing him up.

"Who can?"

"Only one who knows for sure is the sheriff, but he's bein' real close-mouthed 'bout it. Just says Miss Windsor decided not to wait for the folks from Iowa."

"Nothing else? Like where she went?"

"No, but rumor has it she and—" He stopped himself, pressing his lips together. "I don't like to spread gossip."

Hating to part with any of limited funds in his pocket, Hershel placed a dollar on the counter. "I give you my word whatever you say will go no farther."

"Well," the clerk started, reaching for the bill.

"The rumor first," Hershel said, covering the money with his hand before the clerk could take it up.

A flash of temper flitted over the man's face, and for a moment Hershel thought he might decide not to say anything more. Fortunately, greed won out. "Word is she helped break that Injun out of jail, and then took off for Canada with him."

Hershel had only thought the knot in his stomach was bad before. "Canada? An Indian? None of this makes any sense!"

The clerk looked over his glasses at Hershel and lifted his eyebrows in a look that said *No more information until I get my money.*

"Sorry." Hershel removed his hand from the desk. Consciously fighting to remain calm, he went on in the most controlled tone he could manage, considering the fact that his insides were on fire and that what was probably his last chance for greatness was being ravaged by this man's casual words. "Why would she go to Canada with an Indian? You must be mistaken."

The clerk shrugged and pocketed the bill. "Accordin' to the wire the sheriff sent to the folks in Fairfield, that's what happened."

"But why?"

"Beats me. All I know is that he was with her when they found her in the mountains after her balloon crashed. Someone heard her tell the sheriff he was her assistant and that he come with her in the balloon from Iowa."

"What does the sheriff say about it?"

"He don't say nothin'. If you ask me, he's just glad to git rid of both of them. With the election comin' up, one thing he didn't need was a coupla

226

lynchins his last weeks in office."

"Lynchings!?" The pain in Hershel's gut intensified. "Where did you get this information?"

The clerk smiled and patted his pocket. "There's only so much you can buy for a dollar."

Hershel considered spending another dollar to see if the clerk had anything else worthwhile to say, but he decided against it. Surely we wasn't the only person in Keene Valley who knew something. Hadn't the clerk mentioned a wire being sent? Maybe he'd just amble over to the telegraph office and see what he could learn there.

"Thanks for the help," Hershel said, placing his new black derby on his head and turning to go.

The clerk's mouth fell open in surprise. "You mean you don't —"

"I'll get back to you later if there's anything else I want to know." His posture straight and confident, he tipped his hat and strode out the door.

Outside, Hershel stopped on the boardwalk and clutched at his belly. It took all his remaining willpower not to double over and drop to his knees in agony as the growing pain in the area where his ribs came together tightened into a violent cramp.

Was this it? Was he doomed to fail yet again?

He pressed his fist to his middle and swallowed back the acidy bile that rose in his throat as he waited for the pain to subside.

No! I can't give up. Pearl had enough faith in me to buy me a train ticket and a new set of clothes so I would make the right impression when I approached Aerial Windsor. One way or another, I've got to find her. I can't let Pearl down.

"What are you doing out of bed?" Rye asked, coming into the kitchen from outside.

Aerial looked up and smiled. "I'm heating some

227

water for a bath." She dropped her hold on the indoor water pump lever and started to lift the kettle of water she had drawn.

In a flash, Rye was across the room, brushing her hands away from the handle. "I'll do it." He easily hefted the kettle from the sink and carried it to the stove. "You're not strong enough yet. You shouldn't even be out of bed. You need your rest."

Aerial hoisted a second kettle into the sink and began to pump more water into it. I've been resting for three days. If I don't get a real bath and out of this house soon, I'm going to go crazy.

He hurried over to the pump and relieved her. "But your arm . . ."

"Is healing beautifully, thanks to you. I don't think a doctor could have done any more for me." She covered his hand on the pump and stopped his work. "But you've done enough. It's time for me to start taking care of myself again."

"All right," Rye finally said, returning control of the lever to her. "But, only on one condition."

"What's that?"

"No matter how strong you think you are, you're not to lift those kettles once that water gets hot. I'll do it. Is that understood?"

Aerial smiled. "It's understood."

Rye frowned as though he'd expected her to argue more. "Good," he said, turning toward the small bath closet off to the side of the kitchen. "I'll uncover the tub for you."

"I already did it," she said breathlessly as she continued to pump water.

"And I guess you found the towels in . . ."

". . . the cupboard to the right of the tub," she finished for him. She carried another kettle of water to the stove, then began to fill a third. She decided that, mixed with just enough cold to keep it from scalding her, three ought to be enough to

228

give her a wonderful bath. She could hardly wait. The closest thing to a real bath she'd had in days was in the creek on Mount Marcy after the crash, and that water had been icy cold. Of course, there had been the lukewarm baths she had taken in the room upstairs using the water pitcher and bowl, but she was more than ready for a good long soak in a real tub—and in *hot* water.

An hour and a half later, Aerial emerged from the tub, her toes and fingertips wrinkled and pale, her hair freshly shampooed and wet, and her skin softly pink from the scrubbing she had given it. She felt revitalized and alive. Never had any bath been more appreciated.

Or needed, she thought with a soft chuckle as she bent over to flip her long wet hair forward so she could wrap a towel around her head. Giving the towel ends a quick twist, she flung it back over her crown.

Using a fresh bath sheet, she briskly dried herself, then turned to put on the clothing she had found in the wardrobe in her room. She hated using someone else's things without permission, but surely the owners would understand when they read the note of explanation she intended to write to them. She vowed right then to find a way to repay them for their hospitality.

"Oh, no," she groaned, picking up the white petticoat, then dropping it onto the stool. "I left the chemise and drawers upstairs."

Whisking the bath sheet off the floor, she hurriedly wound it around her and opened the door to the kitchen. Poking her turbaned head through the door, she peered cautiously around the empty room. "Rye?" she called. "Are you here?"

She waited a moment for his answer. When none came, she grabbed the dress and petticoat and stepped out of the bath closet.

229

Tiptoeing on bare feet, she scampered across the green linoleum kitchen floor into the hallway. She paused at the foot of the stairs. "Rye? Are you up there?"

He must be outside she decided, relieved. Clutching the clothing and bath sheet to her bosom, she hurried upstairs.

"Thank goodness," she sighed as she stepped into the bedroom and closed the door behind her. Then she giggled. What was she so worried about? It wasn't as if Rye hadn't seen her in much less than a towel when he had put the nightgown on her that first night they had come to the island, or when he had made love to her in the shack in the Adirondacks.

Of course, that was different. It was night and I was unconscious, and it was dark in the shack. Broad daylight is quite another thing!

She pushed away from the door and walked directly to the dresser where the rest of her underthings lay. Just as she started to remove the bath sheet to step into her drawers, a deep sigh, followed by a soft moan, broke the silence of the room.

Startled, she whirled around. Her gaze snapped immediately to the long, lean masculine body stretched out on the bed. "Rye!" she squealed. "What are you . . . ?"

In answer to her unfinished question, Rye's bare chest expanded as he sucked in a deep breath, then fell as he slowly released the air.

Suspicious, she studied him more closely. His full lower lip hung slightly open, his fingers were interlaced over his flat middle, and his eyes were closed. He was asleep!

Grinning, she relaxed. *Poor thing, he must be exhausted.* Her gaze roamed lazily from his bare feet up the length of his tightly trousered legs to his trim waist.

Her eyes were immediately drawn to where the buttons of his fly had been undone, exposing his deep navel and a tantalizing vee of flat belly.

Just then, a gust of wind stirred the curtains and the lock of black hair on Rye's forehead. A shiver shook his broad shoulders, and the centers of the flat, copper nipples on his smooth, muscular chest contracted into tiny kernels.

Touched by the sleeping man's total vulnerability, she crossed to the bed. Noticing that he had changed the sheets while she'd been in the bath, she felt a place deep inside her swell with emotion.

How could this be the same violent man she'd had to stop from killing her three attackers? And how could this man, who'd saved her life and cared for her more tenderly than even her mother would have, be guilty of murdering that man in Iowa?

She drew a light cover over his chest.

Without warning, Rye grabbed her wrists and jerked her off her feet. "What are you doing?" Flipping her over onto her back, he rolled on top of her, pinning her to the mattress with his weight, her wrists clamped together above her head with one punishing fist.

Fear pounding wildly in her chest, Aerial stared into Rye's angry, black eyes. "I . . . I . . ."

Recognition dawned on Rye's features almost immediately, and the viciousness in his eyes melted into an apology. "Aerial."

Aerial nodded her head weakly, finally able to speak. "You're hurting me."

He loosened his grip on her wrists, but he didn't move off her. His eyes darted uncertainly over her face. Then just as suddenly as he had grabbed her, he released her and rolled off her.

"I'm sorry. I thought—" He threw a forearm

back over his eyes. "Hell, I don't know what I thought. I just don't like anyone to sneak up on me."

"I wasn't sneaking up on you." Her voice trembled as she fought the tears that threatened to spill from her eyes. She swung her bare feet off the other side of the bed and stood up. "You looked cold and I just wanted to cover you up."

Behind her, she heard the bed ropes creak in the frame. Her feet rooted to the floor, she tensed. Even without seeing him, she could feel him moving toward her.

"I'm sorry," he said huskily. "I didn't mean to scare you."

"I thought you were going to kill me," she admitted.

"Hey," he said, his breath on her cheek and shoulder as his hands covered her arms. Slowly he turned her to face him. With gentle fingers, he lifted her chin so she had to look into his eyes. "Don't you know by now that I'd never hurt you, and that I'd kill anyone who did?"

His mouth was so close to hers that when she breathed in, she felt as if she were inhaling the very essence of him. It left her weak down to the tips of her bare toes. "Then why did you . . . ?"

"Shh." He silenced her with a brush of his lips over hers. "I didn't mean to frighten you."

The brief kiss sent erotic ripples charging through her veins. Her stomach somersaulted, and the heart of her femininity was immediately moist with passion. Incapacitating desire coiled tightly inside her, and intuitively she moved her hips closer to him.

"But you did," she murmured, her attention on his mouth. If only he would kiss her again. "My heart is still racing."

Rye's black eyes dropped to the point between

her breasts where she had secured the end of the bath sheet around herself.

Spontaneously, she straightened her shoulders and ever so slightly thrust her breasts forward.

Rye's surprised eyes flew back to her face, the look in them a question. She was surprised to see they contained something she had never expected to see.

Then it hit her. Rye was afraid. For some crazy reason, he was afraid of her!

A new sense of protective emotion welled in her chest. Unflinching, she left her own hands hanging limply at her sides, waiting for him to act.

Moving as if he were hypnotized, Rye brought his hands around to the front of her and tentatively placed his fingers on the twisted towel. Then he looked into her eyes again, his own filled with uncertainty.

A tiny little voice inside her head told her she was behaving in a totally immoral manner, but another more pressing need told her this was right — right for her and right for Rye.

Running her tongue nervously over her lips, she raised her arms and removed the towel from around her head. She dropped it to the floor, then threw back her head and shook her mane of wet hair before running her fingers through it.

"Oh, God, Aerial," he gasped, sitting back down on the bed and hauling her between his open thighs. His hands at the curve of her waist, he pressed his face to her breasts and rocked his head distraughtly from side to side. "Don't do this to me. I promised myself I wouldn't let this happen again. I can't give you what you want. You deserve so much more than someone like me."

Touched by the pain in Rye's voice, Aerial trapped his face between her palms and bent her head to kiss his black hair. "Don't you think I should be the one to decide what I deserve. And who I want?"

His fingers climbed up her back and gripped her shoulders from behind. Roughly, he forced her down to her knees in front of him so he could scowl into her eyes. "Stop it! Can't you see that I'll only destroy you? I'll take everything from you and give you nothing in return. Then I'll leave you the first chance I get. Is that what you want?"

His words cut cruelly into her heart, and she dropped her gaze from his face, tempted to pull back from him. But she couldn't.

No matter what he wanted her to believe, she couldn't forget the picture in her mind of the little boy who'd seen his family murdered in cold blood or the angry young man who'd spent his life searching for his family's killer, with no one to love—and no one who loved him.

But most of all, she couldn't forget the gentle man who hadn't been able to leave her when she had needed him most, the man who had risked his life over and over to save hers, the man who had comforted her when she was afraid, the man who had cooked for her, the man who had fed her, clothed her, sheltered her. The man who had changed the sheets for her . . .

She looked up and smiled understandingly. "Do you know what I think, Rye Berenger?" she asked, brushing the backs of her fingertips over his temples to straighten his thick, unruly hair. "I think you're not nearly as unfeeling as you want me to believe you are. In fact, I think that beneath that hard shell of yours, there's a kind and vulnerable man, a man whom life has treated so cruelly that he's afraid of being hurt if he gives his trust to anyone."

Rye grabbed her wrists and wrenched her hands away from his face. His own features were twisted with bitterness and pain. "And I think you're a naive little girl who doesn't have enough sense to know that when she plays with fire she's going to get burned!"

"Rye," she said softly, pressing her hands to his chest and leaning forward to kiss his eyes closed, "Trust me. I won't hurt you. Let me heal the wounds on your soul, the way you have healed mine."

Chapter Fifteen

Rye bolted up from the bed, lifting Aerial off her knees as he stood. Dragging her hips hard against him with one hand on her buttocks, he grabbed a handful of wet hair with the other and yanked her head back, arching her neck.

"You still don't get it, do you?" He brought his face to within an inch of hers. "I'm not who's in danger here. I'm not the one who has everything to lose and nothing to gain! You are!"

Aerial didn't resist, though the tight hold on her hair brought tears to her eyes. She fixed her stare on his face and stood her ground. "You're the one who doesn't get it, Rye. Taking risks and facing danger is all I've ever known. And I'm still here."

She watched as the internal war he was experiencing played across his countenance. Aware of the growing pressure of his manhood against her stomach, she fought the inclination to move closer.

"Damn you, Aerial Windsor!" His eyes bright and threatening, he tightened his hold on her and brought his face even closer to hers. His lips were only a quarter of an inch away now.

"Love me, Rye," she whispered, unable to resist her own need any longer.

With a helpless growl, he surrendered. He ripped the bath sheet from around her and pitched it aside, then brought his mouth down on hers.

His kiss was hard, punishing.

Startled by his sudden assault, Aerial pushed at his chest and tried to take a step back. But it was impossible. His hand tangled in her hair held her head immobile, and his kneading fingers on her buttocks dragged her hard against his grinding hips.

All thoughts of resistance left her. This was what she wanted, what she needed. Moral or immoral, safe or dangerous, crazy or practical, this was where she belonged. It was the reason she had been given a second chance at life.

She opened her mouth to receive his full kiss as she twined her arms around his torso. Possessively and greedily, she mapped the smooth flesh and muscled contours of his back with her open hands.

Her need desperate now, she drew his tongue deeper into her mouth. Delving her splayed fingers into his trousers, she caressed his buttocks and forced him closer to her hunger.

His mouth plundering her neck and shoulders with hungry nibbles, Rye turned her around so that her back was to the bed. As one, they fell to the mattress.

He brought his hands from behind her and lifted her breasts to his lips to cover them with starving kisses. Pinching one thrusting nipple between his thumb and forefinger, he took the other into his mouth and nursed it ravenously.

Electric shocks of ardor sizzled throughout Aerial's body. Instinct ruling her, she opened her thighs and climbed her heels up the side of the bed in a frantic effort to find relief from the burgeoning need at the center of her body.

Once he had thoroughly anointed both of her breasts with his kisses, Rye moved down the length of her body, his mouth and tongue scorching his brand into every inch of her stomach.

He dropped to his knees between her bent thighs. Caressing her calves, he stabilized her heels on the wooden frame of the bed. Then he wrapped his large hands over her slim hips and pressed his thumbs into the hollows where her torso met her thighs.

All thoughts of modesty destroyed, Aerial used the newfound support on the bed frame to lift her hips upward in a provocative plea.

Needing no further invitation, Rye brought his thumbs toward each other. Manipulating, caressing, he separated the moist petals of her body to expose the thrusting bud at the center of her sex. With a relieved groan, he bent his head and took her into the scalding heat of his mouth.

"Oh!" Aerial bucked as his lips clamped onto the vulnerable peak. She strained to lift her head off the bed. "Don't," she pleaded, threading her fingers into his hair as if she would pull it out. "You shouldn't . . . Oh, please . . . I can't bear . . . Ohhhh!"

The explosion came with a force that vibrated through her from head to toe. Her breathing loud and rasping, she collapsed back onto the bed.

Rye wasted no time shedding his trousers. Then, in one swift move, he clasped her knees and pressed her thighs up to her chest as he covered her body with his.

With the hurried assistance of one hand, he entered her swiftly, embedding his full length deep inside her.

Rocking her hips upward to receive each of his thrusts deeper into the straining folds of her body, she clawed at his back, desperate to get him even closer.

Over and over he drove into her body, his plunges frantic with emotion. Again, the tension

238

nside her swelled to volcanic proportions.

She clutched him tighter to her, futilely fighting o keep the ride to ecstasy from ending. But even is she struggled to postpone the inevitable explosion, her body pumped upward. Meeting each of is thrusts with more demanding urgency, her ands pulled his buttocks against her with relentess pursuit.

Then it was there, shattering her, draining her, urning her into a weak, mindless, trembling mass of glorious fulfillment.

"Ohhhh!" Rye dragged out the word through lenched teeth as he convulsively shuddered and pilled his passion deep inside her.

Almost immediately, Rye raised his head and tared down at her. His expression was concerned, is breathing irregular. "Are you all right?" he sked. "Did I hurt you?"

Aerial smiled lazily and stroked his cheek. "I'm ine." Her expression became mischievous. "Of course, I may never be able to straighten my legs gain. But otherwise . . ."

Rye immediately reacted by leaping off her so he could lower her legs. "I . . ." His eyes fell to er love-swollen sex and he swallowed back a fresh urge of desire.

"Hey!" She laughed and reached out to grab his and. "Come back here." She scooted to a more onventional position on the bed and tugged him oward her. "I was just teasing you. I'm fine! In act, I've never been so fine!"

Unable to resist, Rye joined her on the bed and overed their naked bodies with a sheet. He drew er against him and kissed the top of her head. 'In that case, I guess it's time to think about finding a way off this island."

His words sent an arrow of reality spearing into er euphoria. Her mood spiraled downward. He

239

was right. There was no reason to stay here any longer.

"Not yet," she whispered, propping herself on an elbow so that she could look down into Rye's sad black eyes. "Let's not think about it yet."

"We have to—"

She put two fingers to his lips. "Shh. Let's forget all the reasons why we should leave. For just a little bit longer, let's pretend we're the only two people in the world and that we are going to stay here forever."

Rye tightened his hold on her arm and caressed her cheek. "Like Adam and Eve in the Garden of Eden?"

She gave her head a sassy little tilt to the side and grinned. "Sounds tempting, doesn't it?"

Falling victim to her fantasy, Rye cast his common sense aside for a moment. He raised his eyebrows and poked the tip of her nose with an index finger. "Don't forget who else was in the Garden."

"The serpent? We don't have to worry about him. We left the snakes all on the mainland! But just in case, I swear I won't touch a thing that even remotely resembles an apple! Can we stay?"

He brought her head back down to his shoulder. "I guess tomorrow's plenty of time to think about leaving."

"Or the next day." She smoothed her hand over his chest and kissed the pectoral bulge closest to her mouth. "Or maybe even the day after that."

"Just a minute, now!" He chuckled, her playful mood wearing off on him. He lifted her chin and looked suspiciously into her eyes. "Did you already eat that apple when I wasn't looking?"

Aerial gave him a secretive smile. "Who, me? Why would you think that?"

A grin threatening to split his serious features, Rye shook his head in defeat. "I can't imagine!"

PEARL O'HARA STOP . . . BROOKLYN
CAFE STOP . . . HENRY STREET STOP
. . . BROOKLYN NEW YORK STOP . . .
BASED ON INFORMATION GATHERED
IN KEENE VALLEY HAVE DECIDED TO
STEAMBOAT UP CHAMPLAIN TO
ROUSES POINT IN HOPES OF INTER-
CEPTING FRIEND AT THE BORDER
STOP . . . YOUR SERVANT HERSHEL
ZIMMERMAN STOP . . . WESTPORT NEW
YORK STOP . . .

A smile on his face, Rye paused as Aerial,
wearing a gray serge bathing dress and calf-length
trousers she had found in the wardrobe, ran ahead
of him toward the private lagoon they had discovered on the island.

Letting him teach her to swim had been one of
the conditions he had forced on her before he had
agreed to extend their stay on the island. And she
had done quite well, considering the fight she had
given him at her first lesson five days before. He
still had the scratches on his back and arms from
the experience.

A lazy, contented grin stretched across his face.
Well, maybe a few of those scratches weren't from
the swimming lessons!

"Come on, slow poke!" Aerial shouted, turning
around and backing toward the water's edge.

"Don't tell me you're starting to enjoy swimming!" He continued his easy stride in her direction.

Struggling not to laugh, Aerial assumed a
haughty stance and tilted her nose in the air.
"Don't be ridiculous. What woman in her right
mind would enjoy spending a sweltering summer
day cavorting in a cool, refreshing lagoon with a

241

handsome man teaching her to swim? Especially when she could be at home doing the wash or baking or some other equally wonderful thing. Enjoy, indeed!"

"You're getting pretty sassy, Miss Windsor." Rye's expression changed to a predatory leer. Dropping their towels, he continued his purposeful amble toward her. "Maybe it's time I gave you an advanced lesson."

Giggling, Aerial backed into the water. She held out her hands, her palms toward him. "Don't you dare."

Slowly, silently, he advanced on her, his features calculating. A cat stalking a mouse.

Unable to stop laughing, Aerial checked over her shoulder to calculate her whereabouts in the lagoon, then returned her attention to Rye. Doing her best to look serious, she retreated deeper into the water. "I mean it, Rye. You'd . . . Ohhhh!"

Without warning, she tripped and toppled over. No sooner did the water close over her face and head than she felt strong, familiar arms lift her up from the bottom of the shallow inlet — waist deep for Rye, chest deep on her.

"You made me do that on purpose," she sputtered, laughing in spite of herself and slapping at his chest. "Put me down!"

Rye's face assumed a conniving wince. "If you say so." With a shrug, he released her and took a step back.

This time when Aerial emerged she came up spitting and wiping at her face. "Now you're really going to pay, Rye Berenger!" She lunged at him, her hands grabbing at his head to dunk him.

Standing firm, Rye caught her at the waist and lifted her out of the water, hooting and wiggling and squealing. He held her so that her face was even with his. "Are you sure that's what you want

242

to do?"

Her footing on the soft bottom lost, she hung from his grasp, her legs dangling helplessly in the water. To support herself, she automatically clasped her hands around his neck and circled his hips with her calves.

Without warning, their playful mood was transformed. Stunned by the passion that flared anew as she caught him between her thighs, they stared at each other for a long moment, neither of them moving. Rye's eyes turned blacker than they had ever seen them, so black that she could see her own reflection in them and could feel them penetrating to the very core of her soul.

He reached up and removed the bathing cap from her head and tossed it onto the beach. "That's more like it," he whispered, weaving his fingers through her hair to untangle it. "To swim your best, you shouldn't wear all this clothing."

She licked her lips suggestively and grinned. "And what would you suggest I wear?"

Trusting her hold on him and the water itself to keep her from falling, he released his grip on her waist and trailed his hands up her spine. His eyes never leaving hers, he unbuttoned one button on the bathing dress, then another. "That smile on your face is quite enough." He quickly slipped two more buttons through their holes.

"What are you doing?"

"I'm going to introduce you to the real joys of swimming." He slipped the dress off one shoulder, then the other.

Feeling naughtily intrigued, Aerial glanced nervously from side to side at the thick greenery surrounding the hidden cove. "You don't expect me to . . ." She stopped as he drew one of her arms from his neck and slipped it through the sleeve before returning it to his shoulder.

Her eyes opened in shock. "You mean. . . ? You can't be serious!" Without thinking, she bent her other arm to assist him as he drew it through the sleeve. "It's broad daylight! What if someone sees us?"

A taunting grin slithered across Rye's mouth. "We're the only two people in the world. Remember?" He slid the dress down to her waist.

"Still . . ." she murmured, her newly exposed breasts peaking with desire as his gaze caressed them.

"You're beautiful." His ragged breath a tribute to her, he lifted her higher so that he could kiss the objects of his adoration. "I want you," he murmured, his lips stamping his fiery brand on her water-chilled flesh.

Her mouth stretched in a surprised, mischievous grin. "Here?"

"Here and now." He fused his lips hungrily to hers, arresting any further resistance.

Aching with the fire he'd ignited, she relinquished her fragile hold on rationality and leaned into him.

Disentangling her legs from around him, he quickly peeled the bathing dress and trousers down the length of her body and pitched them onto the bank. He fumbled with his breechcloth, then added it to the growing pile of scattered clothing on the water's edge.

Dipping his head to cover her face and neck with kisses, he tenderly caressed her back and buttocks. His mouth melded to hers, he lifted her out of the water then lowered her onto his eager shaft with one sure thrust. "Oh, yes," he moaned as the tight muscles of her body grabbed at and closed around him.

Quivering with the desperate need to consume him, she clasped him to her with her ankles locked

244

around his hips, her fingers tangled in his dark hair.

Returning her kiss with equal urgency, he curved his fingers into her waist and lifted her away from him until only the pulsing tip of his manhood was inside her, then brought her down on him again.

Delirious with ecstasy, Aerial arched her neck and cried aloud. She was certain she would die. But she didn't. Again and again he lifted her almost off him, then with demanding force sheathed himself to the hilt inside her.

The fire in her blood raged hotter and hotter with each relentless drive. She was certain each breath she took would be her last, but still she survived. Then it was happening: "Rye!" she wailed aloud. The bright lights behind her closed eyelids intensified and expanded into another blinding explosion of every nerve in her.

"Yeeeessssss," he hissed through clenched teeth, as with one final plunge he spilled his seed inside her. "Oh, God, YES!"

Their hearts beating violently, their breathing ragged and their bodies still joined, Rye carried her to the bank. He carefully lowered her to a patch of downy soft moss and collapsed onto her.

Threading his fingers through her wet hair, he spread it in a halo around her head to dry.

The tremors of her climax ebbing, Aerial realized he was watching her. She opened her eyes. His handsome face wore an expression of such pure love that it brought tears to her eyes. Never in her life had she even dared to dream of knowing the joy of having someone look at her like that.

Reaching up, she caressed his face. "I lo—"

He pressed his fingers to her lips before she could finish. "Don't!" he ordered her sternly. To emphasize the one word, he raised himself off her and walked away.

Hurt and confused, Aerial sat up and stared at his back. "I don't understand. I thought—"

"That's the trouble with women," he said irritably as he retrieved the towels. Wrapping one around himself, he brought the second one to her. "You think if a man gives you physical pleasure it must be lo . . ." He cleared his throat, unable to say the word. He turned away from her again. ". . . going to last forever."

"Why are you doing this?" she asked from behind him, her voice small and injured.

Using every ounce of willpower he could muster, Rye fought his agonizing desire to go to her and tell her he had waited all his life for someone like her to love him, tell her that he wanted nothing more in this life than to spend it with her. But he didn't; he couldn't. He loved her too much.

He balled his fists tightly at his sides and forced his feet not to move. "Because it's time you understand what I've been trying to tell you. I don't want what you want."

"You don't know what I want!" she said bitterly.

"The hell I don't!" He whipped around to face her again. "Do you think I can't see it in your eyes every time you look at me, and in everything you say and do? You want a husband, Aerial!"

Embarrassed, Aerial looked down at her hands. Was she that obvious? "Is that so terrible?" she finally asked.

Feeling like a villain, Rye walked to her and lifted her chin so that she had to look at him. "No, Aerial, it's not so terrible, not if you set your sights on a man who needs a wife. I don't. You want marriage, a house and babies, and a man who wants those same things. But because I'm the only man who's ever made love to you, you've decided I'm that man."

She tried to turn her head to the side, not wanting him to see her tears, but he wouldn't let her.

"Look at me, Aerial," he ordered through clenched teeth, his grip on her face tightening. "For the first time, open your eyes and really look at me! I'm not that man. The truth is, I've enjoyed your company and your body, but I can't imagine anything worse than spending the rest of my life tied down to a wife and a brood of screaming kids. I've been on my own too many years. In fact, I'm already getting restless being stuck on this island."

Aerial searched her mind for something to say, something ugly and cruel, something that would help her cut Rye's heart out of his chest—the way he had hers. But the only words she could think of were, *No. You don't mean it. You love me. I know you do. I saw it in your eyes, in all the things you've done for me, in the way your face lights up when you see me, in the way . . .*

Fortunately, pride gave her the strength to remain silent. Instead, she turned away from him, gathered up her swimming clothes and started back for the house without speaking.

She wouldn't think about Rye or this entire unfortunate experience. She would concentrate on getting off this island, on getting back to Fairfield to claim the glory—and hopefully some financial gain—for her record-breaking flight, and on starting a new life for herself.

"I'm Hershel Zimmermann of New York City," Hershel announced to three rough-looking men at the Rouses Point boat dock. "I'd like to talk to you."

"Yeah?" one of them answered, his attention on the passengers unloading from the most recently

247

docked steamboat. " 'Bout what?"

Hershel swallowed nervously and adjusted his bow tie. Maybe this wasn't such a good idea after all. But he'd come this far. He couldn't turn back now. "I thought we might do some business."

"What kind o' business?" the second man asked, his eyes roving over Hershel's neat black suit and shoes.

Clearing his throat, Hershel stiffened his shoulders slightly. "People in town tell me you've been asking questions about an Indian traveling with a white woman . . ."

All three men jumped to attention and excitedly closed in around Hershel. "You know where that filthy bastard is?" the first man asked.

"Uh . . . not exactly . . . but I had hoped we might join forces in locating them."

The first man hooted loudly. "And just what makes you think we need another partner."

Hershel assumed his most confident air, doing his best to ignore the recurring cramp that tightened in his gut again. "For one thing, four can cover more territory than three can, and for another, I don't want a share of the reward. I just want the girl."

All three men looked at Hershel in surprise. "Who told you there was a reward?" the first man asked.

"Let's just say I have a way of getting people to share information with me, a talent that might come in handy to you if we decide to form a partnership. From what I've heard, folks aren't always too eager to talk to you. I might be able to get some information they wouldn't give to you."

The second man turned to the first. "Maybe we should give him a chance, Ned. It's been over a week since we lost 'em, and we ain't no closer to findin' 'em. For all we know, they're—"

Ned jerked his head around and glared at his partner. "Shut up, Clem. How many times I gotta tell you? They ain't dead."

"Then where are they?" asked the third man, who wore a dirty bandage wrapped around his head and over his ear. "Have you thought they might not even come this way? They coulda cut cross country to get to Canada and not even follered the lake at all."

"I'm with Sid," Clem offered. "They coulda headed due west and follered the New York Central tracks north to Canada. Or that Injun mighta jest said he was on his way to Canada to throw us off his trail."

"When he said it, he wasn't 'spectin' you to be on his trail. He was plannin' on killin' you!" Ned snarled impatiently. " 'Sides, they're on foot, and one of 'em is probably shot. You 'spect 'em to traipse across the state on foot when there's steamboats chuggin' up an' down this lake every day o' the week?"

"They could have stolen more horses," Hershel suggested.

Ned scowled at Hershel. "They're out there. I feel it in my gut." He gazed south over the lake. "They're holed up somewhere, thinkin' we'll give up and leave. But I got news for you. I'm gonna be here waitin' when that filthy bastard what killed my little brother crawls out o' his hole." He turned to Clem and Sid. "Now, are you boys gonna listen to this weaselin' stranger, or are you stickin' with me?"

"I'm with you, Ned," Sid assured him, reaching up and cupping his thickly bandaged ear. "I wanna git that Injun much as you do, and you ain't let us down yet."

"Yeah." Clem cast a disgruntled squint down at his bandaged hand. "Me too. I got my own score to handle with him, an' I guess if you're that sure, I'll hang around too. You ain't been wrong yet."

In the soft part of his belly, just below his sternum, the acidy burning that was always with Hershel reached a boil and started to spew and spit scalding pain to the surrounding areas: abdomen, ribs, chest. These men didn't know any more than he did! Still, he had no choice but to try to join up with them. After all, even if he found Aerial Windsor and her Indian companion, he couldn't take on the murdering savage by himself. He would have to have help.

Determined to ignore the bitter taste in his mouth and the burning belch wedged in his throat, he raised his eyebrows. "I assume you've talked to the steamboat operators who've docked here and asked them if they remember seeing a couple who fit Miss Windsor's and the Indian's descriptions."

"A few." Ned's answer was guarded. He obviously didn't intend to share any information with Hershel. "But they didn't tell us nothin'."

"Once they found out we wasn't wantin' to hire on, they didn't talk much," Clem offered.

Hershel stroked his chin thoughtfully. "Then that's where we should start, with the captains and the crews, maybe even with some of the passengers. If Miss Windsor and the Indian are anywhere on the lake, someone is bound to have seen something. Perhaps they saw them boarding a different steamboat, or saw them walking or riding near the shore, or heard some gossip about an Indian traveling with a white woman. I understand he's taller than average, and that she's quite beautiful and very blonde. An Indian and a white woman would stand out in a person's memory under any circumstances, so these two should be doubly memorable. They even could have left a steamboat south of here, especially if the Indian knows you know he was bound for Canada."

Ned gave Hershel a sullen glare. "You think you know so much, you talk to 'em. Me, I'm gonna have a drink and wait for the next boat to dock."

Sid and Clem both shot Hershel apologetic glances. "He's real tore up 'bout his brother gittin' killed."

"I can see that he is," Hershel said stiffly, covering up his disappointment. "So I'll have to find them on my own."

"Well, I guess that's everything," Aerial mumbled to herself as she looked around the clean kitchen. All the pots and pans had been returned to the proper shelves and cupboards; the bathtub had been covered and tucked back into its cubbyhole in the bathroom; borrowed clothing and bed linens had been washed and returned to the beds and wardrobes; and her letter had been written to the anonymous owners explaining the missing food, medical supplies, clothes, and money they had found in the desk, for which she had promised to send restitution as soon as possible.

Releasing a long sigh, she bent to pick up the carpet bag she had "borrowed" to carry extra clothing and a few toiletries. "Good-bye, house," she whispered, taking one last regretful glance at the only home she had ever known, memorizing every detail. "I'll never forget you."

A gentle hand on her shoulder startled her.

"Are you ready?" Rye asked, his voice raspy.

"Yes," she snapped, taking a hasty swipe at the tears beneath her eyes. Straightening her posture, she turned to face him. "I'm ready."

"Good. Then let's go. The boat I signaled is sending a rowboat for us. We don't want to keep them waiting, do we?"

A plea for him to send the boat away on the tip of her tongue, she opened her mouth to speak, then closed it again. She would not beg him.

A vast empty space was created in her chest by his last words. "No, we wouldn't want to keep anyone waiting." Biting back her tears, Aerial brushed past Rye through the door, knowing she was leaving her heart behind in a house on a nameless island in the middle of Lake Champlain.

Chapter Sixteen

Her vision blurred by tears, Aerial stared through the dirt-streaked train window. With a heart that was breaking, she watched Rye take two long-legged steps onto the platform of the train the next track over and one car down. She pressed her cheek to the glass in order that she might watch him until the last possible moment before he walked out of her life forever.

As if cruel, mysterious forces were conspiring to emphasize the fact that she was a fool for still clinging to the hope that he would come back for her, a huge cloud of smoke billowed from under his train, obliterating him from view — and from her life.

Long after the smoke had cleared and Rye had disappeared, Aerial continued to scan the train windows for one more glimpse. She knew it was crazy, but even now, with the obvious staring her in the face, she couldn't believe he was really gone.

All the way up Lake Champlain on the boat, she had never given up hoping he would change his mind and take her with him. Then, when he had decided it would be easier to slip unnoticed into Canada on a train than by water or on foot and had bought tickets for them both on the train out of East Alburg, Vermont, she had known for certain he intended to stay with her.

A bitter smile twisted her mouth as she thought about her own stupidity — again. He had never had any intention of taking her with him. The only reason he had come this far with her was because he'd had no choice. The northbound train out of East Alburg he had hoped to take wasn't due through there for several days. So, rather than risk staying in the States to wait for it, he had boarded the westbound train with her, planning to transfer to the Canada-bound Delaware and Hudson at Rouses Point.

He didn't even tell me how to get in touch with him to let him know when I've cleared his name and it's safe to return to the United States, she thought dejectedly. *Not that he has any right to expect me to help him after what he's done to me. It would serve him right if I just let that deposition stand.*

Having run out of ideas for how to find Aerial Windsor, and not wanting to waste any more of Pearl's money on a wild-goose chase, Hershel had come to the depot that morning to buy his return ticket to New York City. Since there wasn't a train leaving until much later in the day, he had decided he might as well hang around the station and ask a few questions.

Of course, he hadn't really expected to learn anything new. Surely by now Aerial Windsor and the Indian were either a long way from here or had indeed met the same fate in Lake Champlain her parents had met in the Mississippi River five years ago.

But what the hell? He didn't have anywhere else to go, and asking people questions was better than just sitting on a wooden bench in the depot thinking about his latest failure, not to mention the constant pain in his belly.

And there was the fact that the train station

was the only place in Rouses Point he hadn't checked during the last three days. There could be a conductor or porter who might remember seeing Aerial Windsor and the Indian on a train or in some town along their route. They might even be able to tell him if they had heard of any unidentified bodies being washed up on shore in the past few weeks.

However, after several hours of talking to conductors and porters and passengers with no results, Hershel had finally come to the conclusion that he needed to sit down and rest, even if it meant he finally had to face his own inadequacies.

Just as he was about to lower his weary body onto a hard depot bench, the station master announced that a train out of Rutland, Vermont, had just pulled into the station. Exhausted, Hershel had decided to let this one go. That is, until he learned to his surprise that the Rutland tracks ran the entire length of Grand Island, *in the middle of Lake Champlain!*

His energy miraculously revived, Hershel's mood soared with new optimism. He knew it was a long shot, but like a gambler about to end a lengthy losing streak, he had a gut feeling this would be the hand that was going to change his luck.

Minutes later, Hershel rushed along the walkway between the two tracks, his rapidly beating heart battling with the constant gnawing in his belly for attention. "It's just a coincidence," he mumbled to himself, afraid to believe what the last porter he had spoken to had told him. His eyes darted frantically over the windows of the passenger cars of the Rutland train. "There must be dozens of blond women with dark-haired companions on these trains."

He paused as a billow of smoke filled the space between the trains. "Besides, the porter said the man didn't dress or even talk like an Indian," he reminded himself over and over as he waited for the air to clear. He was determined not to let his expectations run away with him, not this time. *The man he saw with a young blonde woman could be a Mexican, or an Italian or even a Mediterrian Jew, like me."*

As if in a dream, the smoke from the train rose and cleared. And suddenly, there she was. Aerial Windsor!

Hershel's heart stopped for a full second. He would have recognized the face staring out the train window anywhere. She was more beautiful and grown up now than he remembered her from five years before, but it was her. There was no doubt.

He had found Aerial Windsor!

Stunned, Hershel couldn't move for several long moments. He broke out in a sweat. What if he hadn't followed his instinct and checked this last train? What if he'd given up and left town yesterday? Tomorrow? What if . . . ?

Another puff of smoke spit from beneath the train, shaking Hershel out of his paralyzed state. Breaking into a run, he made a dash for the nearest steps onto the train, a train that carried his future within its interior.

"Aerial Windsor?" a man's voice asked from her left.

Aerial froze. Her heart leaped into her throat and formed a strangling bottleneck in her windpipe. There was no doubt in her mind that the people from Keene Valley had come to arrest her for her part in Rye's escape.

256

Her gloved hands knotted into tight fists in her lap, she shot a frantic glance at the train across the way to make sure Rye wasn't in sight. Even if she'd been found, she knew she still had to protect him. After all, no one was going to hang her.

Reasonably confident that Rye wasn't where he could be seen from her window, she slowly turned her head toward the aisle.

"I beg your pardon," she finally answered. "Were you spea—?" She stopped, her eyes springing open wide. "Mr. Zimmermann?"

A relieved smile stretched across Hershel Zimmermann's face. "I knew it!" he crowed. "It *is* you!" He collapsed into the seat beside her.

"What are you doing here? Where did you come from?"

"I've been looking for you!"

"For me? Why?"

"I read about your record flight in the New York papers and wanted to tell you personally how proud I am of you and to talk about your future plans." He placed a business card in her hand and shook his head. "I can't tell you how relieved I am to see you. Everyone was certain you were dead."

A shot of alarm raced through Aerial. "Everyone? Who is everyone?"

"I ran into a three-man posse from Keene Valley at the boat dock who're looking for that murdering Indian who kidnapped you. There's a five-thousand-dollar reward for his capture—dead or alive."

Thinking back, Aerial remembered Clem or Ned mentioning the huge increase, but the horrible significance of having such an outrageous reward on Rye's life only now registered in her conscious mind. A cold chill of terror shimmied up her spine. "Three men from Keene Valley

257

here? In this town? Are you certain? Do they know I'm here?"

"No, of course not, not unless one of them followed me. But that's not too likely, since I told them I was going back to New York. But why do you ask? I would think you'd be anxious to know they've come to rescue you from that heathen." He paused, a terrified expression suddenly transforming his face as his eyes nervously scoured the car. "Where is he? How did you escape from him?"

She chanced a quick peek at the other train, then directed her eyes back to Hershel. It was obvious he believed Ned and Clem and Sid were legitimate lawmen and that Rye was a murderer. For all she knew, he could even be working with them!

"Relax, Mr. Zimmermann. He's gone," she lied, doing her best to keep her voice even. "But I didn't have to escape. He put me on this train in East Alburg and took another train from there into Canada. By now, he's safe."

"Safe?" Hershel repeated, his features puzzled. "That's an odd thing for you to say about a savage who kidnapped you and dragged you all over the country against your will." He paused, suddenly looking quite worried. "It was against your will, wasn't it?"

Aerial peered into Hershel's eyes, trying to decide how much she should tell him, if anything. Could she trust him?

When he worked for her parents, she hadn't really known him that well. While the family had performed in one town, Hershel had usually been in the next town they were scheduled to play so he could set up advance promotion for their act. In fact, Aerial had only seen Hershel when the family first arrived at each stop on their tour.

258

Once the balloonists were settled in their hotel, Hershel had quickly explained the newest setup to her father, then was immediately off to a new destination, sometimes the same day. But he had always been good to her when she was a little girl, and her father had trusted him totally.

Her eyes shifted to the right to look at the other train, then to the left to the man beside her. If he had found her, so could the men from Keene Valley. Besides, she didn't exactly have anyone else to turn to.

"Those men aren't real lawmen," she said. "And Rye Berenger isn't a murderer *or* a kidnapper. I wasn't his prisoner. He was defending me from them, but they're determined to kill both of us."

By the time she had quickly told Hershel the entire story, minus certain personal details and the fact that Rye was on the next train over, Aerial sensed that Hershel was on her side. "So, will you help me get back to Iowa to clear his name, Mr. Zimmermann? Don't you see? It's the least I can do after the havoc I caused in his life when I signed that deposition."

His face looking as if he were going to be sick to his stomach, Hershel gripped his middle. "What about the havoc he's caused in *your* life? Because of him, your life is in danger. You've lost your balloon, and your reputation has no doubt been tarnished almost beyond repair."

"None of it was his fault. Because of me, he had no choice but to do whatever it took to survive. Still, in spite of what I did, he risked his own life more than once to protect me when he could have left me and gotten safely away. Don't you see? I owe it to him to right the wrong I've done him. Now, will you help me or not?"

His olive complexion turning a sickly green,

259

Hershel patted her hand consolingly. "Of course I'll help you, my dear."

"Thank goodness." She breathed a sigh of relief and sagged back in her seat. Idly, she scanned the area outside between the trains. "Oh!" she squealed, sitting up straight.

"What is it?" Hershel asked, looking past her.

"One of them is out there!" She held her hand up to the side of her face and presented the back of her head to the window. "It's the one named Sid. What's he doing here?"

Hershel leaned past her, straining to see. At first he thought it had been her imagination, but then he saw the man Aerial had seen coming in their direction, all the while searching the windows of the other train as he did.

"Evidently they had the same idea I had. It doesn't look like he's seen you, though. Just keep your head turned this way and he'll go on by. Besides, he's looking through the Canada-bound train. They think that's where you're going. He won't come over here."

"You don't understand!" Aerial hissed, on the verge of doing something, anything, to call Sid's attention away from the other train, even if it meant exposing herself. She just knew she couldn't take a chance that Rye would be beside a window.

Hershel gave her a thoughtful frown. "What don't I understand?"

"If Sid is here, that means the others are, too. He's always with them. They must be searching this train for us. I've got to do something!" She started to rise.

Hershel contemplated the problem for a minute. "Maybe I can distract them." Giving her arm a pat, he bolted up from the seat. "I know! I'll tell them I saw you get on that other train. It's about to leave the station, so they'll have to get on if they want to search it thoroughly. By the time they realize they've been fooled, they'll be miles north of here and we'll be gone."

Aerial gasped, grabbing at his sleeve to stop him. "No! You can't tell them that!"

"Why not? I think it's a good idea."

Think, Aerial! Why not? she screamed to herself over the panic roaring in her ears. "Uh . . . because . . . uh . . . because they might see you coming from this train and know you're lying. They'll think you're trying to trick them so you can collect the reward for yourself!"

"I'll make sure they don't see me!"

"*And* they'll expect you to search the train with them!"

Hershel silently pondered her logic.

"Maybe you could tell them you thought you saw me board this train and followed me, but that the woman you saw turned out to not be me!"

"I don't know. They might not believe me and come looking for you anyway."

"I'll hide in the restroom!" Her tear-filled eyes implored him. "Please, Mr. Zimmermann! There's no other way!" She gave him a long, tearful look. "For the sake of my parents!" she pleaded.

"All right. I suppose it could work. Pull down your shade and wait here. I'll be back to escort you to Iowa just as soon as I've gotten rid of them."

"I'll be forever in your debt, Mr. Zimmermann. I know my parents would rest easier if they could know I'm in your care now."

A triumphant smile skittered across Hershel's face and he hurried down the aisle.

The instant Hershel disappeared through the front exit, Aerial stuffed his card into her pocket, grabbed her carpetbag, and bolted for the rest-room at the opposite end of the car. She had to find Rye and warn him! Moving as quickly as she could in the tight space, she put on the black, hooded cape she had brought from the house on the island.

Seconds later she stood on the platform at the rear of the car, feeling slightly guilty for running out on Mr. Zimmermann. But it couldn't be helped. She had to warn Rye.

Making a mental note to write Hershel a note explaining her disappearance, she clutched the cape and hood tightly at her throat and peered up and down the walkway, looking for her pursu-ers.

With a loud hiss of smoke and the clangorous strain of car couplings, Rye's train lurched for-ward a few feet, then stopped. Frantic to get to him, she stepped off the train into the concealing vapor that filled the walkway between the tracks.

Running blindly, she slammed into the hard wall of a male chest. Before she could stop her-self, she screamed.

The man cut off her scream with his hand over her mouth and whisked her up into his arms "Shut up! It's me!" He removed his hand and made a dash toward the other train.

Immediately recognizing Rye's voice, Aerial sagged against him with relief. "Rye! Thank goodness! Sid is here in the station looking for us on these trains! And the others are probably here too!"

"I know." He picked up his stride toward the Canada-bound train, which was starting to move out. "I saw Clem and Ned talking to a conductor, who was pointing in the direction of your car." Tightening his arms around her, he quickened his pace and leaped onto the slowly rolling train.

Suddenly it occurred to her that it had been no accident that Rye had been there. He had been coming back for her. At another risk of exposing himself and missing his own train to safety, he hadn't been able to leave her at the mercy of the bounty hunters. That had to mean something, didn't it?

Of course it did! It meant he loved her!

Her heart singing despite the danger that still threatened them, she smiled to herself and pressed her face to his chest. Whether Rye Berenger knew it or not, he loved her. And sooner or later he was going to admit it to her and to himself, because she was never going to let him leave her again!

His feet rooted to the ground in the shadows of the Ottawa, Ontario depot, Rye stared down the tracks long after the caboose of the train carrying Aerial Windsor out of his life had disappeared from view. Putting her on that train had been the most difficult thing he'd ever done in his life, even more difficult than it had been when he had left her in Rouses Point.

In Rouses Point his resolve had been bolstered by his anger at her for not understanding why they didn't belong together. But now, after three days of constantly being with her and denying himself the comfort of her body while they had waited for the train to take her back to the United States, he couldn't feel anything but loneliness.

If he could have made love to her just one more time, maybe the loss he was feeling wouldn't be so bad. Unfortunately, the knowledge that he had done the right thing by restraining himself didn't help. Right that minute, knowing that if he'd allowed himself the luxury of making love to her again he wouldn't have been able to put her on that train didn't help one damn bit!

"You look like you just lost your best friend," a throaty female voice cooed from behind him. He felt a woman's hand on his sleeve.

Rye tensed, then relaxed. Maybe a woman was exactly what he needed to blot Aerial out of his mind once and for all.

Lazily, he began a slow turn to face the woman.

"As a matter of fact I . . ." His eyes widened. "What the hell!"

A combination of happiness and anger such as he'd never known roared through him. He twisted his head to view the tracks where the train had been, then returned his intense stare to the smiling woman. "What are you doing here? Why aren't you on that train?"

Aerial grinned sheepishly and shrugged her shoulders. "Would you believe me if I told you I couldn't find my ticket when the conductor came by to collect them, so he put me off the train?"

Fighting his impulse to squeeze her to him and cover her face with kisses, Rye did his best to look furious. "No, I wouldn't."

Aerial rolled her eyes as if she were thinking. "Well, then, what if I told you I had to come back because I forgot my carpetbag?" She held up the case for him to see.

Rye arched his eyebrows and crossed his arms over his chest. He shook his head.

Her eyes twinkling with mischief, Aerial thought for a minute more. "I'm afraid to travel alone?" she finally suggested.

"Aerial!" He grabbed her by the arms and jerked her to him. "I'm not in the mood for your games. Now tell me the truth! Why aren't you on that train?"

"The truth?"

"The truth."

Aerial's playful expression grew serious and she caught his cheeks between her palms. "Because, whether you like it or not, Rye Berenger, it's your fault I'm here and you have an obligation to get me safely back to Iowa."

He felt himself mellowing in spite of what common sense told him his reaction should be. "I thought that's what I was doing when I put you on that train." Unconsciously, he slid his hands around her and interlaced his fingers at the small of her back to bring her closer to him.

"Do you realize what terrible things could happen to a woman traveling across the country by herself? As a matter of fact, there were some very shifty-eyed passengers on the train with me."

The corner of Rye's mouth twitched up in a half grin. "I didn't see any shifty-eyed passengers."

"That's because they got on after you left," she said with a winning grin that said, *I can match every argument you give me.*

"Do you really expect me to believe that?"

"Are you suggesting I would lie?" she asked, her eyes open in wide-eyed innocence.

He clicked his tongue against his teeth and shook his head fatalistically. "Now, why would I do that?"

Looping her hands around his neck, Aerial raised up on her toes to bring her face closer to his. "Face it, Mr. Berenger. You saved my life, so now you're stuck with me."

"Oh, really?" he asked with an arched eyebrow. "And how exactly did you come up with that peculiar little bit of logic?" He grinned in spite of himself.

"When I was a little girl, a wise old Chinese man who worked for my father when we were in San Francisco told me that if one person saves the life of another person, then from that day forward, that person's life belongs to you."

"Neither one of us is Chinese, Aerial."

She shrugged, obviously confident that she had won him over. "That's an unimportant technicality. So! Are you going to live up to your responsibility and take me with you? Or are you going to leave me *alone* and *defenseless* in a strange country with Ned and Clem and Sid apt to show up here any time now?"

Rye knew she was fully aware of how her subtle threat would affect him, but he was just too happy to see her to be angry.

He held his hands out to his sides in defeat. "I must be crazy."

"Yes!" she squealed, throwing her arms around his neck and kissing him on the mouth. "I knew it!"

Gripping her upper arms, he held her away from him. "This is only a trial. The minute it gets too dangerous or you start to slow me down, I'm putting you on the nearest train. Is that understood?"

"Understood."

"Good!" He had the feeling he had just made the decision to step off the steep ledge of a cliff. There would be no turning back for him — ever. "Then I guess the first thing we should do is cash in your ticket and buy you a horse and some clothes more suitable for riding."

"I already did that," she announced with a smug grin. "My horse is in the stable with yours. We can leave any time you're ready."

"It'll be interesting to see how long that confidence of yours lasts once your butt's black and blue from sitting in a saddle all day; and your eyes are so dried out from the wind you can't blink them; and that fair skin of yours gets sunburned and starts to peel like fish scales, and you have nothing to eat but hardtack and water for days on end, and—"

"Why, Rye Berenger! Are you trying to frighten me into changing my mind?"

"I'm not trying to frighten you. I just want to be sure you know all the facts. I don't want you to be able to say I didn't warn you."

Chapter Seventeen

Unable to fathom the abject poverty and misery she saw, Aerial halted her horse and stared at the isolated Indian village before her. Using the back of a wrist, she wiped the sweat from her forehead and out of her eyes, as if she thought she could wipe away the bleak scene.

None of this made any sense. Where were the bright feathers and beautifully beaded clothing the Indians wore in the Wild West shows she had seen? Where were the healthy, well-fed children who were supposed to live on the reservations now that the government was supplying their food and medical care and clothing? Where were the beautiful Indian princesses and handsome young braves she had read about in Ned Buntline's dime novels?

She took off the man's hat Rye had insisted she wear and used it to fan herself. "I don't understand," she mumbled, shaking her head as she continued to survey the colorless terrain. "It's all the same color."

There wasn't a single tree to break the monotonous, dun-colored hue of everything in sight. The tepees, the clothing, the cracked, arid soil, the dead prairie grass that stretched for miles around them, the animals—everything seemed to be the same grayish brown color. "I thought . . ."

"What, Aerial?" Rye asked, his own hurting gaze riveted on the bedraggled old people, the hollow-eyed youngsters, and the wary young women who huddled outside their teepees watching the two visitors at the edge of their village. "Did you think there would be a happy celebration to welcome us? Maybe a huge feast and wild dances?"

Confused and embarrassed by the bitterness in Rye's tone, Aerial shook her head. "No, of course not. It's just that . . . Why are they living like this? Where are the schools and supplies and homes I've read the government has given them?"

"Propaganda printed in the newspapers to make the government look good and to keep the truth a secret."

"And what about the men? The only ones I see are either very old or just little boys. Where are the others?"

"The ones who aren't in the army stockades sneak off the reservation to hunt for food for their families, since the People would starve if they didn't have more than the meager rations the government provides."

"This is disgraceful. Isn't there anything that can be done about it?"

Before Rye could answer, an old woman pushed her way through the crowd and hobbled toward them. *"Hau.* Hello," she said, her voice unexpectedly strong, considering her frail-looking body. *"Nituwe he?*—Who are you?" she asked. *"Taku ca yacin he?*—What do you want?"

A wave of sadness covered Rye's face and he dismounted. "It is Walks Two Trails, Grandmother," he answered in Lakota.

The black of her eyes murky with old age, the woman squinted and leaned forward to examine better the tall stranger.

"Walks Two Trails?" she repeated, obviously not trusting him. "How do I know you tell the truth? You wear the clothing of the *wasican*—white

269

man—and your woman is white."

"*Ohan, Unci.* Yes, Grandmother. My woman and my clothing are white, as was my father, Hair of Fire. But my heart is Lakota, as was my mother's."

Aerial didn't understand what Rye had just said to the old woman, but she saw when recognition dawned in the nearly blind eyes. She felt relieved for Rye.

She had known he was uneasy about coming back, afraid there would be no one who knew him after his long absence. Thank heavens, at least this one woman remembered him. Hopefully, there were others.

After a few more minutes of conversation Rye reached up to lift Aerial from her horse. "This is my grandmother. We can stay in her teepee. The agent isn't due back to take a head count for the next allotment shipment for at least two more weeks, so we'll be safe. It would be hard on the whole tribe if the authorities found a wanted man in their midst."

"What about your grandfather?"

Rye's expression darkened. "We're too late. He's gone."

"Gone? Hunting with the others?"

Rye shook his head sadly. "No. He died in his sleep a month ago."

"Oh, Rye, I'm so sorry."

"Don't be. It was for the best. He started dying when the government forced him to live like a prisoner in his own land. He's finally free again. Now, say *hau* to my grandmother."

Aerial approached the older woman and took her gnarled hands in her own. "*Hau,* my name is Aerial. Rye has told me so much about you."

"My grandson and his woman are welcome in my teepee," the woman said in broken English,

270

drawing Aerial's face down close to her own. "But do not stay long. It is not safe for my grandson here. He must leave this evil place before many days go by. The old ways of his mother's people are dying, and he must live in the ways of his father if he is to survive."

That night, after a meager supper of boiled roots and herbs, Aerial lay beside Rye on the blankets they had shared the past two months as they had crossed Canada on horseback, before entering the United States to visit his grandparents on the reservation in the southern part of the Dakota territory. He had decided that he needed to see them one more time before he rode into Iowa with her, just in case things didn't go as planned.

"Are you asleep?" she whispered.

"No," Rye answered, rolling over onto his back to wrap his arm around her and rest her head on his shoulder. "What's the matter?"

"Nothing. I was just thinking about some things your grandmother said." She gently caressed his muscular chest.

"What things?"

"Did you tell her I was your woman?"

Rye's chest rose as he breathed in deeply, then fell as he released the air from his lungs. "I thought it would set her mind at ease about me if she believed I wasn't alone."

"I am, you know."

"What?"

"Your woman." She propped herself up on one elbow and gazed down into his dark eyes. They glistened in the moonlight that filtered in through the smoke hole at the top of the teepee. Though it was customary for Lakota families to sleep in the same teepee, his grandmother had chosen to spend the night with her daughter to give Rye and his new bride some privacy. "I am your woman."

"Aerial, don't start this again," he said with a weary moan. "We've been over it too many times. We're wrong for each other, and once we get you back to Iowa and you've cleared my name, we're going our separate ways."

"Why can't you admit you love me, Rye?"

"Because I don't," he said through gritted teeth, his gaze avoiding hers.

They'd had this argument so many times, Aerial wasn't even hurt by his words. "You do! And we both know it."

"I don't! How can I make it any clearer?"

She caught his jaw in her hand and rolled his head toward her so that he had to look at her. "Maybe I'd believe you don't love me if you could look me in the eye and tell me, Rye. But you can't do that, can you?"

His jaw clenching, Rye stared directly into her eyes. "Aerial, I don . . ." his eyes shifted involuntarily to the side, ". . . 't love you."

"Aha! I knew it! You can't do it, can you!? See? You do love me!"

"All right!" he snarled, twisting his face out of her hand and sitting up. "I give up. I admit what I feel for you *might* be more than just lust. And if we were two different people I *might* even do something crazy like ask you to marry me."

Aerial's heart soared. This was the closest he had come to admitting how he felt for her. The idea of marriage had even occurred to him!

"But we're not two different people," he went on. His elbows propped on his bent knees, he held his head in his hands. "And no matter what we think we feel right now, it's all going to change once you're back with your own kind of people."

Aerial slipped her arms around his waist and

272

pressed her cheek to his stooped back. "You're wrong, Rye. Nothing's going to change the fact that I love you."

"I'm not wrong, Aerial. You'll see. Once the good citizens of Fairfield begin to stare at you and whisper about you and avoid you on the streets like you have smallpox because you've spent all these weeks in the company of an Indian, you'll end up hating me because of what I've done to you. Believe me, you'll want to get as far away from me and that town as you can so you can start over where no one knows about me."

Aerial sat up and reached around to turn Rye's head so he looked back over his shoulder at her. "And where is that town, Rye? Between the wanted posters and the telegraph wires and the newspapers, do you really think there's anywhere in the United States where they haven't heard about my balloon flight and the Indian who 'abducted' me?"

"As long as they believe you were held against your will—and if you stick to the story that there was nothing physical between us—they'll forget. Without me there to remind them what happened, you'll be able to put this all behind you and have the kind of life you're looking for with a man who can give you the things you deserve."

"You've got my future all figured out for me, don't you, Rye? But you've overlooked a couple of not-so-minor details that are going to put a kink in your plans."

His dark brows arched. "Oh? And what would those details be?"

Aerial shrugged and dropped her hold on his face. "For one thing, I don't intend to come all this way to clear your name of murder charges, just to see you arrested, and probably hung anyway, for kidnapping. And that's what will happen if I lie and say you forced me to stay with you."

He didn't answer right away, and she could see he hadn't thought of that. "In that case, I'll only take you as far as Sioux City and put you on a train back to Fairfield. I'll be long gone by the time you get there. They'll never find me to arrest me."

"You promised to see me safely back to Fairfield."

"I promised to see you back to Iowa. You don't really expect me to ride into a town where they have a noose with my name on it already strung up, do you? They'd have me tried and hung before you could tell them the truth. Now what's the other detail I overlooked?"

Aerial closed her eyes and sucked in a deep, fortifying breath. "No one's going to believe we didn't make love."

"Of course they won't. But it'll be your word against what they *think* happened. They won't know for sure unless one of us tells them, and as time passes, it'll all die down."

Aerial winced slightly. "I'm afraid that whether we tell them or not, time is going to work against us, rather than for us. The more time that passes, the more obvious it's going to be that our relationship wasn't platonic." Unconsciously, she caressed her tummy.

Rye's eyes dropped to her waist, then jumped back to her face, his expression disbelieving—and horrified. "You mean. . . ?"

Aerial nodded her head and smiled, suddenly shy. "I'm going to have your baby."

Rye squeezed his eyes closed and shook his head. "God, this can't be happening." He snapped his eyes open and explored her face. "Are you sure? How long have you known? Why didn't you tell me before now?"

"Up till now, I only suspected I might be. But while we were preparing supper I talked to your grandmother, and now I know for sure that I am going to have a baby. She says it should be a spring baby—late March or early April."

As if he were touching something holy, he gently placed his hand on her flat stomach. "A baby. My baby."

Aerial covered his hand with both of hers and pressed it to her. "*Our* baby. A baby conceived from our love, Rye. Now do you see why we can't go our separate ways when we get to Iowa? Our baby needs a father and a mother. Together we can give him, or her, all the love and security you and I never had."

"God, Aerial. You're so innocent and trusting. Don't you realize it will never happen that way? When people learn the father of this baby is a half-breed, he'll become an outcast, belonging nowhere, accepted nowhere. Is that what you want for your child? Or for yourself?"

"No, of course not, but—"

"Aerial! There are no *buts* here. No one can ever know the child you carry is mine!"

Aerial bristled to hide the hurt she was feeling. "For the baby's sake or for yours, Rye?"

"What are you talking about?"

"Isn't it obvious? Life with me is such a distasteful thought for you that you would stand by and watch your own baby branded a bastard rather than marry me and give him your name." She took an angry swipe at her tear-drenched cheeks.

Stunned, Rye shook his head and reached for her to embrace her. "No, you've got it all wrong."

"Do I, Rye? I don't think so." She turned away from him. "And I have no one to blame but myself. You told me from the beginning you didn't care. But I was too stupid and too stubborn to listen, wasn't I? Like everything I've ever done, I actually thought determination and perseverance were the answers. I really believed that if I worked hard and stayed with you long enough I could make you love me and want me. Crazy, huh?" Draping a blanket over her shoulders, she walked over to the raised side of the teepee and gazed out onto the vast Dakota prairie. The sky was so clear, the stars so bright that they seemed to be close enough to touch. Had stars ever been more beautiful, or made her feel so lonely and forsaken? She didn't see how.

"Aerial?" he asked from just behind her. His breath tickled the tiny hairs on her neck as his hands clasped her upper arms.

"What?!" she spat out, flinching at his touch.

"I do love you. More than life itself."

She tensed. Her heart skipped and the air remained trapped in her lungs. "You do?"

He rested his chin on the top of her head and crossed his arms over her waist, drawing her back against him. He released a soft chuckle. "I tried not to."

She felt him shake his head.

"God, how I tried not to. But I was probably lost from the first time I set eyes on you, when you were dangling from that balloon over Fairfield. But for sure from the moment I looked down the barrel of my revolver and saw those beautiful blue eyes of yours glaring back at me, daring me to fire."

Refusing to believe the hope that soared anew in her blood, Aerial didn't move. "Then why—"

"It's because I love you . . ." He dropped his hands lower on her body and splayed his fingers over her belly. ". . . and because I love this baby that I have to go away and never see either

276

of you again."

She tried to protest, but he stopped her.

"Just hear me out, Aerial. For once listen to me with your mind and not with your heart."

Aerial nodded her assent, knowing nothing he could say would lessen the glow she felt from hearing him say he loved her and their baby. If that was true, there was no obstacle life could deal them that they couldn't overcome.

"Our baby will only be one-quarter Indian," he pointed out softly, "so that means there's every chance he, or she, could inherit your family's coloring, or even my father's red hair and light skin. And if that's the case, no one ever has to know about his Indian blood unless I'm there to expose the truth."

"But—"

"Don't you see, Aerial? Without me there to poison his life, our child can live as a white in a white world. He can have all the opportunities and advantages that come with being white. He can go anywhere, do anything, be anything he wants to be—*as long as no one knows he has Indian ancestors*.

"But if we reveal his true heritage, it will be the same thing as condemning him to a life of discrimination. He'll have only two choices: he can come back to the reservation and live a degrading life of poverty, or he can work for men who will treat him as if he has no feelings and is no better than an animal. In fact, whites won't treat him with as much respect as they give their horses and hunting dogs.

"He can be falsely accused, beaten, whipped, arrested, or even hung at the slightest whim of a white man, and his attackers will be applauded. And God forbid he should find a white woman attractive, or catch a white man cheating at a

277

game of cards, or try to get a room in a decent hotel or a meal in a family restaurant or a drink of whiskey in a saloon. God forbid he should kill a white man in self-defense . . ." He paused. "Should I go on?"

"No," Aerial whispered hoarsely, the tears streaming down her face. They were not only for herself and for her unborn baby, but for the man whom she knew without a doubt had personally suffered every one of the injustices he had just listed. No wonder he was so bitter; no wonder he was afraid to love her; no wonder he thought he wasn't good enough for her.

She turned in his arms and took his face in her hands. Gently, she wiped the pads of her thumbs under his eyes to wipe away his tears.

"All right. I've listened to you. Now, you listen to me. I'm telling you right now, Rye Berenger, I don't intend to raise this baby alone, and I refuse to stand by and let you walk out of our lives. This baby is going to know who both his mother and his father are, even if we have to follow you from one end of this country to the other. Life may not be easy for this baby, but in one way or another life is hard for everyone. We can do our best to protect and shelter our child, but in the long run he'll survive and take care of himself because he'll know he has the strength of both the whites and the Indians flowing in his blood—and the love of both his parents."

She kissed him on the mouth and smiled. "Now, are you going to ask me to marry you? Or are you going to add the stigma of being illegitimate to this child's burden?"

Aerial rubbed her thumb back and forth over the thin silver band Rye had slipped onto her finger, and a feeling of such happiness washed over her that she actually felt her knees go weak.

"Therefore," the elderly minister from the reservation's Episcopalian mission continued, "by the powers vested in me, I pronounce you man and wife." He gave Aerial and Rye a sympathetic smile and took their joined hands in his. His tired eyes were warm with concern. "May God go with you. You have chosen a very difficult road to follow."

It had been a very brief ceremony, with only the reverend's wife as a witness. No music, no flowers, no guests, no white dress. Yet none of that mattered to Aerial. Even the makeshift wedding ring Rye had fashioned from a silver coin was perfect. The only thing that mattered to her was that she was married to the father of her child and that he was the man she loved with all her heart.

Aerial stepped off the noon stagecoach out of Ottumwa, Iowa. Breathing a sigh of relief, she canvassed the Fairfield town square. It wouldn't be long now. All she had to do was visit the sheriff's office to rescind the deposition against Rye then go by the bank to close her account and claim the reward the town merchants had put in trust for her to show their appreciation for the publicity they had expected her flight to bring to Fairfield.

She grinned and lightly touched her stomach. *We'll be back with your daddy and on our way to our wonderful new life in no time at all,* she silently promised her baby. Though Rye was hidden nearby, they had decided it would be best for her to come into town alone to clear the way.

After all she had witnessed the past three months where white justice for Indians was concerned, Aerial had finally realized that having right on her side was no guarantee it would be

279

safe for Rye in Fairfield. It had taken her long enough to learn, but now that she had, she had no intention of telling anyone where Rye was before she had a paper in her hands declaring him innocent of any wrongdoing in Iowa.

Looking neither left nor right, Aerial strode directly toward the city jail, her posture and demeanor determined. She briefly paused outside the sheriff's office and straightened her hat. Adjusting her jacket, she took a deep breath and placed her gloved hand on the door latch. *This is it!* she told herself and whisked open the wooden door.

Inside the jail, nothing had changed. Same two scarred desks, same hat and coat rack beside the door, same scuffed plank floor. The officer on duty sat with his chair tilted back on two legs, his own booted ankles crossed on his desk, his fingers interlaced across his paunchy middle, his hat pulled down over his eyes.

Aerial cleared her throat.

The thud of the third and fourth chair legs hitting the floor resounded through the room as the man clumsily knocked his hat back on his head and tried to look alert. "Can I hel—?"

The sleep immediately cleared from the sheriff's eyes as they grew round with disbelief. "Miss Windsor?!"

She smiled cordially. "Good afternoon, Sheriff Riley."

"My God!" he gasped. His chair scraped loudly across the wooden floor as he stood up. His expression aghast, he rounded the desk and rushed toward her. "Where'd you come from? We figgered you were dead!" He clutched her arm and pulled her toward a chair. "Here, sit down! Are you all right?"

He inspected the office as if he were at a loss for what to do next. "No one's gonna believe this!

How'd you get here? Where've you been? What happened to the Indian? God! Wait'll Chester Hagen hears you're all right."

Aerial frowned. "Who's Chester Ha—" Her expression changed as the vague memory of a white-haired older gentleman dawned on her. "The man who represented the Chamber of Commerce at my sendoff ceremony?"

The sheriff nodded, his grinning face red and glistening with sweat. "That's him, all right. I don't mind tellin' you he's been drivin' me plain loco ever since we got word that Injun took you. He's been in here pretty near ever day sayin' he wouldn't rest 'til he knew for sure that Injun was dead for what he done. He even offered a five-thousand dollar reward to whoever brung him in—dead or alive."

"That brings me to what I must talk to you about, Sheriff. There has been a serious mis—"

The sheriff held up his hand to stop her from proceeding. "Hold that thought, Miss Windsor." He hurried over to the door that she knew led back to the cells, since it was through that door Aerial had first seen Rye up close. "I better send one o' the boys to get Chester. He'll already be after my hide if he finds out I took even this long to let him know you're back."

Aerial bit back the rest of her statement. The sheriff was obviously too excited to listen to what she had to say right then. She would just have to wait until the shock of her sudden appearance wore off some before she completed her business with him.

It was only a matter of minutes before Chester Hagen rushed into the sheriff's office. Puffing with exertion, he went directly to Aerial's chair. He gripped the arms of her chair and brought his muttonchop-whiskered face down close to hers.

"Where's the Indian? Is he dead?"

Surprised as well as offended by Mr. Hagen's inappropriate questions and tone of voice, Aerial tilted her head to the side and eyed him curiously. "Why, hello, to you, Mr. Hagen," she answered pointedly, smiling deliberately. "It's good to see you again. How have you been?"

Realizing he had overreacted, Chester straightened his spine and cleared his throat self-consciously. "Please forgive my rudeness, my dear," he apologized, nervously threading his fingers through his thinning white hair at the temples.

"It's just that I've been so distraught over your disappearance that I haven't slept a wink since this horrible ordeal began. I am so eager to see to it that what happened to you at the hands of that vicious savage won't happen to anyone else that I completely forgot my manners. Are you all right?" he asked solicitously.

Hagen's concern was so artificial that Aerial had to bite her lip to keep from laughing in his face. "Why, I'm perfectly fine, Mr. Hagen," she said with a smile every bit as saccharine as his attitude. "In fact, I've never been better. Don't I look fine?"

The two men exchanged confused glances, then both looked at her. Chester pulled a chair around and positioned it beside Aerial's. Sitting down, he took her hand between his. "Of course, you *look* well, my dear. You're putting up a very brave front, which is quite commendable. But this is not the time to pretend. You must be totally truthful with us if we're going to make certain that murdering savage gets what he deserves. Now, do you know where he is?"

Ignoring Chester Hagen's last question, Aerial removed her hand from between his sweating palms and smiled stiffly. "If I'm going to be totally truthful, I must tell you that Rye Berenger is not only alive, but that he is not a savage or a murderer. Nor is he a kidnapper. And the reason I'm here today is to rescind the deposition the sheriff coerced me into signing against him."

Chapter Eighteen

"Coerced?!" the sheriff shouted. "What're you talkin' about?"

"Rescind?!" Chester wheezed, his face turning an apoplectic shade of red. "You can't mean that!"

"Oh, but I do. As I told the sheriff three months ago, I didn't actually witness *anyone* being killed in that alley. I only saw a man running out of the alley. But the sheriff convinced me that Mr. Berenger was guilty and that if I didn't sign the statement he would have to let him go. He told me that as long as I was the only witness who could put him in the alley at that time, my life would be in danger. I signed the deposition in spite of what I knew to be the truth, so I've come to appease my conscience and right the wrong I've done."

"The truth?" Chester growled. "Conscience? Right? Wrong? The truth is that Indian bastard killed a white man in the alley behind my office, and now he's made you his accomplice by getting you to lie for him! Now tell us where he is or I'll have the sheriff arrest you for obstructing justice!"

Aerial and the sheriff both stared at the irate businessman, their expressions equally confused.

"Hold on there, Mr. Hagen," the sheriff drawled. "You don't mean that. How would it look to the rest of the country if we put our local heroine in jail after all she's done for this town?"

His breathing labored, Chester didn't speak right

away. When he did, he gripped the arms of his chair and spoke through his teeth. "I apologize, Miss Windsor. I have been under a terrible strain. Not only have I been frantic with worry since you disappeared, but the man murdered in the alley worked for me occasionally, doing odd jobs. I feel responsible for his death because he was in that alley working for me that day, cleaning out my storage shed. So, you see, you must reconsider your decision and tell me where that Indian is."

"I'm sorry, too, Mr. Hagen. But I did *not* see Rye Berenger kill that man and cannot in good conscience disclose his whereabouts until the papers I signed saying I did are returned to me."

Chester bolted up from his chair. "Why you Indian-loving little wh—"

"Whoa there, Mr. Hagen," Sheriff Riley interrupted with a hearty chuckle. "You don't wanna go sayin' somethin' you're gonna be sorry for later, do you? If Miss Windsor wants to reverse her statement, then she's got that right, and there's nothin' we can do about it."

Surprised by the sheriff's attitude, Aerial suspected he was up to something. She didn't know what it was, but she knew she had better stay on guard.

"I'm glad one of you has decided to be reasonable," she said, her voice quivering slightly.

"I'll get the deposition outta my desk," the sheriff said, not releasing Chester Hagen's arm until he was sure the man wasn't going to do anything stupid. "Okay, Mr. Hagen?"

"We need to talk, Riley." Hagen prodded the sheriff toward a far corner of the office, where they proceeded to have a heated conversation that Aerial only caught snatches of.

When the two men turned back to face her, Hagen was obviously making a Herculean effort to control his words. "Again, I owe you an apology, Miss Windsor. I don't know what came over me."

"Your apology is accepted, Mr. Hagen," Aerial said stiffly, her gaze shifting suspiciously from man to man as she tried to figure out what the sheriff had said to cause the man's sudden change of attitude.

The sheriff nodded his approval and stepped over to his desk. "Let me just get that deposition for you, Miss Windsor, and you can be on your way."

He quickly shuffled through a stack of papers and wanted posters until he found what he was looking for. "Here it is!" he announced, holding a paper out to her.

Aerial took the offered document and quickly scanned it to be sure it was the one she had signed. "Sheriff, I'd also like a statement signed by you clearing Rye Berenger of murder charges in your town," she added hastily, bracing herself for another attack from Chester Hagen.

"What?!" Hagen bellowed. "Of all the—"

The sheriff held up his hands to silence the older man, then grinned ingratiatingly at Aerial. "Now, why would I wanna do that, Miss Windsor? With or without your statement, your Injun killed that man, an' sooner or later he's gonna pay for what he done."

Aerial's mouth dropped open in surprise. "But I thought if I—"

"Oh, it's real clear what you thought. But you figgered wrong. We ain't droppin' the charges."

"But you have no witness!"

The sheriff shrugged. "Maybe I do an' maybe I don't. But that don't matter. As long as there's a dead-or-alive reward for him, we probably won't even git a chance to try him. Fact is, if that Injun o' yours is within a hundred miles o' here, he's

286

already a dead man."

Aerial felt the blood drain from her face. Lord, what had she done to Rye? She'd been so sure she would be able to clear his name, and now she had just made things worse by bringing him here. "In that case," she managed to say, "it's a good thing he decided to stay in Canada, isn't it?"

The sheriff smiled knowingly. He took her arm and gently but firmly drew her up from her chair. "Don't let us keep you, Miss Windsor." He ushered her to the door.

"By the way," he added as he opened the door for her, "the only chance that Injun's got o' stayin' alive is if he turns himself in to stand trial. Otherwise, if the bounty hunters catch up to him before we do . . . well, you know bounty hunters. When it's a case of dead-or-alive, they shoot first an' ask questions later. You might wanna mention that to the breed when you see him next."

"I told you, Sheriff. I left Rye Berenger in Canada. I won't be seeing him again."

Riley flashed that knowing grin again. " 'Course you did. How'd I forget that? I'll have one o' the boys walk you over to the hotel. I sent word for them to git your trunks outta the cellar and set up a room for you. You *was* plannin' on stayin' in town for a while, wasn't you? Folks'd be real disappointed if they didn't git a chance to celebrate you bein' alive after all."

"Thank you, Mrs. Wilson," Aerial called cheerfully after the hotel manager who had brought her to the room.

"Damn!" she groaned the instant the door was shut. Her hands balled in tight fists, she made soundless pounding motions on the wood and rolled her forehead from side to side against it.

"Oh, Rye! What have I done?"

She turned around to face the room and slid down the door to the floor. Hugging her legs to her, she closed her eyes and pressed them to her bent knees. "What are we going to do?"

There was no doubt in her mind that the sheriff hadn't believed her when she had told him Rye was in Canada. And she was just as certain that his plan was to just sit back and wait for her to lead him to Rye.

Well, Sheriff Riley had better think again if he thought she was going to be fooled into betraying Rye. If she had to spend the rest of her life in this room, she wouldn't take them to him.

A picture of Rye waiting for her in that deserted shack outside of town filled her mind, and she checked the time on her lapel watch.

He would know something was wrong if she wasn't on that afternoon stage, and the thought of what he would do sent a wave of dread washing over her.

The plan had been for Rye to watch for her signal from the passing stagecoach, then follow it back to Ottumwa, where they would meet. From there, they would begin their trek west, hoping to homestead and start a horse ranch with wild horses Rye would capture, break, and sell.

At the last minute she had gotten him to agree that if for some unforeseen reason she missed that stagecoach he would not come into Fairfield after her. Instead, he was to allow her one more day, then go to Omaha and wait for her at the Maybury boarding house, where she had stayed before and knew she could trust the owners.

However, thinking back on their last conversation, Aerial couldn't forget that Rye had fought against the idea, and had only halfheartedly agreed. But now that it was of the utmost urgency

288

that he follow through as planned, she realized he would never leave her in Iowa and go to Omaha without knowing what had happened to her. In fact, now that she thought about it, she didn't even feel confident that he would give her the extra day before he acted.

"Well, I can't let that happen!" she said aloud, jumping up from the floor. *Somehow, I've got to get word to him that I'm all right and that I'll meet him in Omaha as soon as it's safe.*

She grabbed the door handle, intending to wrench open the door, then paused, realizing there was nowhere she could go, nothing she could do. *The sheriff and his people are going to be watching every move I make!*

A knock on the door to her room exploded through her like cannon fire, setting her heart racing. "Wh . . . who is it?"

"Hershel Zimmermann," an anxious man's voice responded.

"Mr. Zimmermann?" she repeated, stunned and unable to move. "Oh, Mr. Zimmermann!" Her face broke into a relieved smile as full understanding dawned on her.

She yanked open the door and threw herself at the slight man in the hallway. "Thank goodness you're here! I didn't think I'd ever see you again!"

"I don't imagine you did," he said scathingly. "Not after the way you left me without a word in the Rouses Point train station. Do you realize what you put me through when you disappeared without a trace the way you did? If your parents were alive, I can only imagine how disappointed they would be if they knew this was the way you treated an old friend, one who has only your best interests at heart!"

Aerial dragged Hershel into the room and slammed the door, apologizing earnestly as she

289

did. "I'm so sorry. I never meant for you to be worried about me, but I couldn't take the chance that you wouldn't be able to get rid of those men, so I left the train. I sent a letter explaining it all to you at the Brooklyn address printed on the business card you gave me. Didn't you receive it?"

"After a month and a half of not knowing if you were alive or dead," Hershel answered, his tone still injured. "I must admit that I was greatly relieved to receive your assurances that you were alive—though obviously still in serious trouble—but I was tempted to write you off altogether."

He paused in a dramatic play for sympathy. "However, I remembered how much your parents meant to me, and I knew I couldn't do that. Whether you want my help or not, I owe it to them to forgive you and help you escape this danger that seems to accompany you wherever you go. Fortunately, in your letter you stated that you were still determined to clear the Indian, so I was reasonably certain this was where I would eventually locate you."

"Thank heavens you did. I was at my wit's end, not knowing what to do. My reception was nothing like I anticipated. They're watching me like a flock of starving buzzards, just waiting for me to say or do som—"

His expression consoling, Hershel turned her and guided her to a chair. He was in his element once more. He had a client to care for again, and for the first time in years, the pain in his belly was dormant.

"There, there. From now on, I don't want you to concern yourself with incidentals like that. I'll take care of all those things for you. Now that I'm managing your career, I'll schedule all your interviews, set up your bookings, make your travel arrangements. Just leave everything to me."

"Mr. Zimmermann!" Aerial gasped. "What do interviews and bookings have to do with saving my husband's life? Don't you understand the seriousness of—"

"Did you say *husband?*" Hershel wheezed on a cough. His eyes bulging, he grabbed his middle as a sharp cramp attacked him.

"Rye and I were married two weeks ago in the Dakota Territory."

"The Indian? You mean to tell me you married the man who has singlehandedly done everything in his power to ruin your reputation and destroy your career? What were you thinking? Don't you realize what people are saying about you as it is? Now you've gone and married him!"

Shocked by the unexpected tirade, Aerial tried to protest. "Yes, I married him! That's what people do who love each other."

As if he hadn't heard her, Hershel took a deep breath and began to pace. "Don't worry, I'll think of a way to get you out of it."

"What are you talking about? I don't want ou—"

Hershel stopped pacing, a sudden idea obviously hitting him, and blocking out her words. "I know! We'll have it annulled. We can say he forced you to marry him before you escaped." He started walking again. "Maybe we can even get some additional publicity out of this. People will flock to see the woman who—"

Astounded, Aerial stopped Hershel. "Didn't you hear what I said, Mr. Zimmermann? I love Rye! And I have no intention of having our marriage annulled. As far as Rye forcing me to do *anything,* you have it all wrong! In fact, he did everything to try to dissuade me because he wanted to protect me. If anyone was forced, it was Rye, not me!"

"Have you thought about what this will do to your career?" Hershel moaned, his dark, tortured eyes roving over her intensely serious features. "Or what it will do to mine?"

Aerial felt a twinge of guilt. Hershel's desperation hadn't totally escaped her, and she now realized that he had been expecting his association with her to put him back on top, as he had been when he had managed her parents. But she couldn't lie to him.

"My marriage is my career now, Mr. Zimmermann," she said as gently as she could. "Even before I met Rye, I had decided to retire whether I set a new world record or not."

"You can't mean that!"

"I'm afraid I do. Don't you see? Flying balloons is my past. My husband is my future."

"Wait a minute!" Hershel said, his eyes lighting with a new idea. "What if we dressed the Indian up in war paint and feathers and incorporated a reenactment of his abduction of you into your act? Indian attacks are very successful in Wild West shows. Why not in a balloon-flying exhibition?" He broke away from her and started to pace again. "In fact, the more I think about it, this could be just the ans—"

Losing patience, Aerial stomped her foot. "Will you stop it! First of all, 'the Indian' doesn't care for balloon flying; and second, I would never allow him or his people to be exploited that way, no more than I would use my parents' tragic deaths as a part of my act."

"You're right," Hershel apologized, turning toward the door. "It was a thoughtless suggestion."

"Please don't leave," she begged, running after him.

"Why not? You don't need me." He laughed sadly and caressed her cheek with a paternal stroke. "You never really did, did you?"

"But I do need you!"

"I don't understand."

"For one thing, I need someone to handle all those reporters and townspeople who are waiting down in the lobby for me to show my face. Maybe you could set up an interview for tomorrow morning—anything to get them to leave me alone the rest of today and tonight." She flashed her most winning smile. "Of course, I will insist on paying your usual percentage out of the ten thousand dollars the city of Fairfield has promised me for all the publicity I've gotten for them."

Hershel shrugged. At least all wasn't lost. If he were reimbursed for the time he'd wasted on this doomed endeavor he would be able to repay Pearl's loan and have a few dollars left over. "I suppose I could take care of that for you. Is that all you want me to do?"

"Actually, there is one other thing," she said with a slight wince. "I need you to take a message to my husband to warn him that they've refused to drop the charges or to cancel the reward for his capture. He must leave immediately."

"Is he here in town?"

"No, and I've got to make sure he doesn't come here. Will you help me?"

"That depends. Is he somewhere that we can send him a wire?"

"No. But even if he were, it wouldn't be safe. They'll be watching the telegraph office waiting for me to do something like that. What I want you to do is go to him personally and give him my message."

"I don't know. How far away is he?"

"Just west of town, near the Ottumwa road."

"If they're watching you, they'll know I've spent all this time with you, and they'll be watching me,

293

too. I don't see how—"

"We'll create a diversion! You could set up a big interview for me in the lobby—say in an hour. Then when everyone is concentrating on me, you can sneak out and go warn Rye."

"Don't you think someone will notice if I'm not there, especially if I set it up?"

Aerial thought for a moment. "You could escort me to the interview and introduce me. Then, after I've answered a few questions, I could ask you to get me something out of my room. You could leave then. By the time anyone notices you haven't come back you'll be out of town."

He didn't answer right away. "It might work," he finally said.

"Does that mean you'll do it?" she asked apprehensively.

Hershel held his hands out to his sides in good-natured defeat and smiled. "Where exactly am I to find him? I must admit I'm curious to meet the man who could convince you to give up so much." *And who can turn down a thousand dollars?*

Rye squinted, looking east toward town. Damn, would it never be time for that stagecoach? He looked over his shoulder at the western horizon.

Disgusted to see the sun hadn't budged since the last time he had checked, he tossed the twig he'd been chewing aside and strode angrily back to the horses. Even if the stagecoach departed Fairfield on time, it wouldn't leave for at least another hour. That meant he had to kill a minimum of an hour and a half before he knew if Aerial was on board.

"Shit!" he grumbled. "Why'd I ever agree to this crazy idea?"

He quickly rechecked the gear on the horses, for

the hundredth time, then returned to his restless vigil.

Hershel hurried away from the hotel lobby where Aerial was holding court for the press and for as many other people who could crowd into the room. He shook his head in disgust.

What a waste! Aerial Windsor was a natural for the limelight. She had the ability to mesmerize the crowd with the finesse of a great actor. She had it all: beauty, intelligence, personality, talent, fame . . . everything!

And she was going to turn her back on it all— and on him—to homestead with a half-breed! It just wasn't right! If only he could convince her into going on one more tour around the country. With her record and ability to please the public, she would make enough money for both of them to be set for life.

Checking both ways to be sure the alley was clear, he slipped out the back of the hotel and made a quick dash to the horse he had left there. Why was he doing this anyway? What had Aerial Windsor done for him other than promise him a little bit of conscience money? Not one damn thing!

Of course, he reminded himself, ten percent of ten thousand dollars was nothing to sneeze at. He hadn't had a thousand dollars all at one time in several years. *Face it, Zimmermann, it's probably more than you've had in the past five years altogether!*

Still it could be more, *should be more!* If only there were some way to get rid of the Indian. If only . . ."

An idea hit Hershel and his face broke into a sly grin. What if he couldn't find the Indian to give him Aerial's message? The Indian would come into town looking for her, would be arrested, tried and hung; and there would be no one to console his poor widow. No one, that is, except her concerned and indispensable manager!

Hershel placed his foot into a stirrup and stepped onto his waiting mount, but he didn't ride off right away. "A trial could drag on for months, and she'd want to stay here with him," he mumbled aloud. *And there's always the chance he would get off.*

Hershel rode down the alley and out of town following the directions Aerial had given him.

Of course, if Rye Berenger did come into Fairfield, there was the strong possibility someone would kill him for the reward the minute he showed his face in town. But somehow, Hershel's eagerness to make money stopped short of deliberately causing another person's death. Though for the life of him, he didn't know why.

Then it came to him. It was all so simple, Hershel couldn't believe he hadn't thought of it before. He would just tell the Indian that Aerial had changed her mind about the marriage and was having it annulled. The Indian would be too full of pride to go begging her to stay with him. He would simply ride off into the sunset—alone. Meanwhile, he, Hershel, would go back to Fairfield and tell Aerial the Indian had decided he didn't want to be married after all and had left her.

Pleased with himself, Hershel kicked his horse into a gallop and headed west. If he hurried, he could be back in time to console Aerial over dinner.

"You're lying," Rye accused, using Hershel Zimmermann's coat lapels to lift him off the ground. He pushed his face up to Hershel's. "Now suppose you start telling me the truth, you little worm, or I'm going to break your face into little pieces— *bloody* little pieces."

"I only know what I told you," Hershel answered in a trembling voice. "She said it was all a mistake and she wanted you to leave Iowa and not come back."

"Dammit, I knew it! I knew if I let her go alone she would get in trouble. What have they done to her? They didn't put her in jail, did they? It'd be just like them to do something low like that to get to me."

Hershel shook his head. "No, of course not. Don't you think I'd tell you if she were in jail? Why I'd be there trying to break down the bars myself. That girl's like a daughter to me. I wouldn't let anyone harm her. And no one has. She's fine. In fact, when I left town, she was surrounded by an adoring public. They were hanging on her every word as she regaled them with stories of her recent adventures. If you ask me, she's having the time of her life and is simply having second thoughts about rushing into this marriage. I've suggested she can have it quietly annulled, and no one ever has to know."

Rye released his hold on Hershel and spun away from him, disgusted with himself for the hurt he was feeling. Why was he so surprised? Wasn't this exactly what he had told Aerial would happen once she got around her own people again? Hadn't he told her all along that a clean separation was the best way for both of them?

He tightened the cinch on his horse's saddle, intending to ride, but he didn't mount. He was still too stunned.

Damn her and her optimism! She had actually

297

convinced him they might have a chance. For the first time in years he had allowed himself to believe there was hope for the future.

Well, to hell with it. Let her go back to her safe little world where she belonged. She had made the right choice — for herself *and* for the baby. And at least this way their child could be raised white and never have to know the truth about his half-breed father.

A strangling lump formed in his throat as he thought of never seeing his son or daughter, never knowing the joy of holding his child, never being able to teach him the things his own father had taught him . . .

"If Aerial Windsor thinks she can send her flunky to do her dirty work, she's dead wrong!" Rye started to mount his horse.

Hershel ran forward and caught Rye's arm. "What're you going to do?"

"I'm going to Fairfield," Rye spat out bitterly, his eyes focused threateningly at the smaller man's hand on his sleeve. "If she's so anxious to get rid of me, she can damn well tell me to my face. Where's she staying?"

Hershel didn't answer immediately. He knew he should do the right thing and warn Rye Berenger that she was surrounded by lawmen just waiting for him to show up, but after seeing the kind of temper the half-breed had, Hershel couldn't help considering the alternative he had ignored earlier. There was no doubt in Hershel's mind that Rye would shoot it out with the sheriff and his men rather than go to trial. And with the Indian dead, Aerial could be back on the circuit in a month. Maybe even sooner!

Actually, now that he thought about it, what choice did he have? Right or wrong, he had to look out for himself first, didn't he?

"Room 211 at the Fairfield Hotel," Hershel said reluctantly. His guilt getting the better of him, he quickly added, "But you're making a serious mistake. You'll be killed. There's still a reward being offered for your capture."

Rye studied Hershel. "Tell me one thing, Zimmermann. Why haven't you tried to turn me in for that reward yourself?"

"Because—"

"Because that's not the deal we had, is it, Hershel?" A familiar male voice asked with a hoarse chuckle as three men emerged from the gathering afternoon shadows, their revolvers drawn, their mouths spread in victorious expressions. "Our deal was we git the money, he gits the gal. Right, Hersh?"

Raising his hands slowly into the air, Rye smiled coldly at Hershel. "I should have known a weasel like you wouldn't come out here just to do her a favor—unless he had something real big to gain."

Chapter Nineteen

Cowering under Rye's accusing glare, Hershel took a frightened step back. "I never made a deal with them. I didn't even know they were in the state."

"Yeah, I can see that." Dismissing Hershel, Rye fixed his deliberately amused stare on the three men he had thought were still back East. "Good to see you again, fellas. How's the ear, Sid? I see you're wearing your hair longer than the last time we met up."

Surprise converted Sid's features and he made an automatic reach for the side of his head where his ear had been.

"And Clem! I could've sworn you were right handed, son," Rye went on casually. "Why're you holding your gun in your left hand?"

"Shut up, breed," Ned snarled, backhanding Rye across the face with the barrel of his own revolver.

Rye's head snapped back and he tasted blood. The sudden violence sent Rye's horse running in one direction, Hershel in another, but Rye continued to grin deceptively.

"What's the matter, Ned?" he asked, wiping the back of his wrist over his split lip. "Did I forget to tell you hello?"

"You're mighty cocky for a breed," Ned growled, jamming the point of his gun up under Rye's chin. "But let's see how cocky you are after we're through with you. Get the rope, Clem."

Hershel gulped loudly. "You're not going to hang him, are you? Aren't you going to take him in for a trial?"

"Naw, we ain't gonna hang him, leastwise not before we do a little carvin' on him first."

"C-carving?" Hershel's complexion turned a sickly shade of green, and he inched back another pace.

"What about him?" Sid asked, indicating Hershel with a tilt of his head.

"Let 'im go," Ned answered, waving his hand. "The boss said jest foller him, not kill him 'less we got to. 'Sides, Hershel knows if he gives us any trouble we'll hunt him down and do to him what we're gonna do to this breed before we cash in his body for our reward."

Clem waved his gun. "Well, get goin'," he told Hershel. "You got no more cause to be hangin' round here, 'less you got a hankerin' to be gelded along with this Injun filth."

Hershel didn't have to be told twice. Holding his hat on his head, he made a frightened dash for his horse, mounted clumsily and rode away at a breakneck speed.

Laughing as Hershel fled, Sid and Clem came up on either side of Rye, who coldly stared down his nose at the man whose gun was jammed into his jaw. They quickly relieved him of his weapons, then turned to Ned for further instructions.

"We gonna do it here?" Clem asked, snatching a fistful of Rye's hair and jerking his head back as he jabbed his own gun into Rye's ribs. "Or we gonna go somewhere else?"

"Here's good," Ned answered, surveying the small clearing, then pointing. "Put 'im over there."

The instant Ned looked away, Rye brought his knee up, catching the group's leader in the groin.

But surrounded and outnumbered as he was, they quickly overpowered him, despite his valiant struggle.

Working together, the three stripped Rye to his breechcloth and staked him out on the leaf-strewn ground.

Breathing heavily, Ned stood back and surveyed their spreadeagled victim. "I need a drink."

"Me too," Clem agreed, equally winded. "How 'bout we just let the breed lie there and think about how he's gonna feel watchin' us cut him up, bit by bit, finger by finger 'til he bleeds to death like poor ol' Deke did. We might even have us a bite to eat before we go to work."

"That's okay with me," Sid chimed in, squatting down beside Rye's head and knocking his head to the side to expose one ear. "Though I ain't gonna wait too long." He trailed the tip of a knife down the front of Rye's ear for emphasis. "This breed owes me, an' I mean to collect. I's thinkin' 'bout makin' me a lucky charm outta his ears. You know, like a rabbit's foot. Whadda ya think, breed? Ya think I could sell a Injun ear watch bob for a few bucks?"

His expression showing none of the turmoil going on inside him, Rye laughed at Sid. "You know what I think, son? I think you're a yellow shit who'd run and hide if you ever had to make a decision on your own or fight a man who wasn't tied down."

"Shut up, you bastard." Sid cracked Rye in the side of the head with the back of his fist and exploded up from the ground.

His head ringing, Rye looked back at Sid, his vision blurred. Damn, there were two of him. "What's the matter, son?" he asked, managing a steady voice. "Did I hit a little close to home?"

Sid brought the heel of his boot down hard on

Rye' shoulder and twisted it. "You don't know what you're talkin' about, Injun."

"You know the one thing that would make this here perfect?" Clem asked, not really paying much attention to Sid's interchange with Rye.

Ned shrugged and took a slug of whiskey from the bottle, then offered it to Sid. "What's that?"

Clem shook his head regretfully. "It's a real shame the breed ain't gonna get to be there when we git hold o' that gal an' show her what happens to a white woman who ruts with a Injun. I been thinkin' 'bout that gal for months now, and it'd make havin' her even sweeter if he was watchin'. I bet he'd like it, too, wouldn't ya, breed?"

At the mention of Aerial, Rye strained wildly against the tight bindings on his wrists and ankles. "You go near her and I'll—"

"You'll what, Injun?" Ned asked, kicking Rye in the ribs. "Go get her, boys. I think you're right. That uppity white squaw oughta add just the right amount o' fun to our celebration!"

The next hour was pure torture for Rye. It was bad enough that the ropes on his ankles and wrists were cutting unrelentingly into his flesh, and that his head, jaw, shoulder, and ribcage throbbed from where he'd been pistol whipped and kicked, but he was hardly conscious of the pain.

It wasn't even Ned's drunken descriptions of what was going be done to him when his partners got back that had him frantic with desperation. He had stopped listening after only a few minutes.

It didn't even matter that he wore no clothing save a breechcloth and that the temperature had dropped from cool to downright cold once the sun had gone down. He didn't feel that either.

What had him wild with fear was the thought of

303

Aerial at the mercy of these three animals and of not being able to do anything to save her.

Every sound he heard set him off.

The mere flurry of autumn leaves falling to the ground with the slightest hint of a breeze was enough to stop his breathing for seconds. The sudden hoot of an owl or the chirp of a cricket caused every nerve in his body to sizzle with electricity.

Determined to gain control over his reactions, Rye consciously sucked in a deep breath and blew it out slowly. Closing his eyes, he willed himself to concentrate on finding a way out of his deadly plight.

Over and over he inhaled, then exhaled. Inhale. Exhale. Inhale. Exhale. There had to be something he could do. Inhale. Exhale.

Only one other time in his life had he felt so helpless, so worthless. But at least when his family had been killed he'd known that he would be able to seek out his family's murderer and kill him another day. But this time there would be no opportunity for revenge. He would be dead unless he did something—and fast.

Think, dammit! Think! he screamed inside his head.

Something hard and cold touched Rye's left wrist, jerking him out of his self-hypnotized state with a violent jolt.

Before he could release the startled gasp that rose involuntarily from his chest, a hand was slapped over his mouth, accompanied by a sharp, commanding "Shh."

Rye's eyes rolled back in his head as he strained to identify the owner of the hand on his mouth. He could discern the silhouette of a man, but he couldn't quite make out the features.

It took the barest instant for Rye to realize that someone was there to rescue him, and he nodded his head to show he understood the importance of remaining quiet.

Whoever his mystery savior was, he showed that he had received Rye's silent message by removing his hand from Rye's mouth. Immediately he set about sawing at the rope binding Rye's wrist.

The steady scraping of the blade against the strands of the rope sounded loudly in Rye's ears. In fact, he was certain Ned must be able to hear what was going on, too. His eyes fastened on his captor dozing against a tree, obviously unaware that anything was amiss.

Holding his breath as the rescuer worked, Rye kept his gaze leveled on Ned, waiting for any sign that the presence of the third person was known.

Working swiftly now that he could concentrate exclusively on the ropes, Rye's champion quickly cut through the ties on his wrists.

Rye started to sit up, but was pushed back with a hand on his chest. The man then belly-crawled down to Rye's ankles, taking care to keep his head down and his own body on the side away from where Ned still slept.

Realizing that if he moved too soon, he risked waking Ned and having him shoot both him and his rescuer before they could get away, Rye resisted the impulse to try to help and continued to lie spread-eagled as if he were still bound.

The first ankle free, Rye felt his leg lifted slightly so the rescuer could reach under his calf to cut the last rope from below without exposing himself any more than he already was.

His work finished, the man lizarded away from Rye and into the brush. Moving slowly, his stare never leaving Ned, Rye inched over the ground, following the way of the other man.

Hidden safely in the bushes, Rye was finally able to breathe again. "Whoever you are, thanks. I owe you my—Zimmermann! What're you doing here? I thought you were in this with them!"

"An association with that sort would be sinking a bit low, even for me. Evidently, someone knew I spent time talking to Miss Windsor and figured she might have told me where you were. But we can talk about that later. Right now, I just want to get out of here while we can."

"What the hell?" Ned yelled, ending their furtive conversation.

"He knows you're gone," Hershel whispered, his voice alarmed. "Let's go."

"Not quite yet," Rye answered with a menacing scowl. Crouching low, he took off at a silent run through the woods.

"Hey!" Hershel called after him without thinking.

"Who's there?" Ned spun around to face the area where Hershel was hidden. "Clem? Sid? 'Zat you?"

"Wrong!" Rye sprung out of the brush on the opposite side of the clearing, trapping the bounty hunter's neck in a one-armed stranglehold. With his other hand he captured Ned's gun arm and twisted it out to the side and at the same time brought his knee up from the ground to meet the top side of Ned's forearm in a bone-splintering blow.

"Yeow!" Ned screeched as the crack of shattering bone echoed through the stillness of the night. Rye tightened his hold on Ned's neck, squeezing off his air supply and silencing him. "One moan out of you and it'll be your neck I crack next. You got that?"

Ned managed a nod.

"Damn!" Rye cursed, releasing his hold somewhat and shoving Ned to the ground. He forced his face into the dead leaves and held it there. "I was hoping you didn't. I was looking forward to snapping your yellow neck. You still there, Zimmermann?"

Working together, it took Rye and Hershel only a moment to strip Ned naked and stake him out where Rye had been moments before.

Hurriedly stuffing a sleeve of Ned's longjohns into his mouth and securing it with his dirty bandana, Rye had Hershel gather the rest of Ned's clothing and tie it to the back of his horse. Meanwhile, Rye quickly put on his own clothes and made ready to leave.

"Someone's coming!" Hershel announced in a frightened whisper.

"Take the horses and get out of sight," Rye ordered, diving for cover. His heart pounding a frantic rhythm against the walls of his rib cage, he waited, knowing that if the new arrivals were Sid and Clem returning, they might have Aerial with them.

When Sid and Clem rode into the clearing alone, Rye heaved a relieved sigh. Resisting the urge to shoot them both on the spot, he stepped out in the open, a rifle in one hand, a revolver in the other. "That's far enough, boys."

Sid and Clem's gawking stares sliced to the bound man on the ground ten feet away. Recognizing Ned, they both raised their hands in surrender.

Knowing firsthand what Rye was capable of, the two new arrivals allowed themselves to be stripped and bound without resistance. Rye and Hershel were on their way back toward the road in short order, the bounty hunters' horses, weapons, and clothing in tow.

When they reached the road, Hershel brought his horse to a halt. "You're not still determined to go into town, are you? You heard those two say they're watching her every move, just waiting for you to show up. You won't be able to get near her

307

without being discovered."

Rye tilted his head and studied Hershel. "Oh, I'll get to her all right. Being part Indian does have its advantages. She owes it to me to tell me to my face that she's through with me."

Aerial was certain her face would crack if she had to respond to one more compliment or hear one more glowing report of what her success had done for the city of Fairfield. There was even talk of naming a street after her.

Taking care to keep her fixed smile in place, she viewed the hall of the First Christian Church, where she had just spent the most grueling two hours of her life at a supper the town fathers had arranged in her honor.

Actually, it had proved a perfect diversion to keep the town's attention focused on her until Hershel's return, especially after she had said everything she could think of in order to drag out the news conference as long as possible to give Hershel time to reach Rye.

She took a quick glimpse at her lapel watch. What could be taking him so long? He should have been back by now. What if he didn't find Rye? What if he found him but Rye didn't believe he was a friend? What if. . . ?

She was hit by a frightening recollection of the violence Rye was capable of inflicting on his enemies if he was forced into a defensive position.

If by any chance Rye thought Hershel worked for the sheriff and had come to arrest him, he wouldn't hesitate to kill him!

Panic rushing through her veins, she stood up and addressed the people at her table. "If you will excuse me," she said suddenly, "I'm going to have to call it an evening. I am absolutely exhausted."

Rye heaved himself over the windowsill and slipped into the darkened room. It was obvious Aerial was out, but eventually she would be back. Tilting his head back against the wall, he groaned.

God! He ached all over.

Running his tongue over his swollen lip, he shook his head. At least it wasn't bleeding anymore and didn't really hurt all that much. On the other hand, his shoulder was an altogether different story. He massaged his shoulder where Sid had stomped him, still amazed that it wasn't broken.

He breathed in deeply and gingerly shifted his position to keep from making anything feel worse than it did. As he did, a sharp stab pierced his upper torso in the area of his ribs. "I might not be so lucky when it comes to my ribs," he told himself. He would have laughed ironically at his pitiful state, but it hurt too much.

He wrapped his arm over his middle to hold his ribs, hoping the pressure would help, and struggled to his feet. He quickly located a lamp and lit it. The way his day had gone so far, it wouldn't surprise him to find himself in the wrong room.

He pulled down the window shade and scrutinized the room. His attention went immediately to two unfamiliar trunks and several hat boxes he'd never seen, as well as a clutter of feminine toiletries and wearing apparel he didn't recognize. "Shit," he moaned, heading for the window. "All I need is to be found lurking in some strange woman's bedroom." Just then he heard voices in the hallway, one female, one male. He paused and listened. The approaching footsteps stopped outside the door to the room in which he stood.

* * *

Aerial walked briskly to her room, Chester Hagen at her side, still apologizing profusely for his earlier behavior. At the door, she took out her key, thankful at last to be able to escape from the man. But before she could use the key, Hagen snatched it out of her hand.

"Allow me, my dear," he offered magnanimously.

Aerial forced a smile, a very strained smile. "Why, thank you, Mr. Hagen."

Hagen quickly opened the door and indicated with a sweeping gesture that she should enter.

Hurrying through the doorway, she immediately spun around to face him and held out her hand for her key. Again, she was too slow.

Hagen was already through the doorway.

"Mr. Hagen!" She pressed her hand to his chest in an attempt to stop him from coming any farther into the room. "It's really too late for visitors."

"Just a few minutes more, Miss Windsor. I haven't had a chance to apologize properly."

"Believe me, your apologies have not only been sufficient, but I assure you, they have been wholeheartedly accepted. Now, if you don't mind . . ."

Hagen ignored her protests and pushed his way farther into the room, slamming the door behind him. "Don't you think you owe me the courtesy of spending just a while longer in my company? After all, I'm a very wealthy man and quite influential in this town. I could make your success even more profitable than it has been."

An alarm went off inside Aerial's head. Surely, he wasn't proposing what it sounded like he was proposing!

Struggling not to pick up a lamp and hit him with it, she smiled stiffly. "I'm very grateful for all you've done, Mr. Hagen, and I'd like nothing more than to visit longer with you, at a more appropriate time of day, of course, and in more suitable surroundings than my room. Perhaps it would be better if we meet in the morning and talk over breakfast. We don't want to give the gossips anything to talk about, now do we?"

"Come now, Miss Windsor. You and I both know you're not a woman who concerns herself with what other people think." He inspected her room nonchalantly. "Besides, after all those months you spent sharing that Indian buck's blanket, I would think you would be grateful that a white man would still give you the time of the day, much less want to spend time in your company." He sat down in the room's one chair and pulled out a cigar and sniffed it.

"What exactly are you suggesting, Mr. Hagen?"

Hagen threw back his head and laughed, a hard, ugly laugh. "What I'm suggesting, my dear, is a little arrangement between us." He struck a match with his thumbnail and lit his cigar.

"An arrangement," Aerial gasped. "How dare you! Who do you think you are?"

Hagen stared at her, seeming to be genuinely surprised by her reaction. Then his face lit with understanding. "You mean you thought I would want you for a mistress?" He laughed again, this time even more robustly. "That is the most ludicrous thing I've ever heard. Why, the very idea of being in the same room with that breed's leavings turns my stomach."

Taken back by Hagen's open revulsion of her, Aerial stared at him. "Then why are you here?"

"Because, as distasteful as your company is to me, you have something I want, and I need your help to get it."

"What makes you think I would help you even if I could?"

"Oh, everyone has his—or her—price. And I doubt that you'll refuse, once I tell you my proposal."

"Don't count on it, Mr. Hagen. I can't imagine agreeing to anything you would ever suggest."

He went on as if he hadn't heard her speak. "I'm willing to add five thousand dollars out of my own pocket to the ten thousand the city has already given you. My attorney will be here with it first thing in the morning."

"In exchange for what?" Aerial asked harshly.

"Just tell me where the breed is and you'll be a wealthy woman."

"Five thousand dollars? That's a lot of money." She paced away from Hagen as if she were considering his offer. There was definitely more to this than met the eye. Why would a man want to find a vagrant's killer so much that he would offer to pay that much money to do it? It just didn't make sense.

"Well?" Hagen grunted, then took a drag on his cigar and blew it out, his entire demeanor smacking of overconfidence. "Are you going to accept my deal?"

"I might," she answered coyly, turning back to face him. "It depends."

"On what? You want more money? All right, I'll go six thousand."

Now she was really getting curious. "Six thousand?" She made a play at being impressed. "All right, I'll tell you where Rye Berenger is—*if* you'll tell me why you're so interested in finding this one particular man."

Hagen studied her for a moment, obviously trying to figure her out. "Because he killed a friend of mine."

"A friend of yours? From what I learned at the dinner tonight, that man was the town drunk and he had no friends. Why is it so important that his killer is punished?"

312

"And why do you keep defending the bastard?"

Aerial resisted the impulse to shock Hagen by confessing her love for Rye. "Because I believe he's innocent."

"There's no such thing as an innocent Indian. They're all killers. They're the scourge of this great country, robbing and killing and destroying everything that's decent. They're responsible for killing thousands of innocent people. Look at what happened in Minnesota in '64. Hundreds of white settlers murdered in their own homes. If the government had been doing its job right, it would have just killed them all years ago. But instead they put them on the reservations, where they breed their little nits to live off the government and contaminate the rightful citizens of this country."

"I see. So you're telling me you think Rye Berenger should die because he's an Indian, whether he committed any crime or not."

"You got it, lady. The Bible says, 'an eye for an eye,' and as long as I breathe, that'll be the creed I live by where Indians are concerned."

"Just one more question? Would you be willing to offer such a large amount of money for any Indian, or just this one in particular?"

He stood up and took her arm, jerking her to him. "I told you what you want to know. You tell me what I want to know."

Aerial took a deep breath and shrugged. "I'm afraid you're not going to be very happy with my answer, Mr. Hagen, but it hasn't changed since this afternoon." She gave him her most sincere look. "As I told you, the last time I saw Rye Berenger was in Canada. At the Ottawa train depot to be exact. He put me on a train and disappeared before the train even left the station."

"Why you lying little whore!" He raised his hand as if he would strike her. "I ought to . . ."

"What, Mr. Hagen? Strike me? Go ahead, if you must, but be sure to consider the repercussions before you do it."

Before Hagen could answer, a knock on the door reverberated through the room.

Inside, Aerial felt herself turn to jelly with relief, but outside she held Hagen's stare, daring him to act.

"Miss Windsor, it's Hershel Zimmermann. Let me in. I must talk to you."

"Well, Mr. Hagen, now it would seem we even have a witness, don't we?"

Dropping his hand, Hagen wrenched open the door and shoved past Hershel without speaking.

"Did I interrupt something?" Hershel asked, watching Hagen stomp down the hall.

"Thank God you did!" Aerial cried, dragging him into her room. "Where have you been? I've been worried crazy. Did you find Rye? Is he all right? Did you convince him to leave?"

Hershel shifted his gaze from her face to a point behind her. "Uh—"

Aerial jerked her head around to see what had caught Hershel's attention. "What is. . . ? Rye!"

Chapter Twenty

"What are you doing here? How did you get past the sheriff's men?" Aerial sliced an accusing glare back at Hershel. "You were supposed to convince him to leave the state!"

Hershel shrugged. "Believe me, I tried. But—"

Rye stepped out of the shadows of the adjoining bathroom, his expression difficult to read. "Did you really think I'd be so easy to get rid of, Aerial?"

"Get rid of? What are you tal—" As the light from the lamp fell on Rye's face, Aerial fully saw him for the first time since she had discovered him in her room, and her heart contracted with panic.

He was caked with blood and his lower lip was swollen to the size of a walnut. A large, continuous bruise discolored the side of his face from his temple to his jaw. His dark eyes revealing the pain he was experiencing, he held his side and winced as he took another step.

"Oh, Rye," she cried running across the room to him. "You're hurt! What happened? Who did this to you?" She gently clasped his cheeks between her palms.

Rye seized her wrists and removed her hands, holding them firmly between them. "Never mind that. I want to hear you tell me to my face that I was right when I said you wouldn't be able to stand the idea of being married to a half-breed when you got back to your own kind."

Aerial's eyes grew wide with confusion and she

scrutinized Hershel, who stood beside the door also gripping his stomach as if he were on the verge of being sick.

"What's he talking about? Is he delirious?" She directed her attention back to Rye. "Here, let me help you over to the bed." She slipped her arm around his waist.

"Aghh!" Rye groaned as she touched his sore ribs. He twisted away from her. "I don't want to go to bed. I want to hear you admit it." He spoke through clenched teeth.

"Admit what?"

"Admit our marriage was a mistake and that you want it annulled."

"Whatever gave you such a ridiculous id — ?" Suddenly, the word *annulled* sounded a discordant alarm in her memory.

"Mr. Zimmermann?" she asked, her tone accusing as she wheeled about and faced Hershel. "What exactly did you say to my husband when you found him?"

"Oh . . ." Taking a deep breath, Hershel glanced fearfully from Aerial to Rye, then directed his words to Aerial. "Well, you see, I . . ." He stopped to swallow, his eyes shifting nervously around the room. "I . . uh . . ." He drew himself to his full height, which was only an inch taller than Aerial at the most. "I sensed right away that he wasn't the kind of man who was going to go to Omaha and just wait for you to come the way you wanted him to do. And since I knew how dangerous it was for him here, I decided if he thought you had changed your mind about the marriage . . ."

"So you told him I wanted our marriage annulled!?" Aerial's voice was a high, breathy, almost soundless squeal.

"Not exactly. I simply said I had 'suggested' you

316

have it annulled—which is the truth. That you agreed was an assumption on his part."

"An assumption you did nothing to correct. *Why,* Mr. Zimmermann? Why did you deliberately make my husband think I never wanted to see him again?"

"I told you why! I wanted to help . . ." He stopped speaking, unable to proceed under her wrathful glare. "All right! I admit it. My reasons weren't totally unselfish. Though I believed, still believe, you'd be better off without him, I hoped if I could get rid of him permanently I could talk you into flying balloons again and making us both a fortune."

"So for your own personal gain, you decided to destroy my—"

Rye came up behind Aerial and placed a hand on her shoulder, silencing her. "I'm curious about one thing, Zimmermann. Why, if you wanted to get rid of me so much, didn't you leave me for Ned and his pals to take care of?"

Aerial's head swung around. "Ned?! From New York?"

Rye nodded and went on speaking to Hershel. "Why'd you risk your own life to come back and save mine?"

Aerial gawked at Hershel. "You saved his life?"

"If it hadn't been for our friend here, I'd be dead by now—or wishing I were."

"Now I'm totally confused. Would someone please explain to me what's going on? Why *did* you save him, Mr. Zimmermann?"

Hershel shrugged, obviously embarrassed. "I guess I'm not the opportunist I thought I was. It seems I've got a conscience after all, which I might add is a damned inconvenient thing for a man in my line of business to have."

"Maybe it's time we both changed our line of

business, Mr. Zimmermann," Aerial said, her tone sympathetic. "But I would consider it a personal favor if you would stay on as my manager until we figure a way out of this predicament Rye and I are still in."

Hershel considered her, surprised. "Do you mean it?"

Rye nodded his head wearily and staggered to the chair. "She means it. Now, do you think we can get a little sleep? I've had a rough day, and something tells me tomorrow's going to be just as bad."

"Sure," Hershel agreed, stepping to the door. "My room's across the hall if you need me. Just yell and I'll be here."

"Good night, Mr. Zimmermann," Aerial said, walking to the door with him. "We'll see you in the morning."

"Zimmermann?" Rye called.

"Yes?"

"Thanks again. I owe you."

"We both do, Mr. Zimmermann," Aerial added, opening the door for him. She leaned over and kissed his cheek.

Once Hershel was gone and the door was locked, Aerial hurriedly wheeled around to face Rye, her expression a combination of anger and concern. "Now, Mr. Berenger, suppose you start explaining to me how you got yourself in this condition!"

On her knees in front of where Rye sat on the edge of the bed, Aerial secured the bandage she had wrapped around his bruised torso. Her eyes were still spitting fire after the story he had told her while she had cleaned and dressed his wounds. "When I think what they did to you, it's enough to make me want to go out right this minute and shoot them all dead. What are they doing here, anyway? How did they know to come to Iowa in the first place?"

"One of them said something about having a boss who was paying them to kill me but not Hershel. That's why they let him go. They probably didn't figure the little fellow would stop running until he reached the Atlantic coast. But he fooled them, didn't he?"

Aerial wouldn't be deterred from her line of thought. She stood up and stared down at Rye's bruised shoulder, her face pained. "But why would anyone hire out-of-state people to kill you when there must be plenty of guns for hire right here in Iowa? For that matter, why is someone so set on having you killed instead of brought in to stand trial?"

"Evidently, Hackmore had some friends after all. They must be afraid I'll go free now that the only witness has withdrawn her accusation." He trapped Aerial's waist in his large hands and hauled her closer between his thighs. "Come here. Have I told you how much I missed you?" He slid his hands around to her front and began unbuttoning her bodice.

Aerial couldn't resist smiling. "You mean, after all you've been through, you still . . ." She teasingly popped him on his good shoulder. "Rye Berenger, you're out of your mind."

"Totally," he agreed, tearing the bodice front apart and off her shoulders, exposing her camisole. "Totally out of my mind ever to have thought I didn't need you more than life itself. I'll tell you the truth, when Hershel told me you were through with me, I almost did go crazy," he said, concentrating on the ties of her camisole. He pushed it open to expose her breasts.

319

"Ah," he sighed, leaning forward to cover them with a flurry of kisses.

Clutching his head to her breasts, she tried not to lean into his kisses. "Rye, we can't. You're . . . ohhhh, yes . . . injured. You need to . . ."

"I'll rest later," he murmured against her skin, his hands wrestling with the rest of her clothing. "Right now, I need to feel your flesh against mine. I need to find comfort inside you. And I need to know that you're really still mine."

Knowing she couldn't stop him even if she wanted to—which she didn't—Aerial smiled seductively. "At least let me do the work," she offered, slipping one arm out of her bodice and chemise. "Why don't you lie back and relax? Tonight, I'll take care of everything."

Unable to resist her offer, Rye smiled lazily and lay back on the pillows, his eyes glistening with desire.

Keeping her gaze fastened on Rye's enraptured face, Aerial slowly removed the rest of her clothing piece by piece, sensuously prolonging the moment when she would go to him and show him exactly how much she loved him.

When she stood before him, naked and glorying in the worship she saw in his expression, she crawled onto the bed and slid her fingers under his breechcloth. "You won't be needing this," she cooed softly as she freed his manhood.

Rye reached for her, but she shoved his hands aside. Interlacing her fingers with his, she pressed his hands to the pillow beside his head and bent to kiss his eyes closed. "I love you, Rye Berenger," she whispered, covering his forehead and temples with her kisses. "I will always love you."

She continued her assault on his face, paying particularly gentle attention to his bruised temple and jaw, as well as to his swollen lip. "I'll be

320

yours for all eternity." She trailed her lips down his throat. "We belong together." She covered his shoulders and upper chest, again giving his bruises an extra share of her healing touch. "In this lifetime, and in all lifetimes to come, we will be together."

Sliding down his body, she laved his pectoral muscles with her tongue. Not an inch of his torso went unblessed by her loving ministrations.

Finally, she released her hold on his hands and splayed her fingers, trailing them downward to his hips. Holding him, she studied his face and found him watching her, his expression surprised, pleased, apprehensive, as if he weren't sure what he should do.

"I love you, and I want to spend my life with you, Rye," she vowed. "You must believe that no matter what happens to us, my love will be constant."

With those words, she encircled his swollen manhood with her hand and bent her head to give him the ultimate proof of how much she loved him.

"Oh, God, Aerial," he groaned, digging his head back into the pillow and bucking his hips as she took him into her mouth.

Deriving pleasure from loving him the way he had loved her so many times, Aerial was stunned when Rye suddenly grasped her hair and lifted her away from him.

"Enough!" he rasped hoarsely.

Hurt and embarrassed, Aerial raised her confused eyes to Rye's face, which was contorted with obvious anguish.

"Did I do something wrong? I thought you would like it if—"

His expression mellowed into a smile, though his chest continued to rise and fall rapidly as he struggled to control his body's reaction.

"No, love. You didn't do anything wrong. It was the sweetest thing anyone ever did for me. It was wonderful."

"Then why did you stop me?"

Rye laughed softly. "For an old married woman, you've still got a lot to learn about men. If I hadn't stopped you when I did, it would've been too late." He shrugged his good shoulder. "Now do you understand?"

She nodded, then assumed a mischievous mien. Moving gingerly so that she wouldn't hurt his ribs, she straddled him, and bent to kiss his chest. "Is it too late for this, too?" she asked, lowering her hips so that she touched his thrusting manhood with the heat of her sex.

"Not on your life, you little witch." He clasped her hips and brought them downward as he raised his own to fill her to capacity.

Lifting her and bringing her down again, Rye plunged deeper and deeper into her until the only sounds in the room were moans of pleasure, the creaking ropes of the bed, and the slap of flesh against flesh.

Together they soared above the earth to the special pinnacle where only they could take each other. Too soon, they were tumbling back to earth, clinging desperately to each other, murmuring words of love, their breathing loud, and ragged.

After long moments of lying silently in each other's arms, Aerial finally spoke. "Do you have any more doubts about my love that we need to clear up?"

Rye chuckled softly. "As a matter of fact, I'm feeling pretty confident right now. How about you?"

"I've never had any doubts you loved me, Rye

Berenger. Remember? I knew it long before you did!"

No! *Rye's mind screamed as the truth stared at him from his sister's lifeless eyes.*

"Ginny?" *he whimpered, his lips barely moving.* "Say something." *Weeping silently, he gathered the limp body into his arms and rocked her.* "Ginny, please don't be dead."

A loud burst of laughter reverberated through the air, forcing his blurred gaze away from his sister's face to the cabin three-hundred feet from where he lay. Rye's heartbeat accelerated.

Coming from the entrance to his family's cabin was the shabbily dressed man Rye recognized as the town drunk.

"An eye for an eye!" *the man screamed, raising his fist high in the air and shaking it.*

Rye's horrified gaze flew to two scalps the man clutched in his fist, one of them black and mingled with colored ribbons, the other one curly and orangy red; every nerve and muscle in Rye's body cramped and quivered with nausea. "An eye for an eye!" *the man laughed over and over.* "An eye for an eye . . . And a scalp for a scalp . . . An eye for an eye . . . And a scalp for a scalp . . . An eye for an eye. . . ."

Rye pitched himself over onto his back and grabbed his head between his hands. Damn, would the nightmares never stop? Would he never stop being haunted by the memory of that day? That part of his life was over. Why couldn't he put it behind him? Cletus Hackmore was dead. Why couldn't he stop hearing his voice?

As if he'd been splashed in the face with ice

323

water, Rye came fully awake. Throwing off the covers, he sat up and swung his feet over the side of the bed to the floor.

"Rye?" Aerial asked from behind him, her voice husky with sleep. "Is something wrong?"

"It's nothing," he answered, resting his elbows on his knees and holding his head in his hands. "A nightmare. Go on back to sleep. I'm fine."

He felt the bed move as Aerial scooted over to his side and put her arm around his shoulders. "Want to talk about it?"

"Not right now," he answered. "If I just sit here for a minute and don't think about it, it'll go away."

"Then I'll sit with you."

"You don't have to."

"I know that, but I might as well. I wasn't doing anything important."

Rye felt himself smile despite his inability to shake the oppressive weight of the nightmare, and despite the sound of Cletus Hackmore's laughing words still reverberating in his mind.

He tipped his head to the side and deliberately bumped her head on his shoulder with his. "Anybody ever tell you you're daft, woman?"

"All my life. But I'm *your* daft woman, so I guess you're going to have to live with it."

After several minutes of silence Rye finally spoke. "You know what's odd? Except for the night when I had the fever after we crashed in the balloon, the nightmares had stopped ever since I found Hackmore dead in that alley. What made me have it again tonight?"

Aerial caressed his back and kissed his shoulder. "You had a pretty close call with those three today. Maybe that's what caused you to have the nightmare. In both cases you were totally helpless."

"Yeah," he agreed, not sounding convinced. "I guess that could be the connection. It's just that . . ."

"What?"

"Somehow, tonight the nightmare was different—as if it were telling me something."

"How was it different?"

Rye hesitated for a long moment before he spoke. "Maybe different is the wrong word. Basically, it was the same as always. I realize my sister is dead and then I see Cletus Hackmore coming from my house waving my parents' scalps in the air and shouting and laughing." Rye paused and frowned.

"What is he shouting?"

"An eye for an eye, a scalp for a scalp. Over and over. An eye for an eye . . . An eye for a—"

Rye shot up from the bed. "That's it!"

"What's *it?*" Aerial asked.

"The difference! In the past, the dream always ended with me running away. This time I didn't run!"

"What did you do?"

"I woke up."

Unable to keep from showing her disappointment, Aerial said, "Oh."

"I know it doesn't sound like much, but in all these years I never woke up before I ran away . . . until tonight. Why?"

Aerial drew a sheet around her and shrugged. "Maybe you heard a noise outside or in the hallway that woke you up."

He eyed her thoughtfully, though it was obvious he wasn't really seeing her. "Maybe, but I just can't help but think it means something el—" He stopped speaking, his face filled with horror. "My God. What if that man in the alley wasn't Cletus Hackmore after all? What if Hackmore is still alive and here in Fairfield?"

Aerial raced to his side and took his face in her hands, forcing him to notice her. "Rye, don't torture yourself like this. You're scaring me. The man who killed your family is dead! He's not alive. You saw his body yourself!"

"I *assumed* the body I found was Hackmore because he was where my trail had led me to believe I'd find him and because he was carrying my father's knife. But what if the real Hackmore heard I was trying to find him and killed a drunk in the alley and planted my father's knife on him to lead me astray?"

"But you recognized him, didn't you?"

"Actually, now that I think about it, I'm not sure I did. After so many years, his face wasn't all that clear in my mind. And I remember thinking he seemed different from the way I had pictured him."

"Of course he was. Time would account for that," Aerial argued.

"That's what I told myself then, but for some reason I still can't shake the feeling that my dream was telling me Hackmore's not dead, and that I have to stop running from him and face him."

Hating to encourage him, Aerial found herself at a loss. If Rye really believed Cletus Hackmore was still here, it would be impossible to get him to leave town, even if it meant his own death. On the other hand, if there was the slightest chance the murderer of Rye's family was alive, did she have the right to try to talk him out of seeking out the truth?

"What are you planning to do?" she asked, her heart pounding with dread and apprehension. "Even if he's alive, how are you going to find him if you don't even know what he looks like?"

"I'm going to do the only thing I can do. I'm

going to flush him out by making him come to me. Now that I've put his hired guns out of commission for a while, whoever it is that wants me dead is going to be forced to do the job himself!"

A hard lump of panic formed in the pit of Aerial's belly. She knew it. He was going to set himself up as a decoy . . . and probably be killed in the process.

"Please don't do this, Rye!" she begged, throwing her arms around him. "Let the past go. You have a family now to take care of. Do it for us."

He held her out from him. "Don't you think I'd like to let it go? But until I know for certain that the man who killed my family is dead, I can't. I can't do it, Aerial, not even for you and our child."

Tears streaming down her cheeks, Aerial hung her head. "I know you can't." She smiled sadly. "What can I do to help?"

Rye gathered her into his arms, his own eyes bright with tears. "I love you, Mrs. Berenger."

"And I love you, Mr. Berenger. For all eternity."

"Did you send the wire?" Rye asked Hershel.

Hershel nodded, his eyes shifting over the breakfast spread he had ordered sent up to Aerial's room from the nearby restaurant. "Just like you asked."

"And you're sure it got off?"

Hershel nodded again. "The telegraph operator didn't act the least bit suspicious. I stood right there and watched him send it. Of course, after being awakened at five o'clock in the morning to send a telegraph, I doubt he even paid any attention to what it said."

"And you watched from the street to be sure the operator didn't talk to anyone or send any messages to anyone—maybe the sheriff—after you left?"

Hershel slathered a generous helping of dewberry jam on his biscuit and nodded his head again. "Why all the questions? I told you, everything went off without a hitch. The operator sent the wire, he didn't act suspicious, and he didn't pass the information on to anyone in the three hours I watched the telegraph office. Aren't you going to eat that sausage?" he asked Aerial, who sat silently staring at the food on her overloaded plate, her complexion pale.

"No, you're welcome to . . . ohhhh!" She jumped up and made a dash for the bathroom, slamming the door behind her.

Rye's face wrinkled with concern, but he didn't go after her.

"Is she sick?" Hershel asked.

"Mmm," Rye answered, his attention on the bathroom door. "My grandmother says the morning illness should stop once her pregnancy is a little farther along. But in the meantime . . ."

"Pregnancy?!" Hershel choked, spewing coffee all over his own plate. "You mean she's going to have a baby?"

Rye beamed proudly. "So you see, you wouldn't have been able to talk her into flying for a while even if you had succeeded in getting rid of me."

Embarrassed, Hershel stared at the bathroom door. "Shouldn't you go to her? Isn't there something we should be doing?"

Rye shook his head. "She doesn't want me to see her like this. The one time I tried to help she threw a washrag at me and told me to leave her alone. But don't worry. In a minute she'll come out of there smiling as if nothing happened. Neither of us will mention it, and she'll be fine for the next twenty-four hours. Then, tomorrow . . ."

The bathroom door opened, and both men waited expectantly. Exactly as Rye had predicted, Aerial was smiling happily. "Well, what are you two looking at? You don't expect me to eat all this food alone, do you?"

Hershel shrugged and concentrated on his breakfast plate. "So," he said self-consciously, "do we have any other last-minute details to take care of before we leave?"

"Just one," Aerial said, reaching across the table to take Hershel's hand. "Since our baby's natural grandparents are no longer here, would you consider being this baby's substitute grandfather?"

"After what I tried to do, you still want me?"

"Well, you are the closest thing to a family I have, and a baby needs someone besides his parents to help him learn the difference between right and wrong. Who better to do that than a man who has found he has a conscience, no matter how late in life he discovered it?"

Hershel took out his handkerchief and wiped his eyes. "In that case, I'd be pleased to serve as this child's honorary grandfather," he said hoarsely, then hurried to change the subject. "Now, we had better get to work getting that child's father out of the mess he's in."

At the mention of Rye's situation, the air grew tense. All of them knew Rye was taking a grave chance, but Rye had stood firm when Aerial and Hershel had tried to convince him that there had to be another, less dangerous way of clearing his name and finding out the truth about Cletus Hackmore. Consequently, they had agreed to go along with him.

"Is everything set up at the sheriff's office?" Rye asked, his tone serious. "Does anyone suspect what's going on?"

Hershel shook his head. "I simply told the sher-

329

iff that Miss Windsor had had a change of heart and wanted to make a public statement at his office at eleven o'clock. I told the newspaper reporters the same thing. Luckily, most of the representatives of the out-of-town papers are still here, so we should have a good turn out."

"In that case, all we have left to do is toss out the bait and wait and see if Cletus Hackmore bites."

"By the way," Hershel added. "Did I tell you the extra little tidbit of gossip I picked up this morning?"

Rye and Aerial shook their heads.

"It seems that the poor unfortunate fellow in the alley was a chap by the name of Dave Sawyer who's lived in Fairfield all his life. Far as everyone knows, he's never been to Minnesota, never been to Nebraska, and never married or fathered any children—that anyone knows about—so it would seem very unlikely that he was your Cletus Hackmore . . ."

Chapter Twenty-one

An hour later, more nervous than ever now that they knew for certain the man in the alley couldn't be Cletus Hackmore, Aerial squared her shoulders and took Rye's arm. "I hope we're doing the right thing."

Rye smiled and patted her hand where she clutched at his sleeve. "We are. You know we won't be able to have the future we planned until we can put the past completely behind us."

"I know that." She forced a brave smile and lovingly canvassed her tall husband's features. Even with a bruised cheek and a lip that was still slightly swollen, he was the most handsome man she had ever seen.

She had convinced him to let her cut his hair and comb it back in a more conventional—and white—style than the unruly, over-the-ears-and-collar way he usually wore it. Her idea had been that the less he did to antagonize the townspeople, the better chance they would have of being believed.

So, though it went against his principles, Rye had gone along with her, wearing the white shirt and dark suit he had pilfered from the island cottage on Lake Champlain. He even carried a bowler hat, which he had promised to don once they were outside the hotel.

Flanked on one side by his blond wife and on the other by Hershel Zimmermann, who though dark, would never be taken for an Indian, Rye could have definitely passed for white back East, and probably most places in the Midwest. Farther west, he would no doubt have had a bigger problem, but fortunately, they weren't in the West.

As if their actions were orchestrated by one mind, Aerial, Rye, and Hershel all sucked in a deep breath in unison, then stepped out into the hallway.

A reporter who had evidently sneaked past the guard and up the back stairs to get a jump on his competitors appeared out of nowhere. "Miss Windsor!" he shouted. "Is that him? Is that the Indian who kidnapped you? Are you claiming the reward for his capture?"

Resisting the urge to yell the truth at the eager newspaper man, Aerial gave him her most winning smile. "You ought to be ashamed of yourself, young man. You know it wouldn't be fair to the others if I answered those questions before the appointed time. I'm afraid you'll just have to be patient and wait for your answers until we get to the sheriff's office."

"Can't you give me something? I really need this to impress my editor at the *Ledger*. Anything will do. How'd you get him here? What kind of Indian is he?"

Rye narrowed his eyes threateningly and grabbed the reporter by his coat front. "Didn't you hear the lady, son? She said we'll answer all your questions at the sheriff's office!"

His eyes wide with fright, the young reporter nodded his head. "Y-y-yes sssssssir," he whimpered. "I didn't mean anything wrong. I was just trying to do my job."

Rye released the newsman and straightened his coat for him. "Good."

Her expression tense, Aerial tugged on Rye's sleeve, drawing him into the waiting elevator.

Hershel backed in after them, holding out his

hands to stop the reporter from following. "They will answer all your questions at eleven o'clock in front of the sheriff's office." He nodded for the elevator operator to shut the doors leaving the determined reporter to use the stairs.

In the lobby, there were many more reporters and curious townspeople shouting at Aerial and pushing their way forward to get closer. Retaining a firm grip on Rye's arm, a grip that said, *I'll do the talking,* she gave everyone the same answers she had given the man upstairs. They all would just have to wait.

Through it all, Rye remained silent, his fists balled, his teeth clenched. Knowing another loss of control like he'd had in the upstairs hallway could ruin everything, he restrained himself and let Aerial and Hershel fend off the reporters, both verbally and physically, something they were both amazingly good at.

"Clear the way. All your questions will be answered in due time. Let Miss Windsor through . . ." Hershel shouted, elbowing his way forward, his grip on Rye's other arm iron strong. "Clear the way."

With determination and the old-fashioned *chutzpah* that had made him a great promoter at one time, Hershel led them to the front of the crowd, never missing a step. By the time they arrived on the square, they were heading the throng.

Her chin high, her posture stiff, Aerial kept her eyes focused on their objective: the door to the sheriff's office. So far, the sheriff wasn't out front. She gave her watch a brief glance. Two minutes to eleven.

As Aerial, Rye, and Hershel stepped onto the sidewalk in front of the jail, the door to the office flew open. "Miss Windsor," the sheriff greeted her, his suspicious stare on Rye. "What is this?"

"Good morning, Sheriff." She deliberately made her voice loud to be sure it carried over the din of the excited crowd. "We have brought you Rye Berenger to stand trial for the murder of which I wrongly accused him. But before we surrender him, we have a statement to make to all these good people—"

Her eyes darted purposefully to the sheriff's right hand hovering dangerously close to the handle of the gun on his hip. Her smile in place, she leaned toward him. "Who, I should point out," she added for his ears alone, "are watching your every move and would no doubt take a very dim view of a sheriff who would shoot down an unarmed man who was in the process of turning himself in, not to mention how they would feel if a stray bullet hit an innocent citizen!"

"Go on," the sheriff said, relaxing his hand. "But I'm warnin' you, if you and this Injun think you're gonna get away with somethin' . . ."

"I'll take your words into consideration," Aerial answered, turning to the waiting crowd and giving Hershel a nod.

Hershel held up his hands to silence the crowd. "Ladies and gentlemen. Miss Aerial Windsor, the daring young woman who has brought national recognition and attention to your fair city, has a statement to make. If you will kindly give her your attention, I'm certain you will find what she has to tell you very interesting." He stepped back, positioning himself between Rye and the sheriff.

To a round of enthusiastic applause, Aerial, Rye and Hershel moved forward as a unit. Retaining her hold on Rye's arm, she smiled at the friendly reception. After a moment she assumed a serious expression, and the audience grew quiet.

"I'm certain most all of you know that during my last performance in your city I saw a man running out of an alley where another man lay dead. Much to my shame and chagrin now, I must admit I *assumed* the running man had killed the other one, so I allowed myself to be pressured by the sheriff into signing a deposition stating I had actually seen the man murdered, when in fact I had seen nothing of the kind.

"That's a bold-faced lie. I never pressured her into signin' nothin'."

Aerial waited for the sheriff to finish before proceeding. "The sheriff convinced me that if I didn't sign that deposition before I left town, he would have to let the man go because he had no other proof on which to hold him. He then told me that since the man was no doubt guilty, my life would be in danger because I was the only person who could testify that he was in the alley. So I signed it."

She took a deep breath and shook her head apologetically. "I know now that what I did was terribly wrong. Being *afraid* is no excuse for bearing false witness against another human being. Since that time, I have learned my sin was doubly inexcusable because the man I accused wasn't guilty at all. He had merely been the unfortunate person who discovered the dead body. He was running away because he was afraid of being blamed because he was part Indian, a fear we now know was justified." She lifted her handkerchief to her eyes and dabbed them delicately.

"You can imagine how terrible I felt when I learned the truth. I returned to Fairfield as soon as I could, determined to correct my mistake. Upon my arrival, I immediately went to the sheriff, rescinded my statement, and reminded him that I had actually seen very little."

She gave the sheriff a disapproving frown. "However, the sheriff refused to drop the charges against the man I saw running, the man I now know *did not* kill the man in your alley. This man—" She smiled at Rye "—Rye Berenger, stands before you today prepared to face a trial for a crime he did not commit, a crime for which the sheriff has no proof or witnesses. And do you know why?"

Her eyes wide with disbelief, she scanned the crowd imploringly. "Because the sheriff says he doesn't need proof or witnesses to arrest Mr. Berenger. He insists a jury will find Mr. Berenger guilty for the simple reason that he is part Indian, and consequently guilty."

"What makes you so sure he didn't kill poor old Dave Sawyer?" someone yelled from the back of the crowd.

"Yeah," came an agreeing shout. "Fact he was scalped sounds like pretty good proof to me."

Aerial betrayed her confident air with a brief, uneasy glance at Rye, whose loving eyes told her she was doing fine and to go on.

They had already decided she would skirt around the scalping issue if at all possible, so it came in handy that the question and scalping comment were lumped together. She would just ignore that subject and answer the question. She made direct eye contact with different people in the crowd and proceeded.

"For the logical reason that Rye Berenger had no reason to want Dave Sawyer dead, and every reason to want him alive."

"Would you explain that, Miss Windsor?" one of the newspapermen asked.

"Of course. We believe that Mr. Sawyer could have led Mr. Berenger to the murderer of Mr. Berenger's parents and baby sister thirteen years ago in Nebraska, and we are just as certain that fear of exposure is what caused the murderer of

336

that defenseless family in Nebraska to take the life of Dave Sawyer in that alley last July."

"What about the scalp?" another voice yelled. "Is this invisible murderer o' yours a Injun too?"

Damn, there it was again. They weren't going to let it go. She could strangle Rye. That one rash action was going to ruin everything yet. She had better think fast, because it was obvious this crowd wasn't going to give up without an answer!

"No, the murderer isn't an Indian. He's white—as white as any of you standing out there. In fact, he could be your neighbor." She paused and leveled her gaze on the man who'd asked the question. "Or yours," she said, picking out another member of the audience to point to.

Instinctively, the people in the crowd surveyed the citizens around them, obviously trying to figure out who it could be.

"However," she went on with a dramatic flare that would put a traveling evangelist to shame, "being white didn't stop the murderer from scalping Mr. Berenger's mother, father and *eight-year-old* sister thirteen years ago. So why would it stop him from taking Dave Sawyer's scalp, especially if he wanted it to *seem* as if an Indian had done the killing."

The reporters continued to scratch notes frantically in their books, but the townspeople began to shift uncomfortably. They eyed each other suspiciously, each of their covert little glances becoming less and less subtle.

Aerial smiled inwardly. She could see the doubts whirling in every head and decided she couldn't have been any more effective if she'd planned on it happening this way. Thank goodness Rye had gotten rid of that scalp right after he realized the foolishness of what he'd done. If he'd kept it . . . Well, she wouldn't think about that.

"You must remember, there is no evidence Mr. Berenger took the scalp, either. He certainly didn't have it with him when he was arrested."

"That true, Sheriff?" someone asked.

Glaring at the man who'd brought him into it, the sheriff stepped forward. "Yeah, it's true. But it don't mean he didn't do it. He coulda got rid of it when he knew he was gonna be caught."

"The way I remember it," reasoned another voice, "the Injun was caught leavin' town like he had no idea he was gonna be stopped. I saw the arrest. Mater of fact, so did most of the whole town." There was a murmur of agreement from the crowd.

"Besides, it don't make sense for him to throw it away. Everyone knows a Injun keeps the scalps he takes to keep track o' his kills. It's how they count what they call 'coups.' Ain't that right, Injun?" a man asked Rye.

Rye realized now wasn't the time to correct the man's understanding of the facts on counting 'coups,' especially when it sounded like that man was bordering on being on his side, so he shrugged and managed a half grin.

"If you got reason to believe Dave's murderer is one o' us, then we got a right to know who it is!" a woman yelled.

"Yes, who is he?" a second woman cried. "Tell us his name."

Spotting the woman in the crowd, her young daughter clutched to her side, Aerial opened her mouth to answer, but the sheriff cut her off.

"All right, I've heard enough o' this hogwash. This Injun's guilty as sin, an' we all know it. This gal's tryin' to pull the wool over your eyes to get him off."

"Let her talk, Sheriff," a woman cried. "If there's a murderer among us, we want to know

338

who it is."

"Only murderer is that Injun she spent all these months cozyin' up with since last time she was in town," the sheriff replied, his insinuation obvious. He reached across Hershel and took Rye's arm. "Let's go, Injun. You and her can tell the rest o' your story to a judge n' jury."

"Let her talk. Let her talk. Let her talk. Let her talk. Let her talk." The chanting women were quickly joined by the men. Everyone wanted to know whom Aerial was accusing, probably more from morbid curiosity than anything else.

Trapped, the sheriff hesitated and directed his attention toward his office, seeming to be waiting for someone to make the decision for him.

"Your sheriff acts like a man with something to hide," Hershel said, loudly enough to be heard all the way in the back of the crowd.

"Why won't you let her finish, Sheriff?" a reporter yelled accusingly.

"Who are you protecting?" another bellowed.

"What are you afraid of?" still another voice contributed.

Threatened by the shouts, the sheriff had no choice but to defend himself. "I ain't afraid. I jest don't like the idea o' her publicly malignin' innocent folks when any fool kin see she'll say jest about anything to protect this Injun. But if you want to listen to more o' her lies, far be it from me to git in your way." He released Rye's arm and held his hands out to his side in mock surrender. "Go ahead. Show us which one of these good folks is your vicious madman who goes around scalpin' little children."

"Unfortunately," Aerial began, "we don't know what he looks like, but—"

"That's what I thought!" the sheriff said with a triumphant—and relieved—laugh. He gave the crowd a knowing grin. "There now! You folks satisfied?"

There was a disappointed groan from the crowd. Some people even started to leave.

"But we do know his name!" Aerial shouted over the disgruntled hum, causing the departing dissenters to return their attention to the group on the sidewalk.

"Well?" Chester Hagen asked, making his presence known for the first time since the confrontation had begun by stepping up to Aerial's side from behind. "Don't keep us waiting, Miss Windsor. What, pray tell, is the name of this imaginary villain of yours."

Rye narrowed his eyes angrily as he recognized the voice of the man he had heard in Aerial's room the night before. He had been on the verge of attacking him then, despite his own weakened condition and the chance he would have been taking by exposing himself, but fortunately Hershel had come to his rescue—again—and had arrived in time to stop him from doing anything stupid. He only hoped he could stay in control of his anger until they could flush out Hackmore. Then he vowed to beat Hagen to a bloody pulp for the way he had treated Aerial.

"We don't know what name he's using now," Rye answered, his eyes fastened on Hagen. "But when he killed my family in Nebraska, he went by the name Cletus Hackmore."

"Never heard of him," Hagen replied quickly. Then with a sarcastic sneer, he asked, "Any of you know anybody by the name of . . . what'd you call him?"

"Cletus Hackmore," Aerial repeated through her teeth, glaring at Hagen. "But we're sure he doesn't go by that name now."

"Now, let me get this straight," Hagen said,

making a show of keeping a straight face as he scanned the audience to share the humor of the situation with them. "You don't know what this mysterious murderer looks like. You don't know what name he's using now." He glanced back at Aerial, his demeanor deliberately amused. "What exactly do you know?"

"We know he hates Indians, because his—"

"Oh! Now we understand! He hates Indians, does he? That certainly narrows our list of possible suspects down, doesn't it? Down to almost every citizen in the county." He threw back his head and laughed loudly.

Hagen's laugh triggered a memory so vivid in Rye's head, that he felt dizzy. Could it be? Could Chester Hagen be Cletus Hackmore? Could that be what his dream had been telling him? That he would recognize Cletus Hackmore by his laugh?

Stunned, Rye stared at Hagen. Was it him? He searched the man's features for anything familiar, but he found nothing. The man he remembered had scraggly brown hair and beard. Hagen's muttonchop whiskers and hair were snowy white and neatly trimmed, to say nothing of clean. Hackmore was thin and wore filthy, ill-fitting clothes. Though not fat, Hagen was beefy and well-dressed. How could Cletus Hackmore have made such a turnaround from drunken derelict to wealthy businessman? It was impossible.

Rye told himself it had to be another trick his mind was playing on him. He'd been just as sure he'd had the right man in the alley, and he'd been wrong then. A similar laugh wasn't enough to accuse a man. And after all, it had been a lot of years since he'd heard Cletus Hackmore laugh.

But no matter how he argued with himself, Rye couldn't make that unmistakable laugh of his nightmare stop echoing in his mind.

Taking care to hide any inner turmoil he was feeling, Rye spoke. "It's possible, even probable, that most of these people hate Indians," he said, his voice a controlled monotone. "But how many of them had families killed by the Sioux in the Minnesota massacre of '62? Oblivious to the grunts of surprise and whispers sweeping the crowd, Rye watched Hagen for a reaction. "Does that narrow it down enough for you?"

A flicker of discomfort skittered across Hagen's face as his eyes zipped over the crowd, then to the sheriff. "From what I understand," he answered, obviously straining to keep up his amused facade, "over five hundred innocent white settlers were killed by those savages. It stands to reason some of the survivors might have left Minnesota and come to Iowa to start over."

"By way of southeastern Nebraska?" Rye asked pointedly.

"Why not?" Hagen searched the gaping crowd for support. Seeing none there, he turned his scrutiny to the sheriff, who was staring at him with the same puzzled expression everyone else watched him with. "Well? Are you going to just stand there gawking, Sheriff? You gave this breed a chance to produce his murderer and he couldn't do it. Now, do your job and put him behind bars where he belongs."

"I'm not sure I can rightly do that, Mr. Hagen," the sheriff answered, not moving. "Leastwise, not yet. Seems to me this Injun's made some pretty serious points that oughta be answered before I do anything else."

"Don't be a fool! Can't you see what they're doing? They're making this all up to divert your attention from the Indian so he'll get off scot-free."

"What I see is a real interestin' coincidence, in

342

as how you once told me you lived in Minnesota and Nebraska before comin' to Fairfield."

"You two-bit little has-been! Are you saying I killed this filthy breed's Indian-loving old man and his squaw and nit?"

There was a collective gasp from the crowd at Hagen's tirade.

The word "nit" hit Rye square in the head, removing the last of his doubts. Cletus Hackmore and Chester Hagen were the same man. His insides screaming for him to attack Hagen and choke the life out of him, Rye froze, unable to do anything but stare.

Stunned by Hagen's words, Aerial twisted to the side and stared aghast at him. It all made sense now. The exorbitant reward. The out-of-state gunmen. The emphasis on bringing Rye in dead instead of alive. The fact that he hadn't shown himself this morning until they had announced that Rye couldn't identify his face!

"I'm only sayin' there's a coincidence I'd like to see explained," the sheriff went on, unaware of the change in Aerial and Rye.

"You said it yourself," Hagen chuckled, obviously finding it more difficult to keep his composure by the minute. "It's a coincidence. Anyway, what difference does it make if I lived in Minnesota and Nebraska? So have hundreds of other people. That doesn't make any of us murderers! Now, Sheriff, either do what the taxpayers are paying you for and get this riffraff off our streets, or be prepared to find yourself unemployed!"

The sheriff inspected the attentive observers for an indication of what he should do. He didn't like Indians any better than anyone else did, but if the truth were to be known, he liked Chester Hagen even less. Still, Hagen had a lot of influence in this town, and a smart man wouldn't attempt to do battle with him unless he had more ammunition to go on than a simple coincidence.

"Before you give in to his threats, Sheriff," Aerial interrupted, her tone hard, her lips curled bitterly. "I think we should ask Mr. Hagen if it's another 'coincidence' that he knew Mr. Berenger's mother was the Indian, and not his father?"

"Yeah," one of the reporters hollered. "How'd you know his father wasn't the Indian? They never told us that."

His respiration accelerating, Hagen scanned the audience in much the same way a cornered animal would do. "It's obvious," he finally said. "The breed has a white man's name. Besides, only a white man with a squaw wife could have owned a farm in Nebraska, not the other way around."

"No one said anything about the Berenger's owning a farm, Mr. Hagen," Aerial said, her calm smile belying the livid anger and hatred she was feeling at the moment. "No one, that is, except you."

The heads of the audience swerved from Aerial to Hagen to see how he would respond this time.

Sweating profusely, Chester forced a laugh. "It was just a guess. Everyone in southeastern Nebraska farms."

"What do you say to that, Miss Windsor," the sheriff asked, his eyebrows raised questioningly.

"I say a lucky guess on top of your coincidences stretches the realm of possibility to the limits, Sheriff," Aerial declared, reaching into her large handbag. "But since Mr. Hagen is so good at explaining coincidences, I'd like to know if he can explain how this knife stolen from Mr. Berenger's father the day he died ended up in Dave Sawyer's coat pocket." She brought forth Rye's father's knife. "It was crafted by Mr. Berenger's father. Have you seen it before?" She handed the knife to

344

the befuddled lawman.

The sheriff took the offered knife. "Yeah, I seen it."

"Hold the knife up so we kin all git a look," a member of audience shouted.

Holding the knife aloft for all to see, the sheriff went on. "The Injun had it with him when we arrested him. He took it with him when he broke outta jail."

"Yes he did," Aerial said directly to the crowd, "because it was the only thing he had left to remind him of his family. But I'm getting ahead of myself. Let me explain how we think Mr. Sawyer got the knife. We believe the murderer killed Mr. Sawyer because Mr. Sawyer had somehow found out his secret and knew that Mr. Berenger was in town looking for the killer of his family." She paused and surveyed the audience, pleased to realize no one was laughing any longer.

"How much more of this garbage are we going to listen to?" Hagen bellowed. "If there was ever a murderer here, it musta been Sawyer himself. And that's how he got the knife."

"Sawyer wasn't no murderer," someone defended him. "A drunk, yeah, but not a murderer."

" 'Sides, he never got more'n ten miles outta this town in his whole life."

Aerial raised her voice to be certain she was heard at the back of the crowd and went on. "We believe Mr. Sawyer's killer then planted the murder weapon—the knife—on the body in the alley, knowing Mr. Berenger was on his way to the alley where someone told him he would find Cletus Hackmore. Hackmore was obviously counting on the fact that the years would have caused a young boy's memory of his face to fade, and that Mr. Berenger would assume he had found his man when he discovered his father's knife in Mr.

Sawyer's coat."

She took a breath and nodded her head knowingly. "He guessed, correctly I might add, that Mr. Berenger would retrieve his father's knife and try to leave town, never knowing that his father's killer was still alive. If he got away, that was fine with Cletus Hackmore; if he was stopped, he would have the murder weapon on him and would be hung. Either way was all right with Hackmore, as long as he got rid of Rye Berenger permanently and no one discovered his ugly secret."

Aerial eyed Hagen pointedly. "How close am I to what happened, Mr. Hagen? Or should we call you, Mr. Hackmore?"

Chapter Twenty-two

Hackmore's eyes bulged angrily and he took a threatening step toward Aerial, then stopped himself. Instead of attacking her, he eyed her purposefully, his expression saying, *You started this. Now I'm going to bury you alive.*

He turned to the audience in an obvious play for camaraderie. "Are you going to stand there and let this *stranger,* this Indian's whore, get away with this vicious slander?"

There was a united gasp of shock from the crowd at Hackmore's choice of words and his obvious disregard for the ladies present.

His face twisted with rage, Rye moved to lunge at Hackmore. However, Hershel's and Aerial's grips on his arms checked his action.

Aerial gave her husband an encouraging nod, reminding him with her eyes that he had promised not to damage their cause by acting rashly, no matter how difficult it might be. They were here to expose Cletus Hackmore; nothing else mattered. They had both known there was a good probability that name-calling would come into this confrontation sooner or later, and they had decided that as long as they both knew the truth, what others thought about them did not matter. They could not, *would not,* be destroyed by words.

"But you know me, don't you?" Hackmore went on, oblivious to the fact that he was teetering on the edge of death and that the only thread keeping him from toppling over that edge was a woman's gently restraining hand on her husband's arm. "You've known me for years as a decent, law-abiding citizen who has dedicated his life to making this town what it is today. I've been in your homes. You've been in mine. We've done business together. I've lent you money when you were in trouble. Have I ever done anything that would make it possible for you to believe I'm capable of murder?"

He paused and gave Aerial and Rye a deliberately taunting arch of his brows before proceeding. "On the other hand, what do you know about these two *strangers?* An Indian who was caught running from the scene, the murder knife in his possession, and a young woman of *highly questionable morals,* who travels all over the country, unchaperoned I should point out, flaunting herself in revealing costumes and tights. Who knows how many men she was with before she took up with that Indian? I ask you, can you believe anything a woman like that says? I can't, and I don't think you, my friends, can either."

A wave of nausea rocked through Aerial as she considered the collective gathering of unfamiliar faces, unfamiliar and suddenly very unfriendly. She had used her last argument to convince them that Chester Hagen was indeed Cletus Hackmore, but she could clearly see that she had failed. The repulsed and disapproving expressions glaring at her said it all. As far as they were concerned, she was a fallen woman who'd been with an Indian and so was no doubt a liar.

She sagged against Rye's arm, guilt overwhelming the false confidence that had held her up until now. She had let Rye down. They had exposed the real Cletus Hackmore and no one believed her. Now Rye would go to jail and Cletus Hackmore would stay free.

With the speed of a striking snake, Rye wrenched his arm from Aerial's grip and lunged toward Hackmore. "You bastard!" His voice was a low, feral growl. "You killed them and you're going to pay for it."

"No, Rye!" Aerial screamed. "He's not worth it! We'll find another way."

Moving much faster than would be expected of a man half his age, Hackmore grabbed Aerial by the shoulders and ducked behind her to shield himself from Rye. "Better listen to her, breed!"

"Easy now, son," the sheriff coaxed from behind Rye, his revolver drawn and pressing into Rye's back. "You're already in enough trouble as it is. The fact that you turned yourself in oughta help with the judge. Don't go doin' somethin' stupid and spoil your chances o' gettin' off."

"Get your filthy hands off her, you pig," Rye growled through teeth bared in a snarl.

"Not till you back off, filth." Hackmore tightened his grip on Aerial's arms.

Aerial raised her eyes in a desperate plea to Rye—not for herself, but for him. "Please, Rye. Not this way. Whether these people admit it or not, they know we're telling the truth. Sooner or later they'll see him for what he is and do the right thing."

Fighting the white-hot anger with every ounce of control he could muster, Rye consciously relaxed.

"Want me to cuff him, Sheriff?" one of the deputies asked, dutifully rushing forward to grab Rye's arm.

"Before you do that, Sheriff," a woman called out as she pushed her way forward through the crowd, dragging a reluctant man behind her. "Seth here's got somethin' to say that's gonna put a different light on this situation."

Everyone on the boardwalk and in the street directed their curiosity toward the approaching couple.

"What is it, Seth?" the sheriff asked. "You know somethin' that'll clear this up?"

"Yeah, I guess I might." He gave Hackmore an uneasy glance, then averted his eyes to his wife, who nodded her head for him to continue. "Though I didn't think much about it 'til now."

"Well, what is it?" the sheriff asked, surprised to realize he believed the Indian and the woman and was secretly hoping whatever Seth knew was something that would help them, not Hagen.

"Go on, Seth," the woman urged. "Tell the sheriff what you told me."

"Well," the husband drawled, obviously not certain he was doing the right thing. "I was havin' a drink with Dave Sawyer the day he died." Seth gave his wife a nervous glance. "Jest that one. He was buyin' an' I didn't wanna be unpolite by refusin' his invitation. Said he was celebratin' comin' into some money."

"Did Dave say where he got that money?" the sheriff asked.

"He just said he'd learned somethin' about Chester Hagen that Hagen didn't want spread around town, and that Hagen was bein' real friendly . . . 'stead o' treatin' him like dirt the way he usually did. He said things was gonna change for him now. Talked about gettin' cleaned up and maybe openin' a saloon or even goin' in partners with Hagen in his real estate business now that he was gonna have some money comin' in."

"From Hagen?" someone asked anxiously.

"That's the idea I got, though he didn't really say. The only thing he actually said Hagen give him was a knife. He pointed to the knife the sheriff still held. *"That* knife!"

There was a shocked gasp from the crowd as the

meaning of what Seth had revealed sank in.

"This knife?" the sheriff confirmed, holding the knife out for Seth to examine more closely. "Are you sure?"

Seth eyed it carefully, then nodded. "I'm sure. Reason I am is there's a design carved in the handle I thought was kinda clever." He paused and pointed to the handle for the sheriff's benefit. "See, it's a whole line of frontward and backward capital Bs. You can tell someone took a lotta time and care carvin' all them Bs so perfect like that."

The sheriff inspected Seth's face for answers. "I don't suppose Sawyer mentioned how Mr. Hagen came by this knife, did he?"

"Matter of fact, he did. Dave said Hagen told him he got it out west from a squaw man who owed him a debt."

"There, Sheriff!" Aerial cut in. "Now do you believe us? I demand that you arrest Chester Hagen for the murder of Dave Sawyer, as well as the Berenger family of Nebraska!"

Hackmore jerked Aerial back against his chest and brought his mouth to her ear. "Shut your mouth, whore," he hissed, just loud enough for her to hear. "Or you're dead." She felt the hard barrel of a revolver bore into the small of her back, though she didn't think anyone else noticed. They were too intent on Seth and the sheriff.

"Well, now," the sheriff crowed, "looks like we've got another one o' them 'coincidences' here, don't it, Mr. Hagen? Whadda ya say to that?"

Hackmore took a step back, dragging Aerial with him. "That fool's lying. He owes me money and thinks if he can get rid of me he can get out of paying it back. I never saw that knife before today and he can't prove I did."

"You're the one who's lyin', Hagen," another man shouted. "I saw it in your desk drawer a coupla years ago when you took out your whiskey bottle to pour us a drink. I asked you about it and you told me the same thing Seth says you told Dave Sawyer, that you got it out west from a squaw man who owed you."

"Damn you, damn you all!" Hackmore screeched, his eyes leveling on the man who had come forward to support Seth's story. "You'd stand up for this half-breed filth and his white slut against me? Well, to hell with you. You're no better than they are. I don't need you. I don't need any of you."

"He's got a gun!" a woman warned as Hackmore brought the gun he'd been holding in Aerial's back into full view. At the same time, he brought his free hand around her waist and pinned her arms to her sides.

Shouting and screaming, the crowd began to scatter and dive for cover, the people who had spoken out against Hackmore leading the rush.

But instead of firing the weapon at the audience as it appeared his intention had been, he cocked the hammer and pressed the tip of the barrel to Aerial's temple. "I should have hunted you down and killed you thirteen years ago, breed," he said to Rye.

His dark, expressionless eyes darting calculatingly to Aerial, then back to Hackmore, Rye took a step forward, his hands out to his side to indicate that he was unarmed. "Well, here's your chance, Hackmore." He took a second step, his hard mien deliberately challenging.

"No, Rye!" Aerial cried, frozen with fear for her own life as well as for Rye's. "Don't do it."

Rye acted as if he hadn't heard her. "What do you say, Hackmore? Have you got the nerve to kill me here in front of all these witnesses? I'm not armed. Or do you only do your killing in alleys

352

and when you can sneak up behind your victims?"

"Another step and I blow her head off!" Hackmore threatened.

Still showing no sign of emotion, Rye narrowed his eyes at Hackmore. "You could, but you won't. If you kill her, you'll be giving up your one chance to see me dead, because you'll never get off a second shot before every gun trained on your back fills you full of lead." A slow, goading smile stretched across his tight lips. "And you can't stand the thought of knowing that when all the smoke is cleared, the 'breed' you really want to kill will still be alive, can you? You'll go to hell knowing I lived to spit on your bloody, bullet-ridden body. For the rest of eternity you'll be haunted by me laughing over your dead body the way you laughed over my family's bodies."

Rye took another step forward, intentionally calculating that Hackmore could be taunted into aiming the revolver at him and away from Aerial. "How does it feel knowing I'm going to best you *again,* the way I did when I was eleven years old and lived in spite of the bullet you tried to put in me."

A flood of horrified moans and whispers rolled through the cowering audience, but Rye didn't notice. His concentration on Hackmore and Aerial was all-consuming. They could have been absolutely alone, for all he knew.

"The hell you will!"

For an instant, Rye thought Hackmore would rise to the bait, and he tensed, preparing himself.

However Hackmore's actions were no more predictable than those of a cornered animal. Rather than aiming at Rye, he hauled Aerial back harder against his chest and pressed the gun sharply into her temple, forcing her to tilt her head to the side. "I'll see you both dead."

"Not unless you shoot me first." Rye eased two or three inches closer to Hackmore. He wanted to be in the perfect position to kick the revolver out of Hackmore's hand when he did aim it in his direction. It was a risky plan—actually not a very good one at all—but he didn't have any other choice. He had to get that gun away from Aerial.

"Come on, Mr. Hagen," the sheriff coaxed, taking a step toward Hackmore. "We're at a stalemate. Why don't you gimme that gun and we'll go into my office and settle this nice and peaceably. Whadda you say?"

"I say you're a fool if you move another inch. Now, get out of my way, and you and your people drop those guns if you don't want to see this whore's brains splattered all over the sidewalk." He took a pace back. "You know I'll do it, don't you?" he asked Rye directly. "Thanks to you and your whore, I've got nothing to lose now.

Knowing no one could shoot at Hackmore even if they had a guaranteed clear shot, Rye forced himself to breathe deeply in order to release some of the tension building inside his head.

For one thing, he consciously reminded himself, whether or not the bullet killed Hackmore instantly or merely wounded him, his reflex action would automatically release the hammer on his revolver and kill Aerial; for another, if he was shot from behind, the bullet could easily pass through him into Aerial's body. There was no choice but to do as he said.

The sheriff obviously reached the same conclusion and signaled with his head for his deputies and the private citizens who held guns on Hackmore to put down their weapons.

To the sound of dropping revolvers and shuffling boots, the men on the wooden sidewalk stepped aside, clearing a path for Hackmore and his prisoner.

"Anybody moves, she's dead!" Hackmore shouted, dragging her backward.

Everyone believed him; no one budged from where they stood. Helplessly, Rye watched his deadly enemy mount a black horse and haul Aerial into the saddle in front of him.

"Everybody stay put for an hour and I'll let her go once I know I'm safe. But if I even think someone's trying to follow me, I'll kill her and leave her for the buzzards," Hackmore warned, then kicked his mount hard in the sides.

Responding to the signal, the steed leaned back on his haunches, then spurted forward at a full gallop, leaving the dirt street and the stunned citizens of Fairfield in a cloud of dust.

A blinding explosion of unmitigated terror burst in Rye's brain as he watched Aerial and Hackmore round the corner and disappear from view. Oblivious to the frantic, panicked actions of people around him, he didn't wait for the sheriff to tell him he was free to go before he stepped off the boardwalk into the street, his dark features twisted with vengeance and fear such as he'd never known existed.

Hershel, who'd remained silent through the entire encounter, ran up to Rye. "What are you going to do?"

"I'm going to the hotel for my weapons. Then I'm going after my wife," he growled.

"But you heard what he said! He'll kill her."

"You don't really think he intends to let her go, do you? Once he feels safe enough to get by without a hostage he'll kill her anyway. If for no other reason than because he's figured out what it'll do to me if she dies. But as long as he knows I'm on his trail, he'll keep her alive to hide behind."

"Berenger!" the sheriff shouted. "Stop!"

"You're going to have to shoot me to stop me, Sheriff!" Rye shouted back over his shoulder, never breaking his stride.

"I don't intend to stop you. I'm going with you," the sheriff announced, catching up with Rye. "You need a horse? I sent a deputy over to the livery to saddle up one o' my fastest for you in case do."

"Thanks, that'll help. But just you and me. No posse. I can't take a chance on Hackmore hearing us coming and going crazy and killing her if he realizes he can't escape."

"Agreed."

And one more thing. Once we know Aerial's safe, Hackmore's mine."

"We'll see about that, son. But after what that bastard's put you through, one way or another we ain't gonna let him get away with it." He handed Rye his father's knife. "Here, you might be wantin' this."

After an hour of riding at breakneck speed, Aerial's spine felt as though it would snap if it were jarred one more time. Holding herself rigid to keep from leaning on Hackmore, she had felt each jolt of the rough ride. Every inch of her cried out for her to relax, the way she had been able to do when she and Rye rode together. But the instant she thought about who she would be leaning on, she swore she would rather have her back snap in half than show a fraction of weakness to her kidnapper. That one thought gave her the strength to remain erect a few minutes more.

His sides heaving, his nostrils flaring, and his mouth white with froth, the horse Hagen had stolen suddenly stopped, obviously having given his rider all he had to give.

"Come on, damn you!" Hackmore screamed, using the quirt he'd taken from the saddle on the exhausted animal. The horse took a few stumbling steps, then staggered to a halt. Hackmore hit him again, but the animal didn't move.

"He can't go any farther," Aerial shouted, wishing she could get her hands on the quirt to use on Hackmore. "You're going to kill him if you force him! You've got to let him rest. No horse could keep up that pace, especially not carrying two of us!"

"Shut up, bitch!" Hackmore frantically cast his gaze over the surroundings, obviously looking for a place to hide. "When I need your advice I'll ask for it." He vaulted off the horse with the spryness of a much younger man, then dragged her off after him. Without speaking, he wrapped his arm around her middle and hoisted her off her feet. Obviously furious, he carried her into the dense woods that lined the road, leading the winded horse behind him.

"Where are you taking me? You said you would let me go if no one followed us."

"I told you to shut up!" he hissed, tightening his hold on her middle to emphasize his words.

All Aerial could think of was that Hackmore could be hurting her baby. If the rough ride hadn't done it then surely his hold on her waist could. "I can't breathe. Please, put me down and let me walk. I swear I won't make another sound."

No doubt because carrying her was telling on his own strength, and not in answer to her plea for mercy, Cletus set her down hard on her feet.

Before she could gain her footing, he grabbed her arm and tugged her forward, causing her to stumble. Scrambling to keep from falling, Aerial hiked her skirt above her ankles and stretched her stride to keep up.

357

Before long they settled into a pace that was easy for her, though it was obvious by Hackmore's heavy breathing that he was straining to keep it up. She smiled inwardly. Evidently, those months traveling cross-country had conditioned her for this, while Hackmore's years of sitting behind a desk had had just the opposite effect.

Walking behind Hackmore as she was, his fingers digging painfully into her arm, she thought of all the ways she would kill him if she got the chance. She wouldn't even warn him.

A well-placed knife right between the shoulder blades, enough to the left to ensure puncturing his black heart, would be perfect! In fact, the idea gave her a new spurt of energy. Or a gun! Lord, if she only had a gun. She would shoot him in the back! If ever a person deserved to be shot in the back, it was Cletus Hackmore.

Her eyes dropped to Hackmore's revolver in his holster. If she could just get close enough to reach for it. He was slowing down. Maybe . . .

Before Aerial could put her idea into action, Cletus hauled her forward and shoved her in front of him as if he had read her mind. This time, she did fall—flat out on the ground.

Spitting dry leaves and dirt out of her mouth, Aerial crawled to her hands and knees. She peered angrily through the thick blond curtain of hair that hung in her face. "What are you going to do?"

"Shut up!" Cletus demanded, staring down at her as though the sight of her made him physically ill. "I need to think."

Brushing her hair back off her face, Aerial sat back on her calves. "I could walk back to the road and start toward town. If anyone comes looking for me, I'll tell them you released me and kept going on the road."

Hackmore stared down at her, aghast. "What kind of a fool do you take me for, bitch? You don't really think I'd trust you not to tell them where I went, do you?"

"Even if I'm lying, what would I be able to tell them? They're an hour behind us, and by the time they find me it could be dark, and I won't have any idea where you are."

Hackmore pondered the densely forested area as if he might be considering her point.

"And you can travel much faster without me to slow you down," she added, hoping to put a clincher on the suggestion.

"You haven't figured it out yet, have you?" He curled his lip in an ugly smile. "I never had any intention of letting you go."

"But you told them—"

"To *hell* with what I told them! A white woman who ruts with an Indian is no better than one herself, and she deserves the same treatment as the buck she shares a buffalo robe with. Indians are like lice. The only good ones are dead ones. That goes for their squaws and nits, too! If you let one live, first thing you know, the whole country is infested. Besides, for all I know you've got that breed's filthy seed growing in your belly right now, and I couldn't live with my conscience if I thought I'd had an Indian's nit right here in my hands and hadn't rid the world of it and its whore of a mother."

Shocked by the untempered hatred in Hackmore's words, Aerial could only stare at him for several seconds. "If I'm so loathsome, why haven't you already killed me? Surely, you could have traveled faster riding by yourself."

Hackmore threw back his head and laughed, truly amused. "Because as long as you're alive the breed won't touch me. Oh, he'll follow me, all right, but he won't try anything as long as there's a chance you're alive. In fact, you're going to be a big help to me. The way he feels about keeping you alive, he's going to walk right into my trap and let me kill him."

"You're wrong! You'll never get the best of Rye Berenger! Just you wait and see. He won't let you get away with this."

"Oh, yes, he will. There won't be anything he can do to stop me, because until the very last minute, he'll think he's saving you. Then when he realizes you're going to die, too, it'll be too late for him to change his mind."

"You won't get away with this."

"There you go again, making stupid assumptions. Not only will I get away with it, but I'll live to kill hundreds more of you Indian vermin. Now that I think about it, I ought to thank you for shaking me out of the comfortable little life I'd made for myself in Fairfield. It feels good to be free to get back to my original goal."

"Which is?" Aerial asked, hoping to keep him talking long enough to come up with a plan of escape. Now that she knew he intended to kill her anyway, she had nothing to lose by making a break for it—and everything to gain!

" 'Which is' " he imitated her, "to kill as many Indians as I can before I die. But once I'm rid of the two of you, I'm not going to waste any more time just killing them one at a time. They breed too fast for that. From now on, I intend to rub out—that's a Comanche expression—hundreds at a time."

A chill of horror crept up Aerial's back as she looked into Hackmore's deranged eyes. "H-how will you do that?"

"Dynamite!" he announced, his eyes bright with a feral gleam. "I'll ride right onto their reservations and blow their disease-infested villages up. It's so perfect I don't know why the army didn't think to do it before we wasted all our tax money on fighting them and rounding them up and putting them on the reservations. Think of the money and time we could have saved on feeding them all these years, much less on housing and clothing their lazy asses while they lie around doing nothing but breeding more of their kind. I'll be a national hero!"

"My God! You're insane!"

Before Hackmore could respond, a cracking sound caught their attention, as if someone or something had stepped on a branch and broken it. Aerial and her captor both quickly twisted their heads to determine the source of the noise.

"He's here!" Hackmore whispered, yanking Aerial to her feet as he whipped his gun from its holster and stabbed it into her back. "Just like I told you he would be."

"You don't know that!" Aerial's voice was thready as she tried to catch her breath. "It's probably just some wild animal rooting for food."

"It was him, all right. I can smell a Indian a mile off! And he's alone, just like I knew he'd be."

Chapter Twenty-three

"Breed!" Hackmore called out. "I know you're there. I heard you."

Rye leveled his annoyed glare at Sheriff Riley, who flashed an apologetic wince at him and shrugged his shoulders. "Sorry," the clumsy lawman mouthed, freezing where he stood.

Signaling the sheriff to drop down and stay put, Rye indicated he would circle around to the other side of Hackmore and Aerial. With typical Indian stealth, he silently dissolved into the brush.

"I told you it wasn't anyone," Aerial protested after a few moments of silence.

"Oh, he's there all right. Can't you smell him? The only thing that fouls the air worse than a skunk that's been dead a week or two is an Indian!"

"I don't smell anything. It's your imagination. There's no one out there. Besides, Rye couldn't have caught up with us this fast. He wouldn't risk my life by leaving town before you said to."

His gaze intent on the woods in the area where the sound of the cracking twig had originated, Hackmore raised his hand and slapped Aerial soundly across the face. "Shut up! Let me listen."

"Oh!" she yelped.

When the easily identifiable sound of the slap and Aerial's cry didn't bring a response of any kind from the woods, Hackmore relaxed slightly. "Maybe you're right, but he'll be here any time now, and this will give us time to get a nice surprise ready for him when he does get here."

Hackmore whipped a rope off the saddle on the exhausted horse and hurriedly tied Aerial's wrists together in front of her, then cut the rope. With the cut end, he quickly fashioned what Aerial recognized as a hangman's noose.

"What are you planning to do?!"

Hackmore chuckled wickedly, and Aerial knew now what true evil looked and sounded like.

"I'm going to give your Indian lover a choice. He can either stand by and let you hang, or he can show himself and try to save you. Which do you think he'll choose? Your life or his own?"

Hackmore dropped the noose over her head and adjusted it to fit her neck, then threw the free end of the rope over a sturdy branch above their heads.

A triumphant smirk on his face, Hackmore took up the slack in the rope and secured it around his own waist. "You better hope that breed doesn't do anything stupid like try to kill me first, because the minute I go down . . ." He jabbed his thumb toward the sky. ". . . you go up." He grabbed his own throat and made a strangling noise for added effect.

The scratchy rope chafing the tender skin of her throat sent reality storming into Aerial's brain with the force of a tornado. This madman was actually going to hang her, and if Rye tried to stop it he would be killed, too. A wave of lightheadedness rocked through her and her knees suddenly started to buckle.

Immediately, the rough rope tightened on her neck, and she checked her fall in time. Vowing she would not give in to the weakness that threatened to overwhelm her, Aerial brought her bound hands to her neck and closed her eyes. "The Lord is my shepherd, I shall not want. He—"

363

Hackmore cut off her words with a yank on the rope around her neck and the evil laugh Aerial had come to know so well. "Praying won't save you, whore!"

Knowing one false move on his part could end the lives of his wife and child, Rye watched from the dense foliage. He had to make the right decision the first time. There would be no second chance.

His mouth was cotton dry. His entire body had broken out in a cold sweat. His lungs ached, as if the air trapped in them was expanding and couldn't escape. And his heart . . . God, his heart was racing so fast that he wouldn't be surprised if it ruptured in the next instant.

Moving like a ghost, he pitched a rock so that it landed where Hackmore had to turn away from Aerial to investigate the noise.

The instant Hackmore pivoted away, Rye revealed himself to Aerial, praying it wouldn't take but a second to catch her attention.

At first her eyes widened in confusion. Then she shifted them nervously to Hackmore's back, before focusing on Rye again.

"I know you're there, breed," Hackmore yelled, speaking to the spot where the rock had landed. "You've been trying to pass for white so long you've gotten sloppy."

As soon as Aerial acknowledged his presence with a slight tipping of her head, Rye ducked out of view again and waited.

Hackmore watched for another full minute before he checked on Aerial. As soon as Hackmore returned his attention to her, Rye pitched another stone, this time aimed to land a few feet to the right of the location where he had tossed the first stone, hoping it sounded as if someone were walking noisily through the woods.

Hackmore spun around again. "That's it, breed! No more games. Either show yourself or the whore dies right now." He grabbed the taut rope for emphasis. "Are you going to stand there and watch her hang without trying to do anything about it?"

As Hackmore concentrated on where he was sure Rye was lurking, Rye let Aerial see him again. This time he used hand signals to communicate what he planned and how he needed for her to help. His plan—if it worked—didn't require her assistance, but if it didn't work, her aid could make a life-and-death difference.

As soon as Aerial indicated her understanding, Rye stood up, his revolver drawn. "Over here, Hackmore!"

It took only a split second for Hackmore to wheel around, spy Rye, and sight his revolver on him, but the older man was still too slow to match reflexes with Rye.

The instant Hackmore began his turn, Aerial jumped up, and with her bound hands, grabbed the rope above her head. Using her arms, made strong by years of performing on ropes from the balloon, she pulled herself off the ground so that when Hackmore went down her arms would absorb the jolt—not her fragile neck!

At the same time she was preparing herself, Rye fired two bullets in such quick succession that together they made one long whizzing sound. Hackmore didn't have time to get off even one shot.

Both of Rye's bullets hit their marks dead on target, the first square in the left side of Hackmore's chest, the second in the rope stretched above his head, severing it before the man even started his fall.

Hackmore and Aerial dropped to the ground at exactly the same moment, though she landed on her feet while Hackmore crumpled into a defeated heap beside her.

"Oh, Rye!" Aerial ran to her husband and looped her bound wrists around his neck. Covering his face with kisses, she wept. "I was so afraid. I thought he would kill you," she chattered between desperate, salty kisses. "I should have known better. I love you!"

His own eyes gleaming with tears, Rye managed a smile and held her out from him, though he left her arms looped around his neck for the moment. "I love you too, but I have to tell you I don't much care for your taste in jewelry." Crying and laughing at the same time, he lifted the forgotten noose over her head and tossed it aside. Then he gently lifted her arms from around his neck and kissed her fingertips before setting to work on freeing her wrists.

"Watch out!" a man yelled, a fraction of a second before they heard rapid gunfire.

Rye knocked Aerial to the ground, covering her body with his own. They both looked up in time to see Cletus Hackmore's stunned face drop back into the dirt and his raised gun fall from his hand.

Sheriff Riley stepped out of the woods, his smoking gun drawn. "Sorry 'bout the noise, son," he apologized, his eyes gleaming with mischief. He walked over to Hackmore and used the toe of his boot to turn the body over onto its back. "But when I saw Hagen wasn't dead and was gettin' ready to shoot, I just plain forgot all you taught me 'bout bein' quiet when you go after someone in the woods. Guess I'm jest too old to learn new tricks."

"I don't know, Sheriff," Rye drawled. Smiling, he climbed to his feet and helped Aerial to hers.

"There's something to be said for old tricks, too. We're just grateful that you had a couple of them up your sleeve. We owe you!

"In that case, help me get this scum's body on a horse and back to town. He's been holdin' his position and money over too many of us for too long. Folks're gonna be right glad to see that Chester Hagen has moved on to different pastures!"

As Aerial, Rye, and Sheriff Riley rode slowly back toward Fairfield, they passed the place where Rye and Hershel had left the bounty hunters the evening before.

"By the way, Sheriff," Rye said, "I guess I ought to tell you Hershel Zimmermann and I left three of Hackmore's hired guns from out of state tied up over there, about fifty yards off the road. Unless they got loose some way, they ought to still be there. I guess we should do something about them."

"Three men from out of state? One of them wasn't missing a couple of fingers, was he?"

Aerial and Rye couldn't help the glance that passed between them, but Rye kept a straight face. "Now that you mention it, I believe one of them was missing some fingers. Come to think of it, one was minus an ear, too.

The sheriff knocked his hat back on his head and shook his head. "If this ain't your lucky day . . ."

"What do you mean?" Aerial asked.

The sheriff chuckled. "What I mean is those three are wanted for robbin' six different banks in Missouri, Illinois, and Indiana in the past two months, before hittin' two in Iowa. There's two or three rewards, totalin' about thirty-five hundred dollars for their capture, and even more if the money they stole is returned. If they're still there, you could be a rich man, 'specially after you collect the five-thousand-dollar reward Hagen put up for whoever brought you in!"

By the time Aerial, Rye, and the sheriff rode into town, it was dark. At first, no one on the street spotted the three barefoot men who limped along behind the riders, trussed up. But once the prisoners were noticed and it was realized they were wearing nothing but saddle blankets around their hips, the word quickly spread that not only was Aerial Windsor safe and Chester Hagen dead, but that the sheriff had other prisoners.

By the time the weary travelers reached the sheriff's office the street was filled with curious witnesses shouting questions.

"All right, all right!" the sheriff yelled, holding up his hands for silence. "I was hopin' we could wait 'til tomorrow mornin' to do this. These two folks have had a pretty hard day, and I found out I'm not near as young as I thought I was!" Everyone laughed. "But I guess we better give you a quick rundown now, so we kin all go on to bed an' git some rest."

The sheriff quickly recapped the highlights of the hours since he and Rye had left Fairfield to rescue Aerial, closing with, "Now, don't you think we ought to let these two young *married* folks get some sleep?"

As Rye wearily fumbled with the key to their hotel room, the door to Hershel's room was flung open wide.

"What do you think you're do—?" Hershel

started, then stopped, his alarmed features splitting into a huge grin. "It's you!"

"So it would seem," Aerial returned, doing her best not to laugh. She had never seen Hershel Zimmermann when he wasn't groomed to perfection—hair neat, clothing unwrinkled. Actually, she had sort of pictured him looking that way all the time, even when he was asleep.

Unconcerned with his disheveled state and the fact that he was barefoot and wearing nothing but his long underwear, Hershel flew across the hall and embraced them both. "I have never been so glad to see anyone in my life. I've been worried sick. Where have you been?"

"Hershel, honey?" a sleepy female voice called from his room. "Is something wrong?"

With teasing eyes, Aerial and Rye both watched Hershel, their eyebrows raised as they waited for an explanation.

Blushing like a young kid, Hershel stammered. "It's not like it looks."

"Oh?" Aerial and Rye said in unison.

"We wondered why you weren't there to greet us with the rest of the town when we got back," Aerial said. "Weren't we?"

Before Rye or Hershel could answer, a buxom, red-haired woman dressed in a green-flowered wrapper appeared in the doorway to the room across the hall. "Hersh . . . Oh!" the attractive woman squealed, rushing across the hall when she saw Aerial and Rye. "Is it you?"

"I don't know," Rye said, smiling down at Aerial. "Is it us?"

"The last time I checked, it was!" Aerial giggled. "Aren't you going to introduce us to your friend, Mr. Zimmermann?"

"Pearl's not my friend," Hershel hurried to say. "She's . . ."

Rye, Aerial, and the woman all considered him with disapproving stares.

"I mean, this is Mrs. Pearl O'Hara—my fiancée! Pearl, love, this is Miss Aerial Windsor. I've told you all about her. And this is her husband, Rye Berenger."

"Fiancée?" Aerial asked. "When? How?"

Pearl's round face split into a warm smile. "Maybe we ought to take this conversation out of the hallway."

Remembering her manners, Aerial agreed. "Yes, of course. Come into our room and tell us everything!"

Hershel started to accept, then remembered his state of undress and stopped himself. "You go on. I'll be in shortly."

"So," Pearl said a few minutes later after Hershel had returned wearing a robe, "when I finally got it through my head that the only way I was going to get Hershel Zimmermann to marry me was to come after him, I sold my restaurant in Brooklyn and got on the first train heading west out of New York City." She held her hands out to her sides and shrugged. "I got here this afternoon, and Hershel proposed at supper!"

Aerial patted Rye's hand, which rested possessively on her tummy, where they sat snuggled together on a small sofa. "What? No crying or begging or blackmailing to get him to marry you?"

Pearl threw back her head and laughed throatily. "The only one begging and crying was Hershel, when I threatened to sit on him until he proposed!" She grabbed her fiancé, who she obviously outweighed by at least thirty pounds, if not more, and pulled him to her to plant a loud smooch on his cheek. "Right, sugar?"

Hershel beamed happily and returned her kiss. "You know it's not. I've loved this magnificent creature since I first laid eyes on her, and when I saw this red-haired vision getting off that train, the only crying I was doing was from happiness — and for all the time I wasted not asking her to marry me years ago." He shook his head sadly. "To tell the truth, I never thought such a wonderful woman could ever be interested in the likes of me."

Pearl cupped her hand to her mouth as if she were telling a secret and leaned toward Aerial. "Have you noticed yet that men are a wee bit slow when it comes to matters of the heart? I did everything but tie him up and drag him to the preacher to let him know how I felt, but he never noticed."

Hershel shrugged, still embarrassed. "I thought she was being kind because she felt sorry for me when I was down on my luck."

"Well," Aerial announced, "you're not down on your luck anymore. We've got some exciting news for you."

Hershel's dark eyes widened with anticipation. "You've decided not to retire after all?"

"No," Aerial laughed. "It's much better than that. You remember those men from New York you rescued Rye from?"

Hershel rolled his eyes. "How could I forget?"

"What three men?" Pearl asked, all concern. "You didn't do anything dangerous, did you?"

"Just risked his life to save mine," Rye contributed.

"Anyway," Aerial inserted pointedly, giving them all a look that said *Will you let me finish my story?*, "There's a thirty-five-hundred-dollar reward for their capture, and it's all yours!"

"No, I couldn't!" Hershel protested. "That money's more yours than mine," he told Rye.

"It won't do you any good to protest, Mr. Zimmermann. It's already been decided and is a matter of record at the sheriff's office," Aerial stated authoritatively. "Not to mention the fifteen hundred dollars more you have coming to you because we found most of the twenty thousand dollars they stole in the saddlebags you took off their horses and left at the livery."

Hershel blanched. "You mean I had twenty thousand dollars in my possession and I didn't know it?!"

"The stableman's words exactly," Rye chuckled.

Aerial's eyes twinkled merrily. "Tell me, Mr. Zimmermann, what would a man who has discovered he has a conscience after all do with twenty thousand dollars in stolen money?"

Shrugging, Hershel shook his head helplessly. "It's probably just as well none of us got the chance to find out!"

Over the happy laughter that filled the room, a knock came at the door.

"That's our dinner!" Aerial explained, bounding to the door. "Thank heavens! I'm starving!" She whisked open the door.

"Good evening," said a tall man in a white shirt, black suit, and flat black hat. "I was told this is Rye Berenger's room. Perhaps thee will inform him that Matthew P—"

"Friend Padluck?!" Rye asked, stepping from behind Aerial. "You came! I can't believe it's really you." He threw his arms around the older man and hugged him.

"Of course, I came," Padluck laughed, returning Rye's exuberant embrace. "Did thee think I wouldn't? I left Nebraska as soon as we received the wire from Mr. Zimmermann telling us thee might need our help." He stood back and eyed Rye warmly. "Thee has grown some since we last saw thee. Mrs. Padluck and I have often wondered what became of thee, but we always prayed thee would find thy way back to us one day."

"Mrs. Padluck," Rye repeated, his expression warmly reminiscent. "How is Mrs. Padluck?" His voice broke. "When I think what would have become of me if it hadn't been for the kindness you and your family gave me—"

"Pishposh!" a female voice scolded as a black-clad woman stepped out from behind Padluck. "Thee were a good boy, and thee gave as good as thee got."

"Mrs. Padluck!" Rye grabbed the small, slightly overweight Quaker woman and lifted her feet off the floor.

"Young man, put me down this instant!" she demanded with a hearty chuckle. "It is obvious the years have not tempered thy rambunctious nature!"

"Please come in, Mr. and Mrs. Padluck!" Aerial invited. "Since my husband has completely forgotten his manners, I'll introduce myself. I'm Rye's wife, Aerial, and I'm so glad to meet you. Rye has told me so much about you. And these . . ." She indicated Hershel and Pearl with a sweep of her hand. ". . . are our good friends, Pearl O' Hara and Hershel Zimmermann."

Suddenly embarrassed by their own state of inappropriate dress in the presence of the two obviously devout strangers, Pearl and Hershel stood up and made for the door. "We really must be leaving," Pearl said. "We only came by to say good night."

"Don't be silly, dear woman," Mrs. Padluck protested. "Thee mustn't go. We want to know everything about this dear boy. And that includes knowing his friends."

"But we're not really dressed for—"

"Thee are dressed just right," Mrs. Padluck said,

pushing the two back toward their chairs. "In fact, I have a confession to make. I've always had a secret desire to own just such a wrapper as thine."

Friend Padluck and Rye stared at Mrs. Padluck, their expressions equally aghast.

Then everyone laughed and the next hour was spent filling the Padluck's in on all that had happened.

"Before thee makes thy final decision as to where thee will go," Friend Padluck said when Rye explained that he and Aerial were planning on starting a horse ranch farther west, "there's something thee should know."

"Oh?"

"It seems thy father was always worried something would happen to him, so he wrote a will leaving his farm to thee and thy sister, with me as the trustee to keep it for thee until thee could reach maturity."

"You mean. . . ?"

Friend Padluck nodded. "It's still there, just waiting for thee to claim it."

Visions of the last time he had seen his family home flashed across his mind, and Rye shook his head doubtfully. "I'm not sure I'm ready for that. The memories there are still too painful."

Then he happily hugged Aerial to him. "Besides, I've spent the last thirteen years living for the past. I think it's time I finally put the past completely behind me and concentrate on nothing but the future."

"Well, if thee ever change thy mind, the land will be there for thee."

"Thanks, but I'm sure I won't. But do you know what would really make me happy? I want to sign the farm over to you to pass on to your own children. Combined with your farm, it ought to give you enough land to give each of them a decent-sized parcel to raise their own families on. And since I won't be coming back, except maybe for a visit when the memories have faded, nothing would make me happier than to know the land my pa loved and worked so hard for was in good hands. And I think it would make Pa happy, too."

Long after the Padlucks and Hershel and Pearl had gone to their own rooms, Aerial and Rye stayed awake, lying in bed and talking, planning and dreaming about the future.

"You do know that if you'd wanted to go back to Nebraska, it would have been all right with me, don't you?"

Rye cuddled his wife closer to him and kissed the top of her head. "I know, and I love you for that. But I really want to start over somewhere new. New home, new wife, new baby . . . a whole new life. I'm truly a lucky man, Mrs. Berenger."

"You just remember that, Mr. Berenger, when all this 'new' you're looking forward to gets old."

"Somehow, I don't think living with you will ever get old. Your hair may gray, your skin may wrinkle, our children may grow up and have children of their own, but my love for you will always be new. I do love you, Mrs. Berenger!"

"Don't tell me," she whispered, trailing her fingers down his bare chest and below. "Show me."

Epilogue

Wyoming; 1890

"Mama! Daddy's got the wagons loaded!" Aerial's eight-year-old daughter, Gale, announced, her dark red hair gleaming in the sunlight filtering into the bedroom. "Are you ready?"

"Just about," Aerial answered, inserting a final pin into her blond tresses, then checking her reflection one last time in the mirror before donning her new hat. "Though I have to admit, I'm getting too old for this."

"That's what you say every time!" Rye said, a teasing glint in his amused eyes as he came up behind his daughter in the doorway. "But you always say yes every time someone asks."

"Well," Aerial huffed with pretended indignation. "This time I really mean it! In fact, if we weren't celebrating Wyoming's statehood, I wouldn't be going today."

Gale tilted her head back against Rye's belly and grinned up at her dad. "I think she just says that so you'll tell her you think she looks younger and more beautiful now than the day you married her."

"You think so?" Rye asked, giving the girl's freckled nose a loving tweak.

A second little girl appeared beside Rye and struck a theatrical pose. "Don't forget to remind her, no *really* important celebration or function in Wyoming would be complete without an appearance of the *Wind Rose II* and the 'daring, long-distance, world-record-holding Aerial Windsor Berenger and her four *bee-u-tiful* daughters!' " she expounded dramatically.

His expression dotingly amused, Rye patted his precocious seven-year-old on her red head. "You're right, Sky. We can't forget that."

"Or how much money her balloon performances have raised for good causes," Zephyr, Sky's quieter identical twin pointed out with her typical practicality. "Why, the orphanage alone owes its very existence to you!"

Her hands on her hips, Aerial faced her family and eyed them suspiciously. "Why do I get the feeling you sneaky little connivers want something? And speaking of connivers, where's our champion conniver?"

The three girls raised their excited glances to Rye, waiting for him to speak.

"Why're you looking at me? This is *your* scheme, not mine!" he told them. "I'm just an innocent bystander who got roped into being an ally at the last minute."

"All right! What's going on?" Aerial laughed. "Where's Tempest?"

"In the barn," Gale announced, obviously struggling to suppress a mischievous giggle. "Waiting for you."

"For me? Why?" Aerial's eyes fixed on her husband. "What's our girl up to now?"

Rye maintained his conspiratorial silence.

The three girls rushed forward and grabbed Aerial's hands. "Come on, Mama. It's a surprise. You're going to love it!"

Allowing herself to be tugged from the room, Aerial laughed. "All right, but I'm warning you. I take a dim view of your sneaky tactics."

Minutes later, Sky ran ahead of the family and

positioned herself in front of the closed barn doors, then motioned for her sisters to take their places on either side of her. Gale and Zephyr each immediately grabbed a door handle and waited for a signal.

"Ladies and Gentlemen!" Sky announced grandly. "For your viewing pl—"

"Wait a minute!" came a muffled shout from inside the barn. "I'm not ready!"

Aerial regarded Rye and smiled. "What's going on?"

Rye held his hands out to his sides and shook his head. "I've been sworn to secrecy!"

"Ready!" Tempest yelled from the barn.

"Ladies and gentlemen!" Sky began again. "For your viewing pleasure, the Flying B Ranch of Wyoming presents the one and only Tempest Berenger, daughter of the beautiful, world-famous aeronaut, Mrs. Aerial Windsor Berenger, and the handsome, successful rancher, Rye Berenger, in a dazzling performance that is guaranteed to thrill and amaze you."

Gale and Zephyr whisked open their respective doors and held up their free hands in a pose they had seen their mother strike.

Sky took the hands of her smiling parents and drew them into the barn, stopping them just inside.

At first Aerial was surprised not to find her oldest daughter on the little stage Rye had built the girls for the "shows" the children frequently performed for their parents ... and for anyone else they could talk into watching. She shot her husband a questioning glance, then followed the direction his gaze was taking. Up!

"What's—" Aerial stopped, her heart leaping into her throat as her attention focused on her nine-year-old daughter, Tempest. Grinning triumphantly, the red-haired child was sitting on a trapeze bar hung from the barn rafters and many feet from the ground!

Aerial's mouth dropped open with surprise, and she turned her disapproving attention to her husband. "You knew about this and you let her—"

Rye cut off her protestations. "I feel the same way you do, but something tells me how we feel doesn't make any difference. Our first-born evidently has a love for high altitudes in her blood and intends to do something about it—with or without our approval." He wrapped his arm around Aerial's waist and affectionately nudged her ear with his mouth. "Of course, what can we expect from a child who was probably conceived ten thousand feet in the air?"

At his reminder of the first time they made love, Aerial struggled to keep a straight face. "But she could fall."

"She won't. She's wearing a harness!"

"Ta-da-dat-da-daaaah!" the three girls on the floor sang, imitating the trumpets they had heard announcing the acts at the traveling circus the family had attended in the spring.

In the next few minutes, Tempest performed several of the stunts she had seen her mother do dozens of times from the trapeze below the *Wind Rose II*.

"I can't believe this," Aerial said to Rye, beaming proudly up at her daughter as the girl took her final bow from the trapeze and blew kisses down to her applauding audience. "She is really quite good, isn't she?"

"I don't know why you're so surprised," Rye chuckled. "She comes by it honestly."

"What do you think?" Gale asked, rushing to her parents and hugging them as Tempest climbed down the ladder from the hayloft. "Can Tempest do one of the stunts in the show at the celebration tomorrow?"

"Who're you? Her agent?" Aerial asked with a laugh.

"I'm her manager!" Gale announced, her chest puffed with self-importance. "Now, do we have a deal or not?"

Aerial looked from Gale to the rest of the hopeful faces surrounding her, then arched her eyebrows at Rye. "How long has this been going on behind my back?"

Rye winked at his daughters. "I just found out today, but I suspect she's been practicing for quite a while. Our Tempest is like her mama when it comes to going after what she wants!"

"Am I to assume you've given this little scheme your approval?"

"I said it was okay with me, *if* she wore a harness *and* on the condition you said it was all right."

All four daughters surrounded Aerial, hugging her and squealing. "Please, Mama." "You've been saying you didn't want to do it any more. I could learn the act and take your place." "Let Tempest do it. Just one stunt."

Rye joined in the attack. "You said it yourself, love. She *is* good."

Still not convinced, Aerial shook her head. "I'm not sure I like the idea of any of the girls following in my . . ."

Rye put his arm around her shoulders and kissed her cheek apologetically. "I think you're forgetting something you taught me ten years ago: the wind's going to blow in the direction it wants to blow, so we might as well relax and enjoy the adventure, because if we try to turn it, it'll just go on without us."

Her eyes filling with tears, Aerial smiled and patted her husband's cheek affectionately. "And following the wind didn't hurt us, did it?"

"Not once we stopped resisting it and went where it took us."

"Does that mean yes or no?" Tempest asked impatiently.

Aerial shrugged and kissed her oldest. "Who knows better than I do that you can't fly a balloon against the wind? So, I suppose it's a yes!"

Author's Note

While writing this book, I've learned there is a common misconception that hot-air ballooning has been the mode of operating a balloon ever since the beginning. The truth is, however, that hot air was only used to inflate balloons for a few years after the first flight in France in 1783, and did not return to popularity again until the 1950s, with the invention of the propane burners balloonists use today.

Actually, by the 1790s, inflating balloons with hot air from open flames—which resulted in the fiery ends to dozens of balloonists' lives—had been almost entirely replaced by the use of hydrogen. Though hydrogen was expensive and tedious to manufacture, it was a great improvement over hot air because it had a much greater lifting power and was undeniably safer for the balloonist than being trapped hundreds of feet in the air in a small gondola with an open flame in the stove at its center!

Then in 1821, Charles Green of England first made use of coal gas as a lifting agent. A mixture of hydrogen and methane, coal gas became readily available from public gas mains as more and more cities began to light their streets and buildings with gas. Not only was coal gas much cheaper than pure hydrogen, but it was denser and therefore slower to seep through a balloon's cloth envelope.

And an aeronaut could fill his balloon in two or three hours, compared to the day or more it might take with hydrogen.

For the remainder of the 1800s and the first half of the twentieth century, though hydrogen was still used in many instances, coal gas became the preferred fuel of aeronauts, until hot air ballooning made its resurgence in the 1950s.

For those of you who may have wondered about what might seem to be a particulary low timberline on Mount Marcy (little more than five-thousand feet), especially if you're used to the 11,500-foot timberlines in the central Rockies and the Sierra Nevadas, you may be interested to know that every area has a different timberline, depending on climate, temperature, type of soil, drainage, and proximity to the Equator.

SUMMER LOVE WITH SYLVIE SOMMERFIELD

FIRES OF SURRENDER (3034, $4.95)

Kathryn Mcleod's beloved Scotland had just succumbed to the despised James IV. The auburn-haired beauty braced herself for the worst as the conquering forces rode in her town, but *nothing* could have prepared her for Donovan McAdam. The handsome knight triumphed over her city and her heart as well! She vowed to resist him forever, but her traitorous heart and flesh had other ideas.

AUTUMN DOVE (2547, $3.95)

Tara Montgomery had no choice but to reunite with her soldier brother after their parents died. The independent beauty never dreamed of the journey's perils, or the handsome halfbreed wagonmaster Zach Windwalker. He despised women who traveled alone; she found him rude and arrogant. They should have hated each other forever, yet their hunger was too strong to deny. With only the hills and vast plains as witnesses, Zach and Tara discover a love hotter than the summer sun.

PASSION'S RAGING STORM (2754, $4.50)

Flame-haired Gillian Kendricks was known to the Underground Railroad only as "the Guardian Angel." In reality she was a young Philadelphia beauty with useful connections which she doesn't hesitate to use to further her secret cause. But when she tries to take advantage of her acquaintance with the very handsome Lt. Shane Greyson who carries vital papers to Washington, her plan backfires. For the dark-haired lieutenant doesn't miss much. And the price of deceit is passion!

Available wherever paperbacks are sold, or order direct from the Publisher. Send cover price plus 50¢ per copy for mailing and handling to Zebra Books, Dept. 3065, 475 Park Avenue South, New York, N.Y. 10016. Residents of New York, New Jersey and Pennsylvania must include sales tax. DO NOT SEND CASH.